DEAR MISS BREED

True Stories of the Japanese American Incarceration
during World War II and
a Librarian Who Made a Difference

by JOANNE OPPENHEIM

Foreword by ELIZABETH KIKUCHI YAMADA

Afterword by SNOWDEN BECKER

SCHOLASTIC 💡 NONFICTION

An Imprint of

📕 **SCHOLASTIC**

To Clara and those who lived it!
And to Steve, who has been there every step of the way.

Library of Congress Cataloging-in-Publication Data
Oppenheim, Joanne.
Dear Miss Breed / by Joanne Oppenheim.—1st ed.
p. cm.
Includes bibliographical references.
1. Japanese Americans—Evacuation and relocation, 1942–1945—Juvenile literature. 2. World War, 1939–1945—Japanese Americans—Juvenile literature. 3. World War, 1939–1945—Personal narratives, American—Juvenile literature. 4. World War, 1939–1945—United States—Juvenile literature. 5. World War, 1939–1945—Children—United States—Juvenile literature. 6. Japanese American children—Correspondence—Juvenile literature. 7. Breed, Clara E.—Correspondence—Juvenile literature. I. Title.

D769.8.A6O67 2005 940.53'1773—dc22 2004059009

ISBN 0-439-56992-3

10 9 8 7 6 5 4 3   06 07 08 09 10

Printed in Singapore 46
First edition, February 2006

The text type was set in Fournier.
Book design by Emily Waters and Tatiana Sperhacke

CONTENTS

FOREWORD

The "children" of Miss Breed respected her, thanked her, and some knew her well enough to love her. Now Joanne Oppenheim has aptly portrayed this quiet and gentle librarian as a hero, a determined and courageous fighter against racial injustice, who made a difference in the lives of a community of children of Japanese descent—with her personal affection for her children, her gifts of books to them, and her bold protest against the incarceration of American citizens whose only wrong was to look like the enemy.

I was one of Miss Breed's "children." I was almost twelve years old when my family was sent away from our home during World War II. Oppenheim's book about the remarkable Miss Breed will be placed lovingly beside the book *A House for Elizabeth*, which I received from Miss Breed during the war years when more than 120,000 Japanese Americans were incarcerated in concentration camps. The book made a difference in my life. As a preacher's child, I had never lived in an ordinary house. I had lived in parsonages, churches, shabby rental houses, the horse stables in the Santa Anita Assembly Center, and was now living in the black-tarred barracks of Poston, Arizona. Without opening the book, I believed in the promise of the book's title—that someday I, too, would live in a real house, like in the picture books. Every book that Clara Breed sent me was an affirmation that we were not the enemy, the "non-alien"—but American citizens. Every book was more than a story that enlightened, instructed, and/or entertained. Every book was hope.

I have read numerous books about the incarceration: nonfiction, autobiographies, biographies, and fiction. I have viewed videos, films, and exhibits. I participated in the planning and building of the National Japanese American Memorial to Patriotism in Washington, D.C. Yet, I have learned more and responded more to Joanne Oppenheim's book about this time in history. She researched in depth. She interviewed and met many of us, Miss Breed's "children," and used our words from the past and present to tell our story.

After reading Oppenheim's book, I remember more clearly the demeaning life of the horse stables, the inedible squid dinners, and the communal showers. I feel more deeply the pain and hurt of the racial hatred from the newspaper articles she includes. I understand with more sensitivity that we all have different stories to tell, based upon our varying ages, backgrounds, and values of our parents. I am appalled that I did not realize that I was a prisoner of my own government. Focusing on Miss Breed, who loved her Japanese American "children" as her own, and using their voices in a creative and powerful way, Joanne Oppenheim has written a story of the incarceration that is compelling and unforgettable.

My grandchildren have explored the internment exhibits at the Japanese American National Museum in Los Angeles, and found the names of their grandparents and Clara Breed on the memorial windows. Three of them have viewed the National Japanese American Memorial to Patriotism in Washington, D.C. I know, without a doubt, that the most meaningful and effective way for them to comprehend the complete story of the incarceration—the political and social reasons, the description of life in the camps, the personal stories, the post-camp life, the outcomes—will be to read this book. And beyond the internment story, they will appreciate and honor the legacy of the rich cultural heritage of the Issei and the Nisei with their patient endurance, their sacrifices, and their belief in the land of opportunity in spite of the tragic loss of their civil liberties. Most important, they will develop what has been called in our community "something strong within" and recognize that this is the most significant trait that they share with their grandparents, parents, and the remarkable Miss Breed.

Place this book in every classroom. Encourage adults to read the book with their children. Let every individual who visits the Memorial in Washington, D.C., or any Japanese American museum throughout the country be informed about this book. They, too, can make a difference and never allow any group or individuals to be deprived of their civil liberties and rights again.

When the Poston Reunion attendees honored Miss Breed at its banquet in 1991, we ended the tribute with the presentation of an exquisite crystalline-glazed tea set. I placed one of the delicate teacups in Miss Breed's hands with the words, "Our cup runneth over with gratitude to you. . . ." Thank you, Miss Breed. Thank you, Joanne Oppenheim.

—Elizabeth Kikuchi Yamada
La Jolla, California

YOUNG PEOPLE
IN THIS BOOK

Margaret Arakawa

Itsuo Endo

Tetsuzo Hirasaki

Florence Ishino

Margaret Ishino

Richard "Babe" Karasawa

Elizabeth Kikuchi

Aiko Ellen Kubo

Kaizo Kubo

Chiyo Kusumoto

Louise Ogawa

Ben Segawa

Katherine Tasaki

Fusa Tsumagari

Yuki Tsumagari

Hisako Watanabe

Jack Watanabe

Joe Yamada

Ellen Yukawa

*Clara E. Breed as she looked in the late 1920s when she became
the first Children's Librarian of the San Diego Public Library*

HOW I MET THE
REMARKABLE MISS BREED

IN 2001, I met Clara Breed on the Internet. It was quite by chance. I happened to be planning a reunion of my high school class. For months I had been searching online for old classmates, people I had not seen in fifty years.

For some strange reason that I could not then explain, I spent a lot of time searching for one classmate in particular. Her name was Ellen Yukawa, and she came to our little hometown of Monticello, New York, at the end of World War II in 1945. As always, I asked my old reliable friend "Google" where I could find information about Japanese Americans, and moments later I clicked my way into www.janm.org, the Web site of the Japanese American National Museum.

It was there that I met Clara Estelle Breed, who was once the children's librarian of the San Diego Public Library. Miss Breed, as the children called her, was not just their librarian; she was a friend to dozens of Japanese American young adults, teenagers, and schoolchildren when war with Japan began in December of 1941.

The story of what happened to them is largely told through letters that Miss Breed's young friends wrote to her during the war. The more I read of their letters, the more I knew that I had to write a book about them and the remarkable Miss Breed.

She not only served as a lifeline to "her children," as she called them; she was brave enough to speak out against the shameful chapter in American history that they were living through.

This is a true story of friendship and courage that began years before the Imperial Japanese bombed Pearl Harbor on December 7, 1941. But on that day, more than 110,000 Nikkei, meaning all the people of Japanese descent living on the West Coast, found their lives turned upside down. No one in San Diego could have imagined that in just four months to the day, every man, woman, and child of Japanese descent would be forced to leave their homes, schools, and jobs, and the lives they had known.

Clara Breed considered the events that you will read about in this story a terrible injustice. It is a story not just about Miss Breed but also about the young people she had known and cared for over the years. Some were just learning to read. Others were going to junior high or high school. Still others were ready for college but suddenly forced to put their lives on hold. All of Miss Breed's young friends were American citizens, and they had done nothing wrong. Yet for three and a half years they were the victims of hysteria and racial hatred that robbed them of their rights and freedom.

Hours after the war began, the government rounded up hundreds of Issei, first-generation Japanese Americans, immigrants who had come to the United States early in the twentieth century. Many had lived here for more than thirty or forty years, but they were considered "aliens" because the laws did not permit Asians to become citizens as European emigrants had done. Those Issei who were arrested were held in federal prisons as possible spies or saboteurs. Several months later the government removed all the remaining West Coast Issei and their children, the Nisei, those who were born in the United States and were therefore citizens. The government also removed the Sansei, the children of the Nisei, who were also citizens. In fact, two-thirds of those taken away were *citizens of the United States*. They were not charged with any wrongdoing. Their only crime was being born with the wrong ancestors!

My school friend ELLEN YUKAWA, I later discovered, is a Sansei, meaning she is part of the third generation of her family in America. Until she arrived in our small town in 1945 the only Japanese faces we had ever seen were in the movies or newspapers, and they were the faces of our enemies! After all, the United States had been at war with Japan since 1941, when we were seven or eight years old. We had grown up with war movies that portrayed all Japanese as ugly, cruel, and treacherous.

Ellen and her family were the first Japanese Americans any of us ever met. According to the 1940 census, there were approximately 126,947 Nikkei in the United States; most of them lived on the West Coast. I think we were told that Ellen was not from Japan but an American of Japanese descent. Nevertheless, I remember our surprise that Ellen spoke English just as we did. Not only that, she knew how to jump rope, play softball, and, at lunch, ate the same food we did. If or when we asked where she had come from, I think she told us California, and that was true.

What she didn't tell us was that she had spent most of the war in Arizona. We had no way of knowing that she had spent the last three and a half years in a concentration camp. It was not something Ellen ever talked to us about, and since we were children when the war began, we had no idea that such places existed.

Ellen stayed in our town until the end of our sophomore year, when she and her family returned to California. We hated to see her go. She was a good friend, an honor student, and even a class officer. Although she didn't graduate with us, I always considered Ellen a member of our class.

In the years that passed, I sometimes thought of Ellen, especially during the 1980s when Congress appointed a Commission on Wartime Relocation and Internment of Civilians. Newspapers were full of stories about the war years and our government's responsibility for the imprisonment of so many innocent people of Japanese descent. All the quotations marked as "Testimony" throughout this book come from those historic hearings. I remember wondering at the time if my friend Ellen could have been in one of those camps.

Our reunion plans gave me a renewed interest in finding Ellen. Call it luck, chance, or fate, that is why I visited the Web site of the Japanese American National Museum to ask for their help. After writing an e-mail about my friend, I started reading other stories on their Web site and was drawn to the story about Miss Breed. I was sure someone must have already written a book about her. I checked all the online bookstores, but I found no books about Clara Breed.

Every evening I kept going back to the Japanese American National Museum site—reading and rereading the letters that painted a picture of a time and place my friend Ellen must have known.

Through their letters I began to feel that I knew each of Clara Breed's young friends, and I wondered what had become of them over the years.

I wondered if my friend Ellen knew KATHERINE TASAKI, who was ten years old and closer to our age when the war began. After a while I felt as if I knew Katherine. In spite of where she was living, so much of what she wrote about was typical of kids in elementary school. She collected pen pals and movie magazines; so did I. Katherine liked to put on plays; so did I. Miss Breed was always sending Katherine paper dolls and books. I liked those as well. Despite all the colds, cuts, splinters, stomachaches, and leg pains she wrote about, Katherine's letters were full of hope and a breezy sense of humor. Katherine had grown up in downtown San Diego. She practically lived at the library and was clearly one of Miss Breed's favorites. I had great hopes of meeting Katherine, but I was too late. Although she was one of the youngest correspondents, she died in 1993. But I did get to interview Katherine's husband, Ben Segawa.

BEN was eleven years old when the war began. There were ten children in the SEGAWA family, and they lived outside the city of San Diego, on a farm. Ben's family was sent to the same camp as Katherine and her mom, but Ben and Katherine didn't know each other until many years later. Ben was not one of Miss Breed's correspondents, but he is a marvelous storyteller and shared many of his own experiences along with wonderful stories about Kathy, as he calls her.

FUSA TSUMAGARI wrote letters crammed full of information about what was happening—not just to her but also to her family and friends. Fusa was eighteen and a high school senior in the spring of 1942 and would have been going on to college the following fall, as her older sister and brother had done. But like so many graduates that year, Fusa had to put her life on hold. I wondered why her father was being held in a different camp from Fusa and her mother. Many of Fusa's letters were about her brother, YUKIO, who wanted to be a doctor. Had he managed to do it?

RICHARD "BABE" KARASAWA had many answers for me, as well as lively stories about his own camp experience. When the war began, Babe was a fourteen-year-old from San Diego and had known many of Clara Breed's young friends from school and church. He knew both Yukio and Fusa. Babe was not one of the correspondents, but years later, as a volunteer at the Japanese American National Museum, he scanned all of the letters to Miss Breed into the museum's computer. He had also spoken to all the correspondents. Babe told me that Fusa had died in 2000 while he was working on the letters for the museum, but he was able to put me in touch with her daughter, Patty Higashioka, who shared her family's stories and introduced me to her mother's closest childhood friend.

CHIYO KUSUMOTO, Fusa's best friend and classmate, had many stories about what it was like to be a teenager in San Diego and in the camps. Before the war, Chiyo lived outside the city on a farm. Her father grew flowers for local florists, and Chiyo, along with everyone else in the family, helped. She went to school in downtown San Diego and often stayed at Fusa's after school until her father picked her up. The two girls always went home by way of the library. Chiyo remembered sitting on the little chairs in the Children's Room of the library and visiting with their good friend Clara Breed, who was never too busy to talk with them. Chiyo told me many stories about her own family, as well as the Tsumagaris and Fusa in particular.

From the letters it was clear that Fusa knew TETS HIRASAKI, who wrote many long and often cynical letters. It took awhile before I realized that the letters from Tets were by the same person who sometimes signed his letters "Ted." In fact, his full name is Tetsuzo Hirasaki. Like Fusa, his father was being held in a federal prison. From Tets's letters I knew that he was even older than the others. He was twenty-one and eager to join the army. He seemed to know Miss Breed's family—her mother and her sister, Eleanor. Tets's letters were more political and outspoken than Fusa's. I didn't get to meet Tets in person. Sadly, he was too ill to give me an interview. But he did write to me and I was fortunate to meet people who knew him and to have copies of a letter and an article he wrote about Miss Breed—so you will find some of his thoughts in his adult voice and his own words.

LOUISE OGAWA was seventeen and a high school junior when the war began and was one of the most prolific writers. She wrote many moving and amusing letters. Even when she was feeling homesick and blue, Louise managed to put a bright spin on what was happening. I really wanted to meet Louise when I was in California, but she did not seem to want to talk about the past. So I gave it one last try and wrote her a letter. To my great delight, she answered! We began to correspond and every time one of her letters arrives I feel as if Miss Breed would be pleased! Louise and her best friend,

Margaret Ishino, were like sisters. They had lived practically next door to each other in San Diego, and their fathers both worked at the same hotel.

I was lucky enough to meet and talk with MARGARET ISHINO at the Japanese American National Museum. All of Margaret's letters are full of news about her little sister, FLORENCE, and her baby brother, THOMAS. I wondered how Margaret had time to do her schoolwork and all the chores that were expected of her. Margaret was an avid reader and still has some of the books Miss Breed sent to her during those long years. Her letters to Miss Breed often included a little note and a drawing from Florence, six years old and just starting school when the war broke out. Although Margaret had to deal with many demands from her family, her letters are upbeat and full of hope. Margaret Ishino and Louise Ogawa both graduated in 1943, and they are still dear friends—more than sixty years later.

Nine-year-old JACK WATANABE, one of the younger boys, was clearly another favorite of Clara Breed's. His brother William was in high school and wrote to Miss Breed more often; so did Jack's big sister, Hisako, who was a senior and a classmate of Louise Ogawa and Margaret Ishino. Jack spoke with me by phone but couldn't tell me much about Miss Breed, except that she always saved certain books he liked. He explained that he was just a little kid at the time and didn't really remember very much, except that his brother made him write letters of thanks to Miss Breed from time to time. He did remember the books she sent and how much he enjoyed them.

I interviewed AIKO ELLEN KUBO by phone, too. She was in tenth grade at San Diego High when the war began. Aiko, as she was known then, told me an ironic story about prewar San Diego, when she and her girlfriend danced in a high school assembly. They were supposed to dress in clothes from the country their family came from. She and her friend dressed in sailor suits and each carried an American flag in one hand and a Japanese flag in the other. As they tap-danced across the stage, each time they raised their hands with American flags the audience cheered. When they raised the Japanese flags the audience booed. Aiko says it was the first time she understood that many people seemed to hate Japan. That was before Pearl Harbor.

Aiko's two older sisters actually wrote more letters to Miss Breed than she did. That's because she was just fifteen and busy with school and friends. Her sisters were planning their weddings and had more time to write. Miss Breed knew the whole Kubo family. While I was at the Bancroft Library in Berkeley, California, I found a moving essay written by Aiko's brother, Kaizo (also known as George), that you will find in the book. Aiko had never seen the essay.

ITSUO ENDO was twelve years old the year the war began. Its, as his friends call him, came from farm country in Salinas, rather than the city of San Diego. He had many amusing stories about his life on the farm and in the camp. I wanted stories from both boys and girls, and Its had some funny ones as well as sad ones. He was a Boy Scout, had several kinds of jobs, and even helped make the adobe bricks to build the camp school. Although Its was not one of Miss Breed's correspondents, he was in another part of the same camp. Today he is a docent at the Japanese American National Museum and shares his stories with visitors to the museum.

I was tickled by the letters eleven-year-old ELIZABETH KIKUCHI and her little sister, ANNA, sent to Miss Breed about playing library. That was a game my brother and I had enjoyed, too. I wondered if Elizabeth grew up to be a librarian like Miss Breed and if her brother, DAVID, who liked collecting pollywogs, grew up to be a scientist.

Years later, Miss Breed had given all the letters written to her by the children to Elizabeth. I wondered why Elizabeth then gave the letters to the Japanese American National Museum. Perhaps she recognized that together the letters were an untold story of an unforgettable time and place.

Elizabeth was and is still an avid reader. She told me that in camp she would complete a book a day! I visited Elizabeth and her husband, Joe Yamada, who was imprisoned in the same camp. He had great stories to tell, too.

To my deep disappointment, I wasn't able to find Miss Breed's letters, except for one, just as this book was going to press (see page 288). The children moved around so much, and although I heard that some collected her letters for a while, no one could recall what had happened to them after all these years. Still, I felt her warm, generous spirit reflected in the letters the young correspondents sent to her.

Clara Breed never forgot "her children." She not only sent them books to read—she also was like an anchor on the stormy journey they had been forced to travel. I wanted to know more about Clara Breed from them, through their letters, and by talking with them.

Their story was to become my focus for most of the next three years. I felt an immediate kinship to Clara, who shared my love of children and their books. I felt connected to the correspondents who were living through a war that I knew and feared as a child during the 1940s. As I read their letters, I recognized that Clara Breed was an unsung hero, a courageous woman. She didn't fight on the battlefields of Europe or Asia. Yet she battled on the home front against injustice and stood up for her belief in the Constitution.

Several days after sending my e-mail to the Japanese American National Museum, I was thrilled by an answer from Jessica Silver, an archivist at the museum, who found a listing for Ellen's sister, Elayne Yukawa, who had not changed her last name. I left a message on Elayne's answering machine, and a few hours later I heard Ellen's voice for the first time in more than fifty years! That alone would have been reward enough. But imagine my surprise when I learned that Ellen had come to Monticello from the same camp where Miss Breed's children had spent the war.

The coincidences didn't end there. Ellen told me how she and her family came to Monticello to work for the Osborn family, and the first house they lived in was the very house I had lived in for more than forty years—the house where I raised my family.

Ellen and I planned to hold our class reunion at a hotel overlooking the Statue of Liberty and the World Trade Center. But when September 11, 2001, came, those of us who grew up in the 1940s felt a special anguish that the world would once again be plunged into war. That night my friend Ellen called from California to see if we were all right.

We worried together that what happened to Japanese Americans during World War II might happen to the thousands of people of Arab descent. As we talked, I realized that the story of Miss Breed and her correspondents was perhaps more important than ever.

It is not merely a story about long ago but rather one that must be remembered for all time so that it will never happen again.

✈ ABOUT THE CAMPS ✈

Key Words You Will Need to Know

ISSEI first generation of Japanese who immigrated to the United States; the Issei were barred from becoming U.S. citizens, forced by law to remain "involuntary aliens."

NISEI second generation, children of the Issei; Japanese Americans born in the United States, and therefore citizens.

KIBEI children of the Issei, born in America but educated in Japan.

SANSEI third-generation Japanese Americans, children of the Nisei.

YONSEI fourth-generation Japanese Americans.

ISSEI, **NISEI**, **SANSEI**, and **YONSEI** are from the numbers *ichi, ni, san, shi* (for *yon*). *Sei* means "generation." Thus, Issei are the first generation in the United States. Nisei are the second generation in the United States.

NIKKEI all people of Japanese ancestry in America. All Issei, Nisei, Kibei, Sansei, and Yonsei are also Nikkei. *Ni* comes from the word *Nihon* or *Nippon*, as Japan is called in Japanese. *Kei* means "thread" or "lineage."

RELOCATION vs. INTERNMENT vs. INCARCERATION vs. CONCENTRATION

Many people refer to relocation camps as internment camps; others call them places of incarceration; and still others refer to them as concentration camps. Historian Roger Daniels writes that technically only the Justice Department's camps for enemy aliens were internment camps: "In law, internment can only apply to aliens. During World War II, in the United States, internment was individual and presumably based on something the individual had done. . . . Each person interned had the right to an individual hearing, which, in some instances, resulted in release. Although the later mass incarcerations are referred to as 'internments,' that is not really the appropriate term"; in contrast, Daniels writes: "The mass incarceration that took place was based simply on ethnic origin and geography. . . . There would be no hearings for the incarcerated Japanese Americans. Their 'guilt' was their ancestry."

Put simply, the Justice Department's internment camps were only for so-called enemy aliens, whereas the relocation camps were for everyone else. Ironically, young Nisei men inside relocation camps who were eligible for the draft when the war began were reclassified as 4-C and labeled "enemy aliens."

"Relocation camps" was governmental doublespeak. "Internment camps" is also a kind of doublespeak to soften the reality, but it is frequently used, even by scholars. To me, and to others, they are both doublespeak for "incarceration" and "concentration camps." During the same war, the Nazis murdered more than six million people in places they called "concentration camps," which was yet another kind of doublespeak for death camps.

ASSEMBLY CENTERS

These were temporary centers used from late March 1942 through mid-October 1942 to round up the Nikkei community. They were located on fairgrounds and racetracks, and were under the jurisdiction of the U.S. Army and its civilian branch, the Wartime Civil Control Administration (WCCA).

FRESNO, CALIFORNIA
May 6, 1942–October 30, 1942

MANZANAR, CALIFORNIA
March 21, 1942–June 1, 1942
Manzanar was opened as an assembly center and converted into a "relocation camp."

MARYSVILLE, CALIFORNIA
May 8, 1942–June 29, 1942

MAYER, ARIZONA
May 7, 1942–June 2, 1942

MERCED, CALIFORNIA
May 6, 1942–September 15, 1942

PINEDALE, CALIFORNIA
May 7, 1942–July 23, 1942

POMONA, CALIFORNIA
May 7, 1942–August 24, 1942

PORTLAND, OREGON
May 2, 1942–September 10, 1942

PUYALLUP, WASHINGTON
April 28, 1942–September 12, 1942

SACRAMENTO, CALIFORNIA
May 6, 1942–June 26, 1942

SALINAS, CALIFORNIA
April 27, 1942–July 4, 1942

SANTA ANITA, CALIFORNIA
March 27, 1942–October 27, 1942

STOCKTON, CALIFORNIA
May 10, 1942–October 17, 1942

TANFORAN, SAN BRUNO, CALIFORNIA
April 28, 1942–October 13, 1942

TULARE, CALIFORNIA
April 20, 1942–September 4, 1942

TURLOCK, BYRON, CALIFORNIA
April 30, 1942–August 12, 1942

RELOCATION CAMPS

Permanent detention camps, often referred to as relocation centers, were located in remote areas away from the designated "military" areas. They were used from the spring of 1942 until their closing in 1945 and 1946. They were under the control of the War Relocation Authority (WRA).

AMACHE (GRANADA), COLORADO August 24, 1942–October 15, 1945. Peak population 7,318.

GILA, ARIZONA July 20, 1942–November 10, 1945. Peak population 13,348.

HEART MOUNTAIN, WYOMING August 12, 1942–November 10, 1945. Peak population 10,767.

JEROME, ARKANSAS October 6, 1942–June 30, 1944. Peak population 8,497.

MANZANAR, CALIFORNIA March 21, 1942–November 21, 1945. Peak population 10,046.

MINIDOKA, IDAHO August 10, 1942–October 28, 1945. Peak population 9,397.

POSTON (ALSO KNOWN AS COLORADO RIVER), ARIZONA May 8, 1942–November 28, 1945. Peak population 17,814.

ROHWER, ARKANSAS September 18, 1942–November 30, 1945. Peak population 8,475.

TOPAZ (ALSO KNOWN AS CENTRAL UTAH), UTAH September 11, 1942–October 31, 1945. Peak population 8,130.

TULE LAKE, CALIFORNIA May 27, 1942–March 20, 1946. Peak population 18,789.

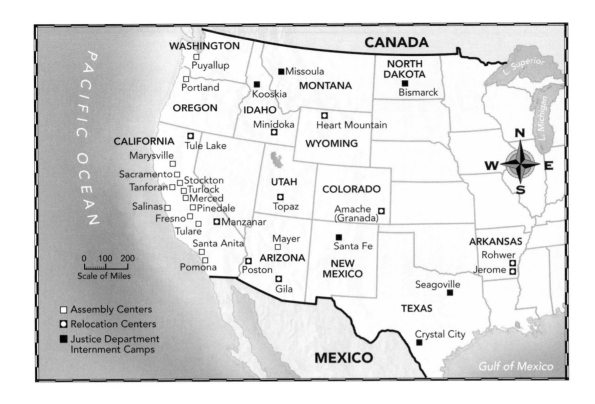

JUSTICE DEPARTMENT INTERNMENT CAMPS

U.S. Department of Justice internment camps were used to incarcerate 2,260 so-called "dangerous persons" of Japanese ancestry.

BISMARCK, NORTH DAKOTA	**KOOSKIA, IDAHO**	**SANTA FE, NEW MEXICO**
CRYSTAL CITY, TEXAS	**MISSOULA, MONTANA**	**SEAGOVILLE, TEXAS**

(Names and numbers were adapted from http://www.momomedia.com/CLPEF/camps.html.)

ABOUT THE LETTERS

In reprinting the children's letters, we have kept the original misspellings, punctuation, and grammatical errors to reflect the full flavor of the authentic letters sent to Clara Breed. All are from the collection of the Japanese American National Museum.

ABOUT THE TESTIMONY

You will find quotes throughout the book labeled as "testimony." These are just a sampling of the moving accounts by 750 witnesses who testified during the 1981 congressional hearings of the Commission on Wartime Relocation and Internment of Civilians (CWRIC), whose mandate was to investigate the policies of the government directed at Japanese Americans during World War II.

CHAPTER ONE

"WE WERE FILLED WITH A TERRIBLE FEAR"

THEY WERE MARKED AS DIFFERENT from other races and they were not treated on an equal basis. This happened because in one part of our country they were feared as competitors, and the rest of our country knew them so little and cared so little about them that they did not even think about the principle that we in this country believe in—that of equal rights for all human beings.

—ELEANOR ROOSEVELT

Chances are you can remember exactly where you were on September 11, 2001. It is a day that will forever be etched in your memory. Even if you lived nowhere near New York City, Washington, D.C., or Pennsylvania, the images of that dastardly attack on the United States will not be forgotten.

For my generation, born in the 1930s, another date was forever seared in our hearts and minds. Our president, Franklin Delano Roosevelt, called that date, December 7, 1941, "a date that will live in infamy." On that unforgettable Sunday morning the Empire of Japan launched a sneak attack on the American naval base in Pearl Harbor. It was just before 8:00 A.M. in Hawaii when the first wave of Japanese fighters, bombers, and torpedo planes swept down from the sky, dropping bombs and sinking five of the eight battleships, the pride of the U.S. Pacific fleet. Half an hour later, a second wave of enemy planes, their wings painted with the symbols of the Rising Sun, hammered dozens of U.S. combat planes before most had a chance to take off and defend the army, navy, and marine airfields. In less than two hours, twenty-one ships of the U.S. fleet were damaged or sinking. More than 180 U.S. planes were destroyed, and another 159 were damaged. Thousands of soldiers, sailors, and civilians lay wounded on airfields and aboard ships ablaze in the harbor. By 10:00 A.M., the attack was over; in the first two hours of the war, 2,390 Americans were already dead.

In towns and cities all over America, people were stunned by the news they heard on their radios as they drove home from church or sat down to Sunday lunch. Americans feared that the war already raging in Europe would now spread to our shores. Hitler's Nazi German blitzkrieg, his "lightning war," which began in 1939, had by June of 1940 gobbled up most of Europe, conquering Norway, Denmark, the Low Countries, and France. While many Americans were opposed to going to war, defense factories in the United States were already turning out planes and tanks and weapons for the British, who were desperately waging a battle for their very existence. With the attack on Pearl Harbor, going to war was no longer a choice Americans could avoid.

I was just seven years old, but I can still remember my terror that bombs would soon be falling on the street where I lived. We sat next to the radio and listened as the first reports were repeated again and again. My big brother tried to assure me that the war was halfway across the world. He showed me on his globe that Hawaii was far, far away from where we lived in a little town ninety miles from New York City. But if planes could fly to Hawaii, I wondered, why not here?

My childish fears, I've since discovered, were shared by thousands of Americans on that day. Especially on the West Coast, where there was an expectation that planes and ships would attack at any hour. For Japanese Americans in California, Washington, and Oregon, the events of December 7 were to change their lives in unimaginable ways.

Although Hawaii was thousands of miles from the West Coast, and no bombs were falling on San Diego, for those of Japanese ancestry the news was even more frightening and immediate.

We were filled with a terrible fear. The question was: What will happen to us now? That night an FBI agent with our town sheriff appeared at our door in the middle of the night to arrest my father. Without a word of protest, he got dressed and went with them into the dark night. We did not see him again for two and a half years. —Testimony of **SALLY KIRITA TSUNEISHI**, Los Angeles, August 4, 1981

The San Diego Public Library, where Clara Breed first met "her children"

"IT WAS AS IF THE WORLD FELL ABOUT OUR EARS"

From the moment she heard the news, Clara Breed worried about all the Japanese American families in San Diego, dozens of whom she knew as friends as well as library regulars.

Just two weeks before, Tetsuzo Hirasaki, along with his father and sister, had celebrated Thanksgiving with Clara and her family. Tets was now a young man of twenty-one, but Clara had known him since he was just a little boy. Tets never forgot the upstairs children's library on 8th and E Streets:

Miss Breed introduced me to the magical world of books. . . . What an ironic fortune I had to be a "neglected child." My mother had died when I was five and my father was working sixteen hours a day. I was on strict orders not to stray and get into trouble. Thus, I became a bookworm. I started at one corner of the library and went along one shelf to another indiscriminately. When summer was over and school started, I found the school library. However, when summer vacation came again, I was back at the children's library downtown. All the while there was Miss Breed quietly, gently, and kindly shepherding me.

Tets was just one of the many Japanese Americans whom Clara worried about that evening. During the past fourteen years, as San Diego's first children's librarian, she had watched Tets and so many others grow from little children who could barely write their names to big teenagers ready for college. The downtown branch was one of thirteen branches of the San Diego Public Library, but it was the one that Japanese American children could walk to in their neighborhood. Clara had given these children their first library cards and shared story hours with them. Miss Breed, as they all called her, helped while they spent long hours bent over encyclopedias and searched through the *Reader's Guide* to find that last little fact for their term papers. They were as devoted to her as she was to them. What would happen to them now? she wondered.

December 7 was a blow to everyone, but to the young Japanese Americans "it was as if the world fell about our ears."—CLARA BREED, *Library Journal*, June 1942

ARRESTS WERE SWIFT AND SUDDEN

Before the sun had set on the West Coast, FBI agents were pounding on the doors of those they suspected of being spies. They rounded up hundreds of leaders in Japanese American communities up and down the West Coast. Before the war, the FBI had made a list of aliens who were considered a risk to the security of the United States and were to be arrested in the event of war. There were three thousand aliens—Germans, Italians, and Japanese—on the list. Half of these so-called enemy aliens were Issei, first-generation Japanese Americans, who had immigrated to the United States more than thirty years before. They were "enemy aliens" only because anti-Asian laws prohibited them from becoming citizens, solely on the basis of race. They were newsmen, ministers, teachers, fishermen, and businessmen who worked for Japanese companies or traveled to Japan often. By morning, dozens of Issei leaders had been taken from their homes and families. Some would not be reunited for years.

Fusa Tsumagari's father was one of the first to be taken away. Fusa was a high school senior who suddenly had to take charge. Patty Higashioka, Fusa's daughter, was not alive then, yet the events of that day are a part of her family's history that she was able to share with me.

My grandfather, Harry Tsumagari, was out fishing that day and was wondering why there were so many ships leaving port. When he got home from fishing (still not knowing about Pearl Harbor), FBI agents were waiting for him at the hotel that he ran in the Japanese section of San Diego. Since many of the guests were from Japan and because he had made frequent trips to Japan, my grandfather was suspected of being a spy. Like dozens of other leaders and businessmen in the Japanese American community, the agents took him away that night. Fusa and her mother had no way of knowing what happened to him. They spent their days going to all the jails trying to find him. Fusa's mother, my grandmother, didn't speak too much English, so Fusa, a senior at San Diego High School, had to do all the talking. Eventually they found him in a jail and before long he was sent to an internment camp in Texas. He had not done anything illegal, nor was he charged with any crime. Dozens of others like Fusa's father were taken away on the chance that they might be spies or saboteurs.

Fusa Tsumagari's father was a successful Issei businessman in the 1920s. Fusa, the youngest, is the little girl on the dashboard. Her brother Yuki is the younger son. Their older brother, Minori, died early, inspiring Yuki to become a doctor.

Fusa's best friend and classmate, Chiyo Kusumoto, still remembers how frightened she was when her father was also taken away that night.

My father was not involved in the Japanese community as a leader, but he liked to play a game called Go, it's like chess.

He happened to be at the wrong place at the right time. He would play Go every Sunday and he just happened to be with these people who were dignitaries—maybe from Japan. My father was not released until a few months later. He didn't have any connection to those people. The FBI was very quick in rounding up many people who they thought were involved with Japan in any way.

By Monday morning, dozens of Issei leaders in the Japanese American community had been taken away to local jails or north to Los Angeles, where they were held for interrogation. In a matter of days or weeks they were sent in a heavily guarded train to distant places such as Fort Abraham Lincoln at Bismarck, North Dakota, or Fort Missoula at Missoula, Montana. Both were internment camps run by the Justice Department. Their only way of communicating with their families was through heavily censored mail. One man wrote this moving poem to his family:

Leaving a city of everlasting spring.
I am buried in the snow of Montana
In the Northern Country.
You in San Diego, I in Montana.
The path of my dream
is frozen. —**KYUJI AIZUMI**

Long before the war began, the FBI had been making up lists of aliens they considered serious security risks. Those on the so-called A-B-C Lists were taken away right after the attack on Pearl Harbor. But the arrests did not stop there. By February the FBI had rounded up thousands of the Issei. They took away anyone connected to the Japanese government, Japanese businesses, and Japanese newspapers. Issei leaders of Buddhist and Christian churches, fishermen, and those who taught in Japanese language schools were rounded up. Although some were eventually reunited with their families, who were themselves incarcerated in so-called relocation camps, many would not see their families again for several years.

Day after day more and more fathers were arrested by the FBI and sent east to internment camps within forty-eight hours, so there was hardly time for hurried shopping expeditions for warm sweaters and woolen socks against the Montana cold. No hearings were held on the Coast because of public hysteria. Arrests were swift and sudden and included everyone who had knowledge of the coastline or waterfront, or who had made regular trips to Japan, or had been a member of a Japanese society. Meanwhile the young Japanese Americans collected money for the destitute, acted as interpreters for the FBI and the immigration authorities, and helped in the alien registration. Their cooperation has been repeatedly praised by government authorities. —**CLARA BREED**, *Horn Book Magazine*

Margaret Ishino, a high school junior who had known Miss Breed since grammar school, recalled in our interview that so many of her father's friends were taken away right after the war broke out that her father had his suitcase ready to go.

When the FBI came to our house, that was a very traumatic experience. Two agents came. My mother was lying in bed because she had just given birth to my brother. They threw the sheets and blankets off her. They said maybe she was hiding something in the bed, that's why they did that. And they took anything that had anything to do with Japanese—anything written in Japanese, scrolls, my mother's things that she brought from Japan. My father's books—my father was an avid reader—he loved to read—they took all his books. Nothing Japanese was left in the house.

For eleven-year-old Elizabeth Kikuchi, the arrival of the FBI at the church was even more frightening. The "G-men" not only took her father, Rev. Kenji Kikuchi, away; they took her mother, Yoshiko, as well. Her teenage sister, Mariam, tried to assure Elizabeth, her twelve- and ten-year-old brothers, Thomas and David, and her little eight-year-old sister, Anna, that they would be all right. They had only moved to San Diego in July, yet their father, the pastor of the Japanese Congregational Church of San Diego, was considered one of the community's key spiritual leaders and their mother, Yoshiko, was an active teacher in the church.

Reverend Kikuchi had graduated from Divinity School at Princeton and returned to Japan to marry Yoshiko in 1926. Ten years later they went back to visit family in Japan. Nikkei who had traveled to Japan at that time were now automatically considered suspects. Elizabeth remembered that trip and her impressions of the Japanese patriotism and loyalty to the emperor on his white horse. But she knew her loyalty was to America. She had no idea where her parents were taken or when or if they would be back.

Oddly enough, the FBI released Reverend Kikuchi before long but they held Elizabeth's mother longer. Why was Mrs. Kikuchi being held? There were no charges. People were simply arrested and held on suspicion. They were given no hearing, no way to defend themselves. And there was no way of knowing how long Mrs. Kikuchi would be held.

I AM AN AMERICAN!

At 12:30 on the afternoon of December 8, 1941, little more than twenty-four hours after the attack on Pearl Harbor, Pres. Franklin Delano Roosevelt delivered a six-minute

HOW TO SPOT A JAP

Racist cartoons began to appear in magazines and newspapers, many depicting Japanese people as ugly, or even as monkeys or vipers. This one was created by Milton Caniff, best known by millions of kids for his daily cartoon strip, Terry and the Pirates. *During World War II, he created cartoons for the military, and pilots put his images on their planes.*

speech asking the Congress of the United States for a declaration of war against the Empire of Japan. Four days later the Germans and Italians declared war on the United States as well. The whole world was now plunged into a war that was to take the lives of millions.

Richard "Babe" Karasawa, who was nicknamed for Babe Ruth, one of his brother's baseball heroes, was fourteen and recalls going to school that day:

. . . first thing before class we used to congregate and Jimmy Papas, my Greek buddy . . . comes up and says to me . . . "Hey Babe, you're an enemy now!" . . . Then he says . . . "I'm only kidding" and he put his arm around me and gives me a hug. . . . That was the only thing said. When Roosevelt was making his speech on Dec 8—we were listening to him in homeroom class. I think I was the chairman of the class and I was the only Asian in the class. I can't remember all that I felt, but I know I felt bad.

In those days . . . practically everyone's parents came from a foreign country. A few guys were Chinese and there was Jimmy my good Greek buddy, his dad used to drive down the street with a vegetable truck and bang a piece of iron and people would come out of the house and buy fruits and vegetables. One of my buddies was Tom, he was German . . . just to give you an illustration how mixed the group was—there were a lot of Italians, Mexicans and a couple of Blacks . . . really, what I like to call an all-American group.

But not everyone had such a warm reception:

. . . on Monday, December 8, I was at the bus stop going . . . for a brush-up course at Knapp's Business college. The driver did not greet me with the usual "Hi Sumie, how's tricks?" I heard someone from the back of the bus yell "Get that damn Jap girl off this bus, Curly." He said "Are you Japanese?" and I said I am an American Japanese. "You got any proof of that?" he sneers . . . "I was born in King County." Then Curly ordered me off the bus saying . . . "You are still a damn Jap." I could not continue my classes. I was suddenly afraid to be alone on the highway. The college . . . refunded my money. —Testimony of **SUMIE BARTA**, Seattle, September 11, 1981

My friend Ellen Yukawa, who at this time lived in the Central Valley, far north of San Diego, dreaded going to school, especially after Pearl Harbor:

There were two schools. One on the West Side where all the minorities lived and then one on the East Side for all the Caucasian kids. Even if you were Polish, you lived on the West Side—it was the poorer part of town. But we shared the same school bus. Everything was fine, as long as the West Side kids were on . . . but the minute it went to the East Side and picked up those kids . . . it's amazing when I think of it now . . . they would call us names and sit on us and pull our hair. It was more so, after Pearl Harbor. The minority people, Mexicans, Blacks, Koreans—didn't treat us that way—it was just the Caucasians.

Remembering the first days of the war, Clara Breed later wrote in *Horn Book Magazine*:

The news was a profound shock to the Little Tokyos. Mothers spent the next few days in tears while they watched their lives crumble around them. Fishermen were arrested as they stepped ashore from their boats. Japanese restaurants and stores were suddenly empty of customers, vegetable markets were deserted, gardeners were told that their services were no longer needed, a fruit market was stormed and wrecked by hoodlums. The Chinese broke out a rash of buttons and printed signs that dangled ostentatiously from their shoulders reading, "I am Chinese," evidence of their fear that they too might be victims of mob violence since few people even claim to be able to tell the difference between a Chinese and a Japanese.

"EVERY MAN, WOMAN, AND CHILD IS IN IT"

On December 9, just two days after the attack, First Lady Eleanor Roosevelt, assistant chief of civil defense, and New York's mayor Fiorello H. La Guardia, chairman of the Office of Civil Defense, began a tour of the West Coast, urging people to be calm but prepared for danger. Mayor La Guardia said, "I'm not saying what to do *if* an attack comes; I'm putting it: *when* it comes." While both urged people not to panic, there seemed to be little doubt in their minds that bombs would soon be falling on the streets of California. At the same time, Mrs. Roosevelt warned about another threat: "Let's be honest, there is a chance now for great hysteria against minority groups—loyal, American-born Japanese and Germans. If we treat them unfairly and make them unhappy we may shake their loyalty which should be built up."

In every city she visited, Mrs. Roosevelt talked about the urgency of preparing for an air raid: ". . . let us not be silly enough to be taken by surprise. It is not a sign of fear to be ready—it is good sense. Go to your homes today and make yourselves ready," she warned.

The Japanese mothers spent the next few days after Pearl Harbor in tears, replying to anyone who expressed sympathy, "We are so sorry, we are so sorry!" They formed Red Cross classes and contributed far more than they could afford to the Red Cross war chest, because that seemed the only way they could make amends and ease a little of their deep humiliation. . . . meanwhile the young Japanese Americans . . . helped in the alien registration assuring their frightened elders that this is America and not Germany and they could expect fair treatment. . . . —**CLARA BREED**, *Library Journal*

On a trip to California, First Lady Eleanor Roosevelt met with Nisei days after the war began. She urged the public to treat these loyal American citizens fairly. She told reporters, "This war is no longer merely a military war. . . . Every man, woman, and child is in it. No one need be ashamed of being afraid. But be secure within yourself and in that way you will learn not to be afraid." (LA Times, *Dec. 11, 1941, p. 2)*

To prove their allegiance to America the Japanese American community volunteered to give blood, to roll bandages for the Red Cross, and to collect money for war bonds. Soon after the war began, the *Rafu Shimpo*, a newspaper read by the Nikkei, urged Nisei to take action, and they ran an ambulance fund, publishing the names of contributors who sent anything from one to five dollars. They proudly collected $3,369.09—a huge sum, considering how many of their readers had lost their jobs.

Newsmen covered the arrests of aliens with plenty of publicity. Their stories were meant to calm the public's fear of possible spies and saboteurs. Although the FBI had made lists of aliens who might be considered security risks, they also told the president that they considered most Japanese Americans loyal to the United States.

President Roosevelt wanted more than one source of information. He asked John F. Carter, a journalist, to gather information on the loyalty of the Nikkei, citizens and aliens. Carter asked Curtis B. Munson, a California businessman, for a confidential report about what the Nikkei community might do in the event of war between Japan and the United States. Just weeks before Pearl Harbor, Munson reported that for the most part the Nikkei presented no threat to America's security. According to his secret report, it was probable that the Issei would do nothing to harm their adopted country or their children, the Nisei, citizens by birth and loyal Americans through and through.

Nevertheless, Munson warned, "There are still Japanese in the United States who will tie dynamite around their waist and make a human bomb of themselves." He warned that the dams, bridges, harbors, and power stations of the West Coast were basically unguarded. This lingering doubt was to weigh heavily on those in power.

"RICE FOR THE LOVELY ONES"

During those early weeks of the war, newspaper editorials and leaders urged Americans to remain calm and be fair to the aliens.

But life for Americans of Japanese descent was anything but calm or fair. During the first week of the war the Treasury Department froze all bank accounts of the Issei. Four days later they were allowed to withdraw a maximum of one hundred dollars a month. This was especially hard on families whose father and breadwinner had been arrested or was out of work. Families were without money for everyday living expenses. Even if the father was not arrested, business in Japanese restaurants, hotels, and shops was very slow.

Truck farmers were not allowed to sell their produce for fear they might poison the food they were selling. Issei fishermen were not allowed to go out to fish for fear they would send signals to Japanese ships, and their wives who worked in the canneries were fired. Some unions refused to accept Nisei as members. In fact, Caucasian employees of the Northern Pacific Railroad said they would quit unless all Japanese Americans were fired. In hospitals on the West Coast, Nisei doctors were fired and patients refused to be cared for by Nisei nurses.

In cities and towns all over the West Coast, Nikkei workers were losing their jobs. President Roosevelt called for a "sane policy" in dealing with enemy aliens, and was said to be deeply concerned over reports that aliens and foreign-born citizens were being fired. "Such a policy is as stupid as it is unjust," he said. ". . . It plays into the hands of the enemies of American democracy. . . . We must not forget what we are defending: Liberty, decency, justice." He cautioned that we not follow the Nazis by pitting "race against race, religion against religion . . . divide and conquer!" Roosevelt added that we need the "services of all loyal and patriotic citizens and non-citizens in defending our land and our liberties."

In spite of those assurances, President Roosevelt did nothing more to defend the Nikkei, and their loyalty continued to be questioned. The statements by the president and by Attorney General Francis Biddle gave the Nikkei a false sense of security that the government would stand by them.

Before long the press complained. In a February 9, 1942, article in the *San Francisco Examiner*, columnist Henry McLemore wrote, "Mr. Biddle does everything but cook the rice for the lovely ones . . . the Japs are doing their best to take their juvenile American born offspring and teach them [in Japanese school] that Emperor Hirohito is the leading citizen of the world, a near god, and completely without wrong."

Attorney General Biddle was receiving a staggering number of letters that said such things as "Don't piddle, Mr. Biddle" and "We are sick of Biddling while Rome burns!"

Clara Breed, like millions of Americans, was a real fan of First Lady Eleanor Roosevelt. Miss Breed and her mother, Estella Breed, went to hear Mrs. Roosevelt speak when she came to San Diego. Clara not only read Mrs. Roosevelt's regular newspaper column, "My Day"; she also clipped and saved some of the columns. During that first month of the war, Mrs. Roosevelt wrote:

My Day . . . December 16, 1941 . . .

. . . the great mass of our people, stemming from these various national ties, must not feel that they have suddenly ceased to be Americans.

This is, perhaps, the greatest test this country has ever met. Perhaps it is the test which is going to show whether the United States can furnish a pattern for the rest of the world for the future. Our citizens come from all the nations of the world. Some of us have said from time to time, that we were the only proof that different nationalities could live together in peace and understanding, each bringing his own contribution, different though it may be, to the final unity which is the United States. . . . Perhaps, on us today, lies the obligation to prove that such a vision may be a practical possibility.

If we can not meet the challenge of fairness to our citizens of every nationality, of really believing in the Bill of Rights and making it a reality for all loyal American citizens, regardless of race, creed or color; if we can not keep in check anti-Semitism, anti-racial feelings as well as anti-religious feelings, then we shall have removed from the world, the one real hope for the future on which all humanity must now rely.

But Mrs. Roosevelt's message did not change the growing tide of anti-Japanese sentiment. It was impossible to miss the hostility in the newspapers, on the radio, and wherever Japanese Americans went.

"GET OUT! WE DON'T WANT YOU!"

Under the door the following note was left . . . "This is a warning. Get out. We don't want you in our beautiful country. Go where your ancestors came from. Once a Jap, always one. Get out." As we became increasingly the target of blind hate, our government failed to come to our aid. Indeed, the government joined in the hysteria by over-reacting, rounding up supposed enemy agents and, above all, keeping silent about the increasing antagonism against all Japanese Americans.
—Testimony of **MINORU TAMAKI**, San Francisco, August 13, 1981

Although the Japanese American children continued to go to school, life was anything but normal. Signs in store windows told them to keep out. During the holiday shopping season that December, Aiko Kubo remembers going to a department store and the clerk "just stared beyond me. She just ignored me and that hit hard."

In Los Angeles, Japanese American children of Little Tokyo no longer came to the library. Clara Breed's friend Zada Taylor, the children's librarian in Los Angeles, wrote that the streets were not safe for Japanese Americans:

"The day after Pearl Harbor most of the Japanese children who usually flood our downtown Central Children's Room . . . turned in their books and walked out empty handed. . . . It is dangerous for them to cross the non-oriental sections of the city and our problem was what to do to give them books." Since these children were such avid readers the librarians dreamed up a solution. Each week they loaded the Library Station Wagon and go to the schools they attended. "So many of the children are from American born parents and have no oriental traits except those of features, but with the war so close to us they have been branded along with the aliens."

Since San Diego's main library was downtown in the Nikkei neighborhood, the children could go there without walking through unfriendly neighborhoods where they might be harmed. Many of the older girls had little else to do but read.

The children came to the library more than ever, but they came in groups as if there were safety in numbers. Little Jack Watanabe, whose fat cheeks always reminded us of a chipmunk's stuffed full of nuts, lost his merriment and became as solemn as an old man, although he still preferred funny books like . . . *The Five Hundred Hats of Bartholomew Cubbins*. Katherine Tasaki no longer danced around the library but walked soberly, even her Chinese friends—for Japanese children do sometimes have Chinese friends—seemed to share her sorrow.

—**CLARA BREED**, *Horn Book Magazine*, 1943

Clara Breed had worked in the San Diego Public Library since 1928. She was delighted to be working in the same old building where Charles Lindbergh had mapped his historic first solo flight across the Atlantic in 1927. There were thirteen branches of the library scattered around the city, but hers was the one that the Japanese American children of the city used. The Children's Room was upstairs, where children from tots to teens came to know Clara as a friend as well as a librarian.

Elizabeth Kikuchi remembers going to the library at least once a week and leaving with a stack of eight to ten books. Liz had a huge appetite for books—she could read through a long book in a day! Miss Breed encouraged Liz's love of reading by suggesting books she thought would interest Liz. After school Liz and her schoolmates worked on their victory garden; it was the patriotic thing to do! By growing fresh vegetables, people all over the country cut back on their use of canned goods, which were needed overseas to feed the troops. But Liz still made time for reading. She was greatly relieved

I NEED YOUR HELP!

All right, nisei, come out of your hiding. All of you who used to rain us with club notices about elections, party plans, basketball practice. . . . Come on out and get into Civil Defense. You'll be surprised to find how few of you will be sworn at, stabbed, stoned or shot! . . . Let's see your notices on how many of your members turned out for state guard, Red Cross, emergency police and . . . Let's hear how much of your treasury went for Defense Bonds and Stamps. Let's hear about your action! You're on the spot!
—*RAFU SHIMPO,*
Dec. 18, 1941

when her mother was released and back home with the family. But many of Liz's schoolmates were less fortunate. Many still had fathers who were being held, and no one knew when they would be released.

FRENZY OF FEAR

Early calls for calm and fairness did not last. The West Coast continued to brace for attacks. There were nightly blackouts. Air-raid sirens wailed in the darkness. Although they were all false alarms, a frenzy of fear and suspicion became a way of life in the cities along the Pacific coast. After Pearl Harbor, there were rumors that Nikkei farmers in Hawaii had cut arrows in their fields pointing the way to U.S. air bases. It was not true, but fear overshadowed truth in those early days of the war, and there was fear that Japanese Americans would send signals by radio or flashing lights to enemy ships or planes off the Pacific coast.

All of this fear did not happen in a vacuum. Off the East Coast in January 1942, German U-boats were sinking American ships almost daily. On the West Coast on February 24, a Japanese submarine shelled an oil refinery near Santa Barbara, California. Though it did little damage, the idea of a sub being that close only triggered or confirmed people's worst fears.

Headlines of Japanese military victories filled the news during the early months of the war. Like Hitler's early blitzkrieg in Europe, the Japanese were triumphing in the Pacific. They had taken Hong Kong and Singapore. Corregidor was bombarded and Bataan fell. Gen. Douglas MacArthur, the commander of the Pacific, was forced to retreat from the Philippines to Australia. America had underestimated the strength of the Japanese, who were moving into the South Sea Islands and southward into Indochina. All through January, February, and March of 1942, the United States was losing the war.

Night after night, air-raid sirens warned of enemy planes about to attack cities up and down the Pacific coast. Newspaper headlines reported the alarms but seldom published a follow-up that reported these were all false alarms.

At approximately 2:00 A.M. on February 23, 1942, my wife and I were awakened by the sound of gunfire. On going outside we saw searchlights converging on a point high up in the sky, antiaircraft guns all around us were shooting at the target. Much, much later we learned that this was a weather balloon that had torn loose from its moorings.

—Testimony of **DR. YOSHIHIKO FRED FUJIKAWA**, Los Angeles, August 5, 1981

"CITIZENS BY ACCIDENT"

. . . With legitimate war fears mixed with racist propaganda, it was a simple step from hating imperial Japanese to hating, distrusting and vilifying Japanese Americans. —Testimony of **J. FRED MACDONALD**, Chicago, September 22, 1981

As the war news from the Pacific grew worse, anti-Japanese sentiments blossomed into senseless attacks on anyone and anything Japanese. In Washington, D.C., four Japanese cherry trees were cut down in the darkness of night. On January 1, 1942, shots were fired into the homes of three Japanese truck farmers in Santa Clara County and two people were wounded.

In late January the president received a report from Owen Roberts, who headed a commission on the causes of the Pearl Harbor attack. Roberts's report was loaded with misinformation. It failed to distinguish between Japanese Americans and those suspected of being Japanese spies of the Imperial Japanese government. When the commission's report reached the newspapers, the call for immediately removing "enemy aliens" from the West Coast was loud and clear.

Soon the Department of Justice, the president, and the First Lady were receiving bags full of hate mail calling for the removal of the Nikkei:

—Everyone should be moved back 500–600 miles—to raise large quantities of vegetables to feed or supply our country, and all of this garden should be under heavy surveillance and guard by true Americans so they cannot poison the vegetables.

—Move them back in the desert and feed them rice.

—We want to see them all sent back to Japan where they belong and leave America for Americans.

Clara could not have missed the constant barrage of anti-Nikkei articles. The *San Diego Union* ran fourteen editorials between January 20 and March 16, 1942, demanding the mass evacuation of the Nikkei.

A delegation of congressmen led by John Rankin of Mississippi told Congress that the Japanese should be removed "even to the 3rd and 4th generation . . . Once a Jap, always a Jap . . . You cannot regenerate a Jap, convert him, and make him the same as a white man any more than you can reverse the laws of nature." California representatives John Costello and Harry Sheppard warned that American Japanese were a "fifth column threat" and a "national hazard."

The anti-Japanese hysteria was stirred by the powerful Hearst and McClatchy newspapers, which had long histories of attacking the Japanese community. They and organizations such as the Native Sons and Daughters of the Golden West, the California State Grange, and the American Legion had managed during the 1920s to bar further immigration of Japanese and demanded laws that prevented the Issei from becoming citizens, owning land, or entering into mixed marriages. Unlike European immigrants, who could become naturalized citizens, the Issei were forced by law to remain "involuntary aliens." For years the Issei worked land they could only lease. Eventually they were able to buy the farmland in the names of their children who were American citizens. Now that the Nisei were coming of age, these same white supremacists were lobbying to get rid of all Japanese from the West Coast forever.

A popular journalist, W. H. Anderson, wrote an article for the February 2, 1942, *Los Angeles Times*, in which he labeled the Nisei as "citizens by accident of birth, but who were Japanese nevertheless . . . a viper is nonetheless a viper wherever the egg is hatched . . . so a Japanese-American, born of Japanese parents, nurtured upon Japanese traditions, living in a transplanted Japanese atmosphere and thoroughly inoculated with Japanese thoughts, Japanese ideas, not withstanding his nominal brand of accidental citizenship, almost inevitably and in the rarest exceptions grow up to be Japanese, not an American. . . . "

Greedy farmers got on the bandwagon, seeing a way to rid the West Coast of Japanese. For years the industrious Nikkei farmers had toiled and turned the arid soil into gardens that produced and distributed three-quarters of the food in California—food the nation depended on. If other farmers could finally push the Nikkei farmers out, they could take over.

Those who would most profit promoted rumors that alien farmers, loyal to the emperor, might poison the food supply. Such rumors gave strength to the argument that the Nikkei should be removed for reasons of security. On the one hand, there was pressure to remove them from their farms, but on the other hand, at the same time the government was making plans to use these same suspected enemy agents to grow crops in their resettlement camps. In truth, there never was a real danger of farmers poisoning the food supply. Once the Nikkei were out of the way, greedy farmers, like vultures, snapped up their orchards and fields for next to nothing.

State employees who were classified as "enemy aliens" were fired from their jobs. One administrator claimed "Japanese employees" disrupted morale and that others refused to work with them. When Japanese American truck farmers arrived in farmer's markets with their produce, they were confronted with signs that said: "This is a prohibited area!"

This billboard could be found at the edge of San Francisco's Japanese quarter. It was photographed on the morning when 600 persons of Japanese ancestry were evacuated from the quarter and placed into assembly centers.

Although some college presidents and religious leaders in California spoke up on Japanese Americans' behalf, the press gave far more coverage to stories that cast doubt on the loyalty of the Nikkei. On February 5, 1942, the *New York Times* carried a story about the Dies Committee on Un-American Activities. A committee spokesman said that they would soon release a "Yellow Paper" to prove there was a spy ring of 150,000 members. Never mind that there were not that many Nikkei in all of the United States! In an effort to embarrass the president, the committee claimed that evidence of the spy ring had been turned over to the State, Justice, War, and Navy departments before December 7. Chairman Martin Dies from Texas predicted that thanks to these spies the West Coast was in for "a tragedy that will make Pearl Harbor sink into insignificance."

Ted Geisel created some characters he would later use in his well-known picture books, which were written under the name of Dr. Seuss. His political cartoons were generally liberal, but not when it came to Japanese Americans.

In the newspapers, *Japs* referred to both Japanese Americans and the enemy. Earl Warren, later chief justice of the U.S. Supreme Court, but then attorney general of California, testified that it was hard to explain as a "mere coincidence" that the Nikkei lived and worked near all utilities, airfields, harbors, bridges, telephone and power lines, and even oil fields. Anti-Japanese organizations saw this as part of a plot designed to take over America. The fact that there had been no sabotage yet did not prove the Nikkei's loyalty. Somehow, Earl Warren managed to turn the idea upside down and claimed that "the very fact that no sabotage has taken place to date is a disturbing and confirming indication that such action will be taken."

In such an atmosphere of hysteria and the need to blame someone, those who looked like the enemy became easy targets. Ted Geisel, who would later become best known as the well-loved children's author Dr. Seuss, worked as a political cartoonist during World War II. His negative images reflected the growing tide of hatred directed at Japanese Americans.

CHAPTER TWO

A SECOND DATE
OF INFAMY

BY LATE JANUARY OF 1942, Lt. Gen. John DeWitt, the military commander of the West Coast Defense Command, considered the presence of the Nikkei a threat to national security. Both DeWitt and Secretary of War Henry L. Stimson believed an attack on the West Coast was imminent and that the Nikkei would help the enemy. DeWitt was convinced that the Nikkei were not to be trusted. Purely on the basis of rumors, he reported that enemy planes were flying over California and Nikkei were sending signals to ships and planes off the coast of California. The FBI quickly established that his reports were untrue. But DeWitt continued to urge Washington to remove the Nikkei from the West Coast, which he considered a military zone and potential battlefield.

On February 19, 1942, the president issued Executive Order 9066, which set the stage for the mass removal of all Nikkei from the war zone, as defined by the War Department and military commanders of the area, namely DeWitt. Although the order did not mention those of Japanese descent specifically, the government handed their fate over to the military. It gave the military the power to remove more than 110,000 people from their homes and send them to unknown destinations because

The Japanese American Citizens League asked Ham Fisher, the cartoonist, to portray the Nisei soldiers who were already in uniform as all-American. Fisher did so, with his world-famous heavyweight champ, Joe Palooka. But anti-Japanese sentiment was powerful, and it soon led to the disarming of many of those who were already in the service.

some might be disloyal. None of them had been tried or found guilty of a crime. Despite the fact that 70 percent of them were U.S. citizens, their rights were forgotten. Their only crime was having Japanese blood—even one-sixteenth of Japanese blood in your veins made you an enemy.

A few weeks later Lieutenant General DeWitt ordered a curfew. All Japanese Americans and enemy aliens were to remain in their homes between 8:00 P.M. and 6:00 A.M. His proclamation also prohibited the same people from traveling more than five miles from their homes during noncurfew hours or from possessing firearms, war materials, explosives, bombs, shortwave radios, signaling devices, codes, ciphers, or cameras.

DeWitt sent a memo to the secretary of war in 1942 that was not printed until 1943 and shows how the lieutenant general's racist bias—not military necessity—had shaped his decision:

The Japanese race is an enemy race and while many second and third generation Japanese born on U.S. soil, possessed of United States citizenship, have become "Americanized," the racial strains are undiluted. To conclude otherwise is to expect that children born of white parents on Japanese soil sever all racial affinity and become loyal Japanese subjects ready to fight and if necessary die for Japan in a war against the nation of their parents. That Japan is allied with Germany and Italy in this struggle is no ground for assuming that any Japanese, barred from assimilation by convention as he is, though born and raised in the U.S., will not turn against this nation when the final test of loyalty comes.

—**WAR DEPARTMENT FINAL REPORT**, Japanese Evacuation from the West Coast

"DON'T WORRY YOSHIO, YOU ARE AN AMERICAN"

All through December 1941 and January and early February 1942, newspapers and radio commentators had continued to spread doubt and fears about the loyalty of people of Japanese ancestry. When they first heard reports on the radio that possibly all Japanese would be moved inland or into detention centers, the Nisei did not believe it. "We are Americans. They could not do that to us." That is what Kay Yamashita and many others believed:

> Well, it did happen, and it happened so quickly that we had no time to think, no time to react . . . we were helpless, as the government of the United States failed to protect the rights of an identifiable group of citizens and resident aliens.
>
> —Testimony of **KAY YAMASHITA**, Chicago, September 22, 1981

"Jap hunting licenses," as buttons or cards, were on sale in many parts of the country. The Tennessee Conservation Department was going to print 6,000 licenses and charge two dollars for each, but in December 1941, it announced an "OPEN SEASON ON JAPS—NO LICENSE NEEDED!"

> My history teacher told me, don't worry Yoshio, you are an American, and the Constitution will protect you from being forcefully moved. The next week I told him I had orders to evacuate. He was stunned. . . .
>
> —Testimony of **YOSHIO NAKAMURA**, Los Angeles, August 6, 1981

Young adults had believed that even if their Issei parents were forced to leave, the Nisei would be free to visit their parents just like all other American citizens.

> As an impressionable 12-year-old in 1942, I had learned about the U.S. Constitution and what it meant. In that period of uncertainty after December 7, 1941, I felt that I could count on our government. The remotest thing on the minds of our family was to be incarcerated under some emotional decision contrary to the Constitution. I could not believe at the time that this was happening to us. This is my country, the land that I love, doing this to us. I hope that I might some day understand, but to this day, I cannot. I was jailed on a trumped-up charge. I was betrayed, not by individuals, but by our United States of America.
>
> —Testimony of **ALLAN HIDA**, Chicago, September 22, 1981

Evacuation was now inevitable—so-called military necessity was just another excuse, based on falsehoods, greed, racist hatred, and political pressure. It was no longer a question of *if* but *when* the Japanese Americans would be removed.

Eleanor Roosevelt wrote the following column from San Diego, where her sons were stationed in the navy and soon to be shipped overseas. All the brutal losses in the Pacific are reflected in her worries as a parent saying good-bye to her loved ones. Although she was publicly opposed to evacuation of the Nikkei, she manages to find something positive about the inevitable:

My Day . . . March 21, 1942 . . .

War has given us . . . an appreciation of the good fortune we enjoy whenever we can be with the people we love. We know that tomorrow, or next week, or next month, they may not only be out of our reach, but beyond our knowledge. . . . These are days to store up memories which will see us through whatever may lie ahead.

I am very happy to see that there is established a War Relocation Authority, which will have charge of the program for relocation and employment of persons who must be moved out of military areas. Unfortunately, in a war, many innocent people must suffer hardships to safeguard the nation. One feels that a program which provides work is certainly better than having nothing to do.

The army supervised the largest mass movement of people in the history of the United States. Once the deed was done, the War Relocation Authority (WRA) would take over the business of running the camps. Milton Eisenhower took charge of the WRA and the fate of the Nikkei community. He was the older brother of a then relatively unknown army officer who would subsequently become a five-star general, Supreme Commander of Allied Forces, and eventually the thirty-fourth president of the United States, Dwight D. Eisenhower.

"WAR CAME LIKE A HURRICANE"

To the children and young people of Japanese ancestry . . . born in this country and educated in our schools, the war came like a hurricane, sweeping away their security, their friends, their jobs, sometimes their fathers into internment camps, and finally their schools and homes and liberty. One day they were living in a democracy, as good as anyone or almost, and the next they were "Japs" aware of hate and potential violence which might strike with lightning swiftness.

—**CLARA BREED**, *Library Journal*

On April 1, 1942, the evacuation order was signed by Lieutenant General DeWitt. Orders were posted on telephone poles and door fronts all over the downtown section of San Diego where most of the Nikkei lived and worked. One was surely posted outside the San Diego Public Library where Clara Breed worked. It happened to be April Fools' Day, but there was nothing to joke about that day. It was more than a cruel joke.

After months of not knowing if the Nisei would be sent along with the Issei or where they would be sent, all persons of Japanese ancestry, both alien and non-alien,* in the San Diego area were ordered to register and be prepared to leave on April 8.

> *** DOUBLESPEAK:** The order says "both alien and non-alien." Didn't it mean "alien and citizen"? It appears that the government couldn't bring itself to admit it was doing this to citizens!

People in other parts of the country knew little or nothing about the Japanese communities on the West Coast. Many people believed that those arrested immediately after December 7 were enemy aliens and agents of the Imperial Japanese. In this climate of anger and fear, it was easy to assume that the FBI was doing the job of protecting national security. Months later, when the evacuation of all Nikkei began, most Americans knew so little about the Nikkei, they believed the camps were for Japanese POWs—soldiers and enemies of the United States.

On April 2, in an article entitled "Japs Register for Evacuation," the *San Diego Union* reported that of the hundreds of Nikkei who waited to register for evacuation at the civil control station on 1919 India Street, some were silent while others said they felt it was for the best. One young man who had been on the wrestling team at Herbert Hoover High felt it was too bad that everyone had to go because of the actions of a few "heels." Another young woman in the crowd, Mary Tanaka, was optimistic that the United States would lick those "Japs" in no time at all and then the Nikkei would be able to come home.

But the upbeat spin in the newspaper did not reflect the feelings of confusion and hurt that many experienced:

Headquarters
Western Defense Command
and Fourth Army

Presidio of San Francisco, California
April 1, 1942

Civilian Exclusion Order No. 4

1. Pursuant to the provisions of Public Proclamations Nos. 1 and 2, this headquarters, dated March 2, 1942, and March 16, 1942, respectively, it is hereby ordered that all persons of Japanese ancestry, including aliens and non-aliens, be excluded on or before 12 o'clock noon, P. W. T., of Wednesday, April 8, 1942, from that portion of Military Area No. 1 in the State of California described as follows:

All of San Diego County, California, south of a line extending in an easterly direction from the mouth of the San Dieguito River (northwest of Del Mar), along the north side of the San Dieguito River, Lake Hodges, and the San Pasqual River to the bridge over the San Pasqual River at or near San Pasqual; thence easterly along the southerly line of California State Highway No. 78 through Ramona and Julian to the eastern boundary line of San Diego County.

2. A responsible member of each family, and each individual living alone, in the above described affected area will report between the hours of 8:00 a. m. and 5:00 p. m., Thursday, April 2, 1942, or during the same hours on Friday, April 3, 1942, to the Civil Control Station located at:

1919 India Street
San Diego, California

3. Any person affected by this order who fails to comply with any of its provisions or with the provisions of published instructions pertaining hereto, or who is found in the above restricted area after 12 o'clock noon, P. W. T., of Wednesday, April 8, 1942, will be subject to the criminal penalties provided by Public Law No. 503, 77th Congress, approved March 21, 1942, entitled "An Act to Provide a Penalty for Violation of Restrictions or Orders with Respect to Persons Entering, Remaining in, Leaving, or Committing Any Act in Military Areas or Zones," and alien Japanese will be subject to immediate apprehension and internment.

J. L. DeWITT
Lieutenant General, U. S. Army
Commanding

Official notices of the "evacuation" were posted on April 1, 1942, in San Diego. But the definition of "evacuate" is to withdraw from a threatened area to protect troops or civilians from harm. The Nikkei were not moved to protect themselves, but supposedly to protect others. Evacuation was doublespeak for an illegal mass arrest of people who were suspect on the basis of only one thing—their race!

I was just 10 years old when I became suddenly a "squint-eyed yellow-bellied Jap" to my fourth grade schoolmates, who had formerly been my friends. I vividly remember the agony of hiding behind the barn and crying after returning home from school and being unable to tell my father. I could see that he was shattered and confused by the order that our family was to pack what we could carry and be taken to what the Government called a relocation center. It helped, only a little, to know that my brother was a good enough citizen to be in the U.S. Army and ultimately wounded in Italy.

. . . I vividly remember wartime propaganda posters and newsreel accounts about the "sneaky, treacherous, rapacious, yellow-bellied Japs" who were the enemy. Nobody in the Government made distinctions between the "Japs" of the Japanese Imperial Army and me. I was one of the enemy, though 10 years old, and placed in a concentration camp.

—Testimony of **ROBERT MOTEKI**, New York, November 23, 1981

WHAT THEY LEFT BEHIND
OR, "UNSCRUPULOUS VULTURES"

In seven days all Nikkei, citizens and aliens alike, had to leave the city. They had just one week to store, sell, or abandon most of their possessions. The order said they could bring only what they could carry. Some people were lucky enough to rent their homes or farms to Caucasian friends or business managers. But most of the Nikkei who were relocated lost everything. With so many houses for sale all at the same time, the prices dropped. The same was true of cars, trucks, pianos, and other possessions they tried to sell:

I witnessed unscrupulous vultures in the form of human beings, taking advantage of bewildered housewives whose husbands had been rounded up by the FBI within 48 hours of Pearl Harbor. They were offered pittances for practically new furniture, appliances, radio consoles, cars and so forth, and many were falling prey to these people.

Rather than submit to these people my mother made a bonfire and with tears streaming down her face, burned articles that I had made at a wood shop, such as a footstool, a small side table, as well as her kitchen table and chairs.

—Testimony of **DR. YOSHIHIKO FRED FUJIKAWA**, Los Angeles, August 5, 1981

Due to the enforced evacuations, many families had to quickly sell most of their possessions.

One young Nisei remembers watching with horror as her mother, weeping, broke the beautiful dishes she had brought from Japan as a bride. She was so offended by the offer, destroying them seemed better than selling them for next to nothing.

Not knowing where they would be sent created great stress for parents and children:

One strong rumor floating in the Japanese community is that we would be sent to the desert, abandoned by the United States Government . . . our fantasy was that we would be made to wander around aimlessly like American Indians in tribal reservations.

As a consequence, my mother purchased canteens for water containers, high boots to protect us from rattle snakes and heavy canvas to be made into bags to carry our belongings. . . .

. . . The pre-relocation days were very confusing for me. One of my best friends was Carmella, a second generation Italian American. When I asked my parents, why didn't Carmella have to be evacuated since Italy was at war with the United States, they replied, Carmella is Caucasian, she doesn't look like the enemy, she doesn't look different like we do.

Even at age nine I realized that some how democracy, my situation, and Carmella didn't make sense.

—Testimony of **BEBE RESCHKE**, Los Angeles, August 6, 1981

In her typical quiet way, Clara Breed did what she could to help many families by storing some of their most prized possessions in her home on Trias Street. Clara's house was not very large, but she made room for sewing machines, barber tools, electric fans, and other valuable treasures of the Hirasaki family. Tets Hirasaki recalled:

I could not take my own small library which was contained in a small apple box. I had accumulated a variety of books—college reference textbooks on mathematics, chemistry, language, plus a few trade journals and how-to books. However, Miss Breed became my personal library custodian. I put a lid on the box and she took care of it until I returned to San Diego!

Miss Breed put one of Fusa's treasured dolls, a samurai warrior, in a safe place where it stayed for the duration.

Although it was risky to do so, many churches took an active part in helping the Nikkei as best they could. The Quakers were especially active in reaching out to the Nikkei. So were the Congregational churches. Clara's uncle, Rev. Dr. Noel Breed, leader of the First Congregational Church in Stockton, California, spoke out against the evacuation and opened the church storerooms for the Nikkei's personal possessions for the duration. Up and down the Pacific coast other churches did the same.

In Berkeley, the First Congregational Church became headquarters for registration and evacuation. Clara's sister, Eleanor Breed, worked there, doing what she could to make the process less painful. On May 1, she wrote in her diary:

Soldiers guarded the First Congregational Church of Berkeley, where Clara's sister, Eleanor Breed, worked to help the Nikkei through the ordeal of registration. Chiura Obata's drawing reflects the belief that many felt the army chose the tallest soldiers to intimidate the Nikkei. Eleanor knew both the artist and his family.

A Methodist minister . . . commented . . . "your church is doing a fine job—if it were in some areas it would be burned to the ground." He cited horror tales of hysteria such as we have feared, but have not found. . . . It came over me suddenly, and with shock, that the soldiers who have been on guard have been here not to protect us from the Japanese so much as to protect the Japanese against us.

Many San Diego families such as Louise Ogawa's stored treasures including Japanese kimonos, furniture, and their *World Book Encyclopedia* at the Buddhist temple on Market and 28th Streets. With so little time, others were forced to take whatever they were offered by greedy junk dealers and bargain hunters who drove away with refrigerators, pianos, furniture, and the hard-earned fruits of the Nikkei's struggle:

. . . On the day before the posted evacuation date, there was a line of cars in our driveway extending about another 200 yards in both directions . . . waiting their turn to come to our house to see what they could get from us for a small fraction of its worth or nothing.

Most of the people were strangers, but some were people we thought were our friends. One man wanted to buy our pick-up truck. My father had just spent about $125 for a new set of tires and tubes, and a brand new battery. So, he asked for $125. The man "bought" our pick-up truck for $25. One friend bought, and I use the words "friend" and "bought" facetiously, one "friend" bought our celery spray rig for $15. We had only a few weeks earlier purchased it new for about $100 . . . the man told my father that he . . . might as well take the $15, otherwise he would be back the next day and pick it up for nothing . . . these vultures were aware . . . we would be limited to $150 per person.

What we did not sell or give away, we stowed in a Caucasian friend's garage and in an old abandoned school bus we had been using as a tool shed. When my family returned to California in 1945, we were able to retrieve our belongings from the private garage, but the boarded up bus had been broken into and everything was either stolen or destroyed.—Testimony of **HIROSHI KAMEI**, Los Angeles, August 6, 1981

ONE PRECIOUS THING

When we got on the bus and started for Bakersfield it was about 4 o'clock in the morning. When we were on the outskirts of Delano I saw my pink stucco house and my white dog sitting lonely in front of the house waiting for us to come home.
—**YOSHI WATANABE**, ninth grade

"Was there one special something you had to leave behind that you still remember?" I asked each of the people I interviewed. Several recalled that they were poor and didn't really have many toys like their grandchildren have these days. But for others the question brought back a never-forgotten sadness. Sixty years had passed, but many spoke of that day as if it had just happened.

Margaret Ishino still remembers:

One thing that was very precious to me was a doll that I had begged my mother to get me. It was in the 1930's . . . during the time of the Depression. I saw this doll in a dry-goods store window and I looked at it every day. She was such a beautiful doll—with beautiful doll curls. I fell in love with her. Then one day the doll was not there. I cried and cried and then on Christmas morning the dry-goods lady's daughter who used to babysit for my younger brother and me came to our house. She had this package wrapped up in Christmas paper, tied with a beautiful bow and I opened it and it was my doll! My mother had sacrificed buying her own clothes so that I could have that doll and I had to leave that doll and I don't know whatever happened to it.

Its Endo remembers his own "prized possession":

I woke up on the day we were leaving but I needed to ride to town to buy a jacket. There was no way of knowing where we were going—only that it might be cold. So, I raced to town and back on my bike. When I returned the buses were there. My family was already on the bus. I was a 12 year old boy at that time, and I guess that bike was my most prized possession! But I had to leave it behind. I still remember how hard it was to leave that bike of mine . . . there were two other bikes just lying on the ground with mine as the bus pulled away. It's a shame—we could have used those bikes in camp!

Chiyo Kusumoto Nakagawa liked collecting popular songs. Teenagers then didn't have CDs or iPods. They used to hear the hits of the week on *The Hit Parade* on the radio:

I used to type all the words to the songs that were popular at that time on the hit parade. That was my hobby. I had all the songs that I copied from *The Hit Parade* magazine . . . my favorite songs in a big binder. You can imagine how heavy that was! I had to leave it behind.

Ellen Yukawa's father had just built a new house, and it was difficult to leave the house and its contents behind:

My dad had bought a console radio and it had a turntable so you could make records. So he used to make records of us singing and that was really something! I remember he had to take it back to Montgomery Ward in Bakersfield because he couldn't pay for it.

Leaving pets behind was probably the most painful parting—especially for young people. Elizabeth Kikuchi Yamada's voice was quiet as she told me that her future husband, Joe, "was just eleven years old at the time . . . he had to give his dog away. No pets were allowed. They took the dog to its new home, in El Cajon, about twelve miles away. Months later, Joe learned that the dog had walked all the way home. Finding the family gone, the dog crawled under the porch and died."

It was a week of unforgettable grief:

Mrs. Ellis, the principal, the teachers, as well as our friends, were in tears as they bid us good-bye and shook our hands. I shall never forget how quiet the group of usually noisy Nisei boys were as we walked home, looking down on the sidewalk to keep others from seeing the moisture accumulate in our eyes. One by one, we escaped into our homes, located in different blocks, closed the doors behind us, to the normal future friendships which could have been but destined never to take place.—Testimony of **CHARLES KUBOKAWA**, San Francisco, August 12, 1981

But for teenagers, the most painful realization was the loss of their identity as Americans:

As I passed my high school, I saw the American flag waving in the wind, and my emotions were in turmoil. I thought of the prize-winning essay that I had written for my English class titled "Why I Am Proud to be an American."

As tears streamed down my face, an awful realization dawned on me: I am a loyal American. Yes, I had the face of an enemy. The trauma of being uprooted from many friends and home and school left me confused with a deep sense of personal loss.

—Testimony of **SALLY KIRITA TSUNEISHI**, Los Angeles, August 4, 1981

SAD GOOD-BYES

In San Diego and cities up and down the West Coast there were sad good-byes. All through that last unhappy week Clara Breed did her best to give the children her usual sunny self. But it was next to impossible to cover the grief she shared with them.

From personal experience Clara knew what it was like to be uprooted from home, to lose loved ones. Before she was fourteen she had lived in Minnesota, Illinois, Wisconsin, Iowa, and New York. Her father, Rev. Dr. Reuben L. Breed, like his own father and brother, was a pastor of the First Congregational Church, so Clara and her family moved often. Born in Fort Dodge, Iowa, on March 19, 1906, Clara spent several years in Brooklyn, New York, while her father worked at Ellis Island with the thousands of immigrants arriving during the early years of the twentieth century. She never forgot his stories about their courage and hardships. Little did she know that in years to come she would be involved with families of Asian immigrants who had arrived at the same time on the other side of the continent.

In 1920, when Clara was fourteen, her father died. Years later she wrote to her sister that their father's death was a shattering experience:

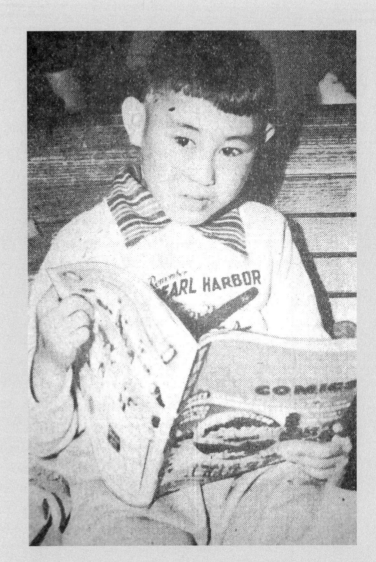

Little Joe Karamoto, with "Remember Pearl Harbor" on his sweater, whiles away a dull moment by reading a comic book in the rail depot. Patriotic propaganda was packed into comics directed at young kids.

I wasn't very grown up, and I didn't talk about it to anyone, but for several years I made a determined effort not to become fond of anybody, any new people I wasn't already fond of that is. It took quite a while before I realized how self-centered and selfish and altogether silly that was. One of the joys of being grown up is the discovery of how much fun it is to love—and how many degrees of loving there are, the close family interwoven with hearth-and-home-and-memory love that belongs to you and Mother, love of friends, of people you work with, and on and on—not excluding the whistling gardener you wave to in the morning on the way to work—But you're special . . . that's why I keep telling you to take care of yourself . . . I hope you do!

With no way to support her family, Clara's mother, Estella Breed, was grateful when her sister "Mate" Cuddeback and her husband insisted they come to live with them in San Diego. Once again Clara's family moved, this time to Southern California.

At San Diego High School, Clara made a new circle of friends. She joined the tennis club, art club, and French club, worked on the 1923 yearbook, and was an honor student. Clara liked riding horses and playing "zookeeper" in her backyard on Trias Street. It was the best kind of zoo, no bars or captive animals allowed. Clara fed the wild foxes, opossums, and raccoons that made the backyard of 4215 Trias Street a part of their wild habitat.

Clara attended Pomona College and graduated in 1927. She went on to earn a master's degree in library science from Case Western Reserve in Cleveland, Ohio. Children's books were a new specialty at that time, and Clara hoped to make a career of it. She also hoped to stay in Ohio, but when the stock market crashed and banks failed, jobs were next to impossible to find. Clara had to earn a living not just for herself but also for her mother. Reluctantly Clara returned to California, where she was offered a job that was to change her life. Her starting salary was $130 a month—but she considered herself lucky to have a job. In 1928, she was appointed the first children's librarian in the City of San Diego Library.

PENNY POSTCARDS

There were two things that Clara loved dearly—books and children—so she had a perfect job. And she was not ashamed to admit that she had an extra-special place in her heart for these Japanese American children in particular. They were among her most avid readers. Now many of the children she had known and loved through the years were about to leave. Sending these children away as if they were guilty of some crime—it was all such a terrible mistake!

There had to be a way of keeping that love of reading alive—even if there was a war on. But how could Clara do that? She could not change the fact that the children were leaving, but that didn't mean they should be without books. In fact, wouldn't they need books now more than ever? Clara was determined to find a way.

Just days before the children left, Clara received a small package in the morning mail. It was a stack of blue postcards imprinted with her Trias Street address. Funny, she had ordered them as a gift to herself just weeks ago, thinking they would be handy for dashing off short notes to friends— never dreaming how perfect they would be! Quickly she licked penny stamps to a fistful of cards and rushed off to work. Her plan was simple. As the children came to the library to turn in their library cards and books, Clara gave each of them a postcard. "Write to us," she told them. "We'll want to know where you are and how you are getting along, and we'll send you some books to read." "OK," they answered as their sober faces brightened briefly.

Clara knew she would never forget the look of their sad faces as they came to the library one last time. For little Katherine Tasaki, who adored Miss Breed and loved filling up her library card and getting a new one, turning in her card was one of the most difficult moments. Years later she recalled, "My library card was one of my most precious possessions." That day, Katherine shoved the postcard into her pocket and held back tears as she hugged Miss Breed good-bye.

"WITH A CHEER AND A TEAR"

The scene was unforgettable . . . the station was packed, the platform overflowing, but there was no confusion, not a baby cried, not a voice was lifted in irritation or complaint. The boys were dressed in boots and dungarees and plaid shirts, while the girls with their slender figures looked dainty and feminine in slacks. Babies were delectable in soft pink and blue, while one little toddler in trousers and coat of bright red looked like an animated doll. The soldiers, who seemed to have been chosen for their height, towered above the crowds, but their authority was courteous and considerate and one saw in the faces honest American interest in the human spectacle, and sympathy for the participants. Only at the very last, when the procession filed slowly toward the train, did one old woman break down and sob uncontrollably. —**CLARA BREED**, *Horn Book Magazine*

It was April 7, four months to the day since Pearl Harbor. No bombs had fallen on San Diego, but the war had touched so many lives. Today was the day they had been dreading. In just a few hours the children Clara had known and loved for years were to leave. No one even knew where they were being sent—only that they had to go where the government took them!

"And everyone, young, middling, and old, wore a tag around his neck or hanging from his lapel, with name printed on and a number, for his family group." (Eleanor Breed diary)

Knowing that the bond between herself and the children had always been books and their mutual love of reading, Clara was determined to keep that bond alive. She tucked more postcards into the book bag. Maybe she had found the way!

By midday the vast waiting room of San Diego's old Mission-style Santa Fe depot was jammed with hundreds of families waiting to board the two trains that would take them away from the only home most of them had ever known. They still did not know what the army had in store for them. Rumor had it that they were going to Owens Valley, to the place that would come to be known as Manzanar.

Fusa Tsumagari and her brother Yuki put on brave faces as Miss Breed took their picture at the train station that day.

Katherine Tasaki and Tetsuzo Hirasaki look happy to see Miss Breed as she snaps their picture.

At every doorway and all along the train platforms, soldiers in battle gear holding rifles with gleaming bayonets towered over the men, women, and children who continued to arrive, their duffel bags bulging with possessions they could carry. With identification tags hanging from their coat lapels they struggled with babes in arms and bags crammed with clothes, bedding, and toiletries.

In this sea of humanity Clara Breed searched for familiar faces. She could only imagine how these families had spent their last night in houses stripped bare of everything but memories. For days she had been struggling with good-byes and trying desperately to find some way to comfort them.

It's not clear if Miss Breed found them first or they found her. As she made her way through the station, she not only gave away all the books, candies, and postcards that she had brought; she also managed to take photographs of several of her young friends before her film ran out.

Louise Ogawa still remembers:

It was a real surprise to see Miss Breed come to the train station. She gave me a warm feeling to know someone cared about us. She passed out postcards and asked us to write to her. She wanted to keep in touch and wanted to know if we were all right. She promised we wouldn't be forgotten. She was such a warm loving person.

Tets still had his arm in a sling. He had been forced to leave his first year of college when an old shoulder injury suffered during his junior high school days became infected and required major surgery. The doctor saved the arm and was able to reconstruct the shoulder. Tets laughed when he spoke about the cast being removed on December 10, 1941: "Boy, did the orderlies cutting off the cast have fun with me, vowing to get even for Pearl Harbor!"

Aiko Kubo was thrilled to see Clara Breed that day: "Yes, yes, I remember talking with her. She said, 'When you have time, write to me . . . if you need anything, just write and let me know and I'll see what I can do.'" Aiko also recalled that one of her sisters was carrying a teddy bear that day: "It was a big bear . . . so big that when we got on the train and they were counting heads—they counted the bear, too."

Miss Breed almost walked right by Jack Watanabe. He was contentedly reading a comic book and trying not to notice the crowd. Katherine Tasaki practically danced circles around Miss Breed, she was so happy to see her one last time! Clara gave Katherine a book, a postcard, some candy, and many hugs good-bye.

There are no pictures of Elizabeth Kikuchi, her brother David, or her sisters, Mariam or Anna, on that day, but we know they saw Miss Breed because a few days later Elizabeth wrote a letter to her saying how happy she was to see her at the train station! Elizabeth was surely also happy since her mother had been released by the FBI. So wherever they were going, at least the whole Kikuchi family was reunited.

Margaret Ishino does not remember seeing Miss Breed at the station. Margaret was probably too busy and nervous about her family being split up. Since her mother had a very small infant, Margaret's parents took little Thomas on the first train. Seventeen-year-old Margaret was left in the Santa Fe station with her fifteen-year-old brother, Henry, and her little six-year-old sister, Florence. Henry was more interested in being with his friends than in taking care of Florence, who was terrified by the sight of the soldiers with their guns. After the Ishino children's parents disappeared into the crowd to board the first train, Florence cried quietly until at last she fell asleep in Margaret's arms.

Clara Breed watched as the long line of passengers walked quietly toward the first train at four o'clock in the afternoon. They still did not know where the train was to take them, only that they were going. Little did they know that it would take several more hours before they would pull out of the station.

Twelve-year-old Ben Segawa said: "As the train began to move, armed Military Police came through the cars. They ordered everyone to pull the shades down so we could not see out. It was hot and cramped and people could hardly move." Before long the old stuffy train was bombarded by some boys who delivered their final nasty farewells by flinging rocks at the train.

It was one o'clock in the morning before the second train pulled out of the station. Louise Ogawa wrote:

> That feeling of sorrow and the emptiness . . . comes back to me every time I think of how I left San Diego. I shall never forget how I spent that night of April 7th sleeping on the train. My sister and I stuck our heads out the window never peeling our eyes off the direction of our home. We filled our eyes with the sight of San Diego to the limit until my pupils gave in and I dozed off.

Although they were to travel only 125 miles that night, it took seven hours. They traveled at a snail's pace, stopping and starting and being sidetracked so that trains with more important "cargo" could go through. In Los Angeles they were transferred to buses that would take them the rest of the way. Rumors that they were going to Owens Valley turned out to be wrong. There were not enough barracks ready at that camp. Instead, they were taken to the world-famous horse-racing arena, the Santa Anita Racetrack in Arcadia, California.

"Only at the very last, when the procession filed slowly toward the train, did one old woman break down and sob uncontrollably." (Clara Breed, *"Americans with the Wrong Ancestors,"* Horn Book Magazine)

Though they tried to put a brave face on their departure, they were sorry to be going. Frank H. Otsuka, president of the Japanese American Citizens League, said, in the words of a Cole Porter song, that it was "just one of those things." Like other JACL leaders, he believed that when the government said they had to go, the Nikkei community should cooperate. In time, the JACL's willingness to cooperate with the government would cause a division within the Nikkei community that lasted for decades.

CHAPTER THREE

WELCOME
TO SANTA JAPANITA!

IN LOS ANGELES THE WEARY passengers from the first train were transferred to old buses that would lumber on for close to another twenty miles. Finally, at 3:00 A.M. they pulled up to the gate of Santa Anita, the largest of fifteen assembly centers that the government hastily opened during the spring of 1942. Ben Segawa recalled:

> All I remember is a mass of people—a great mass of Japanese people. . . . I had never seen so many Japanese people—until I got to Santa Anita. It didn't even dawn on me when I got on the train, but when we finally got to Santa Anita, I thought, Geez—they're all Japanese people. There was no Caucasian or blacks or Hispanic among us. That's when I realized, maybe I am a little different. I thought I was American, but that's when it finally dawned on me that maybe people look at us differently—I was 11 years old then.

Soldiers in watchtowers were armed with machine guns, while military police guarded the gate with rifles and gleaming bayonets. Glaring searchlights turned slowly in endless arcs over the rooftops of the stables that were to be home for most of

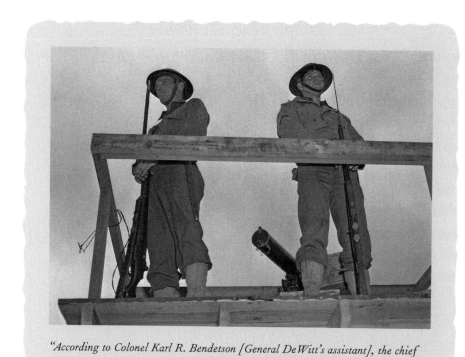

"According to Colonel Karl R. Bendetson [General DeWitt's assistant], the chief architect of the evacuation scam, the soldiers, the weapons, the barbed wire, and the watchtowers were there to protect us. Hogwash." (Testimony, William Kochiyama, New York, Nov. 23, 1981)

the San Diegans. Those in the second group did not arrive until 8:30 A.M. the next day.

Margaret Ishino has never forgotten her first moments at Santa Anita:

Every one of us had a family number when we were evacuated. We had to wear that number where it could be seen. Well, when we got to Santa Anita I didn't have my tag on and there stands this soldier with a bayonet and a helmet and he pointed at me and he said . . . "Where's your tag?" and I didn't have it and he said, "Get out of the line!" . . . So I was carrying my 6-year-old sister Florence . . . she had gone to sleep and I couldn't find my tag! I looked in my coat pocket, I looked in my sweater pocket and my purse. Finally, I found my tag. It was in my sister's sweater pocket. So he says—"O.K. get back in line!" . . . To this day, that memory is vivid and I hate to wear tags of any kind. I won't if I can help it.

In fact, at the Japanese American National Museum where Margaret and I met, visitors are given admission tags, but Margaret chose not to wear one. Florence, who was just a little kindergartner and remembers almost nothing about the war years, still vividly remembers one thing: her family's number—4019.

Like Santa Anita, all of the assembly centers up and down the West Coast were nothing more than converted fairgrounds, livestock exhibition halls, and racetracks. They were to be temporary living quarters. Eventually, the detainees would be moved to relocation centers away from the Pacific coast. All the Nikkei families from San Diego were sent to Santa Anita. They were people from all walks of life—farmers, fishermen, nurses, gardeners, shopkeepers, ministers, doctors, nurses, teachers, lawyers. Rich and poor, young and old alike, all found themselves inside a place they were not free to leave.

From March 27 until October 27, 1942, more than eighteen thousand people from Los Angeles, San Diego, and Santa Clara counties lived in Santa Anita. In just sixty days it became the thirty-second largest community in California. Santa Anita may have been a perfect place for racehorses—but it was hardly a perfect home for people. What had been a stall for one horse now became housing for five to six people.

Six decades later, Babe Karasawa asks as if it happened yesterday:

Did I tell you I lived in a horse stable? Did I tell you there was dried horse crud in the crevices of the asphalt? My mother—all I remember is my mother had tears in her eyes . . . saying . . . "we're not going in there!" When I asked my sister just recently she says Mama was bawling! See, my dad was picked up by the FBI so he wasn't with us. He was held in Santa Fe, New Mexico, for about five months. When he read that we might be forced to leave San Diego he wrote in his diary—"Everyone is worried about the evacuation. . . . I don't know how to stop my tears from flowing. . . . I can't believe this is something occurring in this country of freedom and liberty."

We were fortunate in that stable . . . the adjacent units were occupied by people from Los Angeles and they let us use brooms and buckets. We just kept pouring water on the asphalt and scrubbing it with the broom till we got the asphalt clean and my mother said we could move in. It stunk from the very beginning—you couldn't get rid of the stink! There was manure in there with straw stuck on the side where the walls were spray painted.

Ben Segawa came from a large family of twelve, so they were "lucky" enough to be put in the barracks that had been built in the huge parking lot. Each barrack was divided into four "rooms." Ben's family had two rooms; each was twenty feet by twenty-five feet. Six people lived in each of the two rooms. There were no real walls, only partitions that did not go up to the ceiling or close off the sounds of neighbors in adjoining rooms. But Ben remembers visiting a friend who lived in the stables:

. . . the horse urine was so strong you could never get rid of that smell. So when I'd visit my friend, I couldn't stay there long because the horse urine on the wall of the stall—I don't know how they could stand that—it bothered me at eleven and I still remember it today. And I'm from a farm family—I'm farm bred—I was around horses all the time, you know. I don't know how—some of the sophisticated dignified females that were city bred—how they handled that—they don't talk much about it.

"DEAR MISS BREED"

Miss Breed did not need to wait long for the first postcards and letters to arrive.

Dear Miss Breed,
Thanks a million for coming down to the depot. We left S.D. at 1:15 A.M. Thursday. They are treating us very well. Will write more later. Our address is written on the other side. Very busy trying to get settle.
*   Margaret Arakawa*
*   P.S. Excuse the awful writing. Did it on my lap.*

Dear Miss Breed,
I am writing this postcard to give you our new address. We are still here at Santa Anita but are living in a different part of the camp. Everything is fine up here and wishing you the best of everything I remain,
*   Sincerely,*
*   Yoshiko Kubo*

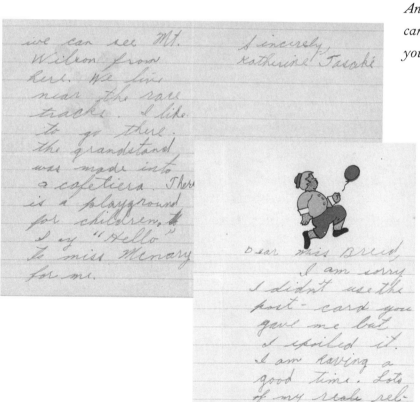

Hello! We arrived in Santa Anita on Apr. 8 about 10:00 in the morning. We are just fine. I had a nice long train ride. The weather here is quite cool. Now that we have a post office I shall write often. I would appreciate your correspondance too. I miss going to the library very much. I often look around for a book to read and soon become disappointed. Good bye for now!
*   Very sincerely yours,*
*   Louise Ogawa*

April 10th, 1942
Dear Miss Breed,

We arrived safely at Santa Anita on the eighth. We have been busy getting settled in our new homes which were formerly horse stables. We have been given good army beds and blankets. The food is getting better as the cooks become more experienced. There are just rows and rows of similar houses and we get lost trying to find our own. My girl friends got lost in the blackout which occurred during our first nite here. I will write a more detailed letter soon.

    Yours truly,
    Fusa Tsumagari

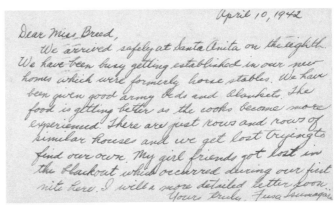

Dear Miss Breed,

I am sorry I didn't use the post-card you gave me but I spoiled it. I am having a good time. Lots of my— reali—relatives live here. we can see Mt. Wilson from here. We live near the race tracks. I like to go there. the grandstand was made into a cafetiera. There is a playground for children. Say "Hello" to miss Mcnary for me.

    Sincerely,
    Katherine Tasaki

Oddly enough, from their first cards and notes it is hard to know just how shocking and uncomfortable their new homes must have been. They write that they are living in stables as if this were not at all unusual. Yet these were city children, who just one day earlier had lived in homes with comfortable furniture and indoor plumbing. They may not have been rich, but they had never lived in stables.

Clearly they didn't complain to Miss Breed, perhaps because they had often been told by their parents and grandparents *"shikata ga nai,"* which meant "there are some things that cannot be helped." As immigrants, their parents and grandparents had learned to live with many hardships—they had to be accepted.

No one wrote to Miss Breed about the communal toilets with no doors or partitions for privacy. Nor did they write about the public showers, although sixty years later Babe has not forgotten them:

Privacy was not to be found anywhere! This drawing by Miné Okubo of the "assembly center" at Tanforan (near San Francisco) depicts the women's latrine as having partitions. However, in Santa Anita, women had to carry a large piece of cardboard to use as a screen since there were no partitions.

I do remember the shower facilities. It was a great big circular structure . . . it had a floor—a dish-shaped concrete floor so the horses could be brought in—and then they had a whole bunch of showerheads. Well, they ran a plywood partition down the middle of it—men on one side and women on the other. When I asked my sister about that within the last year she said, "Mom and I really would go to take a shower after midnight because we were so embarrassed to be in this great big old place with no partitions."

I asked Babe, who was fourteen at the time, about stories I had heard about young boys trying to see over the partition, some even making taller and taller stilts to see over the top.

I know this much: In the washroom facilities there were knotholes and you always saw guys peeking through the knotholes.

"TWENTY THOUSAND SOULS BROODING"

As I was to learn repeatedly, attitudes about life in Santa Anita had a lot to do with one's age. Very young children could not understand the losses their parents had suffered, and they spent their time "outdoors wringing the last ounce of play out of their day," wrote Dorothy Obata, a high school junior.

Those who were teenagers had trouble years later understanding how younger children such as Katherine Tasaki could have written: "I am having a good time." Or how David Kikuchi could say: "It's very fine here." Yet from their nine- and ten-year-old points of view, Santa Anita was like a huge playground, with no school, lots of kids, and nothing to do all day but play!

David's eleven-year-old sister, Elizabeth, even managed to find beauty in her surroundings:

April 18 '42

Dear Miss Breed,

I am very sorry I haven't written sooner, but I was sick in bed from the typhoid fever shot. There was a sudden change in our going to Owens Valley. But we arrived safely at Santa Anita (which we call Santa Japanita). . . . Santa Anita is a very beautiful place. You could see the big mountains. In the morning when you could see the shadows of the mountains it looks like the great preyimeds Egypt. Our camp is right near the racetracks of Santa Anita. The stables that the horses used to live in were fixed over for us to live in. They gave us many things that we needed like beds, blankets, brooms, and buckets. So we are getting along fine. When we eat we always have to get in a long line about three block. We do not go school yet but we go to the Recreation park to play games. So all we do is eat, play and sleep. But in the evenings I read some of the books I b[r]ought. I enjoyed very much to take books out of the library. My mother told me to give your mother her love.

> *Yours always,*
> *Elizabeth Kikuchi*
> *P.S. I was very glad to see you at the station.*

Many letters included special regards to Clara's mother. Liz's and Clara's mothers knew each other through the church—they were both ministers' wives. Clara, like many unmarried women of her day, continued to live with relatives, her mother and her aunt, in the house on Trias Street. As a librarian she would have had limited funds for a place of her own.

Older teenagers and young adults felt their country had turned against them, and the wound was deep. Kaizo Kubo, Aiko Kubo's teenage brother, wrote this when he was a high school senior:

Before my very eyes my world crumbled. From the instant I stepped into the barbed wire enclosures of our destination, I felt that queer alienable presence within me. All the brash bravado I had saved for this precise moment vanished like a disembodied soul. I suddenly felt incredibly small and alone. So this was imprisonment.

The oppressive silhouette of the guard towers looming cold and dark in the distance affected me in only one way. They seemed to threaten, to challenge me. I hated their ugly hugeness, the power they symbolized. I hold only contempt for that for which they stand. They kept poignantly clear in my mind the inescapable truth that I was a prisoner.

Thus my life as an evacuee began . . . At first I was inclined to think my imagination was provoking the wall of silence that seemed to shroud my being, but it was real, as real as evacuation itself. An incomprehensible air of tension hung over the confines of the entire center. Twenty thousand souls brooding. It was not pleasant. The next abruptly discernable phase was a lifting of the silence and in a surprisingly short time, the atmosphere had changed to a noisy, equally unpredictable show of human emotions. Camp life was like that—uncertain.

Some said that the Issei parents and grandparents were having their first vacation in their lives. It was hardly the kind of vacation anyone would plan on purpose. The indignity of having to stand on a line to be fed was especially abhorrent. One Issei felt ashamed that he and his family had been turned into beggars with tin plates waiting to be filled. Another father wrote this letter from Santa Anita to a friend:

I never dreamed I would see my children behind barbed wire. This is a terrible place to raise children. We are not cattle but three times a day, in the morning, noon and evening, you hear the gong, gong, gong, of the bells. Then and there you will see men, women and children come out of stable-like shelters. Every time I see this sight, I cannot help my heartaches.

We were evacuated and imprisoned without cause, without due process. Our rights as citizens . . . were violated. The one and only thing against us was our race. . . . —Testimony of **EMI K. FUJII** for her father, Toshio Kimura, Chicago, September 23, 1981

Medical facilities were not much better than the housing at Santa Anita. In fact, the bad housing and bad health were connected. Hospital records from Santa Anita indicate that about 75 percent of reports of sickness came from people who were living in the horse stalls.

Soon after they arrived at Santa Anita the government inoculated everyone against everything from smallpox to typhoid. The objective was to keep everyone well. But many people had severe reactions to the shots.

One young doctor described them this way:

Morning, noon, and night were spent standing on line. There were lines for everything. Lines to take a shower or use the latrine, lines to do the laundry, lines to get the mail, lines to see a doctor, and, three times a day, there were endless lines for the mess hall.

A long shed that is used for saddling horses, was converted into a hospital. I was one of six MD's and two medical students caring for 18,000 people. . . . We inoculated every person with three shots of typhoid-peri-typhoid, two shots of diphtheria, tetanus and vaccinated them for smallpox.

Hundreds upon hundreds had severe reactions . . . high fever, chills, sore arms and severe diarrhea. . . . We treated these people as best we could. Toilet facilities were inadequate with people fainting and releasing their watery stools while waiting their turn in their own line.

—Testimony of **DR. YOSHIHIKO FRED FUJIKAWA**, Los Angeles, August 5, 1981

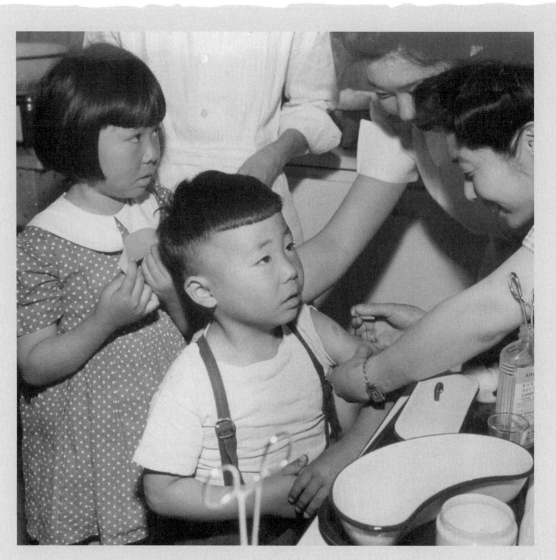

The shots were supposed to be good for you, but Elizabeth Kikuchi was one of many children who became ill from the shots they had to get. Going to the communal latrine was unpleasant when you were well—but even worse if you were ill.

YOU CAN'T BELIEVE WHAT YOU READ . . .

After talking with Ben and Babe, who had both been in Santa Anita, I asked them to read this article from the *Los Angeles Times* (April 4, 1942) that makes Santa Anita sound like a vacation paradise:

Santa Anita Gates Open to 1000 Japs

Multimillion-dollar Santa Anita track—the world's most luxurious racing plant—yesterday opened its gates as an **assembly station*** for Japanese **evacuees**.* Into the verdant grounds of the establishment, nestled amid ancient oaks and peppers at the foot of the lofty San Gabriels, the initial contingent of 1000 aliens removed from the bustling San Pedro–Long Beach harbor area filed to take up **temporary abode*** . . . on the vast garden plot surrounding the imposing grandstand and clubhouse, where a year ago movie stars in silver fox rubbed shoulders with hang-tail followers in checkered coats, has been erected as far as the eye can see, **apartment dwellings*** to house the **guests**.* . . . Most of the new arrivals took to the place at first glance, expressing open admiration at the beauty of the surroundings their **faces wreathed in smiles**.*

*****DOUBLESPEAK: Assembly stations**, better known as "assembly centers," sounds a lot friendlier than calling them what they really were—prisons. People had no choice about going to one of these assembly centers—nor were they free to leave.

Make **evacuees** "prisoners."

Temporary abode sounds like a vacation retreat that people went to for pleasure.

Make **apartment dwellings** "horse stalls or army barracks with army cots for the whole family."

Make **guests** "prisoners."

Faces wreathed in smiles? Nonsense!

"I don't think so," Ben laughed. "That's propaganda they put out there to justify what they were doing."

Babe summed it up in a single word: "Ridiculous!"

In fact, many of the newspapers turned out stories whose whole purpose was to whitewash the truth—but that didn't work any better than the whitewash on the horses' stalls.

An editorial titled "A Chance to Prove It" in the *San Diego Union* just days before the evacuation claimed that the opportunity to go to the centers cheerfully, willingly, and cooperatively gave those who have professed their loyalty to this country a chance to prove it. In fact, the article claimed that the Nikkei were being taken to places that were ideal for their health, and even better than the homes they were leaving. It claimed that they would have a chance to develop their talents and enjoy good food and quiet, comfortable living conditions. Indeed, the article stated that if the Nikkei cooperated, the government would treat them well.

The writer makes it sound like a benevolent Uncle Sam would be providing a safe haven. The camp, instead of being described as a concentration camp, is described as more nearly resembling a settlement of pioneers such as the country saw a century ago. It's unlikely that the person who wrote this article was ever inside any of the places where the Nikkei would be living.

Other newspaper editorials and politicians promoted the myth that sending the Nikkei away was for their own good. Margaret Ishino had friends in Chula Vista whose farms and barns were burned down and who had been attacked while plowing their fields. In the cities there had been some vandalism of Nikkei businesses, insulting name-calling, and physical assaults. So the case was made for removing the Nikkei for their safety. Instead of enforcing the law and protecting them from attacks, the government surrendered to those who would defy the laws of a democracy.

Although she was just six years old at the time, one girl saw through the lie:

> I remember . . . the guard towers, the soldiers with their guns pointed into us . . . weren't they supposed to be protecting us from all the potentially dangerous hostile people outside?—Testimony of **AMY IWASAKI MASS**, Los Angeles, August 6, 1981

Some Nikkei entered Santa Anita believing that going along with the exodus and not complaining was a way to show one's loyalty and patriotism. In years to come, there would be great resentment about this position, which was supported by the leaders of the Japanese American Citizens League. But the wish to prove their patriotism continued inside the camps in many ways:

My Day . . . July 06, 1942 . . .

The First Congregational Church in Berkeley, Cal., has taken a great interest in the American-born Japanese . . . The following story was sent me by them*:

"Arriving in Tanforan with only the clothes he wore, Bill Kochiyama, 21, last week received a $2000 inheritance from a former stage and screen actress, for whom his father had worked for the past 20 years. Kochiyama came from New York City in 1940 to attend the University of California. At Tanforan he is a mess hall worker. 'After deducting income taxes I purchased $1900 in war bonds in order to do my part in the war effort,' Kochiyama stated. Eventually he hopes to use the money invested

to continue his education." *This should remind us that among the group are really good, loyal Americans and we must build up their loyalty and not tear it down.*

*Eleanor Breed, Clara's sister, was the secretary of that church and had been active in trying to ease the registration and departure of the Nikkei in Berkeley. She sent the story to Mrs. Roosevelt and then the clipping to Clara, saying: "The *them* is me."

The *Los Angeles Times* and the *San Diego Union* didn't have an exclusive on "spin-doctoring" news stories. Newspapers sanitized what was happening behind barbed-wire fences—somewhat like the younger children's censoring themselves in what they wrote to Clara Breed. Here's an example from the April 7, 1942 *San Francisco Examiner*:

650 Japs Depart; S.F. Exodus Starts like Giant Picnic
Gray haired men and feeble, tottering old women, middle aged husbands and wives, young girls in slacks, and young men in collegiate garb of sweater and jeans, schoolboys and babes in arms—all had a place in this procession which should have been like a funeral march but wasn't.

It was a festival—a gigantic picnic—a holiday tour—a trip to nowhere—at least on the surface. . . . Everybody wore a grin; everybody had a wisecrack for his neighbor; nobody complained and nobody shed a tear. . . .

But Thomas Minoru Tajiri didn't remember any part of the experience as a picnic. He had grown up in San Diego and had been a member of the army Junior ROTC in high school. This is how he remembers Santa Anita:

My twin brother, James, and I were students. . . . We were 15 . . . we ended up at the Santa Anita Race Track. . . . It was called an assembly center . . . but it was a concentration camp . . . surrounded by barbed wire fence and watch towers with machine guns soldiers with rifles and with fixed bayonets. We were given mattress covers and told to stuff straw in them.

The toilet facilities were terrible. They were communal. There were no partitions. Toilet paper was rationed by family members. Since there was no toilet paper in the latrine, we had to carry it on our persons and lo and behold, for those who ran out or forgot, it was not comical. It was embarrassing and humiliating. It was dehumanizing. —Testimony of **THOMAS MINORU TAJIRI,** Chicago, September 22, 1981

Little children were no less confused and miserable. Clara Breed wrote in a February 1, 1942, article for *Library Journal*, that one child told his mother, "I am tired of Japan, Mother. Let's go back home to America."

A full year later, on April 9, 1943, just before her graduation, Louise was able to express more fully the feelings she had during her very first day at Santa Anita:

Dear Miss Breed,
. . . When I awoke this morning one year ago, I looked up at the ceiling and a funny strange feeling came over me. I knew I was not at home and had a terrible yearning to go home. A little boy next door was crying asking his mother to take him home. That day I felt so lost I was as blue as the deep blue sea. But the sight of a friend certainly cheered me up even though it was just for the moment I saw her. Today that homesickness still is within me but that lost feeling has disappeared. I often wonder how I have changed in thought, actions, knowledge, and facial and physical features during the short memorable one year.
Most sincerely,
Louise Ogawa

Clara put this and each of the letters she received away for safekeeping.

CHAPTER FOUR

"SEABISCUIT'S SIGNATURE"

A S SOON AS THEIR FIRST mail reached San Diego, Clara Breed began sending books and other goodies to her young friends, just as she had promised. Almost every letter she received from Santa Anita begins with thanks:

April 30, 1942
Dear Miss Breed,
Oh! Miss Breed, I think I am the luckiest girl in this camp to have such a kind generous friend as you. I don't know how to begin to thank you. . . . After hearing that the afternoon mail came in, I hurried to the post office. Yes, as usual the line was a block long and that meant I was at the end of the line and oh what a long wait that was. But my patience was rewarded. I was told that I had a package awaiting me. Then such thoughts as, maybe someone sent me something by mistake—could it be a cake or maybe a box of cookies or candies—oh—I know it couldn't be a book rushed through my head. But to my surprise it was a book. And I was so happy I felt like shouting. Thank you ever so much for the nice book! I wish I knew a better word than thank you to show my appreciation. THANK YOU, Miss Breed!

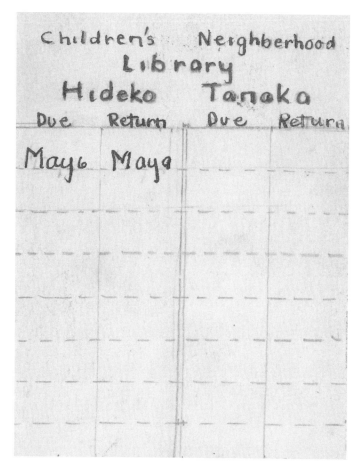

Elizabeth Kikuchi made this library card for Hideko, one of two girls who lived with the Kikuchi family in Santa Anita. By taking in two extra children, the Kikuchis could get a second stall and not be cramped in one stable. The two girls came from large families that were grateful to have one less cot in their own stable.

We have a library now but there are no books as yet just magazines. I imagine there will be books in the near future. At least I hope so. But I am certain no library will be able to replace the San Diego Library.

 Sincerely,

 Louise Ogawa

Even for a young reader such as ten-year-old Katherine, the so-called library was a sad disappointment.

May 4, 1942

Dear Miss Breed,

We have a libory now. But they just have magizines like Colliers, [L]ife, Radio Screen, *and a few old-fashioned books. I think the best magizine is the Geographic magizine. I am reading* Robinson Crusoe *right now. I think it is very nice. Each person is allowed 4 books. I have 3* [L]ook *magizines.*

* The only thing I like about the[m] are the questions. (photoquiz) I always bring home at least 1 magizine because my mother likes to read them. Yesterday we took a walk around the race track, and it was very pretty. On one side, there are lo[ts] of pretty wild flowers. Day before yesterday I went after lunch to practice on the piano, but I left all my books in San Diego, so I couldn't play very goo[d]. And I haven't played for a long time. Lots of new people have arrived in the last few days.*

* . . . Yesterday was so hot, I thought I was on fire. Today it isnt so hot. yesterday I changed my clothes 3 times. Say "Hello" to everybody for me.*

* Sincerely,*

* Katherine Tasaki*

Katherine was not the only one who missed the library. Elizabeth Kikuchi, her little sister, Anna, and other friends missed the San Diego library so much that they made their own and played "library" with whatever books they could gather.

April 25, 1942

Dear Miss Breed,

Thank you very much for the book and the letter. I was very happy when I received it. Yesterday we started a library out of 10 books. The names are Wizard of Oz, Carmen of the Golden Coast, Stella Dallas, Beautiful Bible Stories, Rebecca, Wuthering Heights, The Christ Child *and the three books you have sent us. The library is going to open Monday. We made two cards for each book. One is to be kept in the envelope and the other is to be posted on the cover. We are having lots of fun playing library. Pretty soon there is going to be a big library here. I have already read my book but I'm going to read it all over. My friend and I made rules for the library. Today we got our third typhoid fever shot. It didn't hurt when we took it but now it does. I hope we don't get anymore.*

Yesterday night we went to see a show. There was over 7,100 people there. The show was where they had the horserace. Our seat was clear up high in the grandstand. We couldn't see the show very good but we enjoyed it very much.

Yours sincerely,

Elizabeth Kikuchi

Clara no doubt wanted to help Elizabeth's library grow. Just a week later Elizabeth wrote:

Three days ago I went washing with my mother when I was coming home. I was very tired and hot. When I reached home my sister ran to me and said we got another book from Miss Breed. I was so happy . . . I didn't expect to get another book from you. I ran into the house forgetting how tired and hot I was . . . our library is getting bigger. I think our library is better than the one at the recreation. . . .

Accustomed to returning their books to the library, several of the children asked if they should return the books that Clara was sending. Of course she didn't want the books back. She hoped that they would pass the books from one person to another, at least until a real library got started. In fact, Louise was sharing her books with Margaret and then planned to reread them.

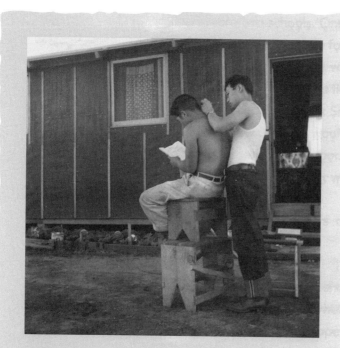
Tets had Clara send his barbering tools, and he set up a shop like this outside his barrack at Santa Anita. There was a camp barbershop, but this outdoor arrangement was friendlier—and cheaper, too.

Almost as soon as he arrived at Santa Anita, Tets sent Clara the first of many requests:

April 8, 1942
Dear Miss Breed,
I have been informed that it is possible to receive small postal parcels at the present time. It seems that the boys here all are asking me to cut their hair, so it seems that the barber equipment is first on the list. Please send me my electric clippers that are in the unpacked box. The razors are not needed just now. My blanket roll is needed as I found that my barber towels are rolled inside.
  Sincerely,
  Ted
  I haven't any place to put books yet.

Tets and his father were barbers, so naturally the San Diego boys preferred going to Tets rather than the camp barbershop. Joe Yamada recalled how they sat outside the barracks on a tall stool that Tets had built from scrap lumber: "We were all 14–15 years old kids. We didn't even have peach fuzz on our faces . . . but Tets would show us how we should shave, pulling the razor downward, so we wouldn't cut ourselves."

A few days later Tets sent Clara a longer and newsier letter:

April 13, 1942
Dear Miss Breed,
. . . Little did I think that I would see Santa Anita, where once trod the millions of pleasure seeking fans of the sport of kings—horse-racing. Why I'm actually treading the ground where the mighty Seabiscuit won his great duels on the track.
  I am in good health and my arm is getting along fine. I received a doctor's order so I am allowed to have milk with my meals. The food here is about the same as the food at the county hospital with the exception of less meat here. Now that we have a number of San Diego men working in the kitchens the food has improved quite a

Yes, that is the world-famous Seabiscuit, and this is a perfect example of a posed WRA photo to make this look like a happy family outing. For those living in horse stables, the stench of past residents like Seabiscuit never faded. No WRA photos show the latrines, overflowing sewage ditches, public showers, or the holes in the walls and floorboards.

bit, especially with the salads. I have heard that we are to receive meat soon, but I think that it will be mostly stew because we are not allowed knives, just a spoon and fork as eating utensils.

The staterooms that we live in are not bad since the roof didn't leak at all during the rains that we had—which reminds me that we certainly [were] lucky that it didn't rain while we were being assigned to our quarters. I think I have the autograph of blue Sun on our walls. I thought it was Seabiscuit's but my friend who lives near the center of town claims that his wall has Seabiscuit's signature . . .

I finally received my messenger's job. The way it requires "pull" is terrific. If one does not have friends or is not able to bluff, he just about doesn't receive a job. Things are changing however because results are not in proportion to the amount of labor hired. Ability will count more and more from now on. I really like this messenger's work. . . . Yesterday I covered the whole section in which living quarters have been established. Pretty close to 80 barracks. What a walk!!!!

I am getting to like this place very much. the view is wonderful with the mountains (I don't know the names yet) practically in our back yard. Santa Anita must have been truly beautiful when it was in session, since it looks beautiful now.

Well I can't seem to think of anything else to write so until the next time I'll say so long with the best wishes to you and your mother.

Sincerely,

Ted

Calling a horse stall a stateroom was Tets's brand of humor. He also considered it something of a joke that just about everyone claimed to be living in Seabiscuit's stall, as if living in a horse's stall—even a world-famous horse's stall—were some kind of distinction! A few weeks later (July 15, 1942) Louise even gives the books Miss Breed is sending a Seabiscuit connection. "The books which you so kindly have sent are now scattered all over this camp and I won't at all be surprised if one of them has entered Seabiscuit's stable."

From their letters Clara began to get a limited view of their day-to-day lives. Fusa's long letter on April 25 thanks Miss Breed for the photos she took at the train station. Photographs were extra-special because cameras were outlawed as contraband, since they could be used for spying. It is hard to imagine what the Japanese Americans might have taken pictures of inside Santa Anita that would have been useful to the enemy. Without cameras, however, there were no pictures of babies such as Margaret

Ishino's brother Thomas or her little sister, Florence. Almost all photos from the assembly centers were taken by government photographers and tend to reflect only what the government wanted to show. There are no pictures of the round horse showers that had been divided in two for men and women. Nor are there photographs of the latrines with long rows of toilets without partitions or doors for privacy. Fusa's complaints are very low-key:

April 25, 1942
Dear Miss Breed,
Thanks a million for everything: the nice letter you sent me, the pictures, and the book. I certainly was glad to receive all of them. . . .

Let me describe Santa Anita to you. It is located on a huge tract of land covering I guess about 75 to 100 acres. There are just rows and rows of houses. Families usually live in two rooms. If there are six or more in a family, they get four rooms. At the present time all the families live in what were formerly horse's stables. They all have new doors and windows in the front of the houses and the floors have been covered with asphalt. A partition separates the various families. We can overhear our neighbor's conversations even though we don't want to. One thing different from the ordinary home is the large door on the inside. The huge door is cut in half and is similar to those that the Dutch people have. These were made so that horses could stick out their head.

The mess hall is located where the grandstand used to be, and where all the bets were placed. It is a huge place and very well constructed. I believe that must be about the only thing that was really well constructed. We have very good food to eat. The quality of the cooked food is getting better, too. You've noticed that I said "cooked food" because the food itself is almost the best. For example today for lunch we had: roast beef and boiled potatoes with gravy, spinach, and cole slaw. However, there are two things that bother me:

1. We don't get a second helping. 2. If the noon meal is very good, supper is terrible! Gee, but really, I'm thankful for getting food free and also housing.

I guess I could ramble on and on and you'd probably be bored to death so I guess I'd better stop. Thank you for sending everything. Your card was so pretty that I have pinned it up in [my] room.
Truly,
Fusa Tsumagari

Although the army failed to plan ahead for regular school classes, before long Nisei teachers and college students, who were not really teachers, used the grandstand for classes to keep kids occupied. With no classroom walls all the students shared one large hall. In order to be heard, teachers had to shout so much that they lost their voices. Nor did they have textbooks or basic supplies such as chalkboards and chalk. Still, the young teachers were determined to give their students some academics so that they wouldn't forget how to study.

Aiko Kubo, a high school junior, remembers:

We would sit in the grandstand and try and have seminar classes. Of course, that was very difficult . . . there were people who were working on camouflage netting . . . on one end of the building and the rest of us were trying to learn whatever the teachers were saying. Most of us were looking out beyond the trees and we could see cars whizzing by and we were wishing we were out there too.

One of the volunteer teachers recalled:

At the first high school assembly, which was held in the grandstand I witnessed an incredible incident. After the morning program was finished, as the students stood to return to the open classrooms, they began to sing "God Bless America." These young people still believed in the country of their birth. We teachers could only gaze at each other, some of us with tears.
—Testimony of **TOYO KAWAKAMI**, Chicago, September 22, 1981

True to her word, Miss Breed wrote letters often, but none of her letters have been found. Katherine collected letters for a while, but as she and others moved many times during these years, old letters seem to have disappeared. But you can almost make a list of Miss Breed's questions by reading Louise's answers:

1. Is the library open to the public? Do they have books yet?
2. Tell me about the mess hall. Is it big? How far away is it?
3. Do you have green tea? That's the kind I like best.
4. Tell me about your family.
5. Have you met many new people?
6. What do you do for entertainment?
7. How do you do your laundry?

No plans had been made for formal schooling, but Nisei college students volunteered to keep students busy and safe. There was a long waiting list to take piano lessons. With no classroom walls, volunteer teachers lost their voices by shouting to be heard.

May 16, 1942

Dear Miss Breed,

Thanks a million for your letter! I was more than glad to hear from you. I am still one of the 16,023 in Santa Anita Assembly Center. We are just fine and I hope you are in the best of health too. I am glad you asked some questions because I was puzzled as to what I could write about that would be of interest. Yes, the library is open now to the public. It has a few books but mostly magazines.

The tables at which I serve seat 16 people on one side—32 people can be seated in one table. I do not know in measurements how large it is. To the kitchen, where I work, it is about two miles, but to the kitchen where I eat (when not at work) is about 8 blocks away from home. No, the tea which we drink is not Japanese tea. It is black tea. Oh, if only I knew you were fond of tea—we had quite a bit of tea at home which we packed in a box and stored. It is useless stored away and I'm sure you would have enjoyed it, but I guess it's too late to think of that now. We were all so busy packing and settling our affairs that we didn't stop to think until we arrived here. I guess we were all too excited to think straight.

Yes, I have one sister and 2 brothers. One brother is in Japan. My sister and brother always went to the main library. I have met many new acquaintances. I have met girls from Gardena, Hawthorne, Downy, San Francisco, Los Angeles, Hollywood, and Long Beach.

There are many entertainments for us. Every Saturday evening there is a dance. It is limited to couples only and all the parents are invited. Clubs of girls and boys as well as boy scouts are being organized. Children between the ages of 3–12 yrs. go to school. On May 13, I attended the community singing. It was very enjoyable. Every night there is a baseball game.

I thought maybe you would like to hear about how we wash and iron. Well, first I'll tell you about washing. There is a large community washing place. . . . About 100 people can wash at one time. I am not artistic so you will have to excuse my awful drawing and use your imagination. Right now the washing place is the ironing house. There are two washing place and 2 ironing house. Stationary ironing boards have been set up. All we have to furnish is the iron and cord. In another part of the ground are rows and rows of clothes lines. So many people go to wash that often a line is formed similar to that of a lunch line.

As I said in my last letter, I have enclosed 2 issues of our paper. I hope you will enjoy reading it. Wishing you always my best.

Sincerely,

Louise Ogawa

Even in Santa Anita, life had its little diversions—especially for the teenagers. There were baseball games and sing-alongs. Every other Friday night movies were shown under the stars, and every Saturday night there was a dance, talent show, or concerts. Church services were held on Sunday morning in the grandstands with guest speakers, and hymns played on a portable organ. On Sunday nights thousands came to the grandstand to watch the sun set and enjoy great concerts featuring some of the world's best-known musicians, thanks to Ruth Watanabe, a college student who used her own classical phonograph record collection. Every week when she needed a fresh supply of records, her friend Edythe Backus brought new choices to the gate.

Going to dances every Saturday evening was a real novelty. Fusa and her friend Chiyo loved the newfound freedom to attend such social events. Before going to Santa Anita, Chiyo explained:

> . . . We were pretty sheltered, I know I was and Fusa was, too. We didn't go out on dates, even though we were teenagers. The only time we were able to go out was if we went with one of our neighbors who was a little older and his sister. My parents would allow us to go to a skating rink as a group. So, when we got to Santa Anita it was just like a dream—having so many people and going to the grandstands where there were records. I remember one time my father came after me. I was in the middle of a dance and he said time for me to come home!

But the dances at Santa Anita didn't make up for the fact that they never got to go to their senior prom or to their graduation from San Diego High School that June. They received diplomas by mail eventually. But theirs was the class that didn't get to march down the aisle in caps and gowns. In 1992, San Diego High School invited those who would have graduated in the class of 1942 to celebrate their class's fiftieth anniversary at commencement. After half a century, those who attended finally got to wear caps and gowns and marched in the academic procession.

During that summer of 1942, older Nisei who had finished high school were able to work in the "camouflage factory," making nets that were used to conceal military installations. Some suffered with skin and breathing problems from the lint flying in the air. The work was dusty and tedious and open only to citizens. However, it was one way of helping the war effort.

High school students were expected to have part-time jobs of some kind. Louise worked in the cafeteria serving tea. "There are so many people to feed," she wrote, "that the cooks have to use shovels to transfer food from one pan to another." Margaret worked four hours a day in the recreation classes for seven- to eight-year-olds. Tets was working as a messenger by day and a barber by night.

Having a job was one way to earn a little money, and very "little" is exactly what they were paid. Skilled workers such as doctors and dentists were paid only nineteen dollars a month! Other workers earned even less—cooks, teachers, and other

"HEPCATS"

In the 1940s, "hepcat" was slang for a cool dancer who did the Lindy Hop or jitterbug to big band swing music. These two hepcats are from Poston's class of 1944 yearbook. Those two-tone shoes she is wearing are saddle shoes and, along with bobby socks, they were "killer-dillers"!

mid-level workers were paid sixteen dollars a month. Waiters, waitresses, snack bar workers, and clerical staff earned twelve dollars a month. Students who worked as teachers' aides or part-time employees earned as little as eight dollars a month. But teenagers such as Louise were thrilled when they received their first paychecks. Many had never had money of their own and took pride in earning a few dollars to pay for things they could order by mail. Some handed the money over to their families—others were able to spend it on sodas, ice cream, magazines, and other goodies at the canteen.

Margaret managed to see the bright side even though she seemed to have more responsibility than most seventeen-year-olds. Perhaps by being upbeat, Margaret tried to convince herself that things would work out. In fact, several of the correspondents seem to put a happy face on their hardship as a way of showing their patriotism to the outside world:

April 23, 1942
Dear Miss Breed,
I find "camping life" very nice. We are all giving a b[u]tton which has a one, a two, or a three on it so that we may have our meals at certain hours. I . . . eat breakfast from 6:30 to 7:00, lunch at 11:30 to 12:00, and dinner at 4:30 to 5:00. The food is simple, but delicious and wholesome. I did not have to cook or wash the dishes as there are many cooks and waiters in the cafeteria. I love cooking, but thanks heavens I do not have to do the dishes! Since I have a two and a half months brother, I wash daily, and sweep out my barrack. About three times a week I iron the family's clothes. There is really not much I may do in the afternoon, but get my exercise playing dodge ball, catch or softball. Once in a while, I type manuscripts for my friends, or write letters. I retire every night between 9:30 to 10:00 P.M. All lights should be out by 10:00 in each barrack.

I went over [to] Louise Ogawa's barrack and saw the two very interesting books you sent her. I certainly love books and miss going to the library every week; so I decided to write you a letter.

Florence is going to school daily from 2:00 to 4:00 and enjoys it very much. She tells me she misses going to the library and asked if I would write to you. If you happen to have any discarded books, Florence and I would certainly appreciate them.

Please keep up the good work in teaching children to read books for that is the pathway to happiness!

I am enclosing dolls that Florence made in school and some stamps.

Sincerely yours,

Florence and Margaret Ishino

As the elder daughter, Margaret learned early about hard work: "My mother always taught me responsibility—to be independent. Since I was 10 years old I was doing the family laundry and things like that." Now "camping life" called for finding solutions to all kinds of problems. When they got to Santa Anita everyone slept on cots with hay-filled mattresses. But Margaret's baby brother was just two and a half months old. To keep him safe she invented a crib:

. . . he slept in a trough—you know where the horses used to drink water—that's where he slept until we sent for a baby buggy from Sears Roebuck. I don't know what we would have done without Sears Roebuck and Montgomery Ward.

I had to bathe my brother—I had to carry two buckets and put water in a big tub and wash him. Sometimes the boys helped carry the water. Every day I had to wash diapers—my mother became ill—but he still needed a two o'clock feeding—so I'd go around begging for milk. Finally, I got the chef in my block to save me some milk everyday—things were rationed—so there was hardly anything to spare.

At Santa Anita we had no privileges—we didn't stick things in the washer or refrigerator—you learn to accept this and you just do the best that you can—otherwise you can't manage.

There was just one laundry area for sixteen thousand people. By 5:30 A.M., the rumble of wagon wheels could be heard. What was it? It was mothers and daughters carting washboards, tubs, soap, and dirty clothes to the laundry area that might be half a mile away. Why so early? Because if they didn't get there early, there would be more long waits on lines. There were no washing machines or dryers. There were no disposable diapers, and most clothes needed ironing. It was a labor-intensive process—all done by hand. First you scrubbed the clothes clean; then you squeezed them out and hung them on lines to dry. Finally, they needed to be ironed smooth. A late start might mean waiting on a line for each step of the exhausting process. Whether it was time to eat, take a shower, brush teeth, collect mail, see the doctor, or iron clothes, there were lines for everything. It didn't matter if it was raining or the sun was blazing hot; they waited on endless lines.

There were no phones for calling out to friends or family in other assembly centers. There were no computers or e-mail. Letters and packages gave them contact with the world beyond the fence. Tets saw the humor of the postal authorities' difficulty with sorting names such as Kuratomi, Takahashi, Miyamoto, Kashiwagi, Izumigawa, and so on.

April 22, 1942
Dear Miss Breed,
The postal setup here is getting better now. At first they had the Japanese boys who had had postal experience prior to coming here to Santa Anita working under supervision of a postmaster from Arcadia. They did very well, and things were going smoothly. Then they decided to bring in postal employees from Arcadia to work in the Camp Santa Anita Post Office. The Japanese boys were released, and boy did those poor Arcadia men take a beating!!! We did too. They did not know one Japanese name from another and we had to stand in line for hours before we could get our mail. Finally the postal authorities "got wise" and placed the Japanese boys back on the job. . . .

At the present time I am a messenger during the day and barber at night. The mud here is not so bad, just in places it is gooey. I have just finished giving haircuts to the hospital staff. I am glad to report that the Dr. Tanaka, our San Diego doctor, was finally placed on the staff. Now that I am barbering my arm seems to be getting better all the time. I am glad you heard from my father. I have not received news from him as yet.

In the same letter Tets fills Miss Breed in on the subject of food. Early reports on food were pretty grim. At first they were fed an abundance of hot dogs, bread, and

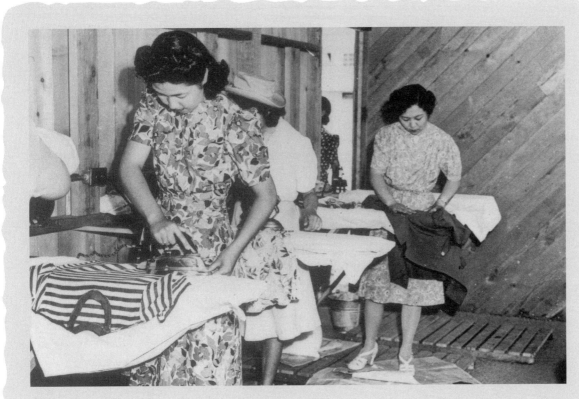

There was a line for washing, a line for hanging clothes out to dry, and still another line for doing the ironing. There were no washing machines or dryers. Having clean clothes for a family was hard work.

little else. For families accustomed to plenty of fruits and vegetables, the lack of fresh produce was difficult. Nor was there an abundance of meat, milk, or rice, one of their mainstays, especially for the older Nikkei. In an earlier letter Tets compared the food at Santa Anita to food at the hospital, but eventually, as more Nikkei chefs began to work in the kitchens, the food improved.

> *The menu here is very nice but—the food isn't prepared as well as could be expected. For breakfast we have coffee, buttered bread, jelly or jam, one egg, and prunes (sometimes we have 1/2 orange or grapefruit or 1/2 banana) For variety instead of the egg we have a box of corn flakes or Wheat-o-nuts (bird-seed to us). For lunch we have tea, bread (unbuttered), stewed vegetables, canned fruit. Sometimes we have rice, with fish. Other times we have beans. On special days we have roast*

meat. For supper we have tea, bread (still unbuttered), beans, and a canned fruit. . . . The tea and coffee are such in name only. So you see the food situation can be improved greatly. I have spoken to the officials in charge and I am sure after talking with them that conditions will improve. The mess halls are cafeteria style if lining up for food is such. Everyone receives the same food. The mess hall that seats 5000 is the RED MESS HALL. It is in the main building where the pari-mutual windows are, under the grandstands.

. . . We are getting up a softball league. Teams are being made up of the people from the various areas. San Diego and Chula Vista are represented. Some of the others are Long Beach, San Pedro, Gardena, San Francisco, Hawthorne, and a few others that I cannot think of at present. Fusa just came in and told me to tell you that she is not going to write to you until you answer her letter. She says that she is "mad as blazes."

We had beef stew this lunch with vegetable salad. It was not so bad. You can disregard the above about Fusa as she went to the post office during the lunch hour and found a letter and a book for her. . . . Mr. Hughes is right about the dust in Manzanar, another camp in East-central California. Mr. Alexander, who is in charge of the housing . . . told me himself that when he went to Manzanar . . . there was dust four inches deep. Every time the wind swept down from the mountains there would be a minor dust storm. Yessir, we are certainly lucky to be here in Santa Anita. . . .

Sincerely yours,
Ted

There was little to look forward to, as one day was much like the last. But for weeks there were letters back and forth about Miss Breed's plans to come visit them in Santa Anita.

CHAPTER FIVE

THE WINNERS ARE . . .

BEING BUSY WAS A BLESSING that kept Clara's days filled, especially during those first weeks when the Children's Room of the library seemed so quiet and empty. All through the early spring of 1942, Clara was busier than ever. She not only sent books and letters to Santa Anita almost daily, but her hours at the library became more demanding also. Because of the war, workers from all over the country moved to San Diego to sign on for high-paying jobs at shipyards and aircraft factories. In just one year San Diego grew from 203,341 people to more than 300,000. Defense workers put in long hours and to accommodate them the library extended its hours and opened its doors even on Sundays. Everyone on staff, including Clara, took turns working weekends.

San Diego was a major military center and naval base from which thousands of GIs shipped out to fight in the Pacific. For all the soldiers and sailors in the area, Clara launched a Victory Book Campaign, a book drive to scrounge up hundreds of used books for the GIs at nearby bases. She called these "war-born libraries."

On top of the war effort, Clara, an active member of the American Library Association, was working on the Newbery-Caldecott Awards Committee. These awards were and still are the most prestigious in children's books, and choosing the winners took months. By March, Clara and twenty-three committee members from all over the country had already read and reread more than five hundred books and cast their first ballots. In fact, Clara read some of her personal favorites to the children at story hour. How they loved calling "Jack, Kack, Lack, Mack, Nack, Ouack, Pack, and Quack," as in the jolly new picture book *Make Way for Ducklings*. Clara and the older children had also loved a new book called *Little Town on the Prairie* and a short but powerful book, *The Matchlock Gun*, the story of a courageous young boy, a Dutch immigrant who must defend his family on the frontier when his father goes away to fight in the French and Indian War.

Just days after the children left San Diego, Clara agreed to take over as acting chairman of the awards committee when Harriet Dickson, a librarian from Texas, became ill and had to resign. Clara was not at all fond of speaking in public or running meetings, but that is exactly what she would have to do at the ALA annual meeting in Milwaukee. By April 22, the votes were final, and although they would not be announced until the meeting in June, Clara wrote to the founder of *Horn Book Magazine*, Bertha E. Miller, to arrange for the publication of the authors' and artists' acceptance speeches for the July–August issue:

> Dear Mrs. Miller:
> The winner of the Newbery Medal is Walter D. Edmonds for *THE MATCHLOCK GUN*. The winner of the Caldecott Medal is Robert McCloskey for *MAKE WAY FOR DUCKLINGS*. I hope you are pleased, and I know I can count on you to guard the information zealously. . . .
> Sincerely,
> CLARA E. BREED, Acting Chairman

This letter to Bertha Miller was one of dozens of letters and cards by which ideas traveled across the continent and grew into a friendship during the next twenty years.

A LOSING BATTLE

During these same hectic weeks Clara not only wrote letters to her young friends at Santa Anita; she began to write about them as well. At the risk of being called a "Jap lover" and aware that some would despise her affection for her Nisei friends, Clara wrote a large part of a *Library Journal* article, "War Children on the Pacific," that was published in June 1942. In it she wrote of the Nisei's patriotism and courage in the face of their lost freedom. "They believe in America," she wrote, "and they believe in democracy, and they intend to prove their loyalty to the doubters."

Weeks later when the article was published, Clara found that most of the other librarians who contributed to the article also had genuine concern for their young Japanese American patrons. However, a librarian from the Fresno area, where snipers were attacking Nikkei farmers, wrote in her part of the article: "The menace of the Japanese warrants their being sent to internment camps as rapidly as possible. . . . At least 70% are Buddhists and are completely loyal to the Mikado: their lives are supervised and directed by Japanese consuls, even though they are American citizens." Getting some people to see the truth seemed to be a losing battle. Clara was upset to think that otherwise bright people would believe such nonsense.

Busy as she was with all her library work, Clara's loneliness for "her children" did not fade. She longed to go and see them, but a trip to Santa Anita was hard to plan. Getting away from the library was not easy. There were deadlines for the article and her remarks for the awards ceremony. And now she had to take a train to Milwaukee.

Week after week, a flurry of letters was exchanged about possible times for a visit to Santa Anita. But getting into the camp required planning ahead. Each family was allowed only one visitor's permit per week and visits were limited to thirty minutes. At first Clara planned to visit in late May and Fusa got a pass, but she didn't manage to notify Clara in time. There was red tape at every turn.

Dear Miss Breed,

You know, things here are changing all the time. In regards to your plans for coming here, I'll have to be a wet blanket again. An announcement came out that Districts 1, 2, and 3 may have visitors on Sunday this week, and the rest of the districts must have visitors on Saturday. Then next week it will be in reverse. Why don't you plan to come up on the 31st, a Sunday. The visiting hours are from 9 A.M. to 11 A.M. and 2 P.M. to 4 P.M. Since you mentioned the fact that you would like to come in the morning, maybe we could arrange to have it that way. Please let me know what you have decided to do. One thing is certain though, I can't meet you this Sunday.

Another announcement just came out stating the fact that we cannot receive any perishable or non perishable food here. The only thing we can bring in from the outside is candy. Gee, that really makes me mad. On top of that, the Canteen has stopped selling cookies, sandwiches, cakes and all sorts of sweets except candy. We have all come to the conclusion that the mess halls will have to serve us better food. Gee, I like stew, but I don't like to eat it three meals in succession. Gee, I always get onto the subject of food— well, don't blame me too much as it is about the only thing we think about.

I was thinking about your being on a sugar ration. At first I thought that we had it pretty soft because that was one thing we didn't have to wait in line for. About a week ago we had sugar for breakfast, but none for lunch or supper. Then, this morning we didn't even have any sugar for breakfast. The waitresses told that they had run out of sugar. I guess you people are better off in the long run.

You asked me what kind of magazine I like. Well, I like any kind which concerns the home and clothes and looks. . . . One magazine I would like is one full of crossword puzzles. My friends in the office are just crazy over crossword puzzles. I'm not very good at them, but it's a lazy person's method of increasing the vocabulary.

I guess my typing must be just driving you crazy. I make so many errors that it really isn't funny any more. Can You imagine, I used to be able to type very accurately, once. I can't blame it on the typewriter because it's a brand new, well, it hasn't been used very much,—Royal. I guess it's just me!

Thank you very much for everything. I really appreciate your very kind interest in me.

Yours truly,
Fusa Tsumagari

May 28, 1942
Dear Miss Breed,
I received your letter this morning—and to tell the truth, was rather disappointed. I had arranged to have you come, and received an O.K., but hadn't informed you on time, so I guess it's my fault. I've had the pass cancelled.

How would it be if we arranged to meet two Sundays from now—June 14, 1942? I realize that it's rather far off—but then there's safety in numbers. Please write to me in the meantime and let me know. The application specifies how many of us can see you, the date, and reason. The reason given is usually business because the only other reason is blood relative.

I wonder if you come up on the 14th you wouldn't be too inconvenienced by getting me a few things. I have enclosed a money order for the sum of $5.00. If you *cannot bring them would you please send them. If you come, please bring them because that is the best excuse I have for seeing you—I hope you know what I mean. I would like the following items:*

- *2 balls (white) for crocheting. (I have included a piece of it as sample) cost about 25¢ each.   Total: .50*
- *2 yds red and white striped seersucker about 40¢ yd .80*
- *1 1/4 yds batiste (or some thin material similar to that) about 35¢ yd about .45*
- *2 hairnets about 10¢ each .20 made of rayon or cotton (black)*
- *2 yds embroidered organdy galloon about 2" wide. (anything that looks good as part of a peasant blouse) abt 15¢ yd .30*
- *1 1/2 yd blue and white striped cotton material abt 35¢ yd .70*
- *1 doz hair curlers abt 5¢ each .60*
- *1/2 doz cotton sox abt 15¢ each .90*

Total approx 4.45

I certainly would appreciate it if you would bring them up on the 14th when (if) you come. We don't need them in too much of a hurry, and they would serve as a good excuse to see you.

> *Yours truly*
> *Fusa Tsumagari*

However, the Flag Day visit didn't work out, either. Clara was about to leave for the ALA conference. In her place, her friend Helen Fay made the trip and saw Katherine, her mom, "who was near tears most of the visit," and Margaret Arakawa, who was teaching fourth grade. Miss Fay brought back two notes for Clara:

Dear Miss Breed,

Thank you for your lovely card. Miss Fay came Saturday and was unable to see me. I was able to see her Sunday at 10:00. She has given me two books. Matchlock Gun *and* Timmy. *She has been wonderful and I appreciate her generosity. Congratulations, Miss Breed, Miss Fay says you are the new head of the Newberry-Caldecott award. I'll write again.*

> *Sincerely yours,*
> *Margaret Arakawa*

Dear Miss Breed,

I wish I could see you and the library, and just finish my card. I sure do miss the library. I remember how I used to climb the stairs.

I will write another letter soon.

Katherine Tasaki

Clara wished she could see her dear Katherine, too. How she missed them all!

"NO LAST CHAPTER—ONLY THE FUTURE"

Clara was relieved when the speeches at the ALA conference were behind her. By nature, Clara was inclined to be quite retiring, so speaking to large groups of people was not something she liked doing, but she was learning to overcome her shyness. After the ceremony Bertine Weston, editor of the *Library Journal*, congratulated Clara for a job well done, with both the conference and her part of the article that had just been published. Bertine asked Clara to try her hand at writing another article about the problems of the Japanese American children on the West Coast. *Why not?* Clara thought. Maybe an article would help people better understand the problems—even if they could not solve these problems all at once.

The ALA conference had been a great success, and Clara decided to spend the Fourth of July weekend with her sister, Eleanor, in Berkeley. Traveling west was like being on a troop train, as most passengers were soldiers headed for the Pacific. Clara could only imagine the courage of these young GIs who had said their sad good-byes to loved ones and now faced an unknown future.

As the train rumbled along, Clara reread some of Walter Edmonds's stirring acceptance speech for his Newbery Medal for *The Matchlock Gun*:

> We American writers have one of the great stories of the world to tell. . . . It has no last chapter, only the future . . . I shall be content if I can get into my books . . . faith in our land, faith in our people, faith in the integrity and the future of America. I have no doubt of them myself. . . .

The last months had given Clara some doubts about the integrity of far too many Americans who were using the war as an excuse to breathe fire and wound any minority. What kind of future would Louise and Tets and Fusa have in a country that could brush aside their rights as citizens to freedom?

Clara and Eleanor were delighted to have a rare weekend together. They had always been extremely close even though they were nothing like each other. Clara idolized her sister, who was very outgoing and always eager to try new and exotic places, while Clara was more of a private person who enjoyed quiet pleasures and her work. Eleanor had hardly been home since her college days. She had an appetite for adventure and like her hero, Richard Haliburton, who crossed the Alps on an elephant and swam the Panama Canal, Eleanor was determined to do it all, to see the world, and she had already done a good part of it! Unlike Clara, Eleanor seldom had one job—she had many. She worked as a teacher, a stenographer, even a writer at the *San Francisco Chronicle*—whatever was needed to pay the rent between her many trips.

Clara always looked forward to seeing the stunning view of San Francisco Bay and the stately Golden Gate Bridge that was for some reason more red than gold. But today Clara noticed how different everything looked from her last visit. A balloon barrage floating over the water was designed to snare any low-flying enemy planes that might try to attack. Off in the distance, a convoy of warships was putting out to sea.

Eleanor said the sights were different every day. At least once she had seen the *Queen Mary*, the Cunard liner painted battleship gray now—even her three huge smokestacks were camouflaged to blend in with the sea and sky. Eleanor told Clara about their friends the Gordons, who had been in Pearl Harbor the day of the attack. Robert Gordon, who worked in Hawaii for Eastman Kodak, had insisted that Millie bring their three children home to the states on the first ship they could find. They had come back on one of the Matson luxury liners that used to carry passengers to and from the Orient. Now it, too, was painted battleship gray and carried wounded troops home from the war.

The first evening, the two sisters talked well into the night—it was such a novelty. In 1942, you couldn't just take off for Berkeley from San Diego whenever you wanted a visit. The only way to get there was by train, and that was an overnight trip. With the war on, travel was more difficult than ever. Soldiers had first preference—seats for civilians were scarce—and with gas and tires rationed, driving long distances in a car was out of the question.

It was like the old days when Eleanor and Clara were girls and stayed up late talking about what they would do one day when they were grown. With the whole world at war, many dreams were on hold and talk was not cheap. In fact, long-distance phone calls were so expensive they were reserved for emergencies. But Clara and Eleanor were never out of touch—they wrote long, newsy letters frequently.

Eleanor told Clara about the project she was working on for International House, a dorm where students from all over the world lived. She was gathering letters from Nisei college students about their experiences in the assembly centers. She was planning to publish the letters if she could manage to contact enough of the students. In fact, Eleanor planned to visit some of them at Tanforan, another racetrack outside San Francisco, if Clara didn't mind going along.

Clara had not yet seen Santa Anita, but the conditions in Tanforan did not come as a surprise. It matched the descriptions her young friends had sent of their assembly center. Months later she would write about this memorable Fourth of July in *Library Journal*:

Barbed wire surrounded what had once been the grounds and parking area. . . . Armed soldiers guarded the gates. Inside there were row on row of identical tar-paper barracks, deserted now except for a few old men who were taking advantage of the unusual quiet to rest. The second floor of the Visitor's House, once the room where pari-mutuel bets were placed, was buzzing with boys and girls who were decorating the room with red, white and blue newspaper stars for a dance to be held that night. Little boys sailed model boats on the ornamental pond. Everyone else was packed into the huge grandstand . . . watching the celebration on the track below, there were many children, for one-fourth of all the evacuees are children under fifteen years of age. It was interesting to notice among the visitors the number of Chinese faces. Waves of laughter and applause swept across the grandstand and greeted the contenders in obstacle races, potato races, and relay races. There were patriotic speeches and songs broadcast over the loud speaker, a parade of Boy Scouts in uniform and the salute to the flag.

Clara felt sick at heart watching the children saluting the flag. One of Eleanor's Japanese American friends was sitting next to them and said, "The Boy Scouts and the salute to the flag and the 'Star-Spangled Banner' mean more to us now that we are behind barbed wire, not less." Clara was reminded of the letter that had come from Santa Anita:

. . . bitter feelings do not enter my head because I know we were sent here for our own protection. I am grateful to the government for gathering us in such a nice place. If I am helping the government by staying here I am glad. I want so much to be of some use to the government.

Clara wondered how they could not be bitter. How long would they remain patriotic young Americans?

"JUST SEEING HER SMILING FACE"

Her trip to Tanforan made Clara all the more eager to visit her young friends at Santa Anita. It was on the way home to San Diego, so why not? Clara wired Tets, hoping he could get her a pass on short notice. As she boarded the southern-bound train, Clara received a telegram from Tets, confirming he had secured a pass.

Clara knew that during the early weeks people visited Santa Anita through the barbed-wire fence. Visitors would send cakes and melons in with the guards, who cut everything open to be sure nothing dangerous was being passed to the prisoners. But now no food was allowed and all visitors had to have a pass to enter the special Visitor's House. It was the only place where friends from the outside could enter.

A long table ran down the center of the room, and visitors had to stay on one side of the table. It was a five-foot-wide barrier that kept friends from even shaking hands! Nothing could be passed across the table from friend to friend. Guards enforced the rules. All visits were limited to half an hour. It didn't matter how far someone had traveled—a rule was a rule and there were no exceptions.

At 1:30 on the dot, Tets and his sister Yaeko came into the visitors' room with Louise, Margaret, and Fusa. Clara could not get over how suntanned they were from being out-of-doors. She was genuinely happy to see them, but it was awkward, too. Trying to make small talk across a table was not easy. She had an armful of books, some candy, and a few magazines, too. She gave them to the guard to inspect and pass along. Tets wanted to know all about her trip to Milwaukee. Fusa asked about San Diego—had it changed? How was Clara's mother? And how was Miss McNary, Clara's assistant? What were they doing for the summer reading club at the library? Clara had questions, too. She wanted to know if they had seen Jack Watanabe and how he was doing. And what about Katherine? Clara had hoped to see her, but Mrs. Tasaki had moved with Katherine to Arizona, to a place called Poston. That was all they could tell Clara. How about David and Elizabeth Kikuchi? Try as they might to have a normal visit, it was uncomfortable. In fact, it seemed Clara had just gotten there when the guard announced, "That's it. Time's up!"

Late that afternoon Clara took the last train back to San Diego. She was glad she had at last seen her friends—although she found it hard to say good-bye and leave them again. She had heard they would all be moving soon, but where would they be sent next? Would it be any better than the place they were in now? How long would the government keep these young people locked away?

Days after she returned to the library Clara received this letter from Louise:

July 15, 1942

Dear Miss Breed,

I shall never forget that day you visited us. At the sight of your smiling face a big lump formed at the pit of my throat never dreaming I would ever see you again. I was very glad to see you in the best of health.

Thank you a million times for the delicious candy, soap, and the most interesting book! I was most interested in the book because I have read, Peggy Covers Washington, London, *and* Peggy Covers News. *I enjoy Emma Bughee's books very much. . . .*

The distribution of our second checks began today. It was, of course, my first check. I felt so proud to receive it because I really earned it all by myself. It makes me feel so independent. We receive about 37¢ a day. For 11 days work I received $3.04.

I am going to take advantage of your generosity and ask you to go on a little shopping tour for me in your leisure time. Will you please send me the following:

1. *2 yards of printed seersucker (something that would look nice when made into a dirndl. I already have 2 striped ones—green + white; red + white—so please do not send striped one.) cost = not over 50¢ a yard.*
2. *1 1/2 YD. of plain white seersucker. (about same price as printed one)*
3. *1/2 YD. of muslin (going to use it for stiffening)*
4. *1 card of snaps .05*
5. *5 Hollywood curlers*
6. *2 shower caps .29*
7. *1 bottle of brown liquid shoe polish—10¢*
8. *1 bottle of Skrips royal blue ink. 15¢*
9. *1 mirror sold at Kress for 15¢ or 25¢ [crossed out]*
10. *BOYS Cooper-Jockey shorts—SIZE: 28 waist STORE: Walkers*
11. *1 small face towel (cheap one is all right)*

Date __Tue. July 7,__ 1942

Wartime Civil Control Administration
Santa Anita Assembly Center
ARCADIA, CALIFORNIA

OFFICIAL VISITING HOURS
1:00 p.m.–1:30 p.m.
1:30 p.m.–2:00 p.m.
2:00 p.m.–2:30 p.m.
2:30 p.m.–3:00 p.m.
3:00 p.m.–3:30 p.m.
3:30 p.m.–4:00 p.m.

Name of visitor __CLARA E. BREED__

Address __S.D. PUBLIC LIBRARY__ City ____ State __CALIF.__

Reason for visit __URGENT PERSONAL BUSINESS__

Signed by __Richard Akutagawa__ Dist. __IV__ Ave. __1__ Barr. __31__ Unit __14__
                    Applicant

YOUR VISITING TIME IS
from __1:30__ p.m.
to __2:00__ p.m.

Signature of official __Donald D. Malready__
                                Donald D. McCready, Executive Assistant

Countersigned __Guy E. Willingson__
                        Guy E. Willingson, Personnel Relations Officer

1.30 Pm   2.00
IN   OUT

BALDWIN Gate   TOWER Gate   TOWER Gate   BALDWIN Gate

Permit Regulations: Good ONLY for date issued. This permit is to be returned to the U.S. Military Guard on leaving the area.

Clara must have considered this a special day since she saved her visitor's pass from Santa Anita. She could only stay for half an hour. It was a long way to come for such a short visit.

    I have enclosed $4.50 in money order. I hope this amount will be sufficient—if not please let me know. I hope I'm not causing you too much trouble. I want so much to repay you for all the nice books, candy, and soap but do not know how I can. In my spare-time I made this book marker. It is made very crudely but I hope you will be able to use it.

    Yours very sincerely,

    Louise Ogawa

    P.S. *If there seems to be some money left over after deducting the shipping expense [I] would like to have some Butterscotch balls or Fruit balls or drops. Thank you again.*

While Clara was away, a letter had come from Katherine and it was from Arizona. Mrs. Tasaki had taken a job as a nurse's aide in Poston. From the little that Katherine wrote, the place sounded dreadful:

Dear Miss Breed,

We arrived at Poston on Sunday yesterday I went with a girl to the ball game. Arizona vs. California. California won 13–1 It was a pretty good game. It is very hot here, and it is very dusty.

I think one of these days I'll write a book for your libay about this kind of life. The other day, we walked to the canteen which is one mile away.

Well, mamma had to go to a certain office, so while we were going, we saw a dead snake. I saw a rat skin too. There are lots of red ants around here. There are Scorpions too. There was on[e] under our house.

I think it is all very nice here except for the heat, sand, and insects.
Sincerely,
Katherine Tasaki

Clara was soon back to her usual routine: shopping, writing, wrapping up packages. She seemed to be sending something to Santa Anita almost daily. Fortunately, the post office was right across the street from the library. Although she earned very little as a librarian, Clara often stopped at the Woolworth five-and-ten-cent store on her way home to stock up on candy, socks, bubble gum, and other goodies to add as treats. She gladly spent her own money for these extras for "her children."

At the library, she kept a notebook with the name of each child and the name of the books that she sent to him or her. In time, Clara filled several notebooks. Most of the books she sent were review copies that children's book publishers sent to her. There were also many discarded books—old titles that were no longer in condition to circulate in the library. Many of these she sent directly to the library at Santa Anita, hoping they would offer more than magazines to her friends.

THE SPARK THAT LIT THE FUSE

In early August, Clara was shocked to learn there had been a riot at Santa Anita. It was hard to know what had happened because the news reports were very sketchy. She was terribly worried that the children might have been hurt, but there was no way to call and speak with them. All she could do was wait for mail to come. A few days later a letter from Fusa arrived:

August 9, 1942

Dear Miss Breed,

On Wednesday, the army (not from Frisco, though) ordered our barracks searched for contraband. Previous to this whenever such an order was issued we were given bulletins and notified on everything. This, however, was done abruptly with no reason given and did not give the people a very good attitude toward the search. Then, they closed certain gates and would not allow the people to pass unless they were searched. This, too, aroused their anger.

Then, to top that, they began to confiscate such things as scissors and knitting needles as contraband. Then, some of the police had the nerve to steal people's money and also remove things from people's houses without allowing the occupant to see what was taken. One policeman in particular aroused the people to such a degree that they began to mob him. Incidentally a Korean was leading the men in their raid. Many people had grievances against him before as he was claimed to be a "stool pidgeon." Unfortunately the mob of people were so aroused that they chased him and beat him with chairs. This was wrong, but a mad mob is very hard to control. Incidentally this led to the discovery of liquor smuggling and jailing of some of the stewards of the mess hall. The army took control for three days and everything was at a standstill. We and also the army were glad they finally moved out. The newspapers did not give this version, but that's the way we saw it. Just a few days before the incident we were all craving for excitement, but now that it is over we are glad that it is over. Once again thank you for the candy and book. If you have time, please write to me sometime.

Sincerely,

Fusa Tsumagari

Clara kept a record of every book she sent with the name of the person she sent the book to along with the date and their grade in school. Almost every letter to Miss Breed starts with thanks for a book, and several of the books on this list are mentioned in Margaret's letters.

Fusa's brother, Yukio, also wrote about the riot. His letter was to Clara's sister, Eleanor, who was gathering letters from former Berkeley college students about their evacuation experiences:

Today the spark lighted the fuse which exploded into a fury of violence. For the first time the camp actually experienced mob violence. This outbreak all started by the searching of each unit by armed men of all personal belongings with utter disrespect for individuals involved. Uncouth treatment of individuals plus theft by those making the investigation created a frenzy in camp. A huge mob of infuriated people gathered to ask for the reason for such doings. Frightened by the large crowd and excited by pointed questions directed to him, the investigator drew his gun and threatened to shoot anyone who might molest him. This threat lit the fuse which angered the crowd to the extent that flying fists were not uncommon. The investigator was not hurt physically however I do believe there was some change of attitude of this gentleman. Another man was hurt from this outbreak. There has been a drastic shake-up in the administration.

Elizabeth Kikuchi was much younger than Yukio and Fusa but when we spoke, it was clear that Liz never forgot the day of the Santa Anita riot, either:

I had been in the hospital with pneumonia and I remember that Miss Breed had sent me a book that kept me from feeling lonesome while I was in the hospital. I recently found some of the letters that friends sent to me during that time. I was still recuperating in bed when I saw the soldiers with rifles driving past our barrack windows. I heard the "commotion" of the riots. I remember my father cautioning my brothers to stay inside.

Tets wrote only a few lines about the riots. In August, he was far more upset with some terrible news of his own. His father had been notified that he was to be interned in a federal prison in North Dakota for the duration. In other words, he would not be released until the war ended! Tets and his dad were unwilling to take that as final. There was a chance, Tets told Miss Breed, of having the case reopened if enough people would write affidavits to the government. He sent Clara the names of people in San Diego who might be willing to write such a letter and the name of the person at the Department of Justice to whom they should write.

Clara immediately wrote a petition to the Honorable William Fleet Palmer, United States Attorney:

August 7, 1942

My dear Mr. Palmer,

. . . Mr. Hirasaki has lived in the United States since 1901. His children were born here, Tetsuzo the boy being over twenty-one now and Yaeko the girl a graduate of high school. In all the time I have known them Mr. Hirasaki has been both father and mother to the children, and he has done a far better piece of work in raising his family than is done by two parents in many families. (Since I have been supervising librarian of the Children's department of the San Diego Public Library for the last thirteen years, I speak with feeling!) The children are thoroughly American, loyal to our government, intelligent, hard-working, fine citizens of whom we can be proud. The family has been scattered since Mr. Hirasaki's internment, since it seemed wise to them to place the daughter in a family who could chaperone and protect her. If Mr. Hirasaki could be sent to Santa Anita the family could become a unit again before they are moved to a relocation center. I believe it is the humane thing to do, and I believe also that the government would run no risk of disloyalty from his family. If Tetsuzo had not had a tubercular lesion in his right arm, he would have been serving in our armed forces.

At the time Mr. Hirasaki was arrested I wanted to appear in his behalf, but hearings were not held here as you know. I understand that Mr. Hirasaki has never been a member of a Japanese society and I know he has never taken his family to visit Japan. Since the charges against him show no evidence of subversive activities, I strongly urge that he be released from Bismarck and allowed to rejoin his son and daughter in Santa Anita.

Please feel free to investigate my reputation for truthfulness and honor by contacting Miss Cornelia D. Plaister, head librarian of the San Diego Public Library, or the American Library Association at 520 N. Michigan Ave., Chicago.

Very sincerely,

CLARA E. BREED

There was little else Clara could do now but hope for the best.

Katherine continued to write often, and her newsy little letters gave Clara a smile. Katherine was busy trying to say tongue twisters such as "Peter Piper picked a peck of pickled peppers" and pig Latin. "You ought to hear me!" she wrote. Clara wished she could hear her. How Clara missed her adorable little Katherine!

"RUMORS FLY THICK AND FAST"

Excitement over the riot was short-lived. More pressing were rumors that everyone would be moving out of Santa Anita soon. All through the early weeks of August the move was on everybody's mind. According to Louise, the deadline was October, but it might be sooner. Tets wrote that he was sure they would be heading for snow country—someplace far colder than Santa Anita. The question was, where would they be going? Fusa didn't know, either:

August 3, 1942
Dear Miss Breed,
. . . As I have told you before, rumors fly thick and fast. Most of us are expecting to be relocated soon. We've heard that we will be moved to Idaho, Colorado, Wyoming, and Arkansas. I think we will move to either Wyoming or Arkansas. I guess we'll have to wait and see how far from right I am. Gee, wherever we go, we all realize that it will be "rough going" because other people have refused to live there before us. We also know that the weather will be nothing like the beautiful California weather. It will probably be very hot or extremely cold. According to rumors the San Diego people will be among the first to be re-evacuated. Officials will not confirm anything because they do not know anything so the obvious result is rumors. Rumors lead to panic—which is really a shame.
You know, I've often wondered what some of the other people write to you. Do they write as corny letters as I? Gee, I hope not! Do you know on August 8 it will be exactly four months since we came here. The days certainly fly fast, but the months just crawl by! I hope this war will be over before long. Once again thank you very much for sending me the lovely dresses.
Sincerely,
Fusa

On the twentieth of August, Fusa wrote again, this time to say that she thinks they are being sent to Utah. But that, like most rumors, turned out not to be true, either.

"We departed from Santa Anita . . . amid a great deal of tears, for we were leaving many friends whom we may never see. The band played 'Auld Lang Syne' as we departed, and throngs of people waved to us until we were well past the gate." (August 1942, Poston III Reunion Catalog, 1991)

"FURTHER AND FURTHER AWAY"

The exact date is missing from Louise's last sad letter from Santa Anita, but sometime after August 20 the San Diegans were notified that they would leave on August 26 and 27, 1942. They would not be going to snow country. Not to Utah, Idaho, Colorado, Wyoming, or Arkansas . . .

Aug. 1942
Dear Miss Breed,
The time has come again for me to say "good-bye" until I hear from you again at my new home. . . . We, San Diegans, are going to leave Santa Anita for Parker, Arizona on Wednesday or Thursday. (Aug. 26, 27) We are going in two groups—one on Wed. the other on Thursday.

It seems that we are going further and further away from San Diego but I hope to be back soon. I never have gone to Arizona and so I am sure it will be a new adventure to me. We are again leaving by train right after our supper—Wed. The camp is in an up roar just talking about evacuation. Today is my last day at work for I must wash, iron, and pack. It reminds me of the day when I left San Diego.

I hope you will write often. Since I'll be far far away from home I will be more than happy to hear from you.

My friend has made a pair of "geta" which I am sending you. I hope you will enjoy it. The so called shallac (glossiness) is fingernail polish.

Most sincerely,

Louise Ogawa

P.S. I shall write the first thing after reaching my destination—Colorado River Relocation Project—in Arizona. The best of luck to you always!

Once again they had little time to get ready for the move. It was the second time they had to pack their possessions and head for the unknown. Arizona sounded like an adventure to some and gave hope to others that their living conditions would be better. It was hard to picture anything worse than the stables they were finally leaving.

CHAPTER SIX

"GREETINGS FROM FAR-OFF POSTON"

*U*PON MY ARRIVAL TO THE Poston Relocation Center, I stood bewildered, glaring at the hot dusty desert, wondering how we could survive. When my family and I were given our barrack number we spread our blankets and tried to put things in order. The first day here was so hot I should not know how I should express how I felt then. Whoever I met carried wet towels on his heads. Even in the mess hall people ate with wet towels on their heads. Small children had not eaten because of the heat. Even grownups lost their appetite.

That night, as I tumbled into bed, I kept thinking how we could ever survive in such a place and how the hot dusty soil could be made into fertile fields.

—**CHIYOKO MORITA,** ninth grade

After twenty hours on a train and another hour on a hot, dusty bus, the Nikkei arrived at the Poston Relocation Center.* It seemed as if they had reached the ends of the earth. To get an idea of how removed from their former lives they must have felt: The nearest town, Parker, Arizona, was sixteen miles away and it had just one telephone! If one were driving toward California, the first service station would be eighty miles away.

Row upon row of black, look-alike, tar paper–covered barracks were built at Poston in record time. Eventually, the Nikkei transformed their "homes" in the bleak desert by cultivating small gardens.

It was so hot on the bus that they had opened the windows, only to be covered by powdery white dust the consistency of flour. When they stepped off the buses, friends didn't recognize one another. When they arrived in the torrid heat of summer, at barracks that were not complete, their hopes that Poston would be an improvement over Santa Anita were dashed. It was ten degrees hotter than the Libyan desert.

> *** DOUBLESPEAK:** *Relocation center* sounds nicer than *prison*, but all ten of the so-called relocation centers were prisons, all located in the middle of nowhere. In fact, President Roosevelt referred to them as "concentration camps" at a press conference in October 1942 and called the Japanese Americans *prisoners*. In another example of doublespeak, during the same period, Nazi Germany used the term *concentration camp* to disguise what were, in reality, death camps.

The buildings had no window screens but plenty of bugs, there was a record-breaking temperature of more than 120 degrees, and windstorms coated everything with fine sand. Almost overnight, Poston became the third-largest community in Arizona. Where there had been nothing, a city of tar-papered barracks was hastily built to house more than eighteen thousand Nikkei. The camp was named for Charles D. Poston, the first congressman from the Territory of Arizona and first superintendent of Indian affairs in Arizona. In 1865, he had helped to establish the Colorado River Reservation.

Built on Indian land, Poston was the largest of all ten relocation centers. It was divided into three parts, officially known as Poston I, II, and III. Five thousand workers on a double work shift constructed the camps in record time. In fact, one builder boasted they had erected sixteen barracks in twenty-two minutes! Due to a shortage of wood, barracks were built with green pine that shrank and left cracks between the boards, allowing sand and insects to seep and creep inside. The heat was so extreme that standard army barracks were redesigned with double roofs for insulation. But even double roofs did not block the oppressive heat. No guard towers were built at Poston since the location was "in the middle of nowhere" and towers were considered unnecessary.

As buses pulled in, a monitor climbed on board to explain how they were to line up for housing and registration. They arrived at odd hours, some in the middle of the night. People had endured a long, hot trip with poor food. They were weak from heat and dust. The shock of the whole experience was overwhelming. Still, a line had to be formed at the mess hall as the head of each family registered. Everyone over seventeen was fingerprinted and had to sign an agreement that he or she would live by the regulations of the center and work. Another line was formed in the recreation hall for housing assignments.

Even nine-year-old Jack Watanabe felt cut off from the world: "We are now in a strange place—Poston, Arizona. I doubt whether this is even on the map."

Afraid that there would not be enough housing to go around, the administration put four to eight people into a single room, twenty by twenty-five feet. In Poston III there were eighteen blocks. Each block had fourteen barracks with separate latrines and showers for men and women, a mess hall, a laundry and ironing room, and a recreation hall. Since there had to be a minimum of four people in an apartment, small families had to share a single room with another family. Almost all the San Diegans were sent to Poston III. Fusa and her mother had to live with another San Diego family until there were more barracks.

Don Elberson, a sociologist who worked for the War Relocation Authority at Poston, could never erase his memory of the misery families encountered when they arrived:

> It was brutal. Some days we had to process five hundred or more people. . . . But nothing mitigated the moment when I had to take them to their new homes. . . . You'd have to take these people into this dingy excuse for a room, twenty by twenty-five feet at best. These were people who'd left everything behind, sometimes fine houses. I learned after the first day not to enter with the family, but to stand outside. It was too terrible to witness the pain in people's faces, too shameful for them to be seen in this degrading situation.

Fourteen-year-old Babe Karasawa never forgot that moment. Here's how he described it to me sixty years later:

> We opened the doors of our barrack and there were weeds growing between the spaces in the floorboards . . . they were three feet tall inside the barrack! I remember that because my two brothers and I, we just ripped those weeds out. We took buckets of water and washed all over the walls—we washed the dust and the grit. All the water goes right between the spaces—through the floorboards—the place is dry in thirty minutes because it was just so hot. This was the end of August in '42. The records show that in '42, in the middle of July, they had a record temperature of 144 degrees! I used to walk like this . . . my head tilted down and sideways so my face wouldn't go straight into the heat. When I drank water, it would just come right out of my arms. . . . Perspiration just poured right out. This was during the hottest time and I used to always have heat rash.

In her first letter from Poston, Louise tries hard to hold on to her rosy view of the world, but finding positive things to say about Poston was challenging. Now she not only missed San Diego; she missed Santa Anita! Still, sixteen-year-old Louise manages to see beauty in the bleakness.

August 27, 1942
Dear Miss Breed,
Greetings from far-off Poston, Arizona! We arrived yesterday about 3:30 P.M.

After the twenty-hour train ride they took a dilapidated bus for another hour in the scalding heat. With no air-conditioning and the windows open, sand coated their hair and skin. When they stepped off the bus, friends didn't recognize them.

It was a very long train ride. . . . After leaving Barstow, we began to feel the heat. They say yesterday was a cool day but to us it was extremely hot.

We traveled through desert after desert. There were many houses which looked as if they were built many years ago. We seldom saw a human being except when passing through a small town. One of the most beautiful scenery was when crossing a bridge which was right above the Colorado River. It is, indeed, a beautiful river.

One common thing you see while coming here is—the beds and beddings are all placed outside the homes. It has been said that the heat is so hot that the people all sleep outside. It is very hot here. We traveled by bus through acres of cotton plants—so you can imagine the heat because cotton has to be grown in a hot climate.

Another round of checkups was required. Everyone over seventeen was finger-printed like a criminal. Then barracks were assigned. When they arrived, Poston made Santa Anita seem like a paradise lost.

After leaving the train, we had to travel by bus—about 20 miles. We are in Camp No. 3. It is not quite yet completed. It is so sandy here that everyone's hair looks gray. Sometimes the wind blows but when it does the sand comes with it. This camp is so far away from civilization that it makes me feel as if I was a convict who is not allowed to see anyone. I'd much rather sleep in the Santa Anita horse stables—this has made me realize how fortunate I was to be able to live in Santa Anita. The nearest town which is a very tiny one is about 20 miles away. This trip has made me realize the wonderful work of nature. Her delicate work in shaping the stone mountains, the beautiful coloring of the surroundings—it seemed as if I was looking at the picture or a painting of a genius.

This place differs greatly from . . . Santa Anita. In Santa Anita we were allowed to keep a bucket and a broom in our homes until the time came to leave but in Poston we are allowed to BORROW a bucket, broom or mop for 1/2 hrs. This makes it very inconvenient because often they run out of them and we have to wait until one is returned. Even in the dining rooms we have to take our own spoons and forks. They provide just the knife and cups + plates and, of course, food. Yesterday I ate rice, weenies and cabbage with a knife. That was a new experience for me! You never realize how valuable a thing is until you experience it. The dining rooms are very small here because there is one to each block.

. . . We have to mop the house every day because of the dust but it does not do any good because before you know it it's dusty again.

My, this letter is getting too long and it's probably getting boring so I'll write again soon. If you have any questions, I'll be glad to answer them if I am able.

Most sincerely,

Louise Ogawa

P.S. There is no water on Sundays. The electricity is also turned off. Sunday morning everyone eats before 6:00 A.M. Water and electricity turned off between 6:00 A.M. to 6:00 P.M. on Sundays. Very very inconvenient. Never realized how valuable water is. This place looked deserted all the time because of the sandiness every[one] stays inside and no one is outside—not even the children so it looks as if no one lives in the barracks.

In spite of all the difficulties, Louise's positive and patriotic spirit rings true in these final words of her letter: "If American soldiers can endure hardships so can we!"

Years later Louise's best friend, Margaret, wrote this about the early days at Poston:

My oldest brother made a bench and table from Manzanita wood. These and our six beds were all the furniture we had in that one little square home . . . There was a rod the width of the room where we hung our clothes. My mother made a "door" from curtains and for the two windows . . . which helped to add color to our home. We were not allowed to tack any pictures on the walls, therefore, many people scotched taped pictures they had saved from calendars or from the Sears, Roebuck and Montgomery Ward catalogues. What would we have done without the catalogues in those days?

Not everyone was so accepting of conditions in Poston. My friend Ellen Yukawa's mother, Phyllis, and father, Sam, were younger than most Issei parents. In fact, they were Nisei, born in the United States, and citizens. That made Ellen and her sister Sansei, third-generation Americans, and also citizens. Most of their parents' close friends were Caucasians. In 1939, Ellen's parents traveled cross-country by motorcycle from California to New York to attend the World's Fair. Like most Nisei, they considered themselves 100 percent Americans. They ate American food, had American names, and liked American music. Sam Yukawa was pretty bitter at first about losing his freedom. On the night they arrived at Poston, Ellen, who was just eight years old, still remembers:

The latrine was right in the middle of the block and they wanted to assign us to a room way over in the corner of the block. I'll never forget that—here we are trudging along and this guy had a clipboard and he said, "You're assigned here." My dad looked at him and said, "No I'm not! I have two small children. I'm going to stay in a barrack close to the latrine." So my dad just marched off and this guy followed him. "This is the one I'm staying in," he said.

It was just a square room—nothing in it and I'll never forget this either . . . they gave us long canvas bags and told us to go fill them up. There was a big stack of hay and we had to fill those bags. That was our mattress.

Ellen remembers the first meals they had at Poston more fondly than some of the older kids did. Her dad worked as a chef in the kitchen:

I remember the first week we got there—nothing but Vienna sausages [hot dogs] and beans. Mom never bought food like that—so we loved it! The army was sending all of this bread. Of course, Japanese people don't eat that much bread . . . they wanted rice. Dad said this was ridiculous . . . we've got to have rice! So pretty soon they quit sending so much bread . . . after that they got it right.

I remember the squid—it's just like chewing on a rubber band! I remember that and mutton. My dad would try to make a mutton stew or a curry.

There was no furniture in the barracks. So the Nikkei got busy building tables, dressers, closets, and chairs. Some of the pieces that were built have become treasured heirlooms. Joe Yamada remembers:

Tets was a craftsman! He made all their furniture and it was perfection—you know all the joints were perfect—no nails showing. It was beautifully made. He picked up the wood from scraps left from building the barracks. There were great big piles of scraps and guys used to go over there to find pieces of wood so they could make furniture.

My friend Ellen, who lived in Poston I, recalls those scrap piles differently. Her dad was not just a chef; he was a good carpenter, too:

He was scrounging around the huge pile of lumber scraps that they didn't use. While he was hauling lumber home a soldier says to him—"You can't do that!" And

Some people were lucky enough to get regulation army mattresses, but many had to use canvas ticks, which they filled with straw and had to change weekly. Scorpions and snakes often came out of hiding in the straw.

my dad says, "Watch me! What are you going to do? Put me in jail?" Soon he was building furniture for his friends, too.

I also remember Mom bringing the hose inside and wetting down the floor. We would get under the bed and just lie there—because it was so hot! And I think about my dad—he cooked in the mess hall, in that heat! It was 120 degrees with no fans, no coolers. Eventually they gave us a linoleum to put down on the floor . . . because it was just a wood floor with knotholes and scorpions used to come up through the holes. So you wouldn't leave your shoes around. You'd turn them upside down so things like that wouldn't crawl into your shoes!

I remember taking a shower about five times a day—because it was so hot I'd get these terrible nose bleeds. So I'd get in a cold shower. But I remember my mom . . . would take a shower with her panties and bra on—you know you just walked into a room and there were showers on the wall—a wooden bench—no privacy!

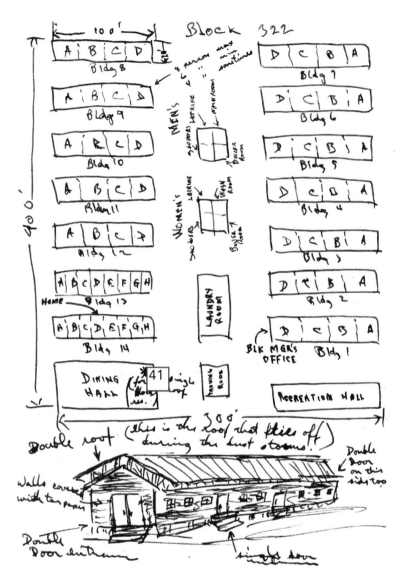

Tets sent this splendid drawing of a typical block in his first letter from Poston to Miss Breed—a fourteen-page tome full of the anger and sadness that he was struggling to overcome.

Often mothers, daughters, and sisters who were modest and did not want to disrobe in front of others would wait for the darkness of night to take a shower. Just as in Santa Anita, there was no privacy in the latrines, either. They were just wooden shelves with cutout holes along the wall. Using three sides of a large cardboard box or holding coats for one another, the women found inventive ways to create a little privacy. In time, partitions were built. In fact, Ellen said that her dad was disgusted with the primitive conditions: "My dad walked into that latrine and said . . . 'We're not standing for this!' So he went down to steal some more lumber and made stalls with doors and everything. I don't know where he got the hinges, but he did!"

It took Tets a few days to write his first letter from Poston. It was hard for Miss Breed to believe that they had now moved to a place that made Santa Anita seem like paradise. Unlike some of the younger correspondents, Tets was blunt about the conditions:

September 7, 1942
Dear Miss Breed,

This is ole prodigal writing to you amid the heat and dust of this h— hole called 'The Colorado River War Relocation Project—Poston Arizona.' . . . at 2:00 Mountain Time we arrived in Parker, Arizona What a jerkwater town, nothing but shanties . . .

The natives . . . told us that we were lucky to have come on a cool day . . . only 104 degrees and not dusty at all!!!! 'Wait 'til it really gets hot and dusty' . . . how true those words—how true!!!!!! After 'signing away my life, liberty, the pursuit *of happiness' (the WRA enlistment documents) we were assigned our quarters in a 12' x 20' room. Then we went to the mess hall for our first supper in Poston. Rice, wieners, pickled cabbage, <u>Bread and Water</u>. Had to eat with a steak knife!!! Dining room seats 300 persons. . . .*

I don't think I mentioned it but my sister and I are living together. After shower flopped on cot and fell dead asleep . . .

Have been keeping busy helping everyone so I won't have time to get heartaches thinking of SANTA ANITA and the friends left behind. Somehow it works most of the time. . . . The evenings are wonderful cool and refreshing. The sky so black that the stars fairly pop out. The Milky Way is really clear. The sunrise here is gorgeous. The purple mountains are all around us but aside from that the view is very drab, unless I look through my green sunglasses. . . . I don't even see cactus growing around here. We have plenty of scorpions, crickets and huge red ants. <u>Lots of dust, too!!</u> We're about 3 mi. from the Colorado River so the thing to do around here just now is to go there to fish and swim. I'm going there as soon as possible.

On Sept. 5 the eve of my birthday I went out for a walk at night by myself/ I sure felt blue. Things around here just 'got me down.' Felt so small and bewildered. Saw a moth fluttering futilely against a street lamp. That's the way I felt. Like butting my head against a brick wall. My whole being rebels against some things— the WRA set up, sloppy, no foresight, red tape, grafting, the weak-kneed bunch of bootlicking Jap farmers in charge under the Caucasian administration at Camp #1 and #2 and #3. They're afraid to stand up for certain things. That's why this Poston is a He——— of a place to live in. We're so d——— far away from the public who are interested that the WRA can get away with it. At an assembly Center on the coast complaints can be seen by a visitor but what fool would venture out to this forsaken land just to see if the Japs are being looked after? Perhaps I'm spoiled by having been in SAAC. But is that a crime?

So ran my thoughts until I just ran out. Then I figures well I'm here so I gotta make the best of it. As I wrote . . . someday sometime I'm going to find my friends by the grace of God. And I'm going to make friends here, too. And SOOOO to the Future may it be what it shall be?????

I hope you have been able to read all this and please don't think that the heat has got me because I have rambled so.

Sincerely yours,

Tetsuzo

This is just a portion of a fourteen-page handwritten letter that included the "inside dope" about the Santa Anita strike and sad regrets about newfound friends left behind at Santa Anita. Although Tetsuzo is sadder than ever, he ends with an upbeat hope for the future.

Their physical discomforts that summer were shocking, but for many their pain was not only from the heat, bugs, and dust storms. The underlying heartbreak was the loss of their freedom.

Since the Nikkei were not allowed to bring cameras, the most memorable images of camp were captured by artists. Miné Okubo had lived in Berkeley at International House before the war. Her drawings of camp life appeared first in a magazine and later in her book, *Citizen 13660*, which was published in 1946. This is part of a letter she wrote to Clara's sister, Eleanor Breed:

> On May 1st, 1942, I was reduced to a number and placed in a horse stall. . . . I arrived here under armed guards. . . . (I have friends who say, 'Why, you are getting free board, free food, free clothing, etc. You have no worries.' Having not been in our shoes how are they to judge our inner feelings?) It isn't so much the material or physical aspects that matter. It is something far deeper. It is the effect on our spirit. It isn't the question of whether we get hot or cold water; beans or stew; feather or straw mattresses, it is the idea of being put away into camps, completely divorced from the National Defense effort. This is what hurts. An act like this only brings greater hatred and greed.

For the second time in less than six months, they had been forced to pack and move to a desolate part of the world that few would ever choose to live in on purpose. How long would they be forced to live in this world apart?

CHAPTER SEVEN

"REAL AMERICAN CHILDREN"

BY LATE SUMMER, even those who didn't especially love school were ready to get back to class. They had been out of regular school since April, when they left San Diego. Classes were scheduled to start the first week of October. Miles Carey, the newly appointed superintendent of Poston's schools, knew it was going to be a close call.

Dr. Carey spent the summer trying to hire the 101 teachers needed for fall. But his job offers backfired, stirring up yet another wave of anti-Japanese sentiments. He traveled to many western states, contacting teachers who might be willing to move to the Arizona desert. But he could not offer them the kind of salary they were being paid in large city public schools. Then he scouted for teachers in smaller school districts. When they said yes, the hate mail began!

One school superintendent complained to his senator, Champ Clark of Missouri, that teachers were being robbed from the "real American children":

I have just learned . . . that two public school teachers have recently been elected to teach in Japanese Concentration camps at much high[er] salaries than they are now receiving. I judge from this that it is the policy . . . of our government which looks after the concentration camps, to provide teachers for most if not all the Jap Camps. If this is true, I want to voice my opposition to the policy and to urge you . . . to prevent further inroads on our diminishing teaching staffs.

In effect it means the education of Japs at the expense of our own American born children . . . some children in some schools are going to be without a teacher, while the Japs in the concentration camp will secure instruction.

Carey contacted seven hundred teachers. Only 72 of the 101 he hired showed up, and 2 of them left when they saw the camp. By December a dozen more resigned. Just 55 of the original group stayed through the first year. Most stayed less than five months. Considering the conditions they found, it's a wonder any stayed!

In the government's great haste to build the camps and remove the Nikkei from their homes, they had totally overlooked the need to build schools or order basic supplies. That first fall, temporary classrooms were set up in barracks that were divided into several classes with partitions that did not go up to the ceiling. As in the barracks they lived in, students could hear everything that was happening in the classrooms next -door. Even worse, they lacked basic equipment such as desks, chairs, books, chalkboards, and maps.

After so many months of "vacation" from school, some students were excited about getting back to their studies. Margaret wrote to Miss Breed in late September that she and Louise were working as waitresses, but they would soon have to quit when school opened for their senior year: "It is really going to be a joy getting back to school with Caucasian teachers. This is going to be a regular school . . . we are going to get credit for attending. I am privileged to have such an opportunity as I have only a year before I . . . graduate High School."

Soon after their arrival, Tets reports that he is not too impressed with the teachers:

October 3, 1942
Dear Miss Breed,
Now that the Caucasian schoolteachers are here in camp we see a few more Caucasian faces than before where two–four days even a whole week went by without sight of a Caucasian face. The first impression of them [the teachers] is rather disappointing. Oklahomans–Texans it seems as if the children will be all drawling "Suthun' Style." Several of the Nisei teachers seemed pretty well disgusted with a

This is one of the WRA photos in Clara's first article, "All But Blind," in Library Journal. *She told her editor that this was her favorite picture. It is not surprising that Clara would love a photo of children and books.*

*few of them. However the "proof of the pudding is in the eating" and school starts
Monday. I hope to meet some of them personally so that I can be more sure of what
to think of them.*

> *Sincerely yours,*
> *Tetsuzo*

This was the first year Fusa would not attend school. If not for the war, she surely
would have started college in San Diego. Instead she had an office job, not even the
library job she wanted but one that gave her a school connection:

October 9, 1942

*I am working in the Construction Office as a so called Secretary. Gee, I really don't
work hard at all . . . Our job here is to keep the time of the Carpenters and to make
requisitions. If anyone needs tables, chairs, or benches, we make out the requisitions
and send them to the Carpenter Shop. Right now the shop is busy making tables for
the schools. The greatest difficulty is getting the supplies. We really are short on
lumber and nails.*

*Last Monday school started. We watched all the students taking their own chairs
to school and regretted the fact that we had already gotten out of school. There are
about 20 Caucasian teachers in Camp 3. They certainly represent a variety of states.
There are some from Oklahoma, New York, Virginia, and California. Most of the
teachers are rather on the old side.*

*There is one male teacher who lives in a trailer. All the students who have him
tell me that he wears a wig. They claim that they can see the stitching on his wig. I
don't know how true that is, but it sounds just like a rumor we used to hear about a
teacher in junior high school.*

> *Sincerely,*
> *Fusa*

Clara noticed a disturbing word that seemed to be in every letter she opened—that
word is *Caucasian*. There was no difference between letters from younger and older
students—all of them referred to "Caucasian" teachers as being more desirable than
Nisei teachers, even though many Nisei teachers were better educated than the
imported teachers.

When school finally opened in October, fifth grader Katherine seemed overwhelmed with "hard work" and her teachers. Miss Breed must have been troubled by Katherine's spelling but even more concerned by the way Katherine referred to her teachers, one being "Japanese," the other being "American." Katherine didn't use the word *Caucasian*, but her meaning was the same. It was clear Katherine thought "American" teachers would be better!

Was this how Katherine thought of herself—as Japanese and not American?

Sunday
Dear Miss Breed,
School has started ever since last Monday, so that is where I spend most of my time. We had been haveing a Japenese teacher until Friday. On Friday the princible brought a american teacher. So starting from monday, we have a new teacher. I have to walk 3 blocks to school. We have scholl in a long barrack. it is cut into 3 sections. (we are in the middle.) When we have singing we go into the next room, which is the 4th gr. By the way, did I tell you I was in the 5th gr.? I had 2 slips. One said to go to the 6th gr. and the other one to go to the 5th gr. We sure do get hard work. Like Fri. we had to write our life history. We had to write the day we were born, the hospital What age we were when we moved from house to house, what age we were when we started school, what the name of the school was, a few other things, and last of all what we liked to do best. Our Japenese teacher wouldn't even let us study any words and she goes and gives us real hard words. Well I guess I'll learn some day. Thank you again.
Yours Truly,
Katherine Tasaki
P.S. For the first time since I came here my mother put on curlers. But I'm afraid it won't turn out good because my [hair] is too long. It doesn't pay to pay $3.00 and get a permanent.

Katherine, like students of all ages, seemed to have bought into the government's view of Nisei teachers as less than equal to their Caucasian colleagues. That attitude would certainly color the children's sense of themselves. The government delivered the message in many ways. Nisei teachers were paid a maximum of $19 a month or $228 annually while Caucasian high school teachers were paid $2,000 annually, $1,620 for elementary teachers with four-year degrees. Even those with only two years of teacher training were paid $1,260 annually.

Like their students, Nisei teachers lived in barracks without bathrooms or kitchens. They used public showers and toilets in the latrines and ate their meals in the camp mess hall. Many, though not all, Caucasian teachers lived on the other side of the camp, "across the road," in more comfortable barracks with furniture, bathrooms, and kitchens. Caucasian teachers were always the lead teachers, with the Nisei acting as assistants, even though many of the Nisei taught a full load and could communicate with the children and parents better.

A few top-notch teachers followed their students from California to Poston. Several were "conscientious objectors," young men who refused to fight on the battlefield but volunteered to serve in other ways. But most were older retired "schoolmarms" who had taught in traditional schools or Indian schools where students were expected to sit in straight rows and answer only when called on. These teachers were trained in two-year "normal schools" rather than teachers colleges. Very few young teachers trained in up-to-date methods were hired that first year. Nevertheless, Ben Segawa, who claimed, "I only went to school to eat my lunch," still admired the many "Caucasian" teachers who were willing to come and live in the desert and face the ridicule many must have experienced.

Miss Breed worried about what kind of future the children would have if their schools and libraries did not improve. Fusa wrote that the library was nice on the outside but had little to offer on the inside. Clara was also bothered to discover that all the "core" subjects in school were taught by Caucasians even though their Nisei assistants were often better educated. Similarly, Caucasians were the head school librarians and were paid WRA wages. In contrast, college-educated Japanese Americans headed the public libraries in each camp and were paid next to nothing!

Clara sent more books to "her children" and directly to the Poston libraries. Fusa and others asked once again if they should return these books. But of course Clara did not want the books back. She hoped that they would be passed along from one eager reader to another inside the camp. That fall Clara started work on her article for the *Library Journal,* hoping to get more teachers and librarians sending books and involved in what was happening to the Nikkei community. Clara feared that the second-class status of the Nisei teachers and librarians might permanently affect the children, eating away their own self-esteem. Months later, in her article, Clara questioned the long-term effect of the government's racist evacuation policy: "This hardening of the children's and young people's consciousness of race seems a great pity. Is it an inevitable counterpart of the evacuation policy? Is it consistent with our war aims?"

The children's letters not only inspired Clara, but she included some of their letters in the article as evidence that they still "hold fast to their faith in America":

. . . I may have complained about my new environment but I know it will be diffi-cult to adapt myself to the new surroundings right away. I am sure everything will brighten up soon and in a few more weeks I will begin to love this place almost as much as my home in San Diego. When I stop to think how the pilgrims started their life, similar to ours, it makes me feel grand for it gives me the feeling of being a pure full-blooded American.
Most sincerely,
Louise Ogawa

Clara knew that her article "couldn't solve the problem—but only state it." In a letter she sent to Bertine Weston, the editor of the *Library Journal,* Clara writes that the problem of the Japanese children of the West Coast affects the whole country: "Many people do not realize that 1/4th of all evacuees are children under 15 years of age. It is these children and their future that I am most concerned with. Those hard-est hit by evacuation in its permanent effect on their idealism and morale are the children and the age group from 15–21."

More than twenty-five thousand Nisei children attended ill-equipped schools in all ten relocation centers. These were racially segregated schools under the control of the federal government, and for most students it was the first time they attended schools where nearly everyone was Japanese.

Older students were accustomed to Caucasian teachers, but attending a segre-gated school came as a shock. Aiko Kubo, a high school junior, recalled: "Most of my friends on the outside were Caucasian. Socially we got to meet more people—not just Japanese. As we got older, there would certainly not be dating between Caucasians and Japanese. . . ."

Indeed, in California interracial marriages were against the law, so interracial dat-ing was taboo. But suddenly a generation of teenagers was thrust into homogeneous classes where everyone was Nisei or Sansei.

Many of those I interviewed, who were not yet in high school, claimed to like their segregated schools. They often had been forced to take a backseat to their white Californian schoolmates. Now they had a chance to become leaders of their groups. Elizabeth Kikuchi, then a seventh grader, has happy memories of junior high:

Poston was rich with activities for children . . . there was the joy of being all Japanese! For the older kids there was bitterness and a struggle—for those who were already on their way to a higher education. Their lives were interrupted. But for the rest of us—the younger kids—there was comfort and security in being able to do anything we wanted to do—you couldn't do that on the outside because we were a minority.

In this world apart, young Japanese Americans played the lead in school plays and were elected officers of their classes and chosen as captains of their teams and editors of newspapers and yearbooks. Teachers stressed English and public speaking to develop their students' ability to speak and write well. Accustomed to being quiet in their former classrooms, the students learned to speak up and express themselves. Their teachers and administrators agreed that such skills were essential in the postwar world the students would live in one day.

As we talked about junior high, Joe Yamada told me about a prank his buddies pulled on old "Baldie," the nickname they gave that teacher with the wig. One night Joe and his buddies went into the shower area and saw that wig sitting on a bench. The water was running in the shower and they started joking about, "What could this hairy thing be?" They kept fooling around and finally one of them said, "Say, we ought to just toss this out!" "Sure, do it!" "Just flush it away!" they all agreed. One guy flushed the toilet and they all ran.

Of course, they didn't really do it. They just left the shower room and poor Baldie, who was no doubt relieved to find his hair right where he left it!

GONE BUT NOT FORGOTTEN

The students often sent Clara clippings from the *Poston Chronicle*, the camp newspaper. If she saw this one, it had to give her hope. She was not the only one who was sending her gift of friendship and caring.

A Medal for Cheesy
Ichiro Yoshimi, 18, and Russell Cleary have known each other since third grade. They went to the same grammar school. In Jr. High they went to different schools, but they were reunited for high school. Both boys tried out for pole vaulting. Russell was always cheering his friend "Cheesy," as he called Ichiro, who surpassed the others by clearing 11' and won his All-star sweater.

That spring of '42 both boys were looking forward to the state-wide championship games when they would match poles with vaulters from other schools. But in May, Ichiro and his family were suddenly residents of Poston. Instead of gripping the slim, strong bamboo pole in his hands, instead of his slim body soaring through the air, Ichiro was holding a paintbrush, working in the sign department after school hours.

One day Ichiro came back to the barracks and found a letter waiting for him. As he tore the envelope open, a piece of metal attached to a yellow ribbon fell out. The inscription said "4th Place Winner in Pole-Vaulting."

Puzzled, Ichiro read the letter. "Dear Cheesy . . . I got fourth place in the meet with 10'6". I'm sending you this medal because you deserve it. I know you could have done as good or better."

Today, Ichiro Yoshimi wears a bronze medal on his watch chain proudly.

As the summer of 1942 turned into fall, Clara felt increasingly lonely as she drove to work through the downtown area where the Nikkei were no more. She passed the hotel that had belonged to Fusa's family, the church where the Kikuchis had lived. All the shops were empty. Overnight that section of the city had been deserted. She knew this was true of all the Little Tokyos up and down the West Coast. Stray cats meandered down the streets with boarded-up windows. Some people had left signs in their windows, thanking old customers or merely saying good-bye.

PATRIOT HARVEST

That autumn when the crops were ready to be harvested in Utah, Nebraska, Idaho, and Colorado, farmers had a huge labor shortage. Young men who would have worked the fields had gone off to fight the war. Others left farming for higher-paying jobs in defense factories. Suddenly those behind barbed wire were asked to do their "patriotic" duty by volunteering to harvest the crops needed to feed both civilians and the troops.

Louise wrote in September: "You may have read about the boys leaving Poston to work in Idaho and Nebraska on the farm. About 45 San Diegans went. We expect them back in a couple of months. But while there, if they find a job they can call their family and stay there."

Harvesting the crops was a chance to get paid more than the usual WRA subsistence wages and an opportunity to get out of Poston, if only for a while. Their work was hard, and the living conditions were primitive. Being patriotic was not always appreciated, as Louise discovered when the boys returned:

November 30, 1942

Dear Miss Breed,

The boys who went out to work on the sugar beets in Colorado came home just in time to enjoy the Thanksgiving dinner with their families. . . . A friend who returned from Colorado related the following incident to me. He said, while in town a few boys entered a restrauant to have a bite to eat. The first thing the waitress asked was "Are you Japs?" When they replied "yes" she turned her back on them and said they don't serve Japs. So they had to go to another restrauant to eat. Here is another incident which disgusted the boys. When the boys asked a policeman where a certain store was he replied—"I don't serve Japs." One of the boys became angry and remarked—"Alright be that way—what do you think we came out here for? We didn't come to be made fun of—we came to help out in this labor shortage." Then the policeman apologized and showed them to the store.

This boy said he certainly was glad to return to camp where there is no unfriendliness. Of course, he knows and we all know that there are people all over the world who hate certain races and they just can't help it. But I am sure when this war is over there will be no ratical discrimination and we won't have to doubt for a minute the great principles of democracy.

Louise Ogawa

Babe told me his older brothers went out and never had any complaints. Maybe they were lucky or they didn't want their parents to worry. Many firsthand accounts by young farm workers who went out are brutal. They endured substandard housing and oppressive work hours. Many young teenagers went looking for adventure and found more hatred:

. . . We heard that workers were needed to harvest sugar beets in Idaho. Being 14, I felt this was my chance to leave the camp and seek the freedom I always thought about. I was the youngest of eight teen-agers who decided to go to Caldwell, Idaho. . . . The farmers would come with their trucks and pick out the number of

With so many young men now in the military, farmers needed workers. Newspaper ads encouraged Nikkei workers to earn extra money or simply get out of camp for a while. It was hard, backbreaking labor where conditions were often even worse than inside the camps.

workers they needed. I was shocked to see the signs around town that said, "No Japs Allow(ed)"

On the way, to the farms, we were harassed and cursed. Here we were, helping out the war effort, harvesting sugar beets, being paid a minimal wage and being treated in this manner. The bitterness and frustration from that experience are still with me. . . . The most painful experience that happened . . . was one evening twelve local punks made six [Japanese American] teens crawl about 250 feet on their hands and knees through the center of the city park . . . they returned to the barn horrified and crying.

—Testimony of **GEORGE TAKETA**, Chicago, September 22, 1981

Outside of the sleepy town of Parker, the cotton crop was ready for picking. But here, too, there were not enough hands to do the job and the army urgently needed the cotton as a war material. Soon residents of Poston went to work picking the crop. The money earned they planned to use to buy chicks, pigs, cows, bees, and other animals that they could use and sell.

It wasn't just the adults who worked the cotton fields. Volunteer groups of Boy Scouts and students from Poston did their part, too. Yuki Kusamoto, a ninth grader, wrote: "My greatest experience since coming to Poston was to go cotton picking!" Yuki picked about thirty-nine pounds of cotton. Her ninth-grade class earned $119.03 for the class treasury! Apparently, the seniors didn't do as well, from the sound of Louise's letter:

November 11, 1942

Dear Miss Breed,

Saturday, Nov. 7th I experienced something which I shall never forget. I went cotton picking with my fellow school-mates to raise funds so the school will be able to have a school paper. We left home at 8:30 A.M. on a cattle truck. We were going bumpity bump down the narrow dirt road when all of a sudden we came to a halt. We quickly jumped to our feet and saw a little house with a military police sitting in it. Then we were counted like cattles and again were on our way. We went winding through the Mosquite trees until finally we were surrounded by cotton plants. Everyone cried out, "Well, here we are—let's get busy!" After piling out of the truck like ants, we were given a large sack in which to put the cotton. This sack was very very long. It weighed 2 lbs and often got in our way. We flung the bag over our left shoulder and began picking the cotton. I often crawled on the ground to pick the fallen cotton. It certainly was a good thing that I wore slacks and a long sleeve blouse because, you get scratched all over. . . .

We stopped work about 4:30 P.M. and were taken to the trading post which is about 8 miles on this side of Parker. The trading post was one of thise country stores where they sold from shoes to food. There were many Indians there. That is where they do their shopping.

It was like being in the middle of a desert. When we arrived at the trading post, we ran in the store expecting to buy a soda. But to our disappointment no cold drinks were sold. Even though I had no water and came home exhausted I enjoyed every minute of it. It certainly felt good to get home!!

My! I am practically writing a book and I do want to hear about you. I imagine the library work keeps you busy as usual. I heard San Diego is a boom town too over-crowded for words. I probably won't recognize S.D. now.

Do write during your leisure hours for I just love to hear from you. Hoping to hear from you soon.

Louise Ogawa

P.S. I enclosed a piece of cotton I picked. It has the seed in it. I wanted to send you a few branches but I was told it would not last so I changed my mind.

For eleventh grader Aiko Kubo, going cotton picking was memorable in another way. It was the first and only time she got to leave Poston. "It was fun to get away from camp," she told me. "The sense of freedom was invigorating. But I wondered what life in the cities 'outside' would be as the war continued."

"A JAP WOULDN'T HAVE A CHINAMAN'S CHANCE"

The new school year also brought unexpected excitement of a different kind. In mid-November there was a serious strike at Poston I. No one I interviewed had memories of the strike, because Camp III stayed out of it. However, Tets and Fusa did write to Miss Breed about the excitement, and from Fusa's letter it sounds like another case of "you can't always believe what you hear or read":

November 23, 1942

Dear Miss Breed,

I guess you have been hearing over the radio about the riot in Camp 1. The version I heard over the radio was quite unlike anything that I have heard in camp. The radio news stated that Mr. Wade Head, head of these camps stated that "pro-Axis elements, a small but well organized group, incited the people to go on strike" or something similar to that. Gee, I was amazed at this report as it was the first of this sort that I had heard. All I know is hearsay, but it comes from reliable sorces so I'll tell you our version.

The first outbreak occurred about two weeks ago on a Saturday night. A band of people were so sick and tired of "Stool-pigeons" going around and listening to private conversations and getting people into trouble that they went to the homes of the "Stools" and brutally attacked them. Then, two men were picked up on charges of "Attacking with Intent to Murder."

They were going to be taken to Phoenix by the FBI for a hearing. The people in Camp 1 heard this and balked. They did not want these men to be taken to Phoenix and tried for two reasons: first, they did not believe these men were guilty of the charges against them; second, if taken to Phoenix they probably would not get a fair trial. The people built large bon fires near the police station and parked all night to be on guard so that the men would not be taken out when everyone was asleep. To date one man has been "unconditionally released." The other has not been released yet. A proposition has been set up to the people in which this man may be given a trial here, but the people still want him unconditionally released, too.

The terrible part of having a trial here is that anyone who goes up on the stand against this man is in for a tough time, and yet the people are unwilling to let this man go to Phoenix cause they think that the jury would be biased before the trial. That is all I know about it. So far the suspense is getting me. Some people wanted us to have a sympathy strike but most people see that it would only hinder us, so they have given it up. You know, the people who spy on their own people may profit momentarily, (is there such a word?) but in the long run they are asking for trouble. . . . Gee, but when situations like this arise we know that they asked for it, yet when crowds get violently mad it really is terrible. I hate to think about such terrible things going on in these camps but outbreaks like this are bound to happen. One thing which does not show but is an emense thing, is the fact that the people have given out some of their pent emotions and feel much more relieved after such outbreaks.

I really don't know what my philosophy is, but I'm trying awfully hard to keep it balanced in these times. Gee, one day I think one way, then the next some other way, but I try to keep my balance.

Yours very sincerely,
Fusa Tsumagari

A few days later Tets sent a letter explaining how things were settled:

December 1, 1942

You have probably read by now in the paper about the strike that was held in Camp I because two men were held on suspicion of beating up an informer. (Sounds like Santa Anita) One man was released but the other was held to face charges at a Phoenix Superior Court. Because a Jap wouldn't have a Chinaman's chance in an Arizona court, the people of Camp I did not want the prisoner to be taken out, therefore the strike.

After 5 days a compromise was reached and the man is to be tried here in Poston II with Jap judge & jury. Camps II & III did not get mixed up with the mess and we are glad of it. Most of the trouble was caused by misunderstanding between the people and the Chief of Police who is anti-Jap, a big blustery fellow who likes to push a small fellow around—a kind of guy who makes criminals so that he can pin something on them.

Wade Head, director of all Poston is a fine man. As yet I have not had the pleasure of meeting him. He was in Salt Lake when this mess occurred. When he came back his efforts resulted in the compromise.

As a young man with a great many opinions, Tets often shared his thoughts with members of the Department of Sociological Research who were attempting to record the effects of the evacuation. Even before the camps opened, sociologists considered them an ideal laboratory setting, where the researchers could study a group from one cultural background in a closed setting. Every now and then Tets had a "bull session" into the night with one of the fellows who worked in the department to discuss why people from different areas don't get along, juvenile delinquency, schools, gossips, human behavior in general, Nisei versus Issei, and so on. Tets had his own opinions about the effects of camp life.

Tets's letter to Miss Breed reflects another aspect of what I found in the letters, testimony, interviews, and essays—age made all the difference in the camp experience:

As a whole everyone is now more or less accustomed to camp life. Proving that the human being is capable of adapting himself to new environments. I think the biggest problem in camp is in keeping the male youth occupied. Those in their late teens and early 20's. This group I think was hit the hardest and this is the group giving the most trouble. Just out of high school or in the last year of high school after being taught democracy, learning how to have fun at dances, parties, their life ahead of them—then suddenly finding themselves behind barbed wire fences . . .

The little tots are having lots of fun. They get to play every day. But once in awhile . . . you hear "When are we going home to San Diego?" "Why do we have to stay here?" However they quickly forget and are off to play. Oh, to be young again to forget the cares of the world!!

I think the oldsters are the ones that in a way benefited by the evacuation. By oldsters I mean those from 50 on. With the exception of those who work, these people for the first time in their life . . . have had a vacation. They have time on their hands. They are having the time of their lives, going to the river to fish, going to the mountains to look for petrified wood, pretty looking stumps, rocks, etc., just sitting in the sun, puttering around the house. Looking after their grandsons and granddaughters. The men carve, play Japanese chess, or just sit around. Yessiree, life is good to them after years of hard work.

One thing I haven't seen as yet (I'm pretty sure there must be some) and that is the moaner. I'll admit lot of people cry about the good season they were anticipating but doggonnit they're doing something to keep occupied. I hope I never see one in this camp—a fellow who has the "what's the use?" attitude and just sits around and does nothing but moan.

"A WONDERFUL THANKSGIVING"

It's hard to imagine celebrating such an all-American holiday as Thanksgiving in a place like Poston. Yet letters to Miss Breed continued to reflect more hope than despair. Clara was haunted by something Louise had written a few weeks before . . . about her life being like the Pilgrims and how grand that is because it makes her feel like a full-blooded American. Louise wrote to Clara of having a "wonderful" Thanksgiving. Margaret also enjoyed her Thanksgiving and made sure that her little sister, Florence, sent special thanks to Miss Breed.

November 28, 1942
Dear Miss Breed,
I cannot express my gratefulness for sending me such excellent books of my favorite American. "The Little Giant" is a very well written book for reading and also history use. "Abe Lincoln's Other Mother" certainly must have been a great insperation to him.

Did you have a nice Thanksgiving? I had a wonderful Thanksgiving. Our dining room was beautiful decorated with flowers made by the mothers of my block. I received light and dark meat of turkey with fruit cake and jello for dessert. After such a delicious dinner I went to an enjoyable party.

Little Thomas is no longer little. He certainly is putting on weight rapidly, tipping the scale at 28 pounds. On the 27th he was exactly 10 months. In two more months he will be a year old; I can hardly wait for that day. Incidentally two more teeth have added making it eight.

I asked Florence to write you a letter. She was in a rush to go to a party so it is not as neat as it should be; but I think she is improving.

Sincerely,

Margaret Ishino

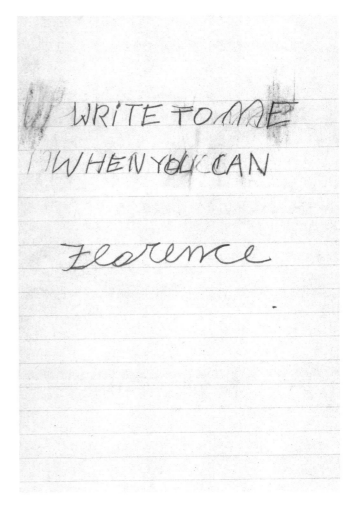

DEAR MISS BREED
HOW ARE YOU?
I HAD A NICE
THANKSGIVING WITH
TURKEY. I WAS 7 YEARS
OLD JUST BEFORE
THANKSGIVING
THOMAS IS A BIG
BABY NOW. I CAN
CARRY HIM. PLEASE
WRITE TO ME
WHEN YOU CAN

Florence

STORMY WEATHER

Just before the Nikkei left Santa Anita, the government gave everyone a clothing allowance to order clothes from the Sears catalog. The rumor mill predicted that they soon would be moving to "snow country." So, ironically, many ordered coats and winter clothing that arrived in Poston while the days were still torrid.

But the heat and their clothes were not the only things they needed to adjust to. The same week that school opened, so did the skies! Nine-year-old Jack Watanabe writes: "We're right in the midst of a thunderstorm . . . rain is coming down in sheets. Lightening is awful. This is the worse storm I've ever been in."

Many wrote to Miss Breed about this and other storms that came all too frequently. Fusa described the same storm this way:

About two nights ago we had an electrical storm. This was our first experience in a storm here. All day clouds formed in the sky. About dusk the clouds were really grey making the place seem dark. Then the winds began to blow. The dust just whirled and began to dance around like a "jitterbug." The wind started to howl almost as loud as the coyotes at night. Then, lightening, then of course, thunder. Then, rain! We were all inside the house, but we were well aware that our top roofs were threatening to blow off. Our stove pipe hole, (which has yet to be filled with a pipe) began to let in the torrent of rain and dirt. We had to move our belonging from there. After that, we were all comfortable and tried to forget the rain. That was rather exciting and quite a change from the usual sun shine and dust flying all over.

Little did they know what winter in the desert would bring. . . .

CHAPTER EIGHT

BITTER WINTER

COLD ACHING WIND THAT CUTS into the pale skin; pure, clean, freezing air that sinks in through the coat, gray lifeless sky that bares a reckless look. This is winter in Poston, Arizona. —**AYOKO SHINTAKU**, ninth grade

After the cruel heat of summer, the bitter cold of winter began early. Keeping the poorly constructed barracks warm was next to impossible. Now cold air seeped in through the cracks and crevices where scorpions and crickets had come in summer. During the afternoons the desert sun pushed the temperatures up to the eighties, but the mercury plunged to the thirties during the nights and early-morning hours. In summer you were baked and fried, and in winter you simply froze. As Katherine put it: "If you ask me which one I'd rather have, I don't want neither."

With a long and newsy letter, Tets got a head start on Christmas by sending some handmade gifts to Clara. Tets was especially angry that a barbed-wire fence was going up. Running away from this desolate place was impossible. So what was the point of building a fence? There's no missing the bitterness that simmers in this letter:

November 16, 1942

Dear Miss Breed,

Guess who? Yup it's ole unreliable again, none other than yours truly, Tetsuzo. Gosh the wind's been blowing all night and all morning. Kinda threatening to blow the roofs down. Dust is all over the place. Gives everything a coating of fine dust.

Heard from dad about a week ago. It seems that there is a possibility that many of the internees are to be released sometime close to Christmas (that's what the rumors have it) Almost everyone who has someone in an internment camp believe that his someone is the one coming home. At any rate the Alien Enemy Control at Washington is considering to allow the families to join the husbands in the internment camp. Many of us have written Edward J. Ennis, Director of the Alien Enemy Control unit asking that it be the other way around.—Yes Fusa's dad is still interned.

I am still working in the mess hall. Brrr to have to get up early in the morning. It is around 38 in the morning and at the middle part of the afternoon it is around 80+. The mornings don't warm up until just about noontime. My arm is all right. Not near so strong as at Santa Anita because I don't do any loading or unloading of supplies. Have been doing a little carpentry as many of us here have no furniture other than cots. Haven't got much made here in my own apt. as most of my work is over where the menfolk have left for the sugar beet fields or where there just ain't no menfolk.

The food has been all right except for quantity. We still have trouble with the warehouse transportation system. Also transportation on the outside to bring food all the way from the Coast here to Poston is limited.

No I haven't hiked to the river yet. I'd better do it soon cause there is going to be a fence around this camp!!!!!! 5 strands of barbed wire!!!!!!!!!! They say it's to keep the people out—ha ha ha what people the redskins?? It's also to keep out cattle. Where in the cattle countries do they use 5 strands of barbed wire??

If they don't watch out there's going to be trouble. What do they think we are, fools?? At Santa Anita at the time of the riot the armored cars parked outside of the main gates, pointed the heavy machine guns inside and then the army had the gall to tell us that the purpose of that was to keep the white folks from coming in to mob the Japs. Same thing with the guards on the watch towers. They had their machine guns pointed at us to protect us from the outsiders, hah, hah, hah, I'm laughing yet.

Enough of this before I go out and murder a white man by killing myself. hah, hah. —Say what is this, just as I wrote that three bombers came roaring overhead flying so low that the barracks shook. Every now and then the Chinese Air Force who are training some where close to Poston, come zooming down at us here in camp. They must think it's funny.

Some day one of us is going to have a gun— A couple of weeks ago one of the bombers (twin motored Douglas attack bomber) crashed on the other side of the Colorado and burst into flame. It wasn't right but a lot of us were kinda glad, in a cynical sort of way. God forgive us for the thoughts that are beginning to run amok in our brains.

Last week a very good friend of mine got to thinking—and he went crazy. He tried to commit suicide by slashing his wrists. His roommates found him bleeding and immediately gave him first aid. He is still alive, but his face is like that of a wild ape caged for the first time in his life. Gosh I get the chills every time I remember how he looked that morning. I think he was sent to an insane asylum in Los Angeles.

Gee, what a morbid letter this turned out to be!

In all of the published photos of Tets, he is wearing a hat. They were taken by Clara at the train station. I wrote and asked Tets if he had a hatless photo, and he sent this, along with a letter telling about his affection for Miss Breed.

I am sending you a few things in appreciation for what you have done for me as well as for my sister and all the rest. The lapel pins are for you, your sister, and Miss McNary. If I remembered correctly Miss McNary's first name is Helen. If I am wrong you may do what you wish with the pin, but please tell me her name. Also what is your mother's name? There are three dogs made by Mrs. Umezawa from pipe cleaners. A longer ribbon may be used so that the dog may be pinned to the lapel or blouse. The corsages are for you and your mother. They were made by Mrs. Ohye (Mrs. Umezawa's daughter) The small roses were made by Mrs. Hirai and Mrs. Kushino and also Jane Kushino (Mrs. Kushino's 14 yr. old daughter) The chrysanthemum was made by Mrs. Nakamura a very good friend of mine. For that matter they are all good friends of mine. The 'mum was made from lemon wrappers and crepe paper. A word about Mrs. Nakamura. A former dressmaker with plenty of time on her hands. Took up knitting also learning English and now making flowers. So busy now she has almost no spare time. If it is possible could you send some simple child primers and a grammar book about 7th grade.

Your name plate I made from mesquite as are also the lapel pins. However the dark pin is made from a pine knot from Santa Anita. The rest are all Poston Products. The evacuation order came just as I was about to send it so it slipped my mind and I thought I had lost it. After all it was the only souvenir from Santa Anita.

Aren't we Japs clever? We are learning to make beautiful things out of ugly scrap, because we are having a hard time to get material like pipe cleaners for dogs, crepe paper for flowers, also soft wire for flowers We get ugly dead mesquite branches and twigs and turn them into a thing of beauty by attaching paper orange blossoms or cherry blossoms made from Kleenex . . . I wish you had been able to attend our handicraft fairs here in Poston . . . Words just can't describe the beautiful carvings, paintings, knitting crochet work, dress making etc If I only had a camera you would have at least a rough idea as to what had been made.

Very truly yours,

Tetsuzo

P.S. Have a nice Thanksgiving dinner. TH

P.S. Do you think you could send me some Welch's peanut brittle? TH

Tets carved this nameplate for Clara from a piece of mesquite. He had no real tools, so he turned a bedspring into a chisel for carving. Clara kept this on her desk until she retired.

Clara was touched by the charming homemade gifts, not just from her children but also from adults who wanted to say thanks for the art supplies she had sent. With so many long hours to fill, crafts became a popular way to pass the time while creating something of beauty. Canes, lamps, and lovely bird pins were carved into useful and beautiful objects. Fusa wrote that she tried making paper flowers but preferred building model airplanes—except for the smell of the glue!

The nameplate Tets made for Clara became a permanent fixture on her desk at the library—long after the war was over, it remained one of Clara's treasures. Although he had no proper tools, he managed to carve the wood with a wire from a bedspring that he turned into a chisel.

Clara hoped that Tets's dad would finally be allowed to move to Poston. Maybe that would give Tets a lift. Was it only a year ago when Tets and his family had shared Thanksgiving in her cozy house on Trias Street? What a sad year this had been!

RED CROSS BOOKS

During that first school year without books or supplies, Poston's Red Cross director, Paul Takeda, and an English teacher, Ray Franshi, came up with the idea to have high school students create books about their lives in Poston, with art and essays. They planned to send these to schools all over the country and hoped that students "outside" would write back. The hope was this exchange would help students know one another—even from a distance.

Although I never found any essays written by Miss Breed's friends, all of the essays and poems are by classmates of the students who wrote to Miss Breed. Since they are "schoolwork," they are more formal than the letters to Miss Breed. But like the letters, they record life as the students saw it through every season, capturing their feelings of loss mixed with hope for the future. Here is an excerpt from a Poston High School junior:

Winter Morning

How everyone dreads to get up, for their beds feel snug and warm. You touch your nose and find it's almost frozen. The sound of the kitchen bell rings, "clang, clang, clang." You just can't miss breakfast, so up you get and rustle about to find the light switch. Your body is shaking just like a skeleton when you are putting on your clothes. Your toes and fingers are practically falling off because of the cold. You hasten to the wash room, and when coming back notice that all the chimneys are smoking their morning pipes. After finishing breakfast you rush near the stove and just about sit on it . . . the stove is not warm enough . . . you dash outside to one of the bonfires. The people of the block are already huddling about the fire, but squeezing yourself through quietly and listen to the older folks talk about war . . . clothing, not to mention pure gossiping, 8:30, it's time for school. How you hate to leave the warmth of the fire and also the fascinating stories the folks are talking about. School is school, and you must go. —**DOROTHY OBATA**

Every child brought something for the Red Cross Drive that fall—even if it was only a penny. Parties with games and dancing were held to raise money for the Red Cross. Teachers gave first-aid programs, and students packed Red Cross first-aid kits. They were also encouraged to write letters to prisoners of war. Through the Red Cross, families could also write to relatives who were in Japan. Letters were limited to twenty-five words and took as long as five months to reach Japan. There was no other way to reach relatives in an enemy country across the Pacific.

FIRST CHRISTMAS IN POSTON

"Christmas won't be Christmas without any presents" the Japanese American Citizens League wrote in an appeal to church groups all over the country. Clara was delighted to read about the success of the toy drive in the American Friends Service Committee's newsletter. Apparently there were lots of people who were as determined as Clara that the children inside the camps would not be forgotten. Sewing groups made bunnies and soft dolls. Others made wooden animals, trains, and trucks. The Friends collected more than eleven thousand gifts in Philadelphia, New York, Chicago, San Francisco, Seattle, and other cities. One very dedicated builder turned out fifty toy trucks. Somehow that story turned into a rumor that the Friends were sending fifty trucks full of toys to the centers.

Knowing this would be a lonely time for her young friends, Clara took special care to send their gifts early. Although she was not a wealthy woman, Clara must have scrimped on many things in order to make the holiday brighter for her children. Fusa was thrilled with a maroon suede jacket and matching belt, cologne, candy, nuts, and even a powder puff—all from Miss Breed! (A suede jacket would have been expensive, but since Clara and Fusa were about the same size, it may be that Clara sent clothes of her own for her young friend.) There were thank-you letters from Tets, Jack,

This is just one of the many cards that came from Poston to Clara, along with paper flowers, carvings, and numerous other items. They were all small tokens of appreciation for Clara's kindness.

Katherine, Louise, and Margaret, who confessed that she and Florence had been "bad girls" and opened their packages early. Nor was the gift giving one-way. Everyone sent Clara small gifts of paper flowers, getas—wooden sandals that they wore in the showers—and carved pins that they had made. These small gifts were sent with thanks for all the things Clara had done for them.

Inside of Poston III a hugely successful Christmas bazaar was held before the holiday to raise money for gifts for every child in all three camps of Poston. Every camp had "block" parties with Santa handing out the gift-wrapped presents to every child under the age of fifteen. Each package was marked with the gender and age of the child who would be likely to enjoy each toy.

But on Christmas Day there was one person who was especially unhappy:

December 25, 1942

Dear Miss Breed,

Some of my girl friends like Louise, Margaret, etc. were talking about receiving presents from you too. They seemed very happy too. Louise was saying she has received quite a few books and she said she would lend me a book since I do not have any. I wonder if it would be too much to ask if I were to ask you to send me any old discarded book you might have at the library. I would appreciate it very much if you would do this for me and I would be grateful to you. The reason I ask this is because my Christmas this year was really awful. I didn't receive a single thing and I thought if you could send me an old discarded book of any kind I would have something to show as being a present from someone. I don't want to put you to any trouble and I do want you to know I appreciate all you have done for the many Japanese children. Thanking you again and hoping to hear from you soon.

> *Sincerely yours,*
> *Hisako Watanabe (Jack's sister)*

Hisako also sent a special New Year's card to Clara:

HAPPY NEW YEAR
Ringing in with best of wishes,
Chiming in with greetings gay,
So you'll know you're not forgotten
On this happy New Year's Day!
> *Yours sincerely,*
> *Hisako Watanabe*
> *I hope you still remember me.*

Soon after Christmas, about the same time as Hisako's unhappy letter reached Clara, the rumor about fifty trucks full of toys having been sent to the Nikkei children backfired in a barrage of hate mail. Day after day the letters-to-the-editor column "Let the Public Speak" in one newspaper contained narrow-minded letters that Clara read with disgust.

Once again, acts of kindness became the object of scorn. Wasn't it enough that the Nikkei were locked away behind barbed wire? Would these hate mongers ever stop their vicious attacks on children whose only crime was having the "wrong" ancestors?

I found this sampling of letters to the editor among newspaper clippings Clara kept. It was amazing to see the many items about the Nikkei that she saved. I sometimes wondered if she was thinking of writing a book or more articles about this time in history.

Certainly the best present we give the Japs for Christmas would be a kick in the pants. Especially, if the obligation were to take place near a large body of water.
—MAE E. COLLINS

I could never look a serviceman in the face if I were to extend Christmas greetings to a Jap.
—A SAILOR'S MOTHER

It is about time that we who are true-blooded Americans, who love this wonderful country of ours and the liberty for which it stands, should let it be known that when this conflict is over that we can very well get along without the Japanese. If ever there was a nation who hates us it is the slimy Japs. . . . As to sending 40,000 Christmas presents to Japs, I feel anyone who has the desire should be living with the slimy devils. . . .
—A MOTHER

Now that you have distributed our Christmas trinkets amongst the Japs, you had better pray to god that some of those trinkets will not be fired at our boys in the forms of bullets. . . .
—MRS. P. E. BAGGE

A very few letters disagreed with the poisonous anti-Nikkei letters:

It seems to me that people who have written in this column consider all Japanese to be alike—the loyal American-born as well as the Jap soldier fighting against our boys, or the disloyal pro-Japanese in our camps. . . . This is ridiculous, as well as un-Christian, and defeats the very ideals we are fighting for. . . . I wonder how some of us can approach this season of the year without more charity in our hearts or does "good will toward men" mean only at certain times and toward certain people, with time out for war?
—MRS. R. C.

Christmas of 1942 was anything but happy. Artist Miné Okubo's drawing reflects how families tried to cheer the children, hanging their stockings near the chimney of a potbellied stove. However, there were no potbellied stoves in Poston. Babe Karasawa recalls, "We had oil-burning stoves, dark brown and rectangular-shaped. It was my responsibility to go to the big tank near the mess hall for the oil, and I recall carrying a bucket less than half full and then pouring it into the back side of the stove."

Letters like the last one were definitely in the minority. And the mean-spirited letters came as no surprise—even in this holiday season, when prayers for peace on earth and goodwill to men did not quite extend to all. In fact, attacks on the Nikkei did not stop after they were incarcerated. Having won their fight to get rid of the Nikkei, the Native Sons of the Golden West and other hate groups were empowered to seek a total victory against the "Yellow Peril." They brought a lawsuit to take away the citizenship of Nisei and to ship every single man, woman, and child of Japanese ancestry back to Japan on the earliest boat possible!

Clara found it hard to understand how people could call themselves Christians and act this way. Would 1943 be a better year or would the war be used as an excuse to push aside the Constitution and all it represented? Clara had grown up hearing stories about her own ancestors who had come to America seeking freedom to worship God in their own way. "Land of the Pilgrims' pride" were not just pretty words in a song to Clara. She had often been told that the real name of Bunker Hill, where the Revolution had begun, was *Breed's* Hill! She had heard the story of Samuel Dwight Breed, her great-grandfather (who like her father and grandfather was a minister), whose home was a station on the Underground Railroad during the Civil War. Those were her roots.

Clara and her family had no false sense of pride or patience for those old families who forgot what their ancestors had fought to build. A few years back, she had been ashamed of the Daughters of the American Revolution who refused to allow the world-famous African American singer Marian Anderson to perform in Constitution Hall because of her race. When Eleanor Roosevelt resigned from the DAR and arranged for Anderson to sing at the Lincoln Memorial, Clara was proud of the First Lady and her stand. America needed more people who did not think of the Constitution as simply a piece of paper that could be forgotten in time of war.

Christmas of 1942 was anything but happy. Thousands of families had already faced the loss of loved ones and uncertainty as to when and how the conflict would ever end. It seemed that no acts of kindness to the Nikkei were allowed to stand without an attack on them or those who wished them well. At the risk of being called a Jap lover, Clara continued to stand up for what she believed. She finished her *Library Journal* article with a simple but often overlooked idea: "Democracy must be defended at home as well as abroad."

Soon after Christmas, ten-year-old Katherine wrote that December 25 was so windy it "almost carried my mother away." Waiting two months for her pay must have been difficult for Mrs. Tasaki, especially during the holidays. She and Jerry Tasaki, Katherine's father, had separated five years earlier. He had moved to Los Angeles and was sent to Gila River, another relocation camp in Arizona. Eventually he went to Detroit, where he worked as a chauffeur. He seldom wrote, but that Christmas he sent Katherine a five-pound box of candy and Chinese checkers. Much as she enjoyed the Christmas party and gifts, the tone of Katherine's New Year's letter is anything but optimistic:

Dec. 31, 1942

Dear Miss Breed,

I can't begin to thank you for all the presents. Please excuse me for not writing sooner, but I just wasn't in the mood for writing. We had a very nice Chirstmas party on our block. A orchestra leader from camp 2 was our song leader. He sang very nicly. Everyone got a preasent. I got a paper doll set, notches, and a book. A girl gave me her paper doll set because she didn't want it.

In the morning it is very cold. I hate to get up to go to school. Sometimes I wish it was vacation, but still I wouldn't want to go to school in the summer because it is so hot. We have a stove in our school room, but it doesn't warm us up. Not even the girl that's sitting in front of it can feel it. We could have got a stove, but there isn't enough, so my mother said to give it to the people who really need it. We have a pail in our room, and we have some sand in it. we put hot charcol in the pail and we have a stove. We go to the "park" and burn wood, then we put it in water, and we have charcol.

My mother washed the kitchen towels for two months, so this month she got 32 dollars for the two months. We didn't get our pay for a long time so when we finally got it, we bought a lot of things now we have only ten dollars left from the pay. I wanted so bad to get yarn to make my doll a pullover sweater, but my mother wouldn't let me. When I go home I'm going to get a lot of yarn and make a lot of things.

We're working harder then ever now at school. We don't have any geography books so we have to make the map of the United States. And we have to know where every state is, and how to spell them.

Well this is the day before New Year, so I wish you a very happy one.
Yours Truly,
Katherine Tasaki

Miss Breed made a mental note to send yarn. But plainly the New Year was not off to a good start for her dear little Katherine. The weeks ahead would bring change—some for the better, some not. The year 1943 was to be marked with difficult choices, high hopes, and bitter disappointments. Their roller-coaster ride of ups and downs was far from over.

CHAPTER NINE

"POSTON SEEMS LIKE A HOME TO ME"

THE WINTER OF 1943 was not just cold but also rainy. Desert sand turns into inch-deep mud that sticks to your shoes, and giant lakes form that float on top of the mud. It was next to impossible to heat the drafty classrooms, so teachers taught with their coats on and often gave up the cold rooms in favor of holding classes standing up around a bonfire outside. Katherine writes that because of the cold, school doesn't start until noon. Poor Katherine has so many colds and misses so much school that her teacher complains she is spoiling her class's attendance records. Miss Breed is more concerned about Katherine's health than the teacher's attendance record.

Elizabeth remembers running from one bonfire to the next to get warm as she and her friends ran to their sixth-grade classes. As always, Louise sends an upbeat letter, happy that Clara liked the paper flowers she had sent and saying that she is beginning to feel at home in Poston even though life is anything but perfect. Once again, you can see Miss Breed's questions in Louise's answers:

January 6, 194[3]

Dear Miss Breed,

I was very glad to hear you liked the flowers. I wish I could have sent 10 dozen Am. beauty roses (red ones) to show my appreciation for everything you have done for me.

In my last letter I said the fence was torn down—well, it is up again. This time a few feet further out. We have been told that the reason for the fence building was so the cattle won't come near our homes. . . . But as yet, we have not seen any. Yes, I think the fence tends to weaken the morale of the people.

Now, I must answer your questions before I forget about them. Yes, many varieties of Xmas cards were made here in Poston. I do not know who the artist is that made the card I selected. I wish I knew. There is no art school here. Yes, there is a famous artist here in Poston . . . his name is Mr. Isamu Noguchi, a famous sculptor. He has gone to New York on a short "furlough."

As time marches on, more and more Poston seems like a home to me. . . . No longer is the thought of being in a camp afloat in my mind. But every time I see the fence, it seems like a dark cloud has lifted and a realization of camp life comes before my eyes. Often I use to think as I laid on my pillow, "What will happen to [m]e if I had to live in this camp for 5 year?" but now, I don't seem to think about camp. I guess I have adopted myself to this situation. But many a time I have wished with all my heart that I could go back to San Diego.

Yes, the food shortage has affected us. We have had no butter or egg for about two months. We have enough meat, though. Just tonite we had steak, mash potato, spinach and rice for supper. Oh yes, about the menu for a week. I am sorry I did not send it to you. To be honest—it slipped my mind. But this time I shall be sure to keep the menu for a week and send it to you . . . We are allowed 1 tablespoon of sugar to 1 cup of coffee. We eat rice only once a day now. We have fresh milk. It comes all the way from California. We have tea too but it is black.

That up-again-down-again fence was offensive to Postonians. After all, they were so far from anywhere, the desert seemed like fence enough! Besides, the camps were so large, it seemed a foolhardy waste to use that much wire when metal was in short supply. Eventually the fence ran around the entrances to the camps but not down to the river or up in the mountains.

Margaret's mother sent Clara a piece of silk for the holidays. But Clara thought it was too extravagant and wanted to return it. Margaret insisted that a few yards of silk was nothing compared to all Clara had done for them. Like her friend Louise, Margaret talked about food shortages that began in December. She asked Clara: "Do you have horse meat in butcher shops yet?"

During our interview Margaret laughed at the look on my face when I asked about horse meat. Then she said, "Yes, we had horse meat—have you ever had horse meat? It's not bad. It's a little like corned beef hash with gristle in it, but it's not bad. But I wouldn't want to have it all the time."

I will take Margaret's word for it. I wouldn't want to taste the pickled beef heart, which was also a regular item on camp menus! Tets wrote that with the New Year they might only have powdered milk. Fuel oil was scarce everywhere; so heaters for the laundry and showers were turned on for only four hours a day.

Clara lost no time in sending a package to Hisako, who sent thanks for more than the books:

January 7, 1943
Dear Miss Breed,

I was overjoyed to hear from you and that lovely book!! you sent me. Thank you very much. When I saw the books it left me speechless with gladness and I cannot find words to express my feeling. You helped to enlighten my holiday spirits. I thank you from the bottom of my heart for all you have done for us. I appreciate the well you feel toward us Japanese. It is in times like these that we need all the friends we can make and it is our duty to keep these friends. I hope I didn't put you to a lot of trouble but in a place like this we haven't anything and I didn't know of any other way to ask you. I am sorry if I caused you a lot of extra work or trouble.

I certainly hope this war is going to be over soon, so that we can all go back into our old mode of living. When we come back to San Diego we shall be sure to look you up because you are one person no one could forget. You have a heart of gold and you believe in making other people happy.

Please write me soon because I shall always be waiting to hear from you.
Sincerely,
Hisako Watanabe

In late January, every day seemed to bring big news. In the bad news department, there was a fire at the Buddhist temple in San Diego where many families had stored their belongings. Such fires, set by vandals, happened in storage places up and down the West Coast. The damage was devastating to people who had already lost so much. Louise asked Miss Breed for the details:

Was it a very big fire? Do you know how bad the damages were? We have been quite worried because all our belongings which we left behind, we left or stored it at the Buddhist Church. I certainly hope the damages were not too severe.

We stored there such things as the World Book Encyclopedia, trunks, little of our furniture, other books, my Japanese kimono. . . . Father is quite worried.

In the good news department, a tofu factory had been built. Louise writes: "Tofu is loved by all our parents. It is made from soya beans."

But the biggest news of all was the dedication of a new school:

January 19th I attended the memorable "ground breaking" ceremony. . . . Mr. Potts, principal of Poston III High School drove the steak into the ground where the new school is going to be built. The first school flag was raised by the Senior Class president, Tots Ishida. The school is going to be built out of adobe bricks. The bricks are being made here.

In the same letter, Louise sent menus of typical meals served in Poston III:

I am enclosing the menus you asked for.

. . . for breakfast we have pancakes and biscuits quite often this has been because of the shortage of bread. If bread is served in the morning it will not be available for noon. Rice is served just at nite.

JANUARY 25, 1943:

breakfast: 2 toast, cocoa, fried potato

lunch: corn beef and cabbage, bread, 2 Japanese biscuits

supper: rice, 2 cubes of tofu (1st one since evacuation), cabbage napa,
   meat and unions cooked together shoyu

JANUARY 26, 1943:

breakfast: 2 pancakes, syrup, 1 cube of butter, fried potato, 1 wienie, cocoa

lunch: bread, jam, 1 ham, spinach, fruit salad

supper: rice, steak (not horse meat—cow meat) peas + carrots cooked,
   5 half sliced can apricots.

Clara's curiosity about their food was probably sparked by a new anti-Nikkei campaign in newspapers that reported that Nikkei got better food than American GIs. In truth, the government spent about forty-five cents a day on each Nikkei's food while the army ration cost between fifty and sixty cents. There were two meatless days a week, and a big part of their diet was starches. "You can see by this that we have quite a bit of potato," Louise writes. "I imagine that's what makes me gain."

Newspapers also failed to report that nearly a third of the food was actually grown in the camp itself, so the actual cost per person was more like thirty-one cents! But lies about the War Relocation Authority's soft treatment of the Nikkei were just beginning.

"AMERICANISM IS A MATTER OF MIND AND HEART"

For Tets and other young adults, the biggest news came at the start of 1943 when the War Department announced a registration program for both the army and leave clearance. When war in the Pacific began in 1941 there were about five thousand Nisei soldiers from Hawaii and the mainland in the army. After Pearl Harbor and all during the winter and spring of 1942, few Nisei were inducted. Those who tried to volunteer were often mistreated:

> Some of my classmates volunteered for the Army air force and some for the Navy air force. So I decided to volunteer also. I went to the army recruiting office in the post office building in San Jose. The recruiting sergeant, with a big cigar in his mouth, was standing in the hallway talking to the cigarette man. I asked him where was the recruiting office. And he answered sarcastically, "Are you a Jap?" And I said yes. Then he said, "We don't want any Japs in our Army; you guys are no damned good, so get out of here."
>
> —Testimony of **YASUKO MORIMOTO**, San Francisco, August 13, 1981

By March of 1942, the army had stopped taking any Japanese Americans. That September after they had settled in at Poston, the Selective Service classified all draft-age Nisei as 4-C: "enemy aliens." Of course, they were neither enemies nor aliens.

But even as this was happening, there were those who believed the Nisei could and should serve their country. Assistant Secretary of War John J. McCoy, who was responsible for Japanese American issues, reported to his boss, Henry L. Stimson, secretary of war, that he did not believe the Nisei could be held indefinitely on the basis of their racial origins. He thought they should be released as soon as possible.

In October of 1942, Elmer Davis, director of the Office of War Information, wrote a memo to President Roosevelt saying: "Loyal American citizens of Japanese descent should be permitted, after individual test, to enlist in the Army and Navy. It would hardly be fair to evacuate people and then impose normal draft procedures, but voluntary enlistment would help a lot."

Finally, in February 1943, an all-Nisei combat team was approved. When some Nisei objected to a "Jap Crow" segregated team, they were assured this was the best way to show the nation they were loyal and brave Americans. Indeed, the 442nd Regimental Combat Team was to distinguish itself for courage on the battlefields of Europe. However, in 1943, General DeWitt still opposed recruiting Nisei into the army or releasing the evacuees for defense work. This time the War Department rejected his opinion. Secretary of War Stimson not only approved a combat team of Nisei; he also sent out a press release that said:

> It is the inherent right of every citizen, regardless of ancestry, to bear arms in the Nation's battle. When obstacles to the free expression of that right are imposed by emergency considerations, those barriers should be removed as soon as humanly possible. Loyalty to country is a voice that must be heard, and I am now able to give active proof that this basic American belief is not a casualty of war.

A week later President Roosevelt wrote:

> No loyal citizen of the United States should be denied the democratic right to exercise the responsibilities of citizenship, regardless of ancestry. **The principle on which this country was founded and by which it has always been governed is that Americanism is a matter of mind and heart; Americanism is not, and never was, a matter of race or ancestry.** A good American is one who is loyal to his country and to our creed of liberty and democracy. Every loyal American citizen should be given the opportunity to serve this country wherever his skills will make the greatest contribution—whether it be in the ranks of our armed forces, war production, agriculture, government service, or other work essential to the war effort.

The very quotable second sentence of this missive was added by Elmer Davis, director of the Office of War Information.

"YESSIRREE ALL OF US ARE ITCHING TO GO"

By early February, teams of army officers arrived in all ten relocation centers to enlist volunteers. Tets, by now twenty-two, could hardly wait to sign on!

February 19, 1943
Dear Miss Breed,
This is prodigal reporting. Things have been popping rather fast lately. A (dust) windstorm, a cold spell, a rainstorm, and good news . . .

When the Army came here to Camp III to register the men under selective service and also to take volunteers for the Japanese American Combat Unit, it was the best piece of news we nisei have had in a long time. We nisei were despairing in ever becoming recognized. But now we have the chance to prove our loyalty, because after the evacuation, nisei were classed as aliens inelegible for military service.

I am proud to say that the San Diego group has the most volunteers than any other group in camp. All together in our block we have just about 15 volunteers including yours truly, which makes about the best record yet. We are going around Feb 23 to (according to those "in the know") Camp Douglas, Utah (near Salt Lake City) for induction then to Camp Shelby, Mississippi (this much is official) for training. This is the bunch to be with because we are all volunteers and there won't be those slackers and pro-axis minded as there would be if the men were drafted. Yessirree all of us are itching to go.

So—if everything goes well I'll be writing to you from an Army Camp instead of a relocation center.
Sincerely yours
Ted

Not everyone shared Tets's enthusiasm and eagerness to sign up. Before they could volunteer for the army, Nisei had to sign a "loyalty oath" that sparked great anger between generations. Basically, the same loyalty questionnaire was sent to all Nikkei who were seventeen or older, men and women; for them it was called "Application for Leave Clearance." This was part of the War Relocation Authority's plan to resettle as many of the Nikkei as possible and as soon as possible. It was not compulsory that they leave, but filling out the form was required. Oddly enough, none of the letters sent to Miss Breed mention the explosive controversy that erupted over these two questions:

QUESTION 27. Are you willing to serve in the armed forces of the United States on combat duty, or wherever ordered?

QUESTION 28. Will you swear unqualified allegiance to the United States of America and faithfully defend the United States from any and all attack by foreign or domestic forces, and foreswear any form of allegiance to the Japanese emperor, to any other foreign government power or organization?

To Issei men who were on average sixty years old, Question 27 was meaningless—they were too old to serve in the army. Although the Issei women were younger, there was no reason to expect they would leave their young children to serve. Nor was it likely that parents of seventeen-year-old girls would allow their daughters to sign up for the Women's Auxiliary Army Corps—the WAACs. While many Nisei men were willing to sign "yes" to this question, many felt that their families should be released and their freedom restored first.

For the Issei, signing "yes" to Question 28 would make them people without a country. Since the United States would not grant them citizenship, signing would mean they were not citizens of Japan. If they were forced to return to Japan, what would become of them? If they were thrown out of the camps, what would they live on? Most had lost their homes, jobs, and means of support.

For the Nisei, signing Question 28 could be interpreted to mean they had *once* been loyal to the emperor. How do you give something up that you never believed in?

The poorly written questionnaire was meant to test the loyalty of the Nikkei and discover who would pledge their allegiance to the United States. Parents often had different opinions from their Nisei sons, as Babe Karasawa recalled during our interview:

I overheard late at night my older brother telling my dad, "Me and the guys are going to volunteer," and my dad said, "That's stupid! They put you in a place like this? And you're going to volunteer? Just ridiculous." Well, under the circumstances that's the way my dad felt. And I think that many dads would have said the same thing whose sons did volunteer. But I also know that there were many, many people that opposed volunteering. In Camp Two, I know one family that when the oldest brother volunteered for the Four-forty-two they were harassed so much by their block that they left camp—that's how much harassment they were being subjected to.

More than sixty-five thousand of the seventy-eight thousand Nikkei over the age of seventeen answered "yes" to both questions and were classified as "loyal." Young men who refused to sign "yes" to both questions were known as the "No-No Boys" and classified as "disloyal." Two thousand did not give outright "yes" answers. Some said they would serve if their families were free to leave the camps. Those who qualified their answers were also listed as "disloyal."

About sixty-seven hundred answered "no" to Question 28 and they were listed as disloyal, too. These are probably the ones Tets considered pro-Axis.

> . . . here I was, a 19 year old, having to make a decision that would affect the welfare of the whole family. If I signed, "No, No," I would throw away my citizenship and force my sisters and brothers to do the same. Being the oldest son and being brought up in the Japanese tradition, it was up to me to take care of my parents, sisters and brothers. It was about a mile to the administration building. I can still remember vividly. Every step I took, I questioned myself, "Shall I sign it 'No, No,' or 'No, Yes'?" The walk seemed like it took hours and then when I got there, a colonel asked me the first question and I cursed him and answered, "No." To me he represented the powers that put me in this predicament. I answered "Yes" to the second question. . . . I have never had to make such a difficult decision as that.
>
> —Testimony of **HARRY TAKETA**, Chicago, September 22, 1981

By the fall of 1943, the War Relocation Authority had separated the "loyal" from the "disloyal." The government's plan was to resettle those who were loyal in the army or at jobs around the country, getting as many people as possible out of the camps. The so-called disloyal were sent to Tule Lake. On August 20, 1943, 458 Nikkei from Poston were sent to be segregated at Tule Lake in Newell, California. Those Nisei who went to Tule Lake were to be stripped of their citizenship. When the war ended, they were all to be sent back to Japan.

More than eighteen thousand from all ten camps were eventually segregated in Tule Lake, but of these, many were young children and family members. A third of them had been sent to Tule Lake as a relocation camp from assembly centers in 1942 and did not want to move a third time.

None of Miss Breed's correspondents were sent to Tule Lake, but several knew people who were sent there. Young people were often caught between their loyalty to America and their parents' fear or anger. Many, such as Elizabeth Kikuchi's future brother-in-law, had no choice but to go with their families.

After loyalty questionnaires were complete, more young people were allowed to go out on "permanent leave." This stirred up protest from those who had long hated the Nikkei and complained that the WRA was coddling the enemy. While war raged in the Atlantic and the Pacific, the WRA leadership was attacked for being too softhearted.

My brother-in-law went to Tule Lake with his family . . . his uncle wanted to take the whole family and all the young Nisei back to Japan—so they all ended up in Tule Lake. Ultimately my brother-in-law rebelled against his uncle; because they were treating his mother unfairly—you know with male domination and he resented that. He was a strong enough young man to say we are leaving. He became a physician—but to this day I think—there is some anger there—that they were put in that position. . . . the cousins all said he was betraying the family—but eventually they all came back from Japan and my brother-in-law ended up helping them. The division within families—was difficult.

In Tule Lake they were treated like the Japanese military—they had to get up at 5 in the morning and run and he had a fever . . . but he had to run and he nearly died from a kidney infection. Later he became a specialist in the kidney. He's the first Japanese-American to win the highest award from the University of California Medical School—Gold Cane Award for the physician student who exemplifies the Hippocratic oath—but he went through that hardship.

The great majority of those who went to Tule Lake during the war never left the United States or gave up their citizenship. Of those who went to Japan after the war, most came back to the United States. Returning to the land of their ancestors, they discovered, was not really an option.

"A SUBJECT CLOSE TO MY HEART"

Clara Breed also had big news in February of 1943. Her article "All but Blind" was finally in print! It was her first big article with her own byline, and it was not just exciting—it led to a second article. That February, Bertha Miller, the founder and editor of *Horn Book Magazine,* wrote to say how much she admired Clara's moving article: "I have to admit, too, that I read it enviously. I wanted to go straight to the telephone and send you a night letter saying 'write the same thing longer for us.'"

Clara answered immediately: "Of course I should love to do a paper for you on the Japanese American children. It is a subject close to my heart." She told Mrs. Miller about Tets, who was so happy about the prospect of joining the army that he wrote: "This is the best news we've had since evacuation." Clara wrote, "His letter had a lift and exhilaration that has been absent from former letters. He is an idealist and this experience has been hard for him."

All through March and April, Miss Breed heard about delays in their induction. Fusa wrote that the boys were impatient to get on with it. On April 9, Tets wrote that he had his physical and was still waiting. But twelve days later, one can only imagine his disappointment when he wrote:

April 21, 1943
Dear Miss Breed,
Regret to inform you that for the good of the country and morale of the U.S. Army I have been "rejected for general military service as a result of the physical examination." I have applied for limited military service although present plans do not include limited service men in the Japanese American Combat Unit. I had hopes of visiting San Diego after induction in Salt Lake City (Fort Douglas). Perhaps later I'll get the chance. At any rate until further orders I am in the rejected class.
Sincerely yours
Ted

His bad arm, the same old problem that had flared up while he was in college, kept Tets out of the service for now. But he was determined to strengthen his arm, hoping they would take him next time.

After the letdown, Tets felt a little happier when he discovered that Miss Breed was planning a trip to Poston. Clara was working on her article for *Horn Book Magazine* and felt that seeing the camps with her own eyes was important. All of her young friends were counting the days till her arrival. Fusa warned Clara to be prepared for the intense heat. In May the temperature was already 100 degrees or worse. Katherine hoped it would be a long visit. It was almost a year since Clara had seen them last, so she was just as eager as they. She had a pass for the nineteenth, but at the last moment her plans had to be changed to the twenty-seventh. But that date did not work out, either.

Clara was crestfallen as a string of emergencies in the library led to one delay after another. We don't know all the details, but during those weeks several new branch libraries were opened for defense workers and their families. Due to limited funds, the library was understaffed and everyone, including Clara, was required to take on additional hours—even on the weekends. Clara could not afford to lose her job, but she didn't want to let her children down, either. Still, there was no way around it. Clara could not take time off to go to Poston. She must have written or wired Tets. In late June, Fusa wrote: "Tetsuzo explained to me why you were unable to visit us. We realize —'business before pleasure' is just one of those unavoidable things." Letters would have to do.

On May 10, the first contingent of Nisei volunteers for the army left for Salt Lake City. More would follow daily. Louise wrote of this memorable farewell:

> *A procession of trucks with one volunteer on each truck left Poston III and headed for Poston I. Camp II joined in the procession—making 24 trucks full of people going one after another. It certainly was a sight to see.*
>
> *In Camp I a talent show was held in honor of the boys. Also at this time administration officials spoke. Then at 8:45 P.M. all the volunteers hopped on the awaiting bus. Leaving a puff of smoke behind them they were off to fight for our country, U.S.A. It was a sad but yet a happy parting. I felt so sorry for the mothers.*

COLLEGE BOUND

From the start, Clara Breed worried that the young people who were ready for college would lose these years. Many of their letters talk about possibly going out to get a job and go to school. California was still off-limits, but the Nisei were being encouraged to apply to college or find a sponsor who would guarantee them a job in the Midwest or the East. Some found work in offices and factories and as domestic workers. For these young adults, "permanent leave" was possible. Few had the funds to pay for full-time college, but they had renewed hopes that eventually they could go to school and learn a trade. From their letters Clara knew that Fusa, Chiyo, Aiko, and Louise were all considering a move, but the decision was not that easy. How could they leave family behind? What kind of job could they find? How could they afford college? How would they be treated? All of these questions kept many Nisei from leaving.

Behind the scenes, Eleanor Roosevelt and her friend Clarence E. Pickett, a Quaker leader of the American Friends Service Committee, shared their mutual concern that the camps might become a new kind of Indian reservation, a permanent way of life whereby the talents of the Nisei would turn to dust in the Arizona desert. The government refused to help directly with funds but officially asked the American Friends Service Committee to take charge and organize the National Japanese American Student Relocation Council in May of 1942. They immediately began helping students make applications, raising funds for scholarships, and persuading colleges to open their doors to these young Americans. (Universities with government research programs could not accept the Nisei.) Some left for college directly from the assembly centers. But for many others it was not so quick and easy. The Student Relocation Council had to convince many Nisei and their parents that it would be safe to leave the camps.

Once again, the good news was turned ugly by a campaign of poison-pen letters and threats by anti-Nikkei groups that got wind of the student relocation movement. Letters from senators, governors, and other citizens objected to "Japanese-American students being sent to college while our American boys are sent to war . . . such discrimination in favor of our country's enemies is absolutely unbelievable."

Letter to the Editor [of the *Sacramento Bee*]:
How do you like this? I came home tired from work with my arms full of groceries on a loaded bus in the rain to find out in your paper that the Japanese are being let out of their relocation centers to attend college. Can you imagine that? Our boys giving up their schools and homes and all good and decent things to go and fight the yellow devils and in their absence, the Japanese are allowed to attend our very own schools.

I have been here a very short time from Honolulu where I was present and witnessed the sneaky way the Japanese got around to do their dirt. I heard the planes over our home. I heard the awful news of the attack over our radio, and as soon as possible I was in the thick of helping our boys who had their very hearts torn out, if not by shrapnel, then by the sight of their buddies and loved ones who were hit in the back by individuals of this very same yellow race whose youths are entering our colleges and taking what rightfully belongs to our own boys.

I am not speaking only for myself. I am speaking for the thousands who feel the self same way.

—MRS. WALTER PERRY

Jan. 16, 1943

My dear Mrs. Roosevelt,

I am enclosing a clipping which has appeared in one of our California papers.

We are all working for Victory and fail to understand how we can extend freedom to this race of people. Our beloved President has so many problems facing him, but this race never should be granted freedom until we have Victory.

I do trust this clipping enclosed gets consideration.

Truly Yours,

GRAYCE E. SIBLEY

Mrs. Roosevelt did not answer directly. She sent the letter to Dillon S. Myer, director of the War Relocation Authority. This is part of his answer:

April 2, 1943

Dear Miss Sibley:

This is with reference to your letter of January 16 to Mrs. Roosevelt which has been referred to this Authority for consideration and reply.

I am sure that every American shares the views of the writer of the letter to the editor which you enclose as it relates to the Japanese attack on Pearl Harbor. I do not believe however that it is in keeping with the democratic principles for which we are fighting automatically to transfer this feeling to all persons of Japanese ancestry residing in this country, and especially to those who are American citizens. The bombs from Japanese planes at Pearl Harbor also fell on American citizens of Japanese ancestry, and their reaction was much the same as that of other

Americans. This is demonstrated by the fact that when given the opportunity to do so a few weeks ago, about 50% of the male American citizens of Japanese ancestry of military age in Hawaii volunteered for service in the United States Army.

For about a year prior to the reopening of military service, Japanese Americans did not have the opportunity of entering the Army and a number left relocation centers to continue their education. The number who have attended educational institutions has always been a very small fraction of the total leaving the relocation centers for employment.

I believe that young men of Japanese descent should not only be given the opportunity to volunteer for military service, as was recently done, but should be drafted as well. Then if any person of draft age of whatever national or racial extraction is attending an educational institution, it will be because of his physical condition or other reasons, which affect all persons alike. . . . I am hopeful that Selective Service procedures will soon be extended to cover American citizens of Japanese descent.

Sincerely,

D. S. MYER

Despite the threats, inside the camps the Nikkei raised funds for scholarships. Their first young people were sent off as goodwill ambassadors for those who would follow. They registered in schools in the Midwest and the East. By the end of the war more than four thousand Nisei would be in college.

Fusa's brother, Yukio, was one of the college students who left that winter:

Jan. 30, 1943

Dear Miss Breed,

On the 28th of January my brother left for Marquette University in Milwaukee, Wisconsin. Since then my mother and I find home lonely and missing something. If it wasn't for my pet radio I think I should go crazy with the unusual quiet. We will, of course, in due time get used to the quiet and probably think nothing of it later. Perhaps in a few months we may move to Colorado to join my sister, but that is still vague.

But going to school was not so simple without adequate funds. A few months later Fusa seemed worried but proud of her brother:

June 27, 1943

Dear Miss Breed,

My brother, Yuki, is now working on a farm in Milwaukee. Due to some tie up with the Federal Reserve Banks he hasn't been able to withdraw the money which was to keep him in school. He is planning to work until about Nov., then enter school again. He claims that to become a doctor (a full fledged M.D.) is an "obsession" with him and he will attain his goal regardless of the amount of years and amount of work he has to do. Mother was worried for fear that after he started working he would not care to go back to school, but now has been rather assured by him that it will not be so. I'm glad for his sake that he plans to become something of value to mankind. I hope and pray that he will make a fine doctor someday.

Well, Miss Breed, don't work too hard. Let me hear from you soon.
Sincerely,
Fusa Tsumagari

Clara wrote about Yukio to her editor and friend Bertha E. Miller at *Horn Book Magazine*:

August 6, 1943

I wish you could know Yukio Tsumagari. He was a student at Berkeley when war broke out but succeeded in getting permission to leave the relocation center to go to college in Milwaukee. The family has been rather well-to-do and had money enough saved up to insure his education, but after a few months he discovered that because his father is an alien the government would allow no money to be withdrawn from his bank account. He is working on a farm in Wisconsin this summer and hopes to save enough money to go back to college for at least one semester next winter. His family has worried for fear he would not finish his education, but he writes that he is going to be a doctor, and that nothing can stop him, no matter how many years it takes. Somehow, I do not think anything will.

In fact, nothing did change his mind. Fusa's daughter, Patty Higashioka, told me:

My grandparents were determined to have their children educated. They had two sons and two daughters. Fusa was the youngest. Their first son, Minori, died because he was misdiagnosed and not treated correctly. I recall my Uncle Yuki telling me that was one of the reasons he became a doctor. He went to Marquette University for his M.D. and then had his practice in Cheyenne, Wyoming. He was very successful and had a large clinic.

But leaving the camps took courage. The students were fearful of how they would be treated and lonely as they faced an uncertain future without their families and old friends:

In April 1943, I boarded the train alone . . . to go to Indianapolis. I sat in my seat, shrunk in its corner, hoping that I was not too visible. I kept my face buried in a magazine. I had feelings of guilt, self-hate and fear. My guilt came from the feeling that I abandoned my aging parents in camp. Another guilt was the old ongoing one of having a Japanese face.

My self-hate came from having allowed myself to be uprooted and interned. Many times I wished I had disobeyed the order and been arrested. My fear came from the past. I had experienced the hate, expressed on a daily basis through the newspapers and the radio, as a death wish on us.

When I was herded into camp and saw the barbed wire enclosures and guns, I lost hope. My citizenship had meant nothing. There was no secure hope for us in America. Even as we were sitting in camp, economic interest groups and racists were demanding that we be, at the end of the war, put on ships and sent to Japan, better still, sink the ships. Sitting on the train I felt like a mauled creature, afraid of what lay before me.

—Testimony of **MONICA SONE**, Chicago, September 22, 1981

"MUDPIE DAYS"

Preparations for new schools at Poston, built of adobe mud bricks, were under way that spring. Students and their families assisted workers in the camp. Its Endo remembers that he and fifteen classmates made adobe bricks after school every day: "Workers taught us how to make the mixture of dirt and hay—we just put in the forms—flattened it out and put it in the sun to dry."

By March it felt more like July; the desert was heating up and so were the windstorms. Louise wrote to Miss Breed about a new and frightening problem:

In the 1940s, polio was a dreaded disease for which there was no real cure and no immunization shots to protect people from catching it. If you got a severe case of polio you might be paralyzed for life. That had happened to Franklin Roosevelt. Although people knew the president had polio as a young man, only a few knew that he could stand only with the aid of braces and that he was essentially bound to his wheelchair. If you were lucky enough to get a mild case, you might recover completely. But the fear of ending up in an iron lung, unable to breathe or move, was very real. In small towns and cities, children were kept away from swimming pools and crowds of any kind. My best friend's mother made "necklaces" of cotton for us that held smelly bars of camphor—in the hope that they would keep the flies away!

Miss Breed was alarmed when she heard that Richard Watanabe, one of Hisako's brothers, was one of the polio victims. Tets had told Clara that the medical facilities in all three of Poston's camps were "pitiful." The main hospital was in Poston I, fifteen miles from Poston III, where there was just one young doctor with limited experience and a student doctor working in the emergency room: "They are supposed to take care of approximately 5,000 people!!!! And they (the Big shots) wonder wh[y] we squawk about inadequate medical attention." Epidemics worried Tets the most.

With limited doctors and supplies, any contagious disease was a worry. When my friend Ellen Yukawa caught chicken pox they quickly took her out of the barracks, where people were living in close quarters: "I had it pretty bad. So they put me in the hospital and then two weeks later my sister, Elayne, came in."

But for the Yukawa sisters it turned out to be a lark:

We were in there together and they forgot us. We were in the isolation wing of the hospital and we had this whole ward to ourselves and we used it to play. My parents would come to the windows and we'd talk to them. It was so funny—eventually an administrator finally came by and asked, "How long have you girls been

"I always thought the dear dead days of mudpies were gone, but . . . anything can happen in Poston. . . . All high school students are helping to build the new adobe school. . . . Everyone was out there pitching mud. A messy job and how! . . . But it's worth all the sore muscles and dirty hands to know that we're doing our best toward the new school." (JuJu, Poston high school junior)

Sam Yukawa took this photo of the Poston hospital with a camera that a visiting friend smuggled in for him. Ellen and Elayne Yukawa spent a month there with the chicken pox. Most residents don't have photos of the early years in camp because cameras were considered contraband.

in here?" And we said, "A month." "Oh, for heaven's sake!" she said. "Get these girls out of here!" We had the best time in there. We just played and friends came by with comic books. I'm sure my parents were very happy. They had peace and quiet for a month! I don't remember the food—but at least we didn't have to go to the mess hall and stand on line. Besides, the hospital had inside walls and plumbing—but the barracks didn't. I spent my birthday in the hospital. It was April, I'll never forget that . . . funny the things you remember as a kid.

All through the spring and summer Clara asked for progress reports on Richard Watanabe. At first he could only get around with the aid of crutches, but in time he walked without them. However, the disease left him with a limp for the rest of his life.

As thousands of adobe bricks dried in the summer sun, everyone looked forward to better school days to come.

While the new schools were taking shape, racist politicians began throwing mud of another kind at the Nikkei. In her *Horn Book Magazine* article, "Americans with the Wrong Ancestors," Clara Breed wrote:

There are those who say that Japanese descendants will never be allowed to return to the West Coast. If this is true, California and Oregon and Washington will be the losers, for there are among these Japanese Americans young people of ideals and courage and creative imagination, young people who may some day be great sculptors, great doctors, great scientists. Some of them could help to interpret East to West, and that interpretation will be needed when the war is over.

As more and more Nikkei became eligible to leave the camps, renewed attacks appeared in newspapers, magazines, and pamphlets with titles such as *The Japs Must Not Come Back*. There were articles designed to enflame public sentiment against releasing any of the Nikkei, now or ever. Not content that the Nikkei had lost their freedom, the Hearst newspapers, the Native Sons of the Golden West, the American Legion, and politicians who depended on their votes began a new and even uglier round of lies and attacks. Their objective was to strip the Nisei of their citizenship and send all the Issei, Nisei, and Sansei back to Japan forever.

In January 1943, Sen. Albert "Happy" Chandler of Kentucky, head of a special subcommittee on military affairs, charged that disloyal evacuees would commit "almost any act for their Emperor" and in some camps he charged "as many as 60% were disloyal." Of course, there was no truth to his charges, nor in rumors that if the evacuees were released they might poison the water of Parker Dam, destroy military installations, or commit other serious acts of sabotage.

General DeWitt was stubborn in his belief that no Nikkei soldiers or civilians should be allowed back in California. "I don't want any of them here. They are a dangerous element. There is no way to determine their loyalty. . . . A Jap is a Jap," he said at a news conference. The *Los Angeles Times* called the release of ethnic Japanese "stupid and dangerous."

Chandler's committee attacked Dillon S. Myer, head of the War Relocation Authority, for "turning loose 'dangerous Japs' on permanent work leave." Committee members referred to the Nikkei as "parolees," but Myer insisted they were not parolees, nor were they "prisoners of war." Of course, many Nikkei, then and now, would not really agree with Myer. They were indeed prisoners of war. Here was another case of doublespeak: The government preferred to call the incarceration "protective custody." But who was being protected and from what or whom? Dillon Myer preferred to say that the camps were temporary housing before the evacuees were resettled in communities east of the Rockies. The government's new plan to get the loyal Nikkei out of the camps was met with anger and distrust by those who hoped they had seen the last of all the Nikkei. For the Nikkei who felt they had no place to go and no way to start over, the idea of leaving the camps was also met with fear and resistance.

In April, news from Tokyo of the execution of American pilots who were prisoners of war provoked a new wave of anti-Japanese feeling. As always, the word *Jap* was used interchangeably to describe both Americans of Japanese descent and the

Japanese military who were committing such barbarous acts. In some newspapers the cry went out to kill Japanese internees for every American GI who was murdered. Others vowed that the release of Nikkei would lead to bloodshed.

It was in that climate of hate that Happy Chandler set out to tour the camps and prove that the War Relocation Authority was coddling these people who he claimed were living in "luxurious conditions."

"I WOULD NOT WANT TO LIVE THAT WAY"

That same month, Franklin Roosevelt, who was traveling to a meeting with the president of Mexico, asked the First Lady to visit Gila River, another relocation camp in Arizona. Eleanor Roosevelt often acted as her husband's eyes and ears by visiting places he was too busy to see himself. She not only reported back to the president; she also reported to the nation. In her "My Day" column and in a long article in *Collier's* magazine, she wrote about her impressions of the camp:

We shared a meal that was served to the staff, minus meat, butter, sugar and coffee. . . . Neither in the stock-rooms, or on the tables did I notice any kind of extravagance.

The people work and around almost every barracks you can see the results of their labor. Sometimes there are little Japanese gardens, sometimes vegetables or flowers bloom, sometimes bushes transplanted from the desert grow high enough to afford a little shade. Makeshift porches and shades have been improvised by some out of gunnysacks and bits of wood salvaged from packing cases.

Ingenuity has been used in the schools. The class in typing only had two typewriters, so they worked out a key-board of card board with holes for the keys and on this the class practiced. The typewriters were rationed, ten minutes' use a day to each member of the class.

. . . Young American born and educated men are now joining the Army division made up of men from Hawaii and from these evacuation camps. Some of the sons of the older people were already in the Army before the evacuation took place and many of the American born girls asked me whether they would have an opportunity in the women's auxiliary services.

Complaints that the Nikkei were being pampered continued. FDR asked Mrs. Roosevelt to visit Gila in Arizona and check the conditions. After her visit with WRA Director Dillon S. Myer, the First Lady told reporters, "The sooner we get the young Japanese out of these camps the better. They are living in conditions which certainly are not luxurious, as some report. . . . I would not want to live that way."

Newspapers around the country ran articles quoting the First Lady saying, "I saw no pampering or coddling."

After her visit to Gila, the First Lady held a press conference during which she asserted, "I think it's a bad idea to institutionalize anybody. . . . Of course, the citizen Japanese in these camps should be checked carefully, but then I think they should be put to work at locations where they are welcomed, and when government officials are willing they should. . . . They are living in conditions which certainly are not luxurious, as some report. . . . I would not want to live that way."

"LIBRARIES ARE NOT PLACES WHERE PREJUDICE GROWS"

As the furor over "coddling" continued to fill the news, Clara Breed was finishing her article "Americans with the Wrong Ancestors." She was appalled to read that the San Diego City Council was protesting the return of Japanese Americans to the West Coast. Would the hatred never end? Clara decided to add a stronger ending to the article; if it sounded too much like propaganda, so be it. In May 1943, she sent "Americans with the Wrong Ancestors" with a letter to Bertha E. Miller, her editor and friend at *Horn Book Magazine*:

Dear Mrs. Miller,

I feel humble in offering it, because the subject is so big, so complicated, and so important that there is more to say than can possibly be said in 3200 words. . . . No one could really know the American born children and young people without deep affection for them. They have been through a great deal. One dares not mention some of the injustices they have been submitted to and which they have endured without complaint, knowing America was bigger than some individuals . . .

The whole experiment has implications for the conduct of the war and for the peace. . . . It's up to the whole country now to accept the young Japanese Americans without stigma, to give them a chance. I believe we'll do it. But public opinion will have to be changed gradually. And perhaps an article in the *Horn Book* will help a little.

Thank you for your interest in this subject, which is close to my heart.

Sincerely,

CLARA E. BREED

Several weeks later Clara was delighted when she received this reply:

On the front page of her article for Horn Book Magazine, *Clara wrote, "Robert Naeda, nine, studying his lessons in a homemade chair, is the son of the first family to arrive at the War Relocation Authority Center at Poston, Arizona." Homemade furniture was made with scrap lumber and food crates. Notice the cracks between the floorboards where sand could seep inside.*

June 1, 1943

Dear Miss Breed:

Your paper pleases us very much. We are more than satisfied with it. Our treatment of our Japanese American is a most important matter, not for today and tomorrow, but for the future of this country. . . . Once more our most cordial thanks to you for the splendid article. We have never had a better one.

Sincerely yours,

BERTHA E. MILLER

When the article was published that July, Clara received letters of congratulations from librarians all over the country. More than one indicated they had had no idea what was going on. Others were eager to do something to help. One librarian wrote that when the Japanese Americans left the Palos Verdes School they gave twenty-five dollars to the school as a parting gift. "The school decided to use the money to buy books that will help children build better racial attitudes. They are to be inscribed . . . 'of one book made He all people,' and a duplicate set will be sent to Poston from Palos Verdes friends."

A librarian from Palos Verdes, California, asked Clara to help her make a proper list of books, and that gave Clara an idea for yet another article, one to help librarians find books that built better racial relations. Clara had been upset by a story she read about a library where children had thrown copies of Japanese fairy tales out the window. "Our library," she wrote to Mrs. Miller, "has not had a single incident of the kind the ALA reported. Chinese children here correspond with the Japanese evacuees, school classes have written them letters. There is much prejudice around of course, and children are not immune but take sides on controversial questions. But I believe that books can influence sanity and that on the whole libraries are not places where prejudice grows."

It may be difficult to appreciate how far ahead of her time Clara was with this proposal. Books in your library and school now reflect the diversity of our people. But as late as the 1960s, most books for beginning readers were only about blond-haired, blue-eyed children who lived in a house with a mom and a dad and a dog, often named Spot.

"MY MOST TREASURED POSSESSION"

Bertha Miller welcomed the idea of Clara's next article. Letters from librarians continued to arrive, but none of the mail Clara received meant more to her than those that came from her young friends at Poston. Clara requested extra copies of her "Americans with the Wrong Ancestors" article so that she could send them to Poston.

By the time the extras arrived, Clara was playing Santa Claus again, packing up gifts to send to Poston. Along with their holiday treats she tucked in a copy of her *Horn Book Magazine* article for each of her young friends. It was a great hit!

That was a very interesting article you wrote in the Horn Book. *Truly it is folks like you who bring peace closer and a better understanding of mankind.*
   Margaret Ishino

Miss Breed, may I compliment you on the fine article you wrote in the Horn Book. . . . *When I read articles like that, it makes me so proud that I am an American having such wonderful friends like you. It gives me confidence and courage that everything will be just fine after this terrible mess is over.*
   Louise Ogawa

Dec. 23, 1943
Dear Miss Breed,
Thank you ever so much for everything. You gave me the nicest Christmas preasent I ever received since I was in Poston. I not only enjoyed the books, but I always like anything that has your name.
   Why, not only are you in the books, but in the magazine as well! Probly the magazine is my most treasured possesion now.
   Everything you said is true. And it certianly made me feel more like "back home." Just think, you have made Poston famous, and also my name in your article. Mama is always proud about the little things which involves our friends or us, so she will probly be doubly happy. Thank you again and again for every thing, and mama joins me also.
   Much love,
   Katherine

WHO IS BEING "PAMPERED AND CODDLED"?

Mrs. Roosevelt's assurances did not silence those who wanted the Nikkei kept imprisoned. In April, when the War Department announced that Nisei soldiers would be allowed to return to the West Coast on furlough, there were more angry attacks on the War Relocation Authority and the Nikkei.

Gov. Earl Warren of California, who owed his election to his anti-Nikkei point of view, complained that the release of "150,000 Japanese now held at relocation centers" may lead to widespread sabotage and a "second Pearl Harbor in California." (Never mind that the 1940 U.S. Census showed that there were only 126,947 Nikkei in the continental United States, 79,642 of whom were U.S. citizens.) Warren charged that their release would lead to a situation whereby no one "will be able to tell a saboteur from any other Jap."

When Gov. Dwight Griswold of Nebraska challenged Warren's statements, saying that "thousands of Japanese had been released with the approval of the FBI without one particle of trouble," Warren replied: "Lack of trouble since the release of the Japanese is no proof at all that they don't intend to commit sabotage. Axis warfare is timed and when the time has arrived and the Japs make a thrust of some sort then we'll feel the full effect of the saboteurs. . . ." That sort of illogical thinking had put the Nikkei into camps, but it was a mind-set that was losing followers.

That summer another so-called fact-finding congressional subcommittee, the Dies Committee on Un-American Activities, began hearings and visited the camps. On the day they were to arrive at Poston, Tets began a long letter to Miss Breed that he would compose over a period of two days. In it he thanked her for sending their sewing machine and fan. Not being able to join the army was especially hard since he felt like the "last of the Mohicans" now that all his buddies had left for the army or jobs as they waited to be inducted. His dad was still being held in an internment camp, and Tets was not even sure where. Rumor had it that he may have been moved to New Mexico. These days Tets was working in the camp barbershop, where he was the only barber. But the big news in the letter was about the Dies Committee:

June 17, 1943 & 6/18/'43
Dear Miss Breed,
"Pride goeth before the fall" or something like that 'cuz a radio news report came in declaring that the Dies Committee has stopped all releases from Relocation Centers pending investigation. What a blow!! Especially for those who had been planning to go out within the next few days.

"Our friends"—the Dies Committee are supposed to come this afternoon to Camp 3. I hope it gets about ten degrees hotter than yesterday. It was only 112 in the barracks. I'd like to have them feel a little of this Poston weather before they leave. We'll see who is being "pampered and coddled."

Sincerely

Ted.

P.S. Checked up on radio report. Found it was untrue. What a relief! Dies Committee was here nosing around. Didn't get to meet any of them. Darn the luck! Gosh, it was hot this afternoon. Heat lightning north of us all afternoon. Looks like a storm coming up. Ugly looking clouds. Feels sultry just now. Maybe we're going to have one of those wonderful desert storms—with 70 + mile winds, thunder + lightning, and dust and rain (2–3 inches in one storm). Oh boy—I hope the Dies Committee gets caught in the middle of it . . .

In fact, the radio report Tets heard was true. Some members of the Dies Committee called for a halt in releasing the "disloyal Japs" until their committee did its work. And what was their work? The committee relied upon testimony of disgruntled former employees at Poston who had a litany of lies. They claimed, among other things, that there were one thousand Japanese soldiers in Poston and that the Japanese were hoarding food and arms; that the evacuees were using autos for pleasure driving and got all the gas they wanted; and that every evacuee got five gallons of whiskey—when, in truth, the War Relocation Authority did not supply or permit the sale of whiskey.

Dillon S. Myer, director of the War Relocation Authority, answered that the ridiculous charges were nothing short of a "willful intent to misrepresent," and he would address all forty-one of the false charges against the WRA and the Nikkei! When a committee member corrected him, saying there were only thirty-nine charges, Myer said he would settle for thirty-nine, and that is what he did.

After Myer was done, the committee itself became the target of the press. East of the Rockies the public was no longer easily misled by racist rhetoric from West Coast politicians. The government was no longer appeasing the anti-Japanese power brokers. The president and the War Department did not end the exclusion of Nikkei from the West Coast but made it clear that would not continue for the duration. Rumors began to surface that General DeWitt would soon be replaced. The government finally took a stand and the national press followed their lead.

An editorial in the *Washington Post* on June 25, 1943, declared: "The outright deprivation of civil rights which we have visited upon these helpless, and, for the most part, no doubt, innocent people may leave an ugly blot upon the pages of our history."

That summer, in the *Pacific Citizen*, Saburo Kido, who was incarcerated in Poston, published an invitation to Rep. Leland Ford of Los Angeles and his fellow congressmen to spend at least a week's sojourn in this "hell-hole of America" so he could experience one of the weekly sandstorms, like the one the previous week that terrified those who had their roofs blown off.

By late summer the issue of coddling was dead. By fall, General DeWitt, who demonized all people of Japanese ancestry, was moved from his command. He was replaced by Gen. Delos Emmons. Almost at once, the army began to investigate ending the exclusion act that prohibited the Nikkei from returning to the West Coast while it was considered a "military zone."

With American victories in the Pacific, the tide of war had turned. There was no longer any threat of attack by the Japanese on the West Coast; it was no longer considered a "military zone." This meant that the door to the West Coast would soon be opened to the Nikkei. However, inside the camps, former Californians were not so sure they would ever want to return to their former homes.

CHAPTER TEN

FIRST GRADUATES, CLASS OF '43

S THE SUMMER SUN BEGAN to scald the desert again and the Dies Committee visited Poston, life for the teenagers centered on the big graduation celebrations. Louise tried to joke about the heat: "Yes, that nickname 'Roastem, Toastem, Postem' certainly is true! I am being roasted and toasted by the ever-shining Poston sun." Louise, Margaret, and Hisako were all about to graduate. Like all graduates, they were busy and excited with plans for the prom and what they would wear: "All the buzz buzz buzzing around school are the bee hives of girls chattering about their clothes for the Prom," Louise wrote. The girls were busy making their pastel dresses for graduation. In fact, Hisako asked Miss Breed to please send her a blue zipper for her dress.

Sixty years later, Louise recalled:

I ordered material from the Sears catalog and made a two piece outfit by hand because at that time there was no sewing machine to use. I sent a piece of the fabric to Miss Breed and asked her to please find me a spool of thread to match. She always wrote and said if there was anything we wanted she would try to send it. Through her kindness I was able to finish my outfit.

Plans for the class of '43 yearbook fizzled, probably due to wartime paper shortages. The photo mentioned in Louise Ogawa's letter could not be found. Maybe one will show up in a scrapbook someday. Margaret Ishino had the next best thing: a group picture of their twelfth grade core class. Margaret is in the second row, fourth from left, and Louise is in the bottom row, second from left. Where was Hisako Watanabe? They don't remember.

June 28, 1943

Dear Miss Breed,

Well, finally I made the grade for graduation day has come and gone. Commencement was held on June 26th, 9:30 p.m. at the newly built amphitheater. All the girls wore sheer, cotton pastel dresses while the boys wore white shirts, dark pants, and dark ties.

I am enclosing a commencement exercise program. I thought may be you will enjoy seeing it. Also I am enclosing a copy of the activities we enjoyed during senior week.

We were very disappointed in being forced to change the hours of the river party. Because of the Dies Committee we could not go to the river in the evening. But we had a wonderful time anyway.

Then came Graduation Day. After graduation, a party was held in our honor. I was in charge of the refreshments. it certainly was a headache but I enjoyed it. Oh there were many delicious things to eat—cake alamo, punch, cookies, doughnuts = food galore!!!! All the mess halls were very generous. . . .

Well finally our group pictures arrived. It is not too good but I am enclosing one. I hope you like it. I'll put my pen aside so I'll be able to hear from you and I hope it will be real soon.

Most respectfully,
Louise Ogawa

Years later, Margaret wrote that the most happy event in Poston was Senior Ditch Day:

We gathered at the Colorado River, sang songs, played baseball, and went on a short hike. The cook made delicious sandwiches and even baked a cake . . . the desert wildflowers were beautiful and the greenery about the River had such a peaceful atmosphere I forgot I was in a concentration camp that day. For our Senior Prom, we danced to the records of Glenn Miller, the Dorsey brothers, and Artie Shaw. Our class . . . received high school diplomas bearing the buffalo seal of the Department of the Interior.

"CHILDREN WHO CONTINUED TO DREAM"

That second summer was quite different from the first. The heat was intense, but small gardens surrounding the barracks provided color and shade. Each of the camps had a swimming "pool" of sorts. A writer from *Liberty Magazine* who visited Poston that August wrote: "There is a swimming pool which is merely a wide place in the ditch." From the uproar in Congress she had expected a marble pool with umbrellas shading tables and waiters serving champagne beside it. "But it's only a ditch and there [are] no alcoholic beverages of any sort." But that did not matter to the kids who enjoyed long stretches of the day keeping cool in the water.

Elizabeth told me about those long summer days with friends:

We were the children who continued to dream. We'd actually get up at 4 or 5 in the morning—before the sun would be too hot and walk about 3–5 miles to the river and spend the whole morning and afternoon there and walk back in the cool of the evening. While we were there we'd make drawings. We were teenaged girls—our dream was a dream of life after camp—when we would live in a dorm at college or have our own house. We would draw a layout of a room in the sand—my bed will be here—with a side table—we just dreamed of a better life beyond the barracks. When Miss Breed sent me the book, *A House for Elizabeth*, I remember saying to my mother—We never had our own house. I lived in a parsonage or in the church and then in the stables and then in the barracks—and so receiving this from Miss Breed was really special—now Miss Breed sent me a book about my own house! She must have thought very carefully about the books that she sent out to each of us.

Reading continued to be a favorite pastime. All Miss Breed's children continued to be avid readers. Almost every letter began with thanks for the books Clara sent and then moved on to other dreams:

August 4, 1943
Dear Miss Breed,
Sometimes I wish I were Webster or Winston so that I could write my appreciation in other words besides "thank you." for all the lovely books you sent me. Then again I am glad I am just plain Margaret Ishino because of the many interesting books I receive from you.

When peace comes again to this world I should like very much to travel to three countries. First of all I would like to go to Alaska—"the Land of the Midnight Sun" and see the Eskimos and their igloo. I would also like to see the salmon going up stream. After reading "Son of the Smoky Sea" I want to go more than ever.

Secondly I would like to see France. I do not know why, but I feel sympathetic toward France. I have always wanted to learn the French language. In our Core class each student chose a country to make a term paper. I chose France and since I have said to myself see Paris and die.

Last of all Japan to see the stream in back of my aunt's home where minnows and water lilies go lazily swimming by. Japan where the four seasons winter,

spring, summer and fall are all different and picturesque. Then I would like to live
contentedly for the rest of my days in America—my home sweet home.
　　Thank you again . . . may God bless you richly.
　　Most sincerely,
　　Margaret Ishino

Summertime reminded Miss Breed's friends of programs they had always attended in the San Diego library. Many asked in their letters if she was still having the summer reading clubs they had attended. Louise remembers:

> I must have been about 8 years old when I started reading books for the summer reading club that Miss Breed started at the children's library. Miss Breed was so friendly, kind, and always greeted us with a smile and happy face. Her summer reading club kept us busy and occupied during summer vacation from school. She would have different programs. I remember one where we would travel around the world reading books. She had a map and selected books from various countries for us to read. We were given numbers when we joined the summer reading club—as we read the books she would put a star with our number on the star and put it on the country we read about. She made our summer fun and not so boring and helped us enjoy reading.

The libraries in Poston were now operating. Miss Breed and other librarians were sending books. A librarian in the camp wrote to thank Clara. That's how Clara discovered that her books were all going to Poston I! After that she mailed books specifically to Poston III, where her children lived.

As always, softball was popular, although no games were played until after 6:00 P.M. Babe recalls that it was 120 degrees at the start of a game: "Playing earlier was definitely unthinkable."

"Speaking of heat—July was terrific!" Tets told Clara. For one whole week it was never below 125 degrees. There was no happy medium, since in the early hours of the morning the temperature plummeted to 69 degrees, enough to wake Tets up "shivering for a blanket." Teams from the three camps played against one another, and Camp III won the championship for two years. Tets wrote to Miss Breed: "The San Diego boys have proven themselves as outstanding ballplayers."

Joe Yamada remembers that Tets was one of the smoothest dancers in the camp!

Joe was so impressed by how many girls liked to dance with Tets that he got Tets to teach him how to dance. But Tets was not just involved with dancing and softball; he also was taking ukelele lessons almost every night. In fact, he sent two dollars and asked Miss Breed to please send him music for "'Stardust,' 'Tuxedo Junction,' 'Anniversary Waltz,' 'Moonlight Serenade' or any new number on *The Hit Parade*."

Summer was also a time when teenagers could earn some money. Its Endo said:

> The summer of 1943, I was almost 15 years old—I took a job in the carpenter shop—the head man is from my same hometown—and I knew him. I worked there with another boy—a grade below me—he and I worked hard. Poston was the only camp where they had double roofs—to keep the heat out so there'd be ventilation—The two roofs were 16–18" apart. We were the smallest, so we had to crawl between the roofs to patch up any holes. I did that one whole summer— we got paid $12 a month—isn't bad when you understand a doctor had to sign up for six days a week and they got $19 a month.

Its and his good buddies also had time for some pranks. When I asked about what they did for fun, Its laughed as he remembered:

> Five to six of us raided the watermelon patch—we went in the evening. Each one of us found a ripe melon—cut it opened and ate the whole thing, except for the seeds! We didn't get sick—it was ripe and nice—and then we said we'll bring some back for the others. You see, in our block one of the families left so we made their barrack into a clubhouse where we played cards. So, we must have taken close to 20 melons. We threw them into the canal and one person had to take off his clothes and swim with the watermelons. He'd help push them if they got caught on the side of the canal. Then another guy took his clothes off and takes the watermelons inside—then we piled them up inside the barrack.

Ben Segawa's memories of that summer are grimmer. He told me about one of his friends, who was a Boy Scout.

> He went around the camp with his troop, collecting newspapers for the war effort. Then they got one of the fellows to drive them into the city of Parker to bring the papers for the war effort. They've got their Boy Scout uniforms on and they

go and deliver these papers for the war effort and after they delivered the paper they go to a restaurant because the scoutmaster wants to treat them. But the restaurant wouldn't serve them at all. Here you are eleven years old—they didn't want us there at all. They had to feed eighteen thousand people—Poston became the 3rd-largest city in Arizona at that time. You know, Parker had to benefit from all of that—but they wouldn't serve us.

Ben was right. One of the first things visitors saw in Parker was a sign on the door of the not-very-grand Grandview Hotel: "Japs Keep Out—You Rats." (It remained on the door until the hotel burned down several years after the war.)

"THE WRONG ANCESTORS"

Morale in the camps has definitely improved, according to my correspondence. One factor has been the gradual, cautious release of carefully selected young people to attend middle western colleges and to take jobs. This policy deserves the support of all intelligent people, for these young people have committed no crime except to have the wrong ancestors . . .

—CLARA BREED, *Horn Book Magazine*

Once the War Relocation Authority sorted the so-called loyal from the disloyal, the government began a serious effort to move as many people as possible out of the camps. One of their main objectives was to "scatter" the Nikkei, to avoid the rebuilding of any "Little Tokyos." The hope was that they would be assimilated into the "melting pot," but without a community of friends, many Nikkei were fearful. Would they be accepted? Of the estimated 126,000 Nikkei in the country, more than 110,000 of them had lived on the West Coast, mainly in close-knit Nikkei communities. During the war the number of people held by the WRA grew to 120,313. Now with relocation they were resettling in places that had only been names on a map to them. Louise found the prospect exciting: "I never thought I would have friends in Boston, Chicago, Cleveland, Colorado, Arkansas, Utah, Idaho, or Wyoming: but I do now! One of these days, I'll be traveling all over the United States just visiting friends. I think that'll be such fun!"

For months Miss Breed noticed their letters were full of uncertainty about "going out." Fusa had almost decided what she would do:

On the door of the not-so-grand Grandview Hotel, in Parker, Arizona, this sign was displayed. In fact, it was still there long after Poston closed down. Tets described Parker to Clara in seven words: "What a jerkwater town, nothing but shanties...."

Dear Miss Breed,

Though many families are planning to join their fathers in internment camps, we probably will not be among them. The only reason for this is that I am unwilling to go. My mother will not go without me so there we are—right back where we started from. Other than being with my father I cannot see any advantage in going to an internment camp, therefore I am reluctant to go. The drawbacks are too many: once we go in we cannot get out until after the war, there would be much closer supervision of our lives, all our letters would be censored, and when we got out we would have absolutely nothing on which to fall back.

The picture in my mind is to join my sister in Colorado. Her husband is doing outside work. We could stay in the center until the time that he could set up house. Of course we are leaning quite a bit on them, but in times like these we cannot help that as my father is interned. When the war ends my father would be able to join us, and we would at least have something to start us off anew. This problem has been bothering me for quite a while, but I feel that I am right in not wanting to go, though my father may not like the decision too well.

I forgot to mention that my brother was granted permission to see my father in Louisiana while en route to school. . . . A great deal of what my brother writes and lets us know will sway our decision whether to go or stay in a relocation center.

Moving airplanes often look like falling stars, but we can hear them as well as see them. In the daytime they often swoop down very low and try to scare us. They don't scare us anymore—just get on our nerves. Now a ruling has been issued that if the swoop down on us less than 200' we should take down the number and report it to the officials. This has helped us quite a bit but there are still some pranksters, but we don't bother with them anymore. I guess we would do the same if we were the pilots and wanted some fun. An airplane was an oddity in Santa Anita but it feel's like home (S.D.!) over here.

All through the spring Fusa's friends continued to leave. Her sister, Fuji, and her husband went out to work in Minnesota, he on a farm and she taking care of twins. They didn't like the work, but they were trying to make the best of it until something better came along.

Tomorrow more of my friends are leaving for Chicago for work of some kind. This leaves me with an empty feeling of wanting to go outside, yet without a definite place to go. It's really tough on people my age who have just gotten out of high school without any specific training. We want to go out and work, but we haven't had enough training or experience and feel rather unsure of ourselves. However, I guess everyone feels this way when they grow up and have to face the world. Our problems are just like anyone else except for the fact that we have to get out of camp first of all. That's more and more red tape just to get out. Everyday we see ads for work outside. Lots of girls take domestic work just to get outside, then they plan to move into some other line of work. I, myself, don't like domestic work and have been told that it isn't the best line of work to go into, even as a starter. I can amble on and on this subject but it won't get us anywhere so this is enough of my troubles.

In May 1943, nineteen families left to join their husbands and fathers for the duration in a "family internment camp" in Texas. Fusa was greatly relieved when her father said she need not come unless she wanted to. That summer Fusa and her friend Chiyo talked of going to a vocational school. They tried to be practical but wanted to do something enjoyable. Secretarial work seemed practical, but Chiyo was more interested in fashion or window designing. They also wondered what jobs would be open to them. On the West Coast, before the war, all too often Nisei with all kinds of professional training ended up working as gardeners or in other blue-collar jobs. Friends and family who had relocated in Chicago told Chiyo and Fusa that typing and shorthand were a must for getting a job in the city. But, Fusa complained to Miss Breed, learning those skills "a la homestudy" was not that easy.

As the idea of "going out" swept through the camp, it was the young, educated Nisei who left first. Many Nisei teachers were in this group. Poston was becoming a dying community. It was inevitable. Relocation gradually made Poston smaller and, in some ways, worse. As one of the teachers put it, "Our children are learning that change is the only constant. There are several teacher-less classes . . . we cannot keep the evacuee teachers here at $16 & $19 a month!"

Tets also had many friends on the move, young men going off to war:

May 26, 1942
Dear Miss Breed,
We have had quite a bit of excitement with all my friends going outside into the world again. The excitement will continue as more and more leave almost daily at times. This evening said goodbye to seven people from our block. Yesterday two left. The day

before, four. The day before that, two more. Come Monday about 14 will leave—All from our block. About half of them are on seasonal leave, the others are out for an indefinite period (almost the same as permanent leave) There are almost as many leaving from other blocks so you see there soon won't be very many people left in camp. The good part of it is that those who have ambition and the courage to brave the uncertainty of outside life are the ones going out. Only the culls are going to be left in camp. Of course there are going to be quite a few people who can't afford to go out because of lack of finances. Then too there are many young people who are held back by parental objections or obligations (by obligations I mean that the condition of one parent is such that they cannot move so the youngster has to stay home to look after the family)

... All in all with the sympathetic help of the WRA I believe that relocation will be on the successful side at least here in Poston. I haven't kept myself well posted on the number of people or the destination of all of them but the meager information that has come to my attention seems to indicate that Chicago Denver, Cleveland, Minneapolis, Cincinnati, and St. Louis are the "big towns," that are attracting the most. Many are out on seasonal leave out there in southern Idaho, northern Utah and far eastern Oregon

What a difference time makes. The cry was "Go West" (young man) now it is "Go East" (young nisei) The outlook for a family to relocate outside is not very encouraging. Many families came into camp with only two to three suitcases per member. They had sold their furnishings for the home. Furnished houses are very rare or are too expensive. As a result if the family goes out, they must start all over to furnish a house on an income that has not increased but decreased during the past year. Another thing many things that were sold are now not available or else priced much higher. This problem alone keeps many in camp. Couple that problem with the uncertainty of the attitude of the people, jobs to support a family (majority of jobs open now are menial.) and then you have the bottleneck to relocation. So at present those who can afford the expense, and those who are single (Bachelors—son— daughter) or are a married couple are the ones who are relocating.

Nothing definite regarding relocation of either my sister or me. Too many things uncertain especially so since word from Washington reports that dad's case is under reconsideration. Then too something may come up for volunteer's who were rejected ...

Sincerely yours
Ted

My Day

Mrs. Roosevelt talked directly to Americans about accepting the Nisei in their communities:

To undo a mistake is always harder than not to create one originally but we seldom have the foresight. Therefore we have no choice but to try to correct our past mistakes and I hope that the recommendations of the staff of the War Relocation Authority, who have come to know individually most of the Japanese Americans in these various camps, will be accepted. Little by little as they are checked, Japanese Americans are being allowed on request to leave the camps and start independent and productive lives again. Whether you are a taxpayer in California or in Maine, it is to your advantage, if you find one or two Japanese American families settled in your neighborhood, to try to regard them as individuals and not to condemn them before they are given a fair chance to prove themselves in the community.

"A Japanese is always a Japanese" is an easily accepted phrase and it has taken hold quite naturally on the West Coast because of fear, but it leads nowhere and solves nothing. A Japanese American may be no more Japanese than a German-American is German, or an Italian-American is Italian or of any other national background. All of these people, including the Japanese Americans, have men who are fighting today for the preservation of the democratic way of life and the idea around which our nation was built. . . .

By the fall of 1943, many of Louise's friends had left for school and jobs. In fact, the War Relocation Authority actively pushed young people to continue the "relocation" process by leaving the camps. Nisei who had finished high school were encouraged to apply to college or find a job in the Midwest or East. All they needed was a sponsor who would guarantee a job and housing. Louise told Miss Breed that she was longing to go out, too:

Sept. 3, 1943
Dear Miss Breed,
As I recall, you asked in your last letter if I applied for leave. Well, I have not as yet. But to my surprise, my Eastern Defense Clearance Papers came the other day. The thing that was so surprising was that I didn't even apply for it. At the present time, I am trying awfully hard to convince my father that I should go out but he feels that I should wait a little while. He believes I am too young, in mind if not in age. But at the rate I am pestering him, he'll give in sooner or later, unless his patience holds out! I talk to him so that he says he even dreams of me talking to him of going out. I can just about imagine how he finally said yes, in his dream of course, but this doesn't satisfy me cause it was not in reality. But just you wait and see, I'll be writing soon saying "I'm finally going out Miss Breed!" Oh what happy days that will be. But on the other hand, the thought of leaving my father leaves me hesitant.

Job opportunities were posted in all the relocation camps.
Here is a sample of the kinds of jobs listed and what they were paying:

OUTSIDE EMPLOYMENT OFFERS, May 8, 1943

JOB	LOCATION	WAGES
Gill Net Fishermen	Chicago, Illinois	$6 days to start
Graduate & Undergraduate Nurses	Holyoke, Colorado	$80 to $125 per month
Registered Nurses	Detroit, Michigan	$85 to $88 per month plus room and board
Orderlies, Internees	Elgin, Illinois	$100 per month plus one meal
X-Ray Assistant	Chicago, Illinois	$18 per week plus meals & laundry
Laundry Workers	Chicago, Illinois	$18 to $20.52 per week
Railroad Workers	Salt Lake & Ogden, Utah	54¢ per hour
Mechanic— Farm Implements	Jerome, Idaho	50¢ to 75¢ per hour
Clerical & Warehouse Girls	Chicago, Illinois	40¢ to 45¢ per hour
Factory Work	Cleveland, Ohio	45¢ to 60¢ per hour
Factory Work	Indianapolis, Indiana	$25 per week
Elevator Operators	Chicago, Illinois	$70 per month
Weather Stripper	Cincinnati, Ohio	$2 per window
Machine Operators, Grinders, Power Machines	Cleveland, Ohio	40¢ to $1.25 per hour

After graduation Louise took a job in the school office with Hisako Watanabe. Both girls wished they, too, could go to the new school. The new building was a huge improvement over last year's scattered classrooms in barracks. Furniture had been built inside the camp, and books and equipment were now more available. Paper shortages limited the number of books that were printed during the war. New books would have to wait, but thanks to librarians such as Clara Breed many books were donated. Even if they had to do their senior year over again, Louise thought it would be worth it! Typing classes were actually going to have typewriters, and home ec classrooms were going to have stoves and sinks! Letters from friends who had relocated made the prospect of leaving all the more intense. Many in Chicago were working in some kind of publishing company. They assured her that most people were friendly, although they did occasionally meet some who were not:

> *. . . but that is to be expected anywhere . . . I'm quite sure it takes loads of courage to go out into the spacious United States again. But I think those who have relocated have advanced one step above us. Here in camp, I think our standard of living tends to become lower, we tend to become less independent, and this certainly does not help to make our future brighter. . . . I certainly would like to go out, but I don't have the slightest idea where I'd like to go. I guess I haven't really given it much thought, since father has not consented to my going. My sister is planning to go out but as yet she has no definite plans. She may go to Chicago where my brother is. Father says he would like to go out, too but he is [not] a little optimistic about the feelings toward him since he is an Issei. Well, only time will tell whether we go out or stay hidden in hot Poston.*

For those "inside," the summer of 1943 was filled with the usual activities. Baseball was a passion enjoyed by young and old alike. Players used a softball, since it is lighter and requires less protective equipment. There were high school girl and boy teams as well as teams of young men and women who were out of school. When they were not playing sports the next best thing was listening to sports on their radios. The bowl games and World Series were popular with young and not-so-young alike. There was no television in those years, but radio brought them all the shows they had enjoyed on the outside. The top pop music on *The Hit Parade* was a must for teenagers, romantic stories on the *Lux Radio Theatre*, mysteries on *The Shadow* and *The Inner Sanctum*, comedy with Bob Hope, Jack Benny, and *Fibber*

Once they got clearance from the WRA, many young adults were able to "go out" to work. Most had to accept jobs that paid little and had no future. Yet, for many, freedom to resume their lives was a welcome option.

McGee and Molly, and for the younger kids *Jack Armstrong the All American Boy, The Green Hornet,* and *The Lone Ranger.*

Comic books were the top choice at the canteen and library. In fact, comics were so popular that the librarian did not allow them to be borrowed. They were like a magnet that drew school-age kids to the library. Crafts also filled their hours, keeping hands busy. Katherine became a "knitting fool," making clothes for her dolls and wishing she had endless supplies of materials.

Some of the younger kids went out to the mesquite trees, bringing back locusts that sounded like buzzing neon lights. Not that they really needed extra bugs around the barracks, what with the crickets that ate holes into clothing and scorpions that popped up through knotholes in the floorboards! There was such an abundance of bugs that Katherine, now eleven years old, offered to mail some to Miss Breed:

If you like bugs, do tell me in your next letter, so I can catch some for you. I'm afraid there won't be much life in them when they reach you. Please tell me the truth if you like them or not, because if you don't, I don't believe you'll want to see so much as a picture of a bug when you see the ones out here.

But Miss Breed must have turned her down, because Katherine writes: "I agree with you that bugs are awful. I tried catching some, but it didn't work out. So now you needn't be in fear that I shall send you any."

The one form of entertainment that just about everyone loved best was going to the movies. It didn't matter if the films were new or old—they were a ticket to another world, a great way to escape for a while from the confines of camp life.

As Louise gazed up at the night sky, waiting for the movie to begin, she surely thought of one of her girlfriends who had relocated to Cleveland, Ohio:

. . . she wrote and said that she just couldn't get use to the indoor theaters. In Poston the movies are shown outdoors, under the stars. She kept looking up at the ceiling thinking she would see the stars. While waiting for the movie to begin, everyone looks up at the sky trying to find the Big Dipper etc. (This is in Poston of couse.) I can imagine how much she enjoyed the picture sitting in the soft-cushioned chairs.

HOMESICK FOR SAN DIEGO

Although Louise couldn't leave Poston in real life, she found another way to leave:

March 20, 1943
Miss Breed, thank you for the wonderful time I had with you last night! I think I better start from the beginning before you think I am not in the right state of mind I had a wonderful dream last night. I left Poston on a short leave of absence and headed for good old San Diego and to you. My first stop after leaving the train was a candy store and you were right behind me too. There I saw rolls and rolls of candy. I kept asking you, "Would this chocolate candy melt before I reach home?"

Before anyone could say [a—] I asked for 5 lbs. of it. I was buying the whole store yet I left the store with the same amount of money I had when I entered it. That was because I never paid. I don't know how I got away with it either. Then I went into the Mayor's office and had my picture taken. It was the first picture I took since evacuation (11 months). Oh, everyone treated me so kindly and they were friendly. I painted the town red, as the saying goes. Yes, I went everywhere—I went to Marstons and Lions for my clothes; Hamilton for all the cakes, cookies and what have you; Jessop for all the rings for all my fingers and wrist watches placed one after another until it reached my shoulder; Boldricks for shoes; haunted the drive-ins every night for a nice juicy steak, ice cream sodas, banana splits by the dozens. Oh, I had a wonderful time!! Then by 6:00 A.M. I was back in my Poston cot again. When I awoke this morning I wondered if it really happened or if it was another one of those wild fantastic dreams. It was so realistic I began to wonder.

Many of the letters, from little children as well as teenagers, included a sentence or more about how homesick they were for the library and San Diego. Nine-year-old Jack Watanabe wrote, "I hope that I can come back to San Diego and see you again."

Every season of the year reminds Louise of San Diego. At Christmastime she tried to imagine how the windows with Christmas trimmings must look and how nice it would be to go window-shopping again. In the summer when Miss Breed ran her reading programs Louise wrote: "I certainly wish I were one of those happy children rushing to your desk with a wagon load of books to check out." What she left behind was never far from her thoughts:

Today [April 13, 1943] we had to write a composition about our home town. This certainly was an easy topic! I had so much to write I didn't know when to stop. Usually I know when to stop but do not know when or how to start. I imagine my English teacher will be waiting to go to San Diego very soon.

I wish we had a copy of that composition!

When Miss Breed writes that she had fun picking and canning figs from the tree in her garden, Louise remembers the fig tree in her own yard where she always got caught out on a limb picking figs. Shortages of canned goods were a problem all through the

"CAMPUS ECHOES"

Students, teachers, and parents pitched in to repair the new adobe school when a storm hit just before opening. The photos of those busy days are from the Parker Valley High School 1944 "annual," or yearbook, "Campus Echoes."

POSTON, 1944

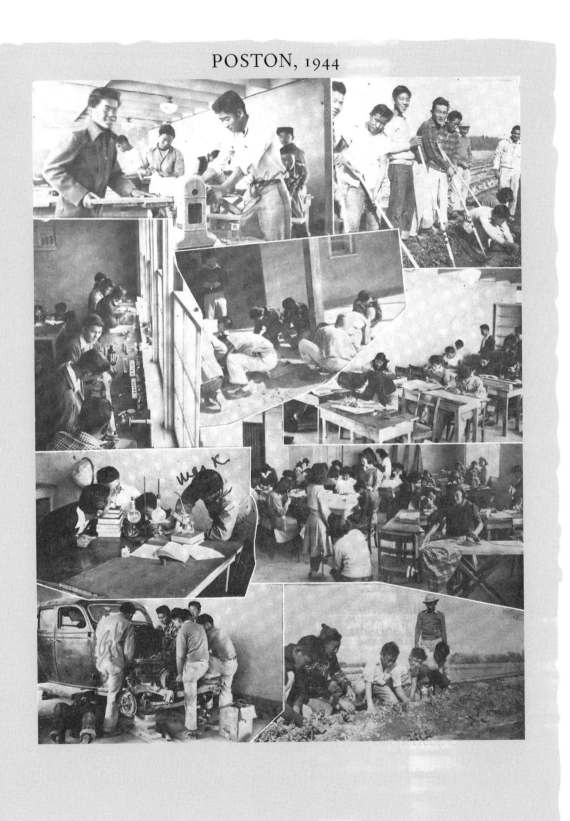

war and millions of Americans tried canning fruits and vegetables from their victory gardens. Food was sealed in glass jars instead of metal cans. I remember my mother making the best canned peaches and the worst, runniest ketchup I ever tasted!

One night at the movies Louise saw a newsreel about the sailors being trained in San Diego: "When I saw Balboa Park and the Naval Training Station, I became too homesick for words. All the former San Diegans began to clap and cheer as soon as they saw a glimpse of our hometown."

Louise, as always, did her best to shrug off her lonely feelings for home, but they kept creeping back:

Often I used to think as I laid on my pillow, "What will happen to me if had to live in this camp for 5 years?" but now, I don't seem to think about camp. I guess I have adapted myself to this situation. But many a time I have wished with all my heart that I could go back to San Diego.

Her friend Hisako felt much the same way:

October 5, 1943
What most of us really would like to do is go to San Diego (home) and work but when we'll be able to, no one knows. I'll be sure to look you up though when the time comes. Please write, I'll be waiting to hear from you.
　　As ever—Hisako

It wasn't just the teenagers who missed San Diego. Young Katherine wrote:

January 6, 1944
I imagine San Diego is just as busy as ever. My mother and I both wish we could go back. We're always saying to each other "Remember when we ————." or "Remember back home ————." We always say "back home" when we mean S.D. Hoping to hear from you soon.
　　Love
　　Katherine

Letters such as these gave Clara and her friend and assistant Miss McNary reason to keep the letters and packages coming. Keeping the young people's hopes and spirit alive was really all they could do to show the children that there were people in the outside world who truly cared about them.

ADOBE SCHOOL OPENS

The way of a schoolteacher is hard. The way of a schoolteacher in a relocation center is almost impossible. To begin with there is a basic dilemma of trying to teach American democracy to children in an undemocratic situation.
—JOHN EMBREE

A new crop of teachers arrived that summer for the second school year. But in August, just weeks before school was to start, three school buildings had their roofs blown off in a windstorm.

To get the new school ready, students, teachers, parents, and laborers hired by the War Relocation Authority rolled up their sleeves and worked together to repair the buildings, make more adobe bricks, dig sewer ditches, wash windows, and paint the woodwork. Martha Hays, one of the new teachers, wrote that thanks to that storm, Poston III was a closer-knit community than the other two camps. Working side by side gave them a sense of pride in their accomplishments, and students got to know their new teachers as people first.

The new teachers were younger than the schoolmarms of the first year. Miss Hays quickly discovered that among the boys, cooperation was considered "apple polishing." If you helped the teacher, you lost your pals. In Poston "slanguage," a good student was "what a brain," "we know you're good," or "too good." Poston itself was "corroded." A tough assignment was a "lost fight." There was "no need" to do anything; everything in Poston was "for free."

School and block parties were held in a mess hall or the school auditorium decorated with crepe paper streamers. The one and only dance step was known as the "Poston shuffle"— done by tipping from side to side. The best way to get everyone to sit down was to play fast music. This was not the jitterbug set—their older brothers and sisters were the true hepcats. Boys and girls lined up on opposite sides of the hall, and boys shyly walked across the floor to ask girls to dance. This was usually not until the record was half over. For refreshments there might be "salad sandwiches," Jell-O, potato chips, punch, or cocoa.

Former students talk fondly of the teachers who came to live in the desert among them. One favorite in Camp III was Barbara Washler, and after speaking with her, it's easy to understand why. Miss Washler was just twenty-one and fresh out of college. "I really wanted to go into journalism," she told me. "But then the war came along and it seemed like everyone besides myself was doing something exciting or different and here I was still in college. So I tried to finish in a hurry and take my practice teaching classes so I could become a teacher. I thought I'd be pretty sure of a job then."

She heard about the need for teachers in the WRA camps as she was about to graduate from Park College in Kansas City. There was just something about the job that appealed to her. "I have an affinity for variety and unusual settings," she told me. "And, I guess . . . unusual circumstances."

There probably couldn't have been more unusual circumstances than what she found in the Arizona desert. But she was young and full of energy and enthusiasm. She didn't teach just English and Social Studies Core in the junior high; she also volunteered to sponsor the two school newspapers and the school annual! So that old journalism dream had a new reality. She also ran a Girl Scout troop. She remembered her scouts making and selling potato chips at a school fair to raise money for the high school annual.

Getting to staff meetings from one camp to another, as teachers often did, meant long, dusty hikes or driving the big black vehicle that the students dubbed the Hearse. Barbara Washler remembers driving herself and others in that big old vehicle. When I asked if she felt cut off from the outside world, her answer was: "It was a busy life! I was just too busy to think that it was something I didn't want to do. There was no place else to go and nothing else to do. You just stayed there and made Poston your life—but that seemed a fair exchange to me. I felt that they had been so misused that I didn't think what we did was enough. I think the parents were grateful to us but couldn't express it in English, and we couldn't speak to them in Japanese. I just felt it was exciting to me to be there and I didn't expect to get any feeling of greatness out of it. Just feeling needed gives an added incentive."

There were two different groups of housing for the teachers. Some chose to live in more comfortable white frame buildings located across the broccoli fields and firebreaks, away from the Nikkei. Others lived in black tar-papered barracks near their students. A single teacher might have as much space as a whole Nikkei family and many more comforts. But many of the "on-campus" teachers welcomed their students' visits, and their rooms became meeting places. While the teacher graded papers, groups of teenagers would hang out together, talking, joking, playing cards, cooking a batch of fudge, and sharing their ideas and dreams.

Not surprisingly, Barbara Washler chose to live in the barracks inside the camp. She had a twenty-foot-by-twenty-five-foot room next door to Frances Cushman, the new principal. By cutting a doorway between the two rooms they had a larger space. Miss Cushman was another favorite of those I interviewed. It was Miss Cushman who managed to get Parker Valley High School accredited, which was important to those who wanted to go on to college.

Most classes in the junior high had thirty to thirty-five students or more. Barbara Washler had an assistant, a college graduate, Takeo Asakawa: "He was six feet tall. I think he was the tallest man I recall. He and I more or less co-taught. He helped me. He was very good with the students and they responded to him really well, so I was lucky to have an assistant like that." Nisei teachers were generally better able to communicate with many of the students' parents, who often spoke little or no English.

Barbara Washler Curry was one of the favorite high school teachers. She not only taught English and social studies, but she ran a Girl Scout troop, two newspapers, and the yearbook. Fresh out of college, she made Poston her life for the duration.

Once the school year got under way, students were occupied with activities much like those in their old schools. But two clubs were especially focused on preparing the graduates to leave. The College Bound Club, run by Miss Hays, helped students prepare for interviews and consider possibilities of relocating at various colleges. A Boys Cooking Club, whose purpose was to teach boys to be able to cook when they relocated, boasted sixty members! A look at the 1944 yearbook includes group photos of the *Hi Times Newspaper* and the junior high paper, *Jr. Hi Spotlight*. Lettermen was an all-boy group that ran a social to raise funds to buy jacket letters for boys who earned them for sports; the No Man's Club was, as you might guess, an all-girl club "for the development of personality and poise." The Photo Tint Club taught students how to hand-tint photographs, and the Skull Club, for football lettermen, sponsored dances to buy letters. There were Senior and Junior Girls Glee Clubs, Orchestra, Senior Radio Club, which discussed only things pertaining to the radio, and an Ag Club that assisted with harvesting Poston's crops. There was a Chess Club, Senior and Junior Girls' Reserve, Dramatics Club,

Art Club, Commercial Club, Model Airplane Club, Girl Scouts, Boy Scouts, football teams, basketball teams, Senior–Junior Girls Athletic Association, and girls' basketball and volleyball teams. As popular as softball was, in 1943–44, it seems the teams were not in the schools but part of the teams set up by barrack blocks. There were clubs for every interest!

I asked Barbara Washler if her junior high students seemed angry about having to live in this world apart. "They were too young—this was their life. I'm sure there was anger and hurt and bewilderment down there," she said. "But they just threw themselves into the life that was there for them." This matches up to what Liz, Ben, Its, Ellen, and others who were in junior high told me about those years.

Senior high students were also enthusiastically involved in school activities, but they had a fuller sense of what had happened to them and their families. Twelfth-grade students were asked to write papers on democracy. The teacher tried to avoid essays with long, angry complaints by asking students to give their definition of democracy and state their contribution to it. Here is a sampling from those papers:

What does democracy mean and stand for? I don't think it is just a scrap of paper on which the constitution is written, but it is the ideas represented in it. That America is a land of freedom, justice, tolerance and brotherhood. Otherwise why are millions of Americans fighting and dying to accomplish the victory of America?—JENNIE NODA

Democracy is a Utopia. The perfect Democratic nation shall, never be. The United States is the most democratic country at the present but it is far from being what I believe a Democracy should be neither economically, politically or socially. The Constitution is by far the most perfect document ever written by man. Its ideals will not and cannot be realized in this day and age. In other words it is too far advanced for this age. . . . I believe that one of the most basic ideals is equality among different races. The common people must . . . come to realize that the color of a person does not make him physically dirty or mentally a moron. . . . When this racial prejudice problem is overcome this nation shall be a truly better democracy. —ALICE TANAHA

. . . Everyone should have the right to voice his opinion and act as he pleases. For a democratic government to be a success we must have citizens who are able to read, write and think straight. By educating myself, I [will be] a good, citizen. When I become of age . . . I am sure I will be able to vote intelligently.

—AKIKO NIMURO

Democracy! What is Democracy? Is it just a type of government? . . . In Social Democracy people might not be born equal but no one should be denied through birth or rank the right to make a place for himself suited to his efforts, character and ability. I think the evacuation of the Japanese was undemocratic.

—SHISUE NATATSUHASA

"WE ARE AMERICANS ALL"

While students inside the camps struggled to define democracy, many brave young Americans entered the battle that was being waged to defend their country. In late September 1943, the first unit of Nisei troops went into action in Italy. A story in the *Los Angeles Times* claimed, "American-Born Jap Troops Take Part in Italy Fighting: . . . every one of them was smiling with satisfaction." Officers were surprised, since men going into battle are usually tense. "These troops looked like they were going to a baseball game which, incidentally, is their favorite pastime." This article has the same over-the-top glow as did earlier articles about how happy the Nikkei were with their new homes in Santa Anita.

But the reports went further, as if to sell the idea that the Nisei soldiers could be trusted—a first step in reshaping the public's tainted perception of all people of Japanese descent:

My Day . . . October 9, 1943 . . .

I wonder if you were as much impressed as I was by a story which appeared in the paper recently. A reporter in Italy asked a Japanese American soldier fighting in Italy with his group, many of them recruited in Honolulu, how they felt about being there. The boy is reputed to have said that he would have liked to take part in the war in the Pacific, but was glad to serve his country anywhere. Perhaps it was wise to have his group in Italy, because they bear such a resemblance to the Japanese that it might be confusing, but his attitude seems to me the perfect one.

You are an American whether your features are those of a Japanese, whether you have Italian or German ancestry, are born or bred in this country, or are naturalized. You are an American and you take pride in "the American Idea," which claims you as its own when you subscribe to the Constitution and the Bill of Rights. We are Americans all, and it is well to bear this in mind as we approach the postwar problems, because they are going to require our close adherence to these ideals.

Their commander says, "They feel they've got a chance to prove they're real Americans and demonstrate their loyalty. . . . They've got something extra to fight for." . . . Officers are unanimously enthusiastic about the quality and spirit of the men. They said they never had seen any troops train harder and more assiduously and never had any doubt as to what to expect from them in combat.

These young soldiers were the 100th Infantry Battalion that had been organized in Hawaii. Later the 100th became the First Battalion of the 442nd Regimental Combat Team. Together they adopted the motto, "Go for broke," and that is what they did! As if they had to prove their courage and loyalty, they made their unit the most decorated military unit in American history for its size and years of service.

While the 442nd served in Europe, there were Nisei soldiers who were serving in the Pacific. Although it was top secret, selected Nisei served as language teachers, translators, and interrogators in the Military Intelligence Service (MIS). Even before the war began, the need for people who could speak, read, and write Japanese was urgent to the military. But as they scouted the relocation centers, the army discovered that most of the Nisei had little or no proficiency in the language of their parents. Even those who had attended Japanese-language schools had limited skills. Most of them were just too Americanized!

Those who did know the language and volunteered risked certain death if they were ever captured on the front lines. Small units of Nisei were attached to larger combat units in the Pacific where they would decipher messages and interrogate prisoners of war. But their work was kept secret for more than thirty years after the war. Gen. Charles A. Willoughby, chief of intelligence under Gen. Douglas MacArthur, said, "The work of the Nisei MIS shortened the Pacific War by two years and probably saved thousands of American lives."

NO WAY OUT

As the population of the camp continued shrinking, there were many who could not consider leaving. Those who had to stay were mostly families with young children or older people who had lost all or most of their possessions and could not face starting over again. Others were caught by obligations to their families. Hisako Watanabe was eager to follow her friends, but with her brother's struggle with polio and being the "next oldest" she was not able to leave.

Margaret was excited that the Women's Auxiliary Army Corps wanted Nisei women. She sent Miss Breed an article all about the WAACs. Would Margaret like to join? It didn't matter. There was no way she could leave. Her mother was very ill, and as the elder daughter, Margaret had no choice but to take charge of running their home and caring for Thomas and Florence.

Tets managed to go out on a temporary leave, working with a crew to save the vegetable crop at Tule Lake. Although he was not free to wander about, he was thrilled to be in California. In fact, he asked Miss Breed to mail him a map so he could trace his travels. He was putting in fourteen-hour days. Because of his arm he wasn't working in the field but on the kitchen crew, as a dishwasher. Still he was thrilled to be out of the heat and monotony of Poston—even when he got stuck with having to clean thirty chickens on top of washing the pots! Yaeko, his sister, was also on leave, working in a restaurant in the eastern part of Washington.

Little did they know what a wonderful surprise awaited them in Poston! On November 15, Fusa wrote to Miss Breed: "Tetsuzo's father returned, but found his home empty. Tets was out working near Tule Lake and his sister was out on seasonal cannery work." Clara's letter must have helped! Mr. Hirasaki was finally released and had already started working in the barbershop. After Tets and Yaeko had waited so long for their father, it's ironic that he arrived when they both were gone. It had been two long years since they were together.

Many young Nisei women believed that joining the Women's Auxiliary Army Corps would prove their loyalty to the United States. Unlike women who serve in the military today, they did not train for combat. About three hundred Nisei women, including Miwako Yanamoto (above) served. Miwako was a member of the first and only all-women Nisei unit of translators. They had all-women classes because the army thought they might distract the men.

For the Hirasakis, Christmas would be a joyous celebration! But for Fusa and her mom, all the gifts in the world couldn't make up for the fact that this year both Fusa's brother and her father were not there. Christmas was just around the corner, and as always Miss Breed made sure that there were gifts for each of her friends.

On Christmas Eve there was a choir concert, but it was neither as elaborate nor as well done as the previous year's because so many of the leaders had left. Still, that night there were forty boys and girls who went around each block singing carols. On Christmas Day there were gifts given to everyone under seventeen or over sixty. Fusa and her friends didn't fit either category. They joked that they were like the pop song about the shortage of available guys, "They're Either Too Young or Too Old." Santa (otherwise known as Mr. Ouchi) had nothing for them—not even a box of candy.

Clara spent a quiet Christmas with her family. Her sister, Eleanor, came down from Berkeley for a visit. They reminisced about Christmases past, when the world was at peace. There are no further letters about Clara trying to get to Poston for a visit. Miss Fay, who worked with Clara, wrote to Margaret saying that Clara was doing the work of two. Rationing of gas and tires made any unnecessary travel difficult—even unpatriotic. Perhaps, after the sad disappointments of having to cancel her summer visit, Clara decided that money for travel might be better spent on extra holiday gifts she could send to Poston instead.

Clara showed Eleanor the cards from Poston, remembering that two years had passed since the Hirasakis had celebrated Thanksgiving with them in their cozy little home on Trias Street. At least Tets and his father were together this year. But how much longer would the war go on?

For those who were left in the camps, Christmas brought with it the hope for peace on earth and goodwill to men. But would that goodwill extend to them? Would peace come with the New Year?

CHAPTER ELEVEN

"THIS PLACE WILL BE . . . A GHOST TOWN!"

$\mathscr{I}$N JANUARY 1944, when so many people were leaving Poston, almost twelve-year-old Katherine worried in a letter to Miss Breed that she and her mother probably couldn't "go out." Getting clearance to leave still involved a lot of red tape:

> *Well, it looks like we may be here for the duration, and we may not. There is a stop list, and if you are on that, you can't go unless the government changes its mind. There are hearings, though, for people on the list. The reason we think we are on the stop list is that we went to Japan between certain years. Two other people on our block had hearings, but they don't know the verdic yet. I bet they're on pins and needles. . . . If we are on the stop list, we won't be called for a long time yet, for they are going by the alphabet.*

Katherine kept busy doing what many twelve-year-olds liked to do—she was an avid collector of jars and bottles, movie star photos, pins, stamps, postmarks, paper dolls, and books. She was proud to say that she now had forty-five books of her own, with six more on the way (she hoped). She was also starting to collect pen pals:

Jan 15, 1944

Dear Miss Breed,

Thanking you a million times isn't enough, so I'll raise it to a billion. But any way I say it, it still amounts to the same thing—thank you for the paper dolls.

A childrens magazine . . . comes in every month at our canteen . . . untill recently, I never noticed the section where the children send letters. . . . I've answered ten letters that were published in the magazine. I'm pretty satisfied, because from the first three I wrote, I got three nice answers. After that, I wrote the other seven.

Really, I never noticed how interesting it was. My mother was born in Oahu, T.H., so I wrote to a girl there, and one in the Canal Zone, at Panama. There were so many from Canada, that it was pretty hard to pick one out, but I did.

Mama says writing ability is a nice thing to have, so I guess if I write a lot of letters, I will get a little ability. But I will have to get a good hand-writing to go with it. I never could write good.

Love,

Katherine

Miss Breed was concerned that Katherine seemed to miss a lot of school. The doctors didn't have any answers about her leg problems, she told Miss Breed, but she was doing all right. Her teacher sent Katherine's work home and she'd made up everything—except the decimal fractions. In spite of her absences, she was happy to report, she was still in the highest reading and math groups. But Poston, she complained, was turning into a "ghost town." Her favorite cousin had left, as had so many of her friends.

Clara noticed how much Katherine's spelling and writing had improved and wondered what dear Katherine looked like now—she no longer wrote like the little girl she had been in 1942. Any day now, she was probably going to give up paper dolls.

By late January, Katherine started taking her writing very seriously. She decided to do more than write letters:

Jan. 24, 1944

Dear Miss Breed,

I've decided to write a book! No kidding. But before I do anything, I would like to have your advise. When you finish with the book, don't you have it typewritten? Thats what bothers me. After that don't I send it to a publisher?

It's lots of trouble to write a book, isn't it? And theres a chance that the book may be turned down.

I think the hardest part is the typewriter. I love to use it, but I really never learned.

I've got lots of time, because I can't go to school. (Walking too much hurts.) My story will be about a little Japanese girl like me. That's another thing. I never knew how hard it was to choose a name. Of course, I can think of lots of Japanese names, but it might be prononced wrong. Can you use true names in stories like: Whitney, San Diego, Santa Anita, Bank of America, etc.?

My goodness, if it takes too much trouble, I guess I'll have to call it off. I don't mind writing the story, but it's the other things. I think I've read enough to know how to hold the reader's interest—I hope.

I hope I'm not putting you to too much trouble with my silly questions.

Love,

Katherine

That same week, Fusa thanked Clara for the two boxes full of clothes she had sent. Fusa was still waiting to hear when her father would be moved from the internment camp in Louisiana to Texas. Until then they had to stay put. Waiting was hard, but she did her job and looked forward to being on the "outside" like Chiyo, who had already left for a job in Chicago.

Fusa also had a problem that she hoped Miss Breed could help her solve. She wanted to find an American name: "The only one that appeals a little bit is Jan. I want a short name, but not harsh sounding. Some gals call me Mabel . . . I answer to it, but I don't like that name. Maybe you can help me pick a name otherwise I'll have to keep calling myself nameless!"

Fusa is one of the few correspondents who didn't have an "American" name. Even if they had Japanese names, many Nisei used them only at home—not in school. It was part of being American. Ben Segawa had brothers named George, Harry, Fred, Art, and Tom. His sisters were named Marion, Elsie, May, and Mary. Ben once asked his parents, who didn't really speak English, why they didn't use Japanese names. Their reason was simple: "We wanted you folks to be Americans."

As you've seen, Tets often signed his letters as Ted. Louise was known to her family as Yoshiko, which means "good child," and her friend Margaret says Louise was that, but she never used that name in her letters to Miss Breed or to me. Margaret was better known as Maggie to her friends—she wouldn't tell me her Japanese name; that was used only by her parents. Miss Breed must have asked Katherine about her name. In a P.S. Katherine explained, "Keiko is my Japanese name. I was named after my father. Only I have a 'ko' on the end instead of 'chi.' My fathers name is Keichi." Her mother called her Keiko, but friends called her Kathy. Aiko Kubo, whose Japanese name means "love," became Ellen Kubo when she left camp. Ellen Yukawa's grandmother gave her a middle name, Shizue, which means "quiet branch." But whenever talkative Ellen went to visit, her grandmother would end up saying, "I gave the wrong name!"

UNCLE SAM CHANGED HIS MIND

To lose our basic principles in wartime is to lose the very reason that we fight. . . . None of us who lived in these camps will ever forget that the American flag flew over them.—Testimony of **SASHA HOHRI**, New York, July 16, 1981

On January 31, 1944, the Selective Service reclassified young Nisei men as eligible for the draft. Those who signed on earlier did so on a voluntary basis. Now the government was saying there was no choice: If you were physically fit and over eighteen, you were expected to serve your country!

Ben Segawa was too young to serve but not too young to understand the irony of the government drafting men whom they had imprisoned without regard to their rights as American citizens. Now they were expected to serve in the same army that stood guard outside the gates of the camps they had been forced to live in since 1942.

All four of my brothers went off to war during World War II. They went out of these camps, just picture that. Here the government has got you locked up in these camps and they feel you are an enemy alien. You're a danger to the American war needs, so they shove us in these camps, but then at the same time, they draft the boys out of camp. "You got to go to war now." And three of my brothers were drafted, one of them volunteered.—**BEN SEGAWA**, Oral History, San Diego Historical Society

In February, Uncle Sam's letters of "Greetings" arrived along with orders to appear in Phoenix for the physical exams. Although there were parents who objected to their sons' signing on, many had taught their children: "Don't bring shame on your family!" I heard this expression from many of the people I interviewed. Ben Segawa explained it this way to me: "This mind-set and the Japanese Americans' need to prove their loyalty as Americans explain the kind of valor they brought to the battlefield."

While the great majority of the men called up by the draft signed on and served with honor, on July 3, 1944, the *Poston Chronicle* reported that 27 percent of all Nisei called refused to be inducted. Of twenty-one Postonians who refused, sixteen failed to appear, while five refused at Phoenix. Nor were these young men in Arizona the only ones who refused.

Close to three hundred draft-age Nisei in all ten relocation centers faced jail and felony charges on their records rather than serve. Their anger over the indignities of the past two years bubbled to the surface. How could the government take away all their rights and then expect them to leave their families and possibly die to defend freedoms they were denied? In 1944, many Nikkei were ashamed of those who resisted, but in later years the resisters were considered heroes who defended their rights with courage. In fact, the Japanese American Citizens League (JACL) recently apologized to those who had dared to say no.

In a letter written from Poston to President Roosevelt on February 19, 1944, the second anniversary of Executive Order 9066, the Committee for Restoration of Civil Rights of U.S. Citizens of Japanese Ancestry sent this appeal to the White House:

We, citizens of the United States of America of Japanese Ancestry, are glad that most of us are no longer excluded from the regular operation of the Selective Service System. We will be happy to join the ranks of the several thousand Americans of Japanese ancestry who are already serving in the Armed Forces of our country. We are glad at this opportunity to give our lives, if necessary, in the cause of our nation and democracy. We hope fervently, however, that this desirable action is but a step in the restoration of full rights as citizens of the United States.

We respectfully request that other civil rights which have been taken from us during the past two years be restored to us as soon as possible. Please give us some incentive for which to fight. We list some of these deprivations in the hope that you may assist us in obliterating discriminations now perpetrated upon us. . . .

They wanted to be free to join any branch of the service, such as the Air Corps, believing that it is "undemocratic to use color or ancestry as a basis for such segregation"; the right to work in war industries; the right to travel in every state as free citizens; and reparations for the losses of their businesses, homes, and injustices.

Mr. President, we will faithfully serve our country, the United States of America, but we firmly believe that the return of our civil rights should be simultaneous with the return of the Selective Service. . . . We believe that the cause of democracy and the winning of the war will be advanced by the elimination of all discrimination based upon race, color or creed. We know that you have been interested in the problems of minorities and have watched our plight, even though you are busy with domestic problems and global war. We have faith that you will understand the justice of this plea, and will grant us equality with other citizens of our native land.

This letter was unanimously adopted at a meeting of one thousand evacuated citizens of draft age incarcerated in Poston.

In February, Louise wrote to Miss Breed that everyone in Poston was talking about the draft and reclassification. Parents were naturally worried, and the morale in the camp was low. A few months later the draft situation became even tenser:

July 14, 1944
Dear Miss Breed,
Speaking of the draft problem—quite a number of boys are being called for the army and together with the relocation this camp is slowly becoming empty. There are quite a number of boys refusing to appear for induction. I just can't imagine young boys just out of school being picked up by the F.B.I. and taken to jail. It just doesn't seem right. For the boys, I know, it is a very delicate problem but I would much rather see them go into the army instead of to jail. I think it is a pity to see such fine young sturdy boys fresh out of high school not yet knowing what life really is being put behind bars separated from the rest of the world. Maybe I am too Americanized to see their view point but on the other hand I know I should respect them for their decision and determination to carry out what they believe should be.

Please give my very best regards to Miss McNary and do write when time permits. I just love to hear about your work and the library, the rapidly changing San Diego—your letters are so full of interesting things.
Most respectfully,
Louise Ogawa

SAN DIEGO—A WOMEN'S TOWN

During the winter Katherine was surprised to see an article in the *San Diego Union* all about women and the way the city had changed. Any news of San Diego was a treat to Katherine. She wrote to Miss Breed:

In the Feb. "Pic" magazine, there were some pictures of San Diego. Mostly were women though, because the title was: San Diego—A Women's Town. I saw one picture of a lady that must have been a Yellow Cab driver. Her cap showed that. Another lady had a "Qaulitee" cap, and had a basket of milk bottles.

Katherine would have been surprised because before the war most women did not work outside their homes. Those who did worked as schoolteachers, librarians, secretaries, nurses, and salesladies. But when the war began, with so many men off to war, women were needed on the assembly lines to make ammunition, planes, tanks, and ships. The San Diego Electric Railway Company also had a serious shortage of drivers. After male employees left to fight in the armed forces, the company began to hire women drivers.

Prewar San Diego had been a sleepy little "border town" with a warm climate that attracted folks who were retired and wanted to spend their days in sunny California. The war made it a boomtown. Between 1943 and 1944, the population reached almost five hundred thousand. At one point three thousand houses went up in two hundred days! San Diego was bursting at the seams. There were shortages of housing, schools, and transportation. The libraries' facilities were being overtaxed as well.

Clara Breed was busier than ever trying to reach all the children in trailer parks and crowded housing units that were hastily built for factory workers and the military. She not only set up small libraries in these areas; she also went out and read stories to the children. To save gas and tires, which were rationed, Clara, like so many San Diegans, traveled more often on streetcars jammed with soldiers, sailors, and factory workers. Clara could not help but notice that there were more people in uniforms than people in civilian clothes like herself.

In February, when Miss Plaister, the head librarian in San Diego, took ill, Clara's extra responsibilities meant she was carrying the workload of two people. Busy as she was, Clara still made time to write and send books along with occasional treats to Poston. Her rewards came in the return mail. In mid-March, Clara was relieved to hear that Katherine was back in school. But she was having some pretty typical troubles:

3/16/44

Dear Miss Breed,

How will I do it? Do what? Why, thank you, of course. For what? For the simply splendid books, naturally. Every single one is almost as dear as you are, but not quite. But for books, they're the best ever.

Well, I haven't even started my book yet, but I wrote a few articles and children's short stories. I figure that's better than just coming out and write a book, all of a sudden.

Miss Breed, did you ever have trouble in the 6th grade? But I guess mine are pretty silly. My worst are the boy's in our class. I never saw such roughnecks—and I'm sure out teacher hasn't either.

My other trouble is the blackboard. Every time I'm asked to write in front of the class, I get the jitters. Making a report is much easier. . . .

The girls in our room have started a club called the Dramatic Damsels—Dee Dee. We have appointed different committees, and I was chosen for one of the play writers. That's quite an honor.

I had an idea for a play, but it was a perfectly impossible one. Three reasons make it very hard for me to think. It has to be our own, it has to be about Norway, Sweden, or Denmark, and I was absent for so long that I didn't get much information on either of those countries. But I'm determined to write a play. I just feel like writing.

I'm pretty proud of my library record. The one at the school doesn't have any blotches, and the public library has only one over-due mark. Of course, there are a few who don't have any over-dues . . . but they all lost at least one card. And I'm already on my third one.

Pen Pals are lot's of fun. I have 20 right now, and every single one is swell. Especially our club. There are 3 others besides me. I feel flattered that I was asked to join, and I happen to be the youngest one—also the silliest.

I've run out of news now, so will close. But not without thanking you again for the books.

Love,

Katherine

A LAST LETTER FROM POSTON

Two years after leaving San Diego, Fusa and her mother were about to leave Poston. After many letters back and forth between her father and her sister and brother, the decision about what Fusa would do was finally made. Her mother was to join her father in Crystal City, Texas, where Fusa would visit briefly, and then go on to her sister, who was in Minneapolis. By 1944, the WRA was eager to send as many people as possible out of the camps if they had a guaranteed place to go and a job. The government gave single people a ticket to their destination and twenty-five dollars in cash—exactly the same amount that was given to criminals after they served time in prison.

With little more than a train or bus ticket and twenty-five dollars, Nikkei faced the uncertainty of having to rebuild their lives. How would they be treated on the outside? What kinds of jobs and homes would they find? For many, leaving was as unsettling as their arrival had been.

April 5, 1944

Dear Miss Breed,

This will probably be my last letter written to you from the fair city of Poston, Arizona. When I think of the good times (and some miserable times) I've spent in Poston I feel sort of sad, yet glad to be on my way. . . . The house looks very bare except for one corner, which has piles of crated boxes. No one seems to know how we've accumulated so much junk in two years!

My mother will probably be happy and greatly relieved to be with father. I'm quite anxious to see him, too, as it is now almost 2 1/2 years since we last saw him. I imagine that he hasn't changed very much in the two years, but I think he'll probably be surprised at how grown up I've become (or have I?)

Crystal City, according to various letters we received, is a very wonderful place. It is quite an improvement over Poston. The buildings are white (not this black tar paper), each family cooks for themself, have a shower in each barrack to be shared by the families occupying the barrack, well furnished, and nice canteen. So much is allowed per person per day for food and this amount is given them in certain coins only good at the local store, and they tell us food is ample. I shall tell you about my experience there after I have left, as we are limited to send out only 2 censored letters a week.—Must admit Crystal City does have its bad point, too!

There is only one thing I regret—that is your being unable to visit Poston while I was here. . . .

. . . . This will be all for now and thanks a million for everything you've done for us in S.D., S.A., and P, A.

Sincerely,

Fusa

When Fusa arrived at her sister's home in Minneapolis, a letter was waiting from Miss Breed. Happy as Fusa felt to be outside, there's no doubt that she was just a bit homesick for good old San Diego. She wrote that she missed her parents "more than I realized or thought I would. These waves come over me every once in a while, but am slowly getting used to living without them. . . ."

Fusa started working in a department store—not as a saleslady but in the mail-order department. It was "monotonous" work, she told Miss Breed, but the people were nice. Fusa also worked that summer on improving her typing speed and accuracy, hoping to attend business school in the fall.

At last, her life was not on hold! For Fusa a new chapter had begun.

"THE PAST, FOREVER GONE; THE FUTURE STILL OUR OWN": CLASS OF 1944

When graduation rolled around that spring, Tets went to the commencement exercises:

June 10, 1944
Dear Miss Breed,
Six years ago today I graduated from San Diego High School—Tonight the first graduating class of Parker Valley High School marched into the partially constructed school auditorium and received their diplomas. They looked splendid in their caps and gowns. The boys were in blue and the girls, in white. Incidently that is the school color combination

Through the relentless efforts of Poston III's school principal, Miss Cushman, and the faculty, Poston III High School this spring became an accredited high school and the name was changed to Parker Valley High School. Poston I and II High Schools are as yet unaccredited. If I am not mistaken I believe Parker Valley High School is the only relocation center high school that has been so honored.

Fusa Tsumagari, above, had to carry this photo ID when she left camp. It said where she was coming from and where she was going, and even had her fingerprints on the other side.

It is magnificent the way the students have striven for higher education. The first year here found them in make-shift barrack classrooms. When construction of the school began the whole community volunteered in making adobe bricks for the school buildings. Even school children helped so that school could open in time for the fall semester of 1943–1944. Yes, the students can rightfully be proud to say "It's my school" for they built it with sweat and toil during the hot summer days that Poston is noted for.

Just a few rambling comments on the graduation ceremony. The class gift was a beautiful American flag. Instead of a vocal selection there was a piano solo by Elain Hibi a very talented pianist from San Diego. I believe this is the first American high school graduation ceremony to have a Buddhist blessing. The class motto: The past, forever gone; the future still our own. There were nine honor students. I didn't get all their names but I did catch one and the name is Aiko Kubo (remember her?)

Miss Breed surely wrote to congratulate Aiko on being an honor student. This is Aiko's reply:

June 20, 1944

Dear Miss Breed,

I just received your lovely note a few minutes ago and would like to take this opportunity to thank you for what you have done, not only for me, but for all of us in Poston. Words cannot express how we feel about you and several others whom the war has not affected in your attitude toward us.

Recently, I applied for college entrance to Hamline University in Saint Paul, Minnesota through the National Japanese American Student Relocation Council. However, I don't know whether I can get in or not, since the quota may have already been reached. I certainly hope not!

Both Shizuye and Yoshiko [her sisters] were married last year, so the house is quite empty now. However, Irene makes enough noise to make up for their absence. I imagine you'd be surprised to see her now—she's almost as tall as I am, and lankier. My brother, George, is hardly ever home, as he spends his time roaming around the camp with his own "gang."

I'm enclosing a snapshot of myself which was taken by a visiting serviceman— (cameras not being allowed on the project for civilian use). Incidentally, all the boys in camp are being inducted into the army every week. Some who volunteered are already overseas and taking active part in the invasion. I'm sure they have quite a lot to fight for!!

I shall end this letter with a "thank you" from the very bottom of my heart.
Sincerely,
Aiko Kubo

The happiness of graduation and her plans for college were soon forgotten. Unfortunately, Aiko became ill not long after graduation. She spent six long months in the Poston hospital recuperating.

The problem of George (also known as Kaizo) not being at home was a common complaint. Teenagers no longer ate with the family but tended to spend their free time with friends. The division between young and old became more and more difficult. Many Nisei told me that language was a barrier, since their parents did not speak English and they spoke only broken Japanese. More than once I was told, "I never could have a real 'heart-to-heart' talk or an in-depth discussion about anything with my parents."

Aiko's brother, Kaizo, expressed it this way:

Our family, like most Japanese families prior to evacuation, was very close. Today, after these years of communal living, I find myself stumbling over words as I make vain attempts to talk to my father. I don't understand him; he doesn't understand me. It is a strange feeling to find such a barrier between my father and myself.

For many, such barriers became permanent. Even if they had not been incarcerated, a generation gap would have existed between the Issei and Nisei. Immigrant parents and their children (not just Issei and Nisei) often struggle over the clash between old ways and new. But life inside the camps made matters worse. Many Issei fathers were imprisoned elsewhere, and even those who were in relocation centers suffered a loss of authority with their teenage children. Even the schools played a role in dividing the generations. One of the objectives of the school and the War Relocation Authority was to further Americanize the Nisei and Sansei to prepare them for life after camp. Adult education classes were also offered to teach English to the older generation. However, the Issei held on to old traditions, and the Nisei wanted no part of the past or customs they considered too "Japanesy." *Ojigi*, their parents' custom of bowing between friends, embarrassed the children. The Nisei wanted no part of arranged marriages, their elders' language, or their food. The Nisei were 100 percent Americans! At least, that was their dream.

CHAPTER TWELVE

"COURAGE BELONGS TO NO ONE RACE"

I REMEMBER QUITE VIVIDLY HOW I spent my last furlough before our regiment went overseas . . . I went to see my family . . . I was two weeks locked up once more behind barbed wire in spite of my uniform. I am sure you can appreciate the irony of that. . . .

—Testimony of **THOMAS KINAGO**, Los Angeles, August 5, 1981

In the Japanese Americans' letters to Miss Breed, the war itself was seldom mentioned—except for the hope that peace would come soon. In fact, both Tets and Fusa complained that people inside the camps felt cut off from the war, except for the steady return of young soldiers. After they finished their basic training, Nisei GIs came back to see their families before they shipped out. Its Endo thought it ironic that these young men who were serving their country should have to spend what might be their last hours with family inside a camp as prisoners.

Before the war one of my brothers was already drafted—at that time he was in Texas. After we're in camp, he came to visit and then went to Georgia, where he was guarding a German POW camp. He was on the outside of the camp with a rifle walking the perimeter of their camp and we were on the inside of an internment camp in Arizona.

Those with sons, brothers, husbands, and fathers in the army did their best to follow the news of the Allied invasion of France that was anticipated by the press and radio newscasters. Like families all over the country, the Japanese Americans put small banners with blue stars in their windows, one star for each son in the service. Walls of honor with the names of those who were serving were built in every camp. Although no relatives of Miss Breed's correspondents were killed, many families in Poston did lose loved ones. Many more suffered serious injuries, especially during the bloody weeks that began with the invasion of Europe on D-day, June 6, 1944.

Its Endo had a brother who went to Italy to fight with the 442nd. Its still recalls the fearful moment when they expected the worst had happened:

I remember when the telegram came—my older sister got it—she was the senior member of the family then—so she read the message to my mother.... "He's alive, you know!" And that was it—the telegram did not say where he was wounded—but he was alive! He was with the 442nd, 100th Battalion.

A hand grenade came in and ripped him—it got his leg and foot—but he lived—with shrapnel that cut his heel. He got a "million dollar wound"—that means he lived without much disfigurement.

A few days later, Tets wrote to Miss Breed that he had been feeling down in the dumps. He had been hoping to work as a barber in an army camp in Minnesota. But once again he was rejected. The doctor said Tets's arm was in a dubious state. He felt so low he "could have walked under a snake's belly!" until he heard the news of the invasion:

June 10, 1944
Yes ma'am I really began to feel sorry for myself but bad. Then I read some articles in the Pacific Citizen, *the JACL newspaper. It told of the heroic deeds of the nisei soldiers, of the hardships they suffered.—I woke up. What I am going thru is nothing compared to the fighting man on the front.*

How did San Diego take the news of the invasion? I didn't know about it for two days . . . I thought it was a rumor around camp. You see I hadn't seen a newspaper in weeks and our radio doesn't work until the early hours of the morning at which time I am usually asleep. Most of the people here in camp were like me—we just didn't know about it, and when people told us we took it more as a rumor. The pro-axis elements went about predicting dire prospects for the allied armies. The "loyalists" can't say much because they don't know any more than what is broadcast over the radio, whereas the "pro-axis" could make up any cock-and-bull story.

Sincerely
Ted

It is hard to know whom Tets is referring to as "pro-Axis." Those who had signed "No-No" had been moved to Tule Lake in 1943. But after the draft was reinstated in 1944, anger created a new group of "loyalists" among both Issei and Nisei.

That summer, stories about the valor of Nisei soldiers ran in many national magazines. This one is from the August 5, 1944, edition of *Collier's*:

GI JAPYANK

Mac Yazawa, a Nisei soldier, says . . . "We weren't like Japanese and German troops who fight only because they were sent somewhere and made to. We knew what we were fighting for—for our country and our homes and families, just like any other American boy. We fought a little harder because we were anxious to let people know we were good Americans, so our families would be better thought of and better treated back home."

FROM BANISH TO VANISH!

Before they left the camps, the Nikkei were given all sorts of advice. First and foremost, they were urged to avoid re-creating tight-knit communities, as they had done in the past. By "scattering" the Nikkei into communities all over the Midwest and East, the War Relocation Authority hoped they would be less visible and vanish into the fabric of American life. In many ways the plan worked. The prewar "Japantown" ghettos were gone. Although they had never been anything but loyal Americans, the fact that they had been incarcerated cast a shadow of suspicion over their loyalty. For many Nisei and Sansei the push for assimilation destroyed much of the pride in their heritage they had managed to hold on to.

For me it meant speaking English only, no Japanese. . . . It meant learning little about Japanese art, language, culture, traditions; learning that I am an American no different than anyone else.

But living it was different. After the questions of who are you, I would answer: "I am an American." But they would insist, "No, really, what are you?" And, at times out of the corner of my eye I could see them pulling up their eyes slanty, making buck teeth, and talking nonsense, and then I began to wonder, American? Japanese? Or what? And, I wished I was different. I wished I had blond hair, round eyes. Yes, at times I wished I wasn't Japanese American. Is that what being an American is all about? Is this how we survive in this society? . . . I was denying my own identity feeling inferior, second class and wishing I was someone else.
—Testimony of **DONNA KOTAKE**, San Francisco, August 11, 1981

I remembered feeling bad about being Japanese, of being even able to speak Japanese, of having Japanese parents. I felt ashamed because I loved my parents. I also loved America. I get goose bumps when I sing the Star Spangled Banner. I believed what our teachers taught about what a great country America is.

[Years later] I tried to understand why so many Americans, Japanese and otherwise were able to justify, rationalize and deny the injustice and destructiveness of the whole event. I have come to the realization that we lulled ourselves into believing the propaganda of the 1940s so that we could maintain our idealized image of a benevolent protective Uncle Sam. We were told that this was a patriotic sacrifice necessary for national security. The pain, trauma, stress of the incarceration experience was so overwhelming we used the psychological defense mechanism of repression, denial, and rationalization to keep us from facing the truth . . . that America was being racist and unfair . . . On the surface we do not look like former concentration camp victims, but we are still vulnerable. Our scars are permanent and deep.—Testimony of **AMY IWASAKI MASS**, Los Angeles, August 6, 1981

All through the long hot summer as the war continued, Louise pleaded with her parents to let her leave. She had hopes they would get so tired of her arguing that they would shoo her out of Poston. Her last letter from Poston is dated July 14, and her next letter to Miss Breed came from Chicago in late October:

October 28, 1944

Dear Miss Breed,

Yes, Chicago is certainly a large city. It seems like a world all by itself! It's a wonderful feeling to be able to walk the streets side by side with all creeds of people again! I never dreamed I would ever relocate but here I am. I know I shall gain much through my experiences in Poston and here in Chicago.

I am rooming with two girl friends. Kikuye Kawamoto, one of the twins, and I came out to Chicago together. Another girl friend formerly from Visalia, California is staying with us. We share a four room apartment. It's very nice. The location is very convenient for the Jackson bus stops right in front of our apt. It takes us a good 30 minutes to get to our place of employment. We transfer twice on the streetcar. We, Kikuye and I, are employed at A.C. McClury & Co. We are doing office work. Kikuye works in the Library Division and I in the Correspondence Dept. We like our work very much.

The business center of Chicago, "the loop" certainly is a busy section isn't it. After going in and out of several stores, we often lose our sense of direction. We found apt. hunting very difficult. It was like hunting for a needle in the hay stack. We looked for one week continuously before one was found.

We haven't done much in the way of entertainment or sight seeing for we are more interested in getting settled at our new home. Some friends have come visiting but as yet we have not gone. Have you heard from Hisako Watanabe? She relocated to Cleveland, Ohio about two weeks before I did. She is at present doing domestic work.

My Day ... May 19, 1943 ...

Many people all over this country must be reading the casualty lists with great anxiety these days. There is one thing which impresses me each time I go through them. I have always known it, but it is something good to bear in mind. There are the names of the men who have given all they had to give for the country in which you and I live, and the names—why, they are Russian, British, German, French, Dutch, Jewish, Czech, Hungarian, Chinese, Italian, Irish, Japanese, Norwegian, Swedish, and from all the rest of the nations of the world!

As you read the stories of heroic deeds, you find again that whether it is Meyer Levin or Jimmy Doolittle, the name, the race, the religion does not seem to make any difference. Courage belongs to no one race or no one religion, but it does seem to be in all our boys, for where one is recognized a hundred go unnoticed. We can take pride in all these young Americans, and if any of us ever had any prejudices we can beat them down and hide them away, shamed by the mute testimony of the names on our casualty lists.

Margaret Ishino is still in Poston. After living like sisters since we were knee-high, I certainly miss her. I hope she will be able to relocate soon too!

Chicago certainly is a windy city. It's quite chilly here. I think I'm going to like the winter. I never have lived in a place where it snowed so it will be quite an experience. This will be my first white Christmas. I imagine everything will be just like a picture. My, I am looking far into the future!

My, how time seems to fly!! Before I know it, it will be morning. I hope this letter finds you in the very best of health! May I hear from you at your leisure! I do miss your letters, Miss Breed!

Most respectfully,
Louise Ogawa

It was not unusual to have trouble finding housing. When Japanese Americans tried renting rooms they ran into comments such as "My son was killed by the Japs, and I don't want you in my house," or, "I don't object, but others won't tolerate it." There were others who were understanding, however, and even helpful.

Being outside was exciting, but it had its lonely moments, too.

Remembrance

You are alone in a strange distant city, far removed from home and friends and things familiar. You feel utterly lost and forgotten as you lean back in your chair to ease a mind weary from study, you cannot help but remember . . . a face that smiled, a simple gesture of friendship, a spoken word. . . . they are all there before you.

You remember the bleak, barren hills far away, the scrubby mesquite trees beyond the firebreaks, the patches of blackened, cindered earth and the sunken craters where trees had been felled and burned; you remember the monotonous rows of barracks, the unpainted wood becoming bleached and shabby under the withering blasts of the hot sun; you remember the fuzzy, orange glow of the street lights, at night, cutting . . . cones out of the darkness; you remember the big cold slab of a yellow moon as it came bounding up and went riding high, the stars in the sky shining bravely, and the puffs of clouds as they slid over the face of the moon turning gold and buttery-like.

You remember these things, but you remember more so the people who are there. You remember them for the unconquerable will with which they are seeking to understand and to embrace a situation for which no honest justification is

Finding housing was no small issue. Many started out in hostels sponsored by religious groups. Kenny Murase (far left), who wrote "Remembrance," found lodging in a cooperative house in Philadelphia, where a mixed group of young people lived together sharing household tasks.

possible. You remember them for their spirit which refuses to be broken, and for the savage tenacity with which they cling to visions of a better day and a better order. You remember them for the imperishable, courage with which they face and master endless adversities of each day of living. . . .

And so you lean back in your chair to ease your tired mind and you find that you cannot help but remember, always.—**KENNY MURASE**

While there was exhilaration in leaving the barbed wired world of Poston behind, there was also genuine loneliness for family and friends left behind. Much as the Nisei had dreamed of freedom, few had been prepared for such independence and its demands. Before the war, young Japanese American women might have attended college, but often they would have lived at home or in a dormitory where there were adult "house mothers" in charge. College girls were known as "coeds," but their social lives were restricted. College dorms had fences around them and strict curfew hours. No young men were allowed past the front desk of the coeds' dormitory. Typically young women married early and moved from their father's house to their husband's house. Suddenly young women such as Louise, Fusa, Chiyo, and Margaret had to find jobs and create a social world without their elders:

> I was the first one in my family to leave. . . . I can always remember my father saying you're going out there and you're on your own, I will not be able to help you anymore. . . . I went with forty dollars in my pocketbook and sat up all night guarding that forty dollars. That's all I had in the world. —MARIAN MUTO

Young men who were waiting to be called for the army often took jobs that called for more brawn than brains. Finding a job and earning their own way became their responsibility. They put up with difficult work and housing conditions with the hope of saving money to send for their families. Many were surprised to discover how much they missed the parents and customs they had been so eager to leave.

THE LOST BATTALION

When school reopened in fall 1944, there were fewer students than ever in Poston. More and more barracks were empty, and those left behind were old people and families with school-age children. For Babe Karasawa, now sixteen years old, October brought a great adventure. Miss Cushman found an opening for Babe at a fine boarding school located in Illinois. Babe was offered the Orson Welles Scholarship, established by the famous actor, who had attended the same school. For Babe it meant giving up being president of the student body, but it was worth it:

> I left Poston October 3, 1944, to Woodstock, Illinois, to finish high school—my senior year. When I left, one of our teachers, the public-speaking teacher, Miss Ellis, who had just graduated from the University of Illinois, said, "Babe, you are going to the best prep school in the state of Illinois!"
>
> It was perfect for me! There were two of us—the other kid came from Topaz —and we were able to go to the Todd School for Boys. My folks worked in the school and I worked in the kitchen.

It was a prep school for rich kids. Grades 1–12. I even have a copy of the letter that says my scholarship was for $1,200! That was a lot of money in 1944! They treated me so nicely. Even in the town, a town of 2,500 people . . . when I walked into the town square, everyone was watching me. They saw me face to face—everyone had a smile. I didn't run into any animosity.

But as Babe told me about how thrilled he was with his new school, his mood shifted. He remembered that his happiness was tempered by sad news from the war front that came in that same month.

In northern France, in a mountainous wooded area, not far from the German border, a battalion from the Thirty-sixth Texas Division was totally surrounded by German soldiers. The 442nd Regimental Combat Team was ordered to go in and rescue the "Lost Battalion." What followed was one of the bloodiest battles of the war. The 442nd lost two hundred men killed in action, and eight hundred more suffered injuries as they rescued two hundred Texans. Their courageous story was reported in newspapers and magazines all across the country.

Babe read about those who were wounded and killed in the camp newspapers that he received in his new school. In fact, the school newspaper had a regular feature that carried letters from those who had left Poston. As I was leafing through these old mimeographed papers, I found this:

Oct 13, 1944

Dear Friends,

Whatta ya say? It's been quite a while since I last saw you all and I really miss seeing you. Everything up here is okay so far (I haven't received grades yet!!!) I hope all is okay in good ol' Parker Valley Hi.

The people here in Woodstock are really swell, regular guys (except when it comes to intellect!! What brains!!!) They like to fool around quite a bit too—that is in class and out. The teachers take quite a bit of something from these guys. And some of the wisecracks slay me!!! Really sharp!

They love sports. Todd is defending champion of the football league and is headed for another crown. What's happening to football in Poston (Hope the HiTimes *can answer that for me)?*

I'm taking college algebra (trig or solid's come next semester), physics, European History (They have real discussions in there . . . their English usage is tops,) and English and Lit IV (I'm in that class now. We write letters every Monday).

I'm going out for football today. I didn't know whether I should or not, because of my studies. The coach made up my mind this morning.

Well, I've said enough. I just wanted you to know that I haven't forgotten you and never will. After I left Poston, I realized a great deal more than before how much it meant to me.

Well take it slow, you guys and gals.

Very Sincerely,

Babe Karasawa

The letters from former Postonians who were on the outside were intended to assure those inside that the world was a safe place. But, of course, few wrote back about problems they were running into, although many people did encounter some less than friendly people:

I remember in particular a high school teacher in Detroit, who was relentless in presenting her version of the Second World War in our history class. She would make such statements . . . those Japs bombed Pearl Harbor, they were sneaky, you can't trust any one. Those Japs can only imitate, they could only produce junk toys. The dialogue went on daily.

. . . many Japanese Americans such as myself felt the way to prevent such devastating occurrences from happening in the future was to become 100 percent American . . . to lose the Japaneseness that we felt was partially responsible for getting us in trouble. We spoke American, ate and cooked American food and associated in the main with non-Japanese.

In fact part of the fantasy was that if our children didn't look Japanese, perhaps they would somehow escape the consequences of racism, which we had to face. . . .

I learned that reject[ion] by one's country can be one of the most painful rejections and have serious psychological consequences.

—Testimony of **BEBE RESCHKE**, Los Angeles, August 6, 1981

That fall still more of Miss Breed's young friends left Poston. Hisako Watanabe was trying to decide if she would go to Cleveland, Chicago, or New York. Her brothers

William and Richard were headed for Cleveland, now that Richard no longer needed crutches. Jack was so big, Hisako doubted Miss Breed would recognize him! It's not clear when he and Hisako's parents would leave Poston. For families with school-age kids Poston seemed like as safe a place as any.

Maryann Mahaffey, a teacher at Poston, got permission to take several girls into Parker. For each of them, it was the first time in three years that they had left the camp. Some were only four years old when they came to Poston. So they had never seen cement sidewalks or store counters with merchandise. They bought their first ice-cream cones that day! But they were given cold and suspicious looks from townspeople.

Miss Mahaffey started a "teen canteen" where teenagers could talk about their fears of racism outside—but, she said, "they wanted to go out" and be "normal American teen-agers."

My friend Ellen Yukawa's father refused to be rushed:

> We were in Poston from '42–'45—three and a half years. My dad always said, "They put me in here—they're going to have to kick me out!" The camp was getting emptier and emptier. I remember my mom saying, "Well, when are we going to leave?" And my dad said, "When they close the place." And that's exactly what happened. I think he felt that way because he was put in there against his will and by G-d they'll have to kick him out. I guess that's the way my dad felt. He still had the property in Delano, but he didn't want to go back there because anti-Japanese feelings were so bad in California. His friends who went back early had difficulty with prejudice.

CALIFORNIA OPENS ITS GOLDEN GATES

In the spring of 1944, California was still off-limits to Japanese Americans. However, those who remained in Poston were asked if they wanted to return to California or not. Some thought that when the war was over, things might be better. No names were given with their remarks, but typically the answer was "No!"

> —To hell with California. I've nothing to go back for. California can keep the damned state to themselves. The opening of the state means nothing to me.

> —Many of the evacuees are under the assumption that California is the only state in the union and do not quite realize that the union is composed of forty-seven

other states. I have been in the midwestern and eastern states and I find people residing in those areas more friendly and willing to accept the Nisei, in fact, quite helpful in lending a "hand."

—I am a fellow that will not be at any one place where it is known I am not wanted. . . . The question of California does not interest me in the least . . . the "hell" with them.

On the West Coast, public sentiment against the return of the Nikkei continued with vicious editorials and threats of bloodshed if they returned. While President Roosevelt still favored assimilation by relocating the Nikkei to many parts of the country, his secretary of the interior, Harold L. Ickes, advised that the West Coast could no longer be considered a possible military zone. There was no longer any real threat that the Japanese could attack the West Coast. Ickes (who had introduced Marian Anderson at the historic concert at the Lincoln Memorial) believed that the exclusion of American citizens of Japanese ancestry from the West Coast was unconstitutional. He warned that American POWs might suffer reprisals at the hands of their Japanese captors. He also cautioned that if the Nikkei were considered too dangerous for California, people in the Midwest and East would not want them, either.

The government also knew that the Supreme Court was about to rule on two Japanese American cases that had been pending in the courts for two years. One was brought by Fred T. Korematsu, a Nisei who was convicted for not reporting for relocation in 1942. After his arrest by the FBI, Korematsu brought a lawsuit charging it was unconstitutional for the government to incarcerate a citizen on the basis of his race. Another lawsuit was brought by Mitsuye Endo, a young Nisei woman with two brothers in the U.S. Army when she was incarcerated in the Tanforan Assembly Center. Her lawyer advised her that they would file a petition for a writ of *habeas corpus**, asking that she be discharged and restored to liberty as soon as she was shipped to a relocation center.

---

*In Latin, *habeas corpus* means literally "you may have the body." The object of a writ of habeas corpus is to bring a prisoner "the body" before the court to inquire into the cause of the person's imprisonment or detention. People cannot be held without cause. According to law, a writ of habeas corpus protects citizens from illegal imprisonment and protects their right to personal liberty.

On December 18, 1944, the Supreme Court held that Korematsu's conviction was legal and that the government had the right in time of war to remove Japanese Americans from a military area. At the same time, Mitsuye Endo won her case, *Ex parte Endo* (323 US 283). The court held that the War Relocation Authority had no right to hold a loyal citizen who was no longer in a military area and deny her constitutional rights, including that which allows citizens to move from one state to another. Justice Frank Murphy put it eloquently when he wrote: ". . . racial discrimination of this nature bears no reasonable relation to military necessity and is utterly foreign to the ideals and traditions of the American people."

On December 17, 1944, a day before the Supreme Court decisions were announced, the government ended the mass exclusion of Japanese Americans from the West Coast. On the eighteenth, the WRA announced that all centers under its jurisdiction were to be closed within six to twelve months. Up and down the Pacific coast the news incited racist hostilities. Newspapers and hate mongers on the West Coast threatened "wholesale bloodshed and violence." Elsie Robinson, a Hearst reporter, wrote that she would "'cut the throat' of any evacuee who dared to return. . . ."

For those still behind barbed wire, the news that the camps would soon close and they could return to California was not greeted with great joy. Tets's letter reflects how unsettled he felt about the prospect of going out into a hostile world:

Dec. 20, 1944

Dear Miss Breed,

Thanks very much for your Christmas package. I am saving it for Christmas so I can have the thrill of opening it on that day.

The big news here is the lifting of the mass exclusion act for persons of Japanese Ancestry. Everything for leave processing has not been clarified as yet. All this rather has me all up in the air. I haven't been able to think much about it. The suddenness and the magnitude of the problem took me by surprise.

Christmas here in Poston will be one of Thanksgiving. However there are many who look with misgiving toward the new year with the prospect of the closing of the centers next year. They have nothing to start anew on the outside.

A Merry Christmas to you and your mother from dad and me.

Sincerely,

Ted

That December, Miss Breed had been hoping to visit Louise in Chicago, but once again, this trip was not to be. Since we don't have Miss Breed's letters, we can only guess that the demands of her job and difficulty in making travel arrangements during the war caused her to cancel her plans. Clara was surely anticipating the end of the exclusion act and wondering if her children, now almost all grown-up, and their families would choose to return to California. But the attacks in the press were not lost on those who followed the news. Louise wrote that she hoped they would meet again soon. But as for returning to California, she had fears of her own:

December 3, 1944

Dear Miss Breed,

Yes, I have heard people [are] returning to California. I am so happy that we are being accepted again in our cities where we spen[t] much of our happy moments. I too would like to go to San Diego and yet hesitate. With public sentiment as it is, I think it might be best to start life anew in a new community. Making wonderful friends like you, I know will take time for we must first prove to them ourselves. Life would be so wonderful if all this hatred and racial discrimination was abolished from the earth. But I believe the war has taught all of us a great deal. I know it has for me. I have come to appreciate so many things that I have taken for granted before the war. My new life here in this vast Chicago, making my own living, depending on myself is something I never dreamed would happen. But it has and in a way I am glad for through my experiences I shall gain much and become that much wiser through my hardships.

This Thanksgiving I enjoyed snow for the first time in my life. It was really a sight to see the housetops covered with white snow. It was just like a picture you see on Xmas cards. But staying in a nice heated apartment takes you away from the icy wind and snow. We have a very nice furnished apt. We all have loads of fun cooking and keeping house. We all do the cooking—taking turns. As yet no one has fallen ill through each others experiments which we are proud of.

Thank you for the advice about isolating myself. I would like to go out and meet people too. Yes, McClurys is a very large firm with many nisei's as their employees. I have not heard of any clubs organized by the co.

It certainly was a surprise to hear Hisako's brothers are relocating. Her oldest brother has recovered though he has a limp. I imagine it will be difficult at first for him walking about but with a car it will be much easier.

. . . I often stop at a florists and gaze at the beautiful flowers in the window! I certainly miss feeling the solid ground with my hands! Well, we can't have everything and I think I have quite a bit!

Respectfully,

Louise

It's hard to know if Louise knew by then that Hisako Watanabe and one of her brothers were going to be more than friends to her in the not-too-distant future. But for now, Chicago remained an exciting and liberating experience.

For Fusa, California was about the last thing on her mind. She had lots of happy news to share from Minneapolis:

January 14th

Dear Miss Breed,

Thank you ever so much for your lovely card and hankie. I don't know how to apologize for not sending you a Christmas card or greetings. I left most of my Christmas shopping to the last minute and then three days before Christmas that nasty cold caught up with me and put me into bed. That is my sad sad story. However, there was a bright side to Christmas—my brother came from Milwaukee to visit us.

We're all very proud of him, and we're certainly glad to see him. He has now graduated from Marquette, and at the present time is trying his hardest to get into Med School there. He was indeed lucky to be asked to join an honorary Biology fraternity—I've forgotten the name. It seems that Nisei's are not accepted at Marquette Med School, but my brother feels that he may be able to break the ice. At least he is trying—we will know in about three or four weeks definitly whether or not he will be accepted.

I should like to tell you some very pleasant news—my sister and Bill are going to have a blessed event some time in May or June. We're all very happy in anticipation—but I think Bill is most excited. My mother is planning to come out in May, which we are eagerly anticipating. Incidentally, my father wrote that at the Canteen raffle in Crystal City my mother won a suitcase and is planning to come up with it. It makes a very good prize, doesn't it? The way my [father] wrote it was so cute it makes me laugh just thinking about it.

Last Friday night my girlfriend gave me one of these so called home permanents. All her previous ones were successful—but mine was an utter flop! When we rinsed it—it was absolutely straight! It makes me laugh just to think about it! I'll have to make an appointment at some beauty shop and get a genuine one. This will cost me more money in the long run!

The news of being able to go back to California has been accepted with mingled feeling. First of all we're more than glad that the ban has been lifted, as it rightfully should be. Those with property are wanting to go back, but wondering how the sentiment will be. Of course we know that good friends like you would be glad to have us back but others who do not know us or understand us may not be as glad to see us. As for us who are not so fortunate to have property in California— we're content to stay here for a while or maybe the rest of our life, but we'll make a point of seeing and visiting California later. My first ambition upon getting back to San Diego is to see you.

Well, this will be all for now. But may I wish you a happy New Year and hope you'll write when you have time.

Sincerely,

Fusa

Unlike Fusa and Louise, Katherine and her mom could hardly wait to return to San Diego. All through the long years they had never stopped thinking of San Diego as their home. In December 1944, Katherine wrote that there would be no schools at Poston after June 1945 and the camps were going to close in 1946. Almost a teenager, Katherine wrote that she was enjoying her home economics classes. She loved sewing aprons and blouses and skirts. But in cooking class she put too much salt in her cookies. She'd learn, she assured Miss Breed.

Katherine now had a little kitten that she found in music class. There were only six people left in her grade—but they made enough noise for three times as many! In her final tally, Katherine wrote that she now had seventy-five books and so many pen pals she had trouble keeping track of them all! She had counted all her letters and had 388! Before she left Poston she hoped to have 400. In a P.S. she told Miss Breed that she was saving the flower seeds she sent for the holiday. She planned to plant them when they got home—very soon!

Soon after the New Year, in February of 1945, Elizabeth's father, Reverend Kikuchi, and two other Nikkei leaders went to San Diego on a "scouting" mission. They visited San Diego for a week, hoping to discover how the Nikkei would be received if they were to return. Traveling by train from Arizona to California, they

Clara E. Breed served as City Librarian of the San Diego Public Library for twenty-five years. This photograph was (probably) taken after the new library was completed in 1954.

worried about rumors that had been spread to keep them from returning. In fact, in some communities there had been fires set and threats of violence directed to returning Nikkei and those who hired them.

While the Kikuchis waited for the reverend's return, Elizabeth's mother, Yoshiko, wrote a poignant poem that captures some of the uncertainty they faced. It was published in a Poston literary magazine:

> Should we go west to our old nest,
> Or should we go east to explore a new land,
> There may be a big storm tomorrow.

When Reverend Kikuchi returned to Poston he was optimistic and assured others that he had not encountered open hostility. He felt it safe to return and encouraged others to do so, too.

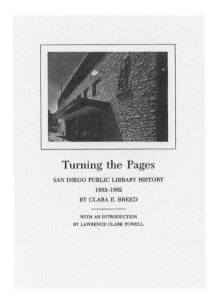

Turning the Pages

SAN DIEGO PUBLIC LIBRARY HISTORY
1882–1982
BY CLARA E. BREED

WITH AN INTRODUCTION
BY LAWRENCE CLARK POWELL

After retiring, Clara had time again for writing. In 1983, she wrote Turning the Pages, *a history of the San Diego Public Library. Her chapter about the war years includes a brief mention of the postcards and her "children."*

It is hard to know why there is only one letter to Miss Breed from 1945—the January 14 letter from Fusa about her brother's visit and the news that she was going to be an aunt. From the 1945 Parker Valley High School Yearbook it appears that the Kikuchi family stayed until the school year was over. So did Jack Watanabe, who was in seventh grade that year. Margaret Ishino was there for at least part of that year, and so was Aiko Kubo. Is it possible that Clara Breed was so busy she stopped writing to those who were still there? Not very likely. In fact, her book log shows that she sent books in early 1945. Yet there are no more letters. Perhaps they were misplaced and will turn up one day. But even without more letters from Poston, I had the use of newspaper articles, oral histories, interviews, and Clara Breed's book, *Turning the Pages*, a history of the San Diego Public Library, that helped me reconstruct what happened to Miss Breed and her friends after January 1945.

In the summer of 1945, Cornelia Plaister, the city librarian of the San Diego Public Library, became seriously ill. She was gone most of that summer. It was Miss Plaister who had hired Clara sixteen years earlier, and now, knowing that she was fatally ill, Miss Plaister selected Clara to be her successor. Clara worried about being up to the task, but Miss Plaister was confident Clara would be a capable leader. Every morning Clara went to the hospital and wrote down the names of all the people Miss Plaister wanted her to contact. Clara had never wanted to become an administrator. She wrote that Miss Plaister ". . . had the worst job in the whole library, fighting battles instead of having the fun of putting books and people together. But someone had to do it." Clara said that the "hardest thing she ever had to do was to call a meeting of the library supervisors and tell them I had been appointed. I dreaded it mainly because it would be an admission that Miss Plaister was fatally ill. . . ."

During that summer of 1945, when the war finally ended, the whole country celebrated. But Clara's joy was marred with sadness. Her good friend's health continued to fail. In October 1945, Clara became the acting librarian of the San Diego Public Library, a job she held until Miss Plaister died in February 1946. Two months later, Clara was appointed City Librarian of the San Diego Public Library, a position she filled for twenty-five years. Although many of Clara's "children" had left Poston for other cities, there were still many families left in camp. Clara wondered if any of them would return to San Diego and, if so, how soon she would see them.

CHAPTER THIRTEEN

"ON THE THRESHOLD OF FREEDOM"

HERE IS WHAT I SAY: there is no need to be bitter. . . . There is nothing to gain by eternally brooding for things that might have been. . . . Evacuation was a pioneering project; re-establishing myself into the American stream of life can be looked upon as another such enterprise. Now I stand on the threshold of freedom; I face the future unafraid, proud of my ancestry, but even prouder of my heritage as an American.

—**KAIZO KUBO**, Parker Valley High School senior

By the spring of 1945, there were not enough players left at Parker Valley High School to play baseball. Hundreds of people were leaving every week. Elizabeth recalls that her family left in June, and once again there were long, long lines, like the ones in Santa Anita, as people waited impatiently for their release cards. They were shoved, pushed, and packed onto one of many trucks jammed full of families heading to the train depot in Parker.

Elizabeth and her family returned to San Diego, where Reverend Kikuchi and his wife worked to help others get started again. He served as spiritual leader of the

Japanese Congregational Church of San Diego at 13th and J Streets. Liz told me that she did not see a lot of Miss Breed when she returned. Being a typical teenager, Liz was soon totally involved with her new life at San Diego High School. Her love of reading continued to grow and eventually led to her majoring in English at Berkeley. She taught at San Diego High School for three years. After college, Liz married Joe Yamada, who was by then a landscape architect. In fact, he was one of the designers of the world-famous SeaWorld. Together they raised a family and Liz worked with Joe in building a successful business. Liz's brother David became an architect and he designed Liz and Joe's beautiful house in the hills of La Jolla, California. Liz finally has the house of her dreams!

On September 12, 1945, those people still left in Poston III who wanted to return to San Diego boarded a special train that took them from Parker, Arizona, to San Diego. There are no passenger lists that tell us who was on that train. It's likely that this was the train that brought Katherine Tasaki and her mother, Jack Watanabe and his parents, Ben Segawa with some of his family, and Tets Hirasaki and his dad.

Fusa eventually moved to Chicago. When her parents were finally free to leave Texas, they moved to Chicago and opened a boardinghouse. Chiyo, Fusa's good friend, was so happy to be reunited with her and her family. Chiyo's own family was not in Chicago, so the Tsumagaris welcomed her and even helped her when she married.

Fusa finally attended secretarial school. She worked for a book-publishing firm, McGraw-Hill, and enjoyed the single life with her friends, known as the Gregory Shorthand Girls. In 1949, Fusa's dad was proud that he was the one who introduced her to a young man he called the "best catch" of the boardinghouse. After a one-year courtship, Fusa married Tom Higashioka, an engineer and recent college graduate.

In time, Fusa and Tom returned to San Mateo in California, where they raised their family. Tom established his own engineering consulting firm and Fusa worked with him as a bookkeeper. Fusa and Chiyo remained lifelong friends. Fusa's daughter, Patty, fondly remembers that when she was ten Miss Breed came to visit them. She brought along Fusa's samurai doll, one that Patty still treasures.

Many of the hobbies Fusa started in camp continued throughout her life. She liked to read, knit, sew, and do crossword puzzles, which Miss Breed always clipped from the newspapers and tucked into her letters to Fusa. She lived until February 11, 2000, long enough to see her first grandchild, Ryan. Her brother, Yukio, became a well-known doctor in Cheyenne, Wyoming. He ran a clinic and lived his whole life as a devoted doctor.

Margaret Ishino waited three months for clearance to leave Poston. Her father left for Seabrook Farms in New Jersey, while Margaret joined her older brother and his wife in Washington, D.C.: "We did not return from the concentration camp to San Diego right after the war. I worked for the Department of Labor and Community Chest and I also witnessed the 442nd when they were being honored by President Truman. It was pouring rain—I remember that. . . ."

On that very special day the 442nd Regimental Combat Team paraded on the White House lawn. They had the distinction of being the most decorated unit of their size and length of service in battle in U.S. military history. The "Go for Broke" GIs were also known as the "Purple Heart Battalion" and the "Christmas Tree Battalion" because they earned so many medals. That day Margaret saw them receive their seventh Presidential Unit Citation from Pres. Harry S. Truman. He saluted these courageous men with words they would never forget: "You fought not only the enemy, but you fought prejudice and won."

However, their battle to overcome prejudice was not over:

When I was honorably discharged from the Army in 1947, I was not able to get a job for many months in SF because of the anti-Japanese propaganda of WWII, even though I was fully qualified as an X-ray technician and jobs were plentiful in my specialty at that time. A compassionate Jew heard my story, and hired me as a darkroom technician at Stanford School of Medicine where I made $150 per month.

When I moved to Southern California again I could not get a job as a technician in a private hospital, even though I had by then five years of college. People with far less qualification and ability were readily given jobs in the hospitals. But the stigmata of disloyalty and traitor is still upon us since the United States committed that grievous error regarding the loyalty of the Japanese in America. We have four in my own family who have served honorably in the U.S. armed forces.

—Testimony of **BEN HARA**, Los Angeles, August 5, 1981

Though many of Miss Breed's children did not return at once, in time most of her young correspondents did come back to California. During those difficult years when the Nikkei community was struggling to start over again, Clara was also starting a new part of her life, as City Librarian of the San Diego Public Library, a job she was to hold until 1970.

Soon after the war ended, the library embarked on a building program. Clara was once again forced to go out and speak to civic groups, juggle financial reports, meet with staff, and plan with the architects. A new library had been one of Miss Plaister's dreams, and it became Clara's great challenge. It took almost another ten years for the new building to become a reality. It was dedicated on June 27, 1954.

Busy as she was with her new responsibilities, Clara was no doubt happy to welcome back her young friends, all of whom were proud but not surprised that Miss Breed was now in charge of the San Diego Public Library.

Margaret returned to San Diego with her family after several years on the East Coast. Her father was offered his old job back at the hotel, and she was ready to return to sunny California. She had always told her little brother, Thomas, that it never rained in San Diego. So when they pulled in and the skies opened up, Thomas didn't believe they were in San Diego! At first the Ishinos had to stay with a woman they knew from long ago, the midwife of all five Ishino children, and her family. Young Thomas was the last one she delivered. The Ishinos stayed at her home about two months and then finally got their own place.

Margaret did not tell me about her father's experiences at Seabrook Farms, but one Nisei remembered it this way:

My family was recruited from the relocation camp with the promise of a good life in a place called Seabrook Farms . . . to work in a factory. At this factory it was not unusual for workers to work 16 hours a day . . . I can also tell you from my personal experience that while working in cold storage, a 24 hour shift was an accepted thing . . . a worker could work 16 hours a day, seven days a week during the peak harvest season . . .

Living quarters with coal stoves for cooking, heating, and hot water were initially free, but were soon assessed a rental fee, which forced every member of the family to work or live without basic necessities. Other families arriving later in the year were housed in temporary barracks sharing community water faucets and outhouses because of the lack of a sewage system.

There were signs in local stores which clearly stated that the Japanese would not be served. There were special seating areas in many public facilities for Orientals and other non-whites as well. Many of the townspeople and school people were seeing a Japanese face for the very first time.

—Testimony of **TADASHI TSUFURA**, New York, November 23, 1981

Life in Seabrook was not any better than life in Poston; in fact, it sounds worse. For many of the Nikkei, starting over meant living in crowded hostels and trailer parks and on farms with substandard housing.

That's how it was for Katherine Tasaki and her mother, as Ben Segawa explained to me:

Life was really tough for them after the war when they came back to San Diego. They had no place to go to, so they elected to come back to San Diego and her mother found a place to live right in the Gaslamp area—in fact, the place she found wasn't much bigger than the units they

Margaret Ishino has never forgotten that proud and historic day when Pres. Harry Truman saluted the men of the 442nd Regimental Combat Team. She lived in Washington, D.C., and was there when the president saluted the men and said, "You fought not only the enemy, but you fought prejudice and won."

housed us in in Poston. The apartment she had was maybe fifteen feet wide and probably forty feet long and that's it. The conditions in the Poston barracks were better than what they were living in there. She didn't have any money. This was the best that she could find. Kathy went back to school and made contact with her dear friend Clara Breed again.

Clara Breed continued to be the one friend Katherine could always rely upon. She had passed the paper doll stage, but Miss Breed hadn't forgotten what it was like to be in high school and not be able to afford any little extras. Miss Breed always seemed to have something special for Katherine on Christmas and her birthday. When she graduated from high school, Miss Breed made sure that Katherine had money for a new dress for the Senior Prom:

Miss Breed had taken me under her wing, and she wanted me to go to Scripps College in Pomona . . . she arranged for me to go for an interview. In those days there were no scholarships . . . going to Scripps was absolutely out of the question. So I figured I would go four years to State and then I wanted to go either to library school at UCLA or Berkeley. That would have been another two years. . . . but it just didn't work out.

Katherine's mother got sick, and Katherine had to leave school.

When I was looking for a full-time job I sent my application around to quite a few places. Back in those days the department store was Marston's, and that was the one place that I went to apply, not realizing that they never would hire me. They had an unwritten code that you had to fit a certain mold to be hired there. And there were other places that I applied back in those days. . . . I think even today civil service is the safest place for a minority to get a job or at least get started and get some experience.

In time Kathy did get a job in Chula Vista Library, one of the new branch libraries, and she loved working with children and books. She said, "I think any of the people you talk to about Miss Breed will say she was a big influence in their life, a wonderful support. You can almost say she is the reason I am working here. I used to practically live in the Children's Room. My library card was one of my most precious possessions."

Katherine's friendship with Clara Breed continued over the years. In 1956, when Katherine married Ben Segawa, Miss Breed was on the guest list, and as Kathy and Ben's family grew, Miss Breed was a regular visitor and dear friend. Ben told me that Kathy was an avid reader all her life and passed her love of books on to their children, all of whom went to college.

Years later Kathy was interviewed for the ReGenerations Oral History Project and she said, "I really have no regrets; my life has turned out very, very well, and I don't think [I] would have changed anything."

Ben Segawa told me a little about his return after the war:

After they said we can leave Poston, 4 years later, we came back to roughly the same area I left and by now I was in the 10th grade—So, I registered as a Sophomore in South West High School with all the class mates that I knew—I was 4 years older. We recognized each other and they welcomed me back like crazy—it was like a homecoming for me. So you see, I think I had a very unusual experience—where most people had a hard time being accepted back into the community . . . I was fine.

Ben's father had to start over again—he had very little and it was a long, hard struggle. Eventually Ben's brothers came home: "We were very lucky; all four of them came back. Nobody got wounded. We were just one of the very, very fortunate ones. . . . When I got out of high school . . . I wanted to join the air force. I felt I wasn't college material." Ben met Kathy for the first time when he returned to San Diego from the Korean War. They never met at Poston because Kathy and her mom left Santa Anita early and lived in Camp I while Ben was in Camp III with most of the San Diegans.

One of the good things that came out of this camp is I met all these people in 1942—and here we are in 2003 and I'm still in contact—I talk to Babe and other friends all the time—How many people can say you have a friend for over sixty years? We see each other at least once a month and the friendships started in 1942 because of the evacuation—we found comfort and security with each other and the bond got stronger.

Aiko Kubo, who is known to her friends now as Ellen, still remembers the train ride from Poston to Union Station in Los Angeles.

At that time it seemed so vast! We were lucky to meet someone from Camp I. He showed us around and told us how to get on the bus for Fresno. I remember thanking him because I was completely confused! It seemed like such a huge place after spending all those years in camp.

My two sisters were married in camp to men who came from Fresno so we went up there to central California and tried to work in the country. My parents worked on a ranch . . . My oldest sister and her husband were with us. Yoshiko and her husband were in Visalia. Then we moved to Reedley in one of the church buildings until we were able to rent a house.

It was just an unsettled period. I was a little apprehensive about going back there. I was there a short time and then I went to UCLA on a scholarship.

Aiko finished college and became an executive assistant in the corporate world. She is retired now and volunteers as a docent at the Japanese American National

Museum. She says as she gets older she becomes more ethnic. One of her passions has become sumi-e painting, a traditional Japanese art form.

In Chicago, Louise worked for the publisher McClury & Company, typing letters to their customers notifying them of cancellations or back orders: "We wrote them in our own words. Everyone was friendly back East and not like the West Coast." Letter writing sounds like a perfect first job for Louise, who loved to write! She was there about two years before joining her dad, who went back to San Diego. He had worked for the Barcelona Apartment Hotel for over thirty years. He was one of the lucky ones who got his job back. After returning to San Diego, Louise encountered some unfriendly people but found work at City Civil Service as a clerk, typing out purchases for the City of San Diego in the Purchasing Department.

It was August 1947 when Louise sent her friend Margaret an invitation to a very special event. Louise was about to marry their friend Hisako Watanabe's brother, Richard! Louise knew Richard before the war, but only to say hello. He's the one who had polio in Poston. They married on September 7, 1947, and raised a family in San Diego. These were busy years and Louise had little contact with her old friend Clara Breed.

Years later, Louise remembers going to visit Miss Breed and bringing her some orchids that she had grown. She discovered that Miss Breed loved orchids, too, but found them difficult to grow: "She was both delighted and 'jealous' that it was easy for me."

Louise recently sent me a photo of her dear friend Maggie, taken at Louise's youngest granddaughter's, Kacie's, graduation from UCLA. Kacie hopes to go to nursing school, and her older sister, Kelly, is teaching English in Japan.

Tets was not well enough to talk with me or to write. However, I had the use of letters and an article he had written to honor Clara Breed. Joe Yamada told me that Tets returned to San Diego soon after the war. His friendship with Clara continued, and he was proud that the nameplate he had carved was still on her desk and remained there until she retired in 1970. Tets took a job at Consolidated, an airplane factory. He later worked for General Dynamics. But he was not working as an engineer. Those who knew him well as a young man still feel it was such a waste! But Tets could never recapture the lost years: "Tets was so smart!" Joe Yamada told me. "He could have been anything he wanted to be—a doctor—a surgeon!" College was interrupted first by his bad arm and then by the long years behind barbed wire. When he came out of Poston he needed a job—college was not in the cards for him. But his love of reading and his affection for Clara Breed never faded.

Years later Tets recalled that "as a children's librarian, she got involved with children. Not just Japanese American children, but all children. Miss Breed believed that every child needed adult guidance. An education. And a belief that as Americans they must better themselves and their society."

In the 1930s, when young Tetsuzo haunted the downtown library, Miss Breed noticed his broken English. "She bought me a pocket dictionary," he said. "I wore it out. Because of that I gained command of the English language and was able to get along." He wrote that Miss Breed was truly a great lady who "believed Americans with literacy could obtain an education to better themselves and their society. I, too, hold that belief—true yesterday, today and tomorrow."

Ellen Yukawa's parents heard about the hostile conditions in the Delano area and decided not to return to California, even though they had property to return to. Nikkei farmers who returned early were not only threatened; some were also shot at by vigilantes who refused to accept their return. Her family left for New York on a train full of soldiers returning from the Pacific. Ellen's mother was nervous about how they would be treated, but the GIs were happy and friendly.

Currently, Ellen Kubo volunteers at the Japanese American National Museum in Los Angeles and does sumi-e painting.

When we got to New York City we got into a cab and went to the Empire State Building. The War Relocation Authority had offices there and that was what you were supposed to do. All we knew was that we had to go to their offices . . . and they had all these religious organizations—churches—set up with private home owners who had "hostels." That's that they called them. So what the War Relocation Authority did was to place you in one of these hostels around the city and then I remember Daddy used to go to the WRA office and look for a job. I don't know how often he went. But they would help him find a job. His first job was as a pot-and-pan man in a hospital. I don't know where it was, but he would put his suit on and his hat and ride the subway to go wash pots and pans. We were

Margaret (left) and Louise (right)—lifelong friends—have shared many happy celebrations. This is the day Louise's granddaughter Kacie graduated from UCLA.

living in Brooklyn for three months. Then he got a job as a cook in a convalescent home in Morristown, New Jersey. We stayed in Brooklyn. I remember it snowed Thanksgiving and that was the first time we had ever seen snow.

In the meantime, I guess my dad was checking back with the War Relocation Authority when he ran across Mr. Osborn. He wanted domestic help, so we moved to Decker Farm, Mom, Elayne, and I, and my dad still had the job in Morristown. He would come to visit us. I don't know how long that went on. Then Mr. Osborn bought the Sho Foo Den, a replica of a Kyoto palace, sent over by the Japanese government in 1904 to the St. Louis Exposition. After the exposition the government made a gift of the palace to a famous chemist named Dr. Jokichi Takamine, who had discovered adrenaline. It was Dr. Takamine who moved the palace to New York and made it his home. A few years later, in 1910, the same Dr. Takamine contributed the cost of thousands of Japanese cherry trees that were planted in the Tidal Basin Washington, D.C.

When the Osborns bought the Sho Foo Den my dad quit his job in Morristown and became the ground maintenance man. All the gardens were overgrown, but my dad uncovered them and brought them back to their original beauty. We stayed in Monticello until 1949, when we went back to California.

We didn't talk about where we had been because my dad believed we had to put it behind us. The past was over and done. There was no point in being bitter.

CHAPTER FOURTEEN

"NO PRICE TAG FOR FREEDOM"

MY STUDENTS ASK ME IF this can happen again to another group of people. I must answer, yes . . . we cannot take freedom for granted. Until you lose your freedom, you do not realize how dear it is. There is no price tag for freedom. —Testimony of **GRACE NAKAMURA**, Los Angeles, August 6, 1981

Forty years had passed since the first bombs fell on Pearl Harbor. For many Japanese Americans, silence surrounded the years of incarceration; some suffered from the shame of having been imprisoned. It was as if they must be suspect, even though they had done nothing wrong. Like Sam Yukawa, most considered the years of exile an unhappy part of their past, not to be dwelt on or even talked about with children and grandchildren:

I could never tell my four children my true feelings about that event in 1942. I did not want my children to feel the burden of shame and feelings of rejection by their fellow Americans. I wanted them to feel that in spite of what was done to us, this was still the best place in the world to live. . . . There are still some bigoted individuals who liken our incarceration in the prison-like atmosphere of the camps to a fun-filled summer camp. They also say that we were there for our protection. If so, why were the guns pointed toward us rather than away from us?

—Testimony of **AKIYO DE LOYD**, Los Angeles, August 4, 1981

Because of their silence this book could not have been written thirty years ago. At that time, most Nikkei would not have been willing to talk with me or share their stories with anyone. But a dedicated vocal minority refused to allow the injustices of the past to be buried in the desert sands.

The process of correcting some of the legal discrimination toward Asian Americans began even before the war ended. Between 1943 and 1946, federal laws that had prohibited the Chinese, Filipinos, and Native Americans from becoming citizens were reversed. In 1948, California's alien land acts that had prohibited Issei from owning land were removed, as were laws against interracial marriages. Finally, in 1952, the McCarran-Walter Act opened the doors to immigration and naturalization for Japanese as well. Ten years after their evacuation and incarceration, the Issei generation could become naturalized citizens of the United States.

In the early 1970s, voices from the Japanese American community began to protest and call for an apology from the government for the injustices of the incarceration. In 1976, when the United States celebrated the bicentennial of the start of the American Revolution, Pres. Gerald R. Ford repealed FDR's Executive Order 9066 with these words:

We know now what we should have known then—not only was that evacuation wrong, but Japanese Americans were and are loyal Americans. On the battlefields and at home, Japanese American names like Hamada, Mitsumori . . . have been and continue to be written into our history for the sacrifices and contributions they have made to the well-being and security of this, our common nation.

While some Japanese Americans considered President Ford's proclamation all they needed, others wanted an apology from Congress. Still others wanted a more traditional kind of redress in the form of monetary compensation. Although there were angry disagreements within the Nikkei community over the demands they should make and who should speak for them, the redress movement continued to gain strength. These formerly "Quiet Americans" were quiet no more. All through the 1970s and early 1980s, individual activists and members within the Japanese American Citizens League (JACL), the National Council for Japanese American Redress (NCJAR), and the National Coalition for Redress/Reparations (NCRR) pressured for action, seeking both money and a public apology from the government. Finally, in 1980, Pres. Jimmy Carter and Congress created the Commission on Wartime Relocation and Internment of Civilians to determine if any wrongs had been done to Japanese Americans during World War II and, if so, to recommend remedial action to Congress.

Hearings were held in cities all over the United States where Japanese Americans had settled and started their lives over again. On January 14, 1981, Sen. Daniel Inouye, a veteran of the 442nd, who lost an arm in battle, gave a stirring opening-day address urging the commission to fill their report with

. . . good words, even great words. Make your report one that will waken this experience enough to haunt the conscience of this nation, haunt it so that we will never forget that we are capable of such an act, so that we will never again be able to do this to ourselves, and so that we will be able to pay tribute to the suffering, the fortitude, the patriotism, and ultimately the triumph of the people who lived through this experience.

You have been reading many of those great words. All the quotations in this book that are marked "testimony" came from those who gave witness during the CWRIC hearings. Their words are eloquent. Whether they favored monetary "redress" or not, the one consistent message they delivered again and again was that such injustice should never happen again.

Chiyo Kusumoto Nakagawa (left) and Fusa Tsumagari Higashioka (right)

But during the hearings the old hatreds resurfaced in the press yet again:

What I wish to address today is the public response to this Commission's activities . . . I am alarmed by the continuing stereotypes and hysteria. In the last two months there has been an outpouring of vitriolic letters to the editors of local newspapers that perpetuate the same stereotypes which led to the internment almost 40 years ago. The predominant stereotype is that "they" were foreigners, either active or potential enemy aliens, and "they" bombed Pearl Harbor and "they" killed our boys in a thousand different battles around the Pacific theatre. Disregarding the restrictions on U.S. citizenship at that time, the proof of "their" loyalty to Japan was that many were not U.S. citizens, and even if "they" were U.S. citizens, deep down somehow "they" were still foreigners. Therefore it was justified somehow to throw them in concentration camps or take almost any action against them. It was "their" own fault. After all, "they" bombed Pearl Harbor. These attitudes are still far too common. How often do you hear Joe DiMaggio blamed for the actions of Mussolini? Nobody assumes that "Mr. Coffee" was an agent of the Italians. Yet, the Japanese Americans are still paying for Pearl Harbor. There are subtle reasons why people distinguish between an American [named] DiMaggio as opposed to a "foreigner" [named] Korematsu . . . but the most important one is probably simple racism.

—Testimony of **ARTHUR WANG**, representative in the Washington State Legislature, Seattle, 1981

Here is an example of what Representative Wang was talking about:

Hearings Set on Internment of Japanese

They were all paid for all properties they owned. They were placed away for their own protection. The Japanese Government was the sole cause of their predicament, not the United States of America. . . . Let's demand the Japanese Government pay for the deaths of each one of these people and also for every bit of property that was destroyed.

All you ungrateful Japs . . . 39 years later should be deported immediately. Not compensated for your ingratitude, having enjoyed the great blessings you have been enjoying in our great United States of America.

—LETTER TO THE EDITOR, *San Pedro News Pilot*, July 8, 1981

But such racist attacks were no longer to shape government policy. In 1983, the CWRIC issued its report. Briefly, it acknowledged that there was no military reason for removing the Nikkei and that the incarceration had been based solely on hysteria and racism. Further, the commission wrote, no Japanese American, alien or citizen, was ever accused or convicted of any act of sabotage or espionage. The commission recommended that the government give a monetary award of twenty thousand dollars to each of those who had spent time in the concentration camps and was still alive. The commission further recommended that money be allocated for education so Americans would understand the tragedy and never allow it to happen again.

While there were many who felt that no amount of money could pay for the pain they had endured, some felt that such payments would stand as a reminder and raise the consciousness of the nation to "remember that when the rights of one American are abridged, the rights of all Americans are abridged."

But money alone was not enough. Another repeated plea at the hearings spoke to the need for educated citizens:

How can we help ensure that innocent people are not put into camps again? First, the true story of the camps must be told. There is absolutely no justification for what happened on any basis; legal, moral, or otherwise. It was purely politically and economically motivated, and the true story must be told and incorporated into every school book that refers to U.S. history. It is not only Japanese American history, but an integral part of U.S. history for all the people of the U.S. to know.

Second, we must all take up the struggle against racism. We as Japanese Americans, Asians, Blacks, Latinos, other minorities and whites, we must unite to wage an uncompromising battle against all forms of racism and discrimination based on national origin. Whether it be taking a stand against rounding up Iranians into camps or opposing budget cuts in social spending that affect our minority communities so sharply.

—Testimony of **SHIRLEY NAKAO**, San Francisco, August 12, 1981

Not surprisingly, among Clara Breed's papers is a letter from the Reagan White House acknowledging Clara's letter in support of redress. Though many years had passed and Clara Breed had retired from the library, at eighty-two, she had not retired from being an activist. In 1988, long after the hearings were over, when the government had still failed to act, Clara Breed wrote a letter to Pres. Ronald Reagan

Ben Segawa and author Joanne Oppenheim

supporting the commission's recommendations for redress. She felt strongly that the payment of twenty thousand dollars to each of the estimated sixty thousand Japanese American survivors was long overdue. A letter from the White House thanked her for her interest. In an interview four years later, she said that she considered the twenty thousand dollars "only a token" but an important gesture.

Eventually there were redress payments. Ben Segawa told me that he and Kathy "... never talked about evacuation but somewhere in the 1980s—during the redress hearings—our children began to hear bits of information about what happened to us and they got curious and some of these children had law degrees and they got their dander up about what happened."

The dollar amount got Ben's dander up, too:

Twenty thousand dollars? That's peanuts compared to what they took away from us. We don't want any money—we just want an apology; that's all. But we applied for it, and it came right away. A lot of people just gave it away—gave it to the churches. I know a lot of people did that. I should have a percentage of what I left—but twenty thousand dollars didn't even begin to compensate for the total loss. But in my case I accepted it and then a few years later we used that money to take my children to Washington, D.C., and let them see where the center of government is—our history. I took twelve of them over there! I rented four suites with my whole family—we spent the whole week there and that's how we spent the money.

By now, I've got four grandkids—the youngest was only four then. Oh, we had a good time. We had a nice vacation and learned all about history and those that were in school—we alerted the schools we were taking them out—and the schools said, "That's OK—the only thing we ask is to have them write an essay about their experiences." So we had three of them do that. So that's how I spent the money— cost me over twenty thousand dollars.

CHAPTER FIFTEEN

HISTORY IN A BOX

B Y 1988, THE HOUSE AT TRIAS STREET had been home to Clara Breed for more than sixty years. Now, at the age of eighty-two, she was packing up and moving out, moving to a retirement home where space was limited. Memories had to be stored in the heart—not in trunks up in the attic or cedar-lined closets. Drawer by drawer and closet by closet, Clara found memories she had put away for safekeeping.

Among those treasures she found a box full of letters she had never forgotten but not seen for years. One by one, Clara examined the penny postcards and envelopes with their three-cent V-for-Victory stamps, postmarked April 1942 from Arcadia, California, and 1942, 1943, 1944, and 1945 from Arizona, Minnesota, Illinois, and Ohio. Printed in the big, scratchy scrawl of six-year-old Florence Ishino; the crossed-out, uneven script of ten-year-old Katherine Tasaki; the sure, steady hand of Tets Hirasaki; the graceful flowing script of seventeen-year-old Margaret Ishino and her good friend Louise Ogawa. As Clara opened one letter after another, she could picture each of "her children."

Rereading their letters for the first time in years, Clara knew again why she had saved the letters. These letters, more than two hundred of them, were a piece of history. They reflected the story of a terrible injustice. In their own way, her children had captured a time and a place that too few people knew about then or even know about today.

Elizabeth Kikuchi Yamada was totally surprised when Clara Breed phoned her. Liz had no idea that the letters existed. In fact, none of the correspondents seemed to know that Clara had saved their letters.

But that day Liz could hear how upset Miss Breed seemed to be: "I can't find anybody to take these letters—would you be interested?" Miss Breed asked. As Liz recalls, "It was as though she was begging me to take these letters—that they were very precious—but that no one wanted them! And I couldn't understand that. There was a part of me that is an historian, too, and I remembered writing to her. I was curious to see my letters again—to see the collection. Even when I went to collect the items—you know, I think I asked her why did she end up calling me?"

Clara really never answered that question. It's something that still puzzles Liz. After all, she didn't write that many letters. But she was thrilled to have them and totally surprised when Clara also gave her the beautiful Japanese dolls that had been sent from Japan to Clara by her sister, Eleanor, so many years ago. They are a traditional set of Hina dolls that are displayed each year on March 3, Girls' Day, Hina-Matsui. Louise remembered that Miss Breed sometimes displayed them in the Children's Room so many years earlier. It happened that the day I visited Liz Yamada was Girls' Day, and in honor of Miss Breed, Liz put them on display so we could both enjoy them!

Liz brought the letters over for Kathy to see. The two of them laughed and cried as they read through more than two hundred cards and letters. Liz recalled that her mother thought Miss Breed was sending books just to the Kikuchi family because her mother and Clara's were friends through the church. They were both wives of Congregational ministers. Mrs. Kikuchi had no idea that Clara was sending books to dozens of children as well as the libraries at Poston. And books were just a part of it.

THANK YOU, DEAR MISS BREED

The letters Miss Breed sent to "her children" during the war years helped all of us keep the faith. I am sure those of us who were touched by her avoided the bitterness over our fate. —TETS HIRASAKI

Elizabeth Kikuchi Yamada and Clara Breed at the 1991 Poston Reunion where Clara Breed was honored

In 1991, Clara Breed was the guest of honor at the sixth reunion of Poston III. Just about all her "children" came to celebrate and see the gentle woman they called Dear Miss Breed. Kathy was hardly able to eat, she was so nervous about having to speak. Clara's hair was white, she was eighty-five years old, but she greeted them with her still-sunny smile and her gentle voice. Her genuine love for them was apparent as she thanked them for the honor of being with them on this special occasion. Fifty years had passed since the war that had changed their lives forever. But it had not changed the affection the Japanese Americans shared for Clara Breed. Seven hundred seventy people gave her a standing ovation on that very special night. Many continued to correspond with her for the rest of her life.

At that time Clara told a reporter from the *Rafu Shimpo* newspaper how powerless she had felt in 1942. "I don't think personally there was much I felt as an individual that I could do. This was a decision of the U.S. government which we had to accept in a way, but not accept without protest." In her own personal way, Clara Breed did what all of us can do. Her story proves that one person can make a real difference in the lives of hundreds of other people.

Katherine Tasaki Segawa, Louise Ogawa Watanabe, and Clara Breed at the Poston Reunion in 1991

I asked each of the people I interviewed what they would want their grandchildren and other young people to know about that time in history and about Miss Breed in particular. This is what they said.

Louise wrote that Miss Breed's friendship was so important to her during the long years when she felt cut off from the world:

Knowing someone truly cares kept me looking ahead—knowing when I returned to San Diego there would be someone there who was my friend. . . . Clara Breed taught me not all people are prejudiced through her kindness and caring ways. By caring and giving of yourself through kindness and reaching out you learn to trust people more and that makes you feel more secure of the future. Showing of love can give you warmth. She has taught me to be more tolerant and show kindness to others no matter who—friend or otherwise. She wanted to do anything she could to help make you happy. She never asked for anything in return.

Barbara Washler Curry, a teacher at Poston, never met Miss Breed in person, but from the first time she heard about Clara she felt a kinship to her:

Clara Breed not only loved the children and understood the terrible upheaval in their lives . . . she did something about it. You know, she put her return name and address on those post cards and went down to the station and handed them out to the children before they got onto the train—and to me that just—many of us would have been in tears about it and we would have felt badly about it—but she did something positive and creative about it.

As he got older, Ben Segawa took schooling more seriously. He and Kathy wanted their children to be educated. They had four children and they got them all through college—two of them earned graduate degrees! Ben has a great deal of pride in his family and what they have achieved. He truly believes that:

Whatever knowledge you can get into your head, nobody can take that away from you. So I tell people, listen to the news, read the newspaper, and keep up with current events, because freedom is not cheap—you always gotta fight for freedom. You think you're going to get it for free, but it's not—someone's always gonna try to take some of it away from you—so you got to constantly be on the alert and fight for freedom. You don't just protect yourself. You have got to protect others—if they are infringing upon them.

That's what Miss Breed did! She was definitely against the evacuation. If you go back all those years, she was only in her thirties—an attractive woman. It took courage for her to be an activist like that, to say it's wrong to put these people in camp—they are not the enemy! It was an uphill battle—but the politicians were all for it. So what are you gonna do? Politicians failed us; the Constitution failed us—we didn't have a chance in this country then.

Clara had a favorite quotation from the Talmud I found among her papers that may have been a comfort when she was unable to win that uphill battle Ben talks about: "It is not upon thee to finish the work; neither art thou free to abstain from it."

Miss Breed encouraged Ben and Kathy Segawa to organize the Japanese American Historical Society of San Diego, with historian Dr. Donald H. Estes, in order to preserve their heritage and so that what happened to them would never be forgotten and would never happen again to any other people!

In 1989, after the letters surfaced, Liz Yamada sent Tets Hirasaki copies of his letters to Miss Breed. True to form, Tets answered with a beautiful letter:

... How lucky I was to have been influenced and loved by such a great lady as Miss Breed who showed me the tools for survival in that great temple of knowledge—the Library. Some one said "Knowledge is free, but you have to bring your own container!" I sure tried to fill mine. The strangest part is that as the filling takes place, the more knowledge is required to fill the voids that keep appearing.

Tets worried that a growing number of people in the United States, as well as worldwide, were unable to attain a decent standard of living: "Mired in poverty and man's inhumanity to man ... this problem is directly tied to the growing numbers of people who cannot partake of the vast fund of knowledge because they lack the key that opens the doors—THE ABILITY TO READ!"

Elizabeth had great hopes about telling Miss Breed's story to another generation:

Itsuo Endo volunteers at the Japanese American National Museum, sharing his stories with students and visitors from all over the world.

I'm hoping that our story will tell them that no matter how dire the situation—how tragic—whenever there is adversity—you know the Japanese expression, "shikata ga nai"—you accept it because there's nothing you can do. But, I think it's more positive than that. There's always hope in human relationships because there are always kind and caring people everywhere wherever you are.

Even though the government did something you know was wrong; still, the teachers showed affection for us. They really cared about us. And Clara Breed was on the outside sending us messages of love and friendship through the books. I, for one, want them to know about the value of literature in life—to heal the soul. Besides learning things, intellectual ideas, books teach you about life.

Of course we loved Clara Breed. What Miss Breed did for me, and for Kathy, too—was to instill the idea of what words do for all of us—she taught us about honoring a love of words. She did so much, sending candy, clothes, and letters, but I don't want to forget the books—and what books and literature can mean to the lives and minds of children. She gave us a positive feeling about books and what they do for you, not just intellectually but emotionally—throughout your entire life!

Miss Breed was always modest about the gifts she had sent her "children." She told a reporter that she hoped the books she sent were able to help them a little bit. "I know I can't imagine life without books," she added. Indeed, her entire career, like that of so many librarians, had been about connecting books and people. As Clara wrote to her good friend Bertha Miller, "Reading is food for the spirit and immeasurable."

Margaret agreed that Miss Breed did much to make her into a reader:

Reading is something like having company all the time. I love to read mysteries. I usually read the last chapter and then I find out—I travel with that person and see how they got there. Miss Breed had a lot to do with making us interested in books—even if I didn't ask for it—she sent books to me and this is how I traveled quite a bit—to Alaska and so many other parts of the world.

Margaret didn't get to travel to all the places on her list when she was a teenager, but thanks to books and Miss Breed she's seen a good part of the world. For Maggie, reading remains a passion.

Richard "Babe" Karasawa scanned the original letters to Miss Breed into the computer for the JANM and serves as a docent at the museum.

When we wrote to Miss Breed we knew that she would take care of us. She was that kind of person that we could really—not take for granted—but appreciate and really respect her for what she had done and this is very, very important—to know you can trust somebody!

Margaret eventually moved to Los Angeles, where she still lives and works part-time for *Rafu Shimpo,* a newspaper serving the Nikkei community. She says that the business courses she took in junior high and high school prepared her for the future. She

Margaret's little sister, Florence Ishino Enomoto, was the youngest of Miss Breed's correspondents.

never regretted taking shorthand and typing in school; in fact, she taught typing after the war. Eventually she earned her adult education credentials and was able to make a living on her own.

Florence has few memories of the war years. She was the youngest of all the correspondents—a little kindergartner at the start. There are just two things she recalls—living in a stable and her family's number, 4019, the number that was on the tag they almost lost when they reached Santa Anita. Florence now lives outside of Los Angeles.

Margaret told me she was so glad she went to the reunion in San Diego in 1991. It was the last time she saw Miss Breed. Soon after the party Miss Breed wrote Margaret a note telling her what a joy it was to see her "to remember those long ago days in the Children's Room when you used to come to the library with your little sister. Do you remember one day when you were embarrassed because she had put her shoes on the wrong feet?" Tucked into the envelope were some photos of Florence and Margaret. Miss Breed thought Margaret would like to send one of the snapshots to Florence.

The photos have been lost, but the note is one of Maggie's treasures.

I would say that Miss Breed was very community conscious. She really fought for what she believed in—she did not think that the evacuation was right—that is very understandable. I think she really, really loved the Japanese people. I'm not saying that she didn't like other nationalities—but I really do think she loved the Japanese people and it showed. She really had great concern for us and she was not afraid. She was a crusader—she believed in what she felt and she had this way about her— people listened to her. She was a beautiful, beautiful person!

I remember seeing a movie called, "Farewell to Manzanar." When I went to work the next day this fellow came up to me and said: "Did you watch 'Farewell

Elizabeth Kikuchi Yamada and Joe Yamada on their 50th wedding anniversary in 2004

to Manzanar'? What a fairytale!" And I said to him, "That was no fairytale—I lived that!" I just walked away because you can't argue with people like that. Their minds are already made up—their mind is prejudiced and they're ignorant—they don't know what happened. And so many people to this day don't understand about what happened and the situation. I hope your book will help them understand what happened so that it will never happen again! Perish the thought!

Like Miss Breed, Margaret had no children of her own, but her little sister, Florence, has a family and several grandchildren and Margaret is very close to all of them. When I asked what she would want them and other young people to know about Miss Breed, her elegant answer was simply this: "We need more Miss Breeds in the world."

In October of 1994, Clara E. Breed died in her sleep. She was eighty-eight years old. She never carried a gun, threw a grenade, or earned a medal for bravery in action. In fact, she thought of herself as a pacifist. She did not believe in solving problems through war. Yet she fought injustice through the power of words and small, but constant, acts of kindness. More than sixty years after the events in this book, she is

Ellen Yukawa Spink (right) and the author (left) at the class of 1951 reunion in New York City. Ellen finally got to see the Statue of Liberty!

still fondly remembered as a brave woman who acted with determination and courage while many of our leaders allowed hate and fear to govern.

After reading all the letters, Elizabeth Kikuchi Yamada knew they were historic documents that she could not keep for herself. Instead, she made a gift of the letters to the Japanese American National Museum, where they would be treasured and preserved so that people would be able to read them for years to come.

This is a poem that Liz wrote and read on the night of the reunion dinner that honored dear Miss Breed.

Poston Revisited: The Colorado River

The coarse talk of river men
Defiles the purity of blue
Flowing swiftly through the desert land;
Defiles the memory of a separate time
When the River was our sanctuary.

Yesterday the cicadas cried in the mesquite trees,
And catfish circled lazily in the crystal pools,
While we traced our dreams in the river sand,
Our bodies warm and brown from the desert sun.

We had won again our race with the sun.
Wakening before dawn to reach the River.
Eager to leave the world of black-tarred barracks,
We conquered boldly the harsh and hostile land.

Under the shimmering shade of the cottonwood,
We talked of the life and time beyond this interlude.
Innocent in our adolescence, invincible in our youth,
We still dreamed the American Dream.

The desert sojourn ended abruptly one day,
The River carried our farewells beyond the bend.
Quietly we left the land, quietly as we had come
And entered a world dark in the shadow of a
mushroom cloud.

AFTERWORD

When I first met Clara Breed, she had already been dead for more than five years. Yet, she taught me some of the most important things I have ever learned about being a librarian, an American, and a friend to others.

For almost a year, starting in late 1999, I worked at a big computer in the collections storage area at the Japanese American National Museum, scanning dozens of letters written to Clara more than fifty years before, many of which appear in this book. I read every word of those letters while I worked on them, and the children who wrote them came to seem like they could have been my friends, too. When I was done with the scanning project, of course I had to know more about their Miss Breed. I was going to be a librarian myself—I was finishing my first year of graduate work for a master's in library science by then—and I was already convinced that Clara was just the kind of librarian I wanted to become: steadfast, principled, passionate, and fearless.

As I researched Clara's personal history, reading the articles she published in *Library Journal* and the *Horn Book Magazine* during the war, her history of the San Diego Public Library, and even letters she wrote to her sister over the years, I knew I'd found the ultimate professional role model. Tough times brought out the best in her: When her Japanese American patrons were forcibly removed to the Arizona desert, she made sure they got their books, no matter what. When the funding initiatives for a new main library building failed, she vowed that next year they'd fight twice as hard for the money. And after the new main library was finally built, Clara kept fighting for new local branches, too. Everything I learned about what Clara did made me proud to be a librarian—like her.

Clara could easily have lost the job she loved for helping her Japanese American friends. Anti-Japanese sentiment was at an all-time high in California after the bombing of Pearl Harbor, and the public library was not thought of as the place for political activism. Yet, clearly, Clara could never consider not helping them. I think it is Clara's choices in life that first made me aware of what I would be willing to fight for—and risk getting fired for. Eventually, I realized I would be lucky indeed to love what I do, and those I do it for, as much as Clara Breed did. That is the sort of love that makes people do great things without even thinking twice.

—SNOWDEN BECKER

Public Access Coordinator, Academy Film Archive; formerly Digital & Media Archivist Japanese American National Museum, Los Angeles, California

Clara (left) with her mother, Estella M. Breed, and her sister, Eleanor. Though undated, it was probably taken when Clara was five years old, in 1911. Formal photographs like this were sent across the miles to grandparents who might not see their grandchildren from one year to the next.

➙➤ ACKNOWLEDGMENTS ◄✦

From the moment I found the story of Clara Breed I knew I had to write this book. But a few weeks later I also discovered that I had cancer. There was no way I could travel to California to read the many letters and papers that were not online. Snowden Becker, then the digital and media archivist at the Japanese American National Museum, gave me the best get-well message—a digital file of all two hundred–plus letters. As one who considered Clara Breed overdue for star treatment, Snowden unselfishly helped me every step of the way, putting me in touch with researchers at the Huntington Library, suggesting other people and sources to track down, and cutting through roadblocks with her enthusiasm and assurances. She is the kind of "librarian" Clara Breed would have appreciated. Without Snowden this book would not have happened.

At the Japanese American National Museum I had the good fortune to work with Toshiko McCallum, a reference librarian at the Hirasaki National Resource Center in the museum. She not only gathered the materials I wanted to see, but she also generously answered questions that seemed to multiply as I worked. My inspiration for this book began online with letters from the "Dear Miss Breed: Letters from Camp" exhibition, curated by Glen Kitayama at the JANM in 1997. Thanks to Cristine N. Paschild, archivist and manager of the Hirasaki National Resource Center, who also answered many questions.

During that first long year, I spent hours reading and rereading the letters until I knew phrases from them by heart! I read many other sources that gave me a fuller picture of what the correspondents had endured. Reading about their losses and courage helped me to face my own struggle. I was determined to get to California to meet as many of these people as I could and to write their story.

I have never worked on a project that brought me in contact with more generous and kind people. So many gave me their time and expertise. I am indebted to Dr. Arthur Hansen at California State University, Fullerton, who put me in touch with Dr. Barbara Kraft and Aiko Herzig. They gave me leads to Postonians who testified at the CWRIC hearings. I read the testimony at the National Archives in College Park, MD. The material was so compelling I included the recollections from other camps.

Thanks to the research librarians at the New York Public Library I was able to read more of the testimony and newspapers of the 1940s that were borrowed from other libraries.

Even before I got to California I was sending questions to Dr. Donald H. Estes, a professor at San Diego City College and historian of the Nikkei community in San Diego. Babe Karasawa considers him "the most important Nisei in San Diego."

My thanks to Dr. Roger Daniels, Professor Emeritus, University of Cincinnati, who clarified some slippery facts at the eleventh hour. His books have been my Rosetta stone! Thanks also to Dr. Setsuko M. Nishi, Professor Emerita, City University of New York, who answered questions as I started on this great adventure.

I am indebted to Clara Breed's two cousins, Allen F. Breed and Margaret Williams, who shared their fond memories of Clara and her sister. I was fortunate enough to connect with them when I sent an e-mail to the First Congregational Church of Stockton, California, where Clara's uncle, Rev. Dr. Noel Breed, was the pastor during the war years. My thanks to the current pastor of that church, Rev. Amy Jayne Johnson, who led me to Clara's cousins.

My thanks to the many people who willingly gave me interviews and shared memories of Miss Breed and their lives before, during, and after Poston. I am indebted to Babe Karasawa, who encouraged some of the more reluctant correspondents to talk with me; to Elizabeth and Joe Yamada, who shared their memories and sent me home with yearbooks, letters, and treasures that added much to this effort; to Itsuo Endo, a docent at the JANM and great storyteller; to Ben Segawa, who shared his stories as well as Katherine's; to Margaret Ishino, who brought not just her memories but also clippings and personal papers that made my job easier. I'm grateful to Fusa Tsumagari Higashioka's daughter, Patty Higashioka, for her family stories and photographs and for putting me in touch with Fusa's friend Chiyo Kusumoto Nakagawa, who also shared wonderful stories; to Louise Ogawa Watanabe and Tetsuzo Hirasaki, who corresponded with me, and to Ellen Aiko Kubo, Barbara Washler Curry, and Miwako Yanamoto for sharing their memories. More thanks to my old classmate Ellen Yukawa Spink, who also sent me home with stories and photos that added so much to the telling of this story.

As a novice in research, I was lucky that Snowden Becker held my hand across the miles, guiding me to and through digital files and archives I needed to visit. I also had the good fortune to meet David Kessler at Bancroft Library, University of

California at Berkeley, via e-mail. He assured me that most of what I needed was there at Berkeley, and he was right! He gave me confidence and guidance for which I am indebted.

My thanks to Fred Romanski, who made my visit to the National Archives in College Park rewarding, and to Aloha South at the National Archives in downtown Washington. At the Franklin Delano Roosevelt Library, several librarians sent me electronic files with Eleanor Roosevelt's articles that focused on the Nikkei. Steve Binns at the Smithsonian mounted an online show while I was working on this project. He helped me connect via e-mail with key people in California. Thanks to John Panter, research archivist at the San Diego Historical Society. My thanks to Irene Kolchinsky of the ALA Archives and to Claire Goodwin, college archivist at Simmons College Archives.

Thanks to Marco Thorne, Clara's successor as Head Librarian, who knew her as a colleague and leader; to Rhoda Cruse, a retired librarian, who was kind enough to give me a copy of Clara Breed's book, which was so useful; and to Richard W. Crawford, preservation specialist of the California Room in the San Diego Public Library. It was so special for me to work in the library that Clara had "built" and to read the letters between Eleanor and Clara.

I am thankful to my friend Jean Marzollo, who not only encouraged me but also helped me find my agent, George Nicholson, who believed in the book from the start.

As always, I owe the greatest debt to my family for their support in this journey. My daughter and business partner, Stephanie, gave me "time off" to wear my other writer's hat. My sons James and Tony gave me technical support with computer problems. My granddaughter Kate converted hours of interview tapes into disks that I transcribed. But most of all, my husband, Stephen Oppenheim, served as cameraman, document copier, and microfilm reader. He listened to my endless excitement about the day's great find or blind lead. He read multiple versions of the manuscript, adding commas and constructive comments. Without his confidence and kind help, this book could not have happened.

I was fortunate to find an editor who knew about and loved Miss Breed and wanted to do this project even before I sent her my first proposal. Liz Szabla gave me a chance to shape a book that would celebrate Clara Breed and librarians everywhere, whose

This is one of my favorite photographs of three of Miss Breed's correspondents. They went to the library and school together as children, and remained lifelong friends. From left to right are Hisako Watanabe, Louise Ogawa, and Margaret Ishino dressed for a Japanese exhibition in San Diego's Balboa Park.

work makes large and small differences in all our lives. Thanks to her team, Jennifer Rees, Chris Hardin, and Alan Gottlieb for their efforts.

From what I've learned of Clara Breed, she would have modestly shrugged off the idea of this book. She did not need or want any special thanks for her acts of kindness. She would have rejected being cast in the role of "Great White Mother." She is rather the very model of a librarian, who represents the best of a profession that has traditionally protected our books and our rights. By telling her story, I hope to inspire future librarians and to honor the many librarians who are devoted to people and their need for books, just as Clara Breed was throughout her life of public service.

My prayer from the start has been to honor Miss Breed and those who lived through this shameful chapter of our history. Remembering their story should keep us from ever allowing such a tragedy to happen again.

—JOANNE OPPENHEIM
New York City

List of Things Sent by and to Clara Breed

Taken from the letters, here is a list of the things Miss Breed sent to the families as well as things that were sent to her between 1942 and 1944. Some letters were very specific in their requests to Miss Breed and included money orders to pay for the shopping and shipping. But the great majority of the packages were gifts from Miss Breed and shipped at her own expense:

- 2 yds of printed seersucker . . . cost = not over 50¢ a yard.
- 1 1/2 yd of plain white seersucker. (about same price as printed one)
- 1/2 yd of muslin (going to use it for stiffening)
- 1 card of snaps 5¢
- 5 Hollywood curlers
- 2 shower caps 29¢
- 1 bottle of brown liquid shoe polish—10¢
- 1 bottle of Skrips royal blue ink 15¢
- BOYS Cooper-Jockey shorts—SIZE: 28 waist
- 1 small face towel (cheap one is all right)
- 2 brown shoe string—21" or 24"
- 1 white "—"
- 2 yds of pique (would like flower pattern or leaves, trees etc.— white or pink, peach or old rose colored background. . . .)
- About 8 or more buttons to match the yarn I enclosed. Size—5/8-1/2" in width. (8 buttons at the least) 10¢ card buttons will do.— something pretty strong—not too fancy for it's for a sweater.
- 1/2 yd of drapery material (It is for a knitting bag—something strong will be fine.) Not too expensive.
- Please buy candies and gums with all the remaining money after deducting the mailing expense. Thank you!!

- A blotter book
  a. Oblong in shape
  b. Different colored blotters
- Two spiral shorthand notebooks
- A pencil eraser
  a. red colored
- Two packages of pencils
  a. Four in a package
  b. Different colored pencils, pencil pouch and 2 spiral shorthand notebook. If they don't have these pencils, any other No. 2 pencils will be all right.
- 2 balls (white) for crocheting. cost about 25¢ each. Total: 50¢
- 2 yds red and white striped seersucker about 40¢ yd 80¢
- 1 1/4 yds batiste (or some thin material similar to that) about 35¢ yd about 45¢
- 2 hairnets about 10¢ each 20¢ made of rayon or cotton (black)
- 2 yds embroidered organdy galloon about 2" wide. abt 15¢ yd 30¢
- 1 1/2 yd blue and white striped cotton material abt 35¢ yd 70¢
- 1 doz hair curlers abt 5¢ each 60¢
- 1/2 doz cotton sox abt 15¢ each 90¢

- Iron
- Radio tubes
- Magazines
- Thermos jug
- Umbrella
- Film
- Safety pins
- Model airplane cement
- Soy sauce
- Lock and keys
- Dictionary
- Road map of California

- A stored fan
- A stored sewing machine
- Barbering tools
- Barber supplies
- Simple primers
- Grammar books for seventh grade
- Zipper and thread for graduation dresses
- *The Hit Parade* music

Many other things were not requested but were mentioned in the letters as thanks for surprises that Miss Breed sent along:

- Paper dolls
- Jump rope rhymes
- Bubble set
- Dresses
- Stamps
- Clips
- Bobbie pins
- Cute little shoes
- Boxes of clothing

- Soap
- Crossword puzzles
- Seeds for flowers
- Pipe cleaners
- Crepe paper
- Candies—coffee and rum and toffee

THINGS SENT TO MISS BREED

- Season's greetings
- A carved nameplate from Tetsuzo Hirasaki
- School newspapers
- An original story by Katherine Tasaki
- Graduation programs and photos
- Crepe paper flowers and corsages of paper flowers
- Getas (wooden shoes that were used in the showers)
- A piece of silk fabric from Japan
- Pictures made by children (Florence Ishino)
- Piece of cotton with a seed picked by Louise Ogawa

FOREWORD

PG. 5 "Most important, they will develop . . ." "Something Strong Within" is the title of a prize-winning video (by Bob Nakamura and Karen Ishizuka) inspired by a quote from a diary written on May 3, 1942, by Yuri Nakahara Kochiyama. The quote is: *"Courage is something strong* that brings out the best in a person. Perhaps no one else may know or see, but it's those hidden things unknown to others, that reveal a person to God and self." The filmmaker added the word *within*.

PG. 10 "No one in San Diego . . ." Slippery numbers: As my work progressed, I found that seemingly straightforward numbers kept changing—i.e., how many Nikkei left San Diego? According to Clara's article, 2,500 left. But the *San Diego Union* reported that 1,150 people left, while Professor Don Estes, a historian, wrote "over 1,150 people." All of this proves that—as your math teacher always says—you should check your numbers!

PG. 11 "Ellen and her family . . ." Eleanor Roosevelt (hereafter ER) wrote that there were 127,500 Nikkei in the continental United States—more than 112,000 lived on the Pacific Coast. I figured ER must be right—after all, she could call the Census Bureau for her information. Maybe she did, but then ER must have rounded the numbers up. According to the 1940 census, there were 126,947 people of Japanese ancestry in the United States, and more than two-thirds of them were American-born citizens; the army took charge of 110,723 who were incarcerated at the start.

But then, why is the number 120,000 generally used for the total number of people incarcerated by the WRA? The difference is that 5,981 babies were born in the camps, and a few thousand other Nikkei arrived from Hawaii, Alaska, hospitals, and prisons. Some were even GIs discharged when the Nisei were reclassified as "enemy aliens." According to the WRA, the number of people held added up to 120,313. Roger Daniels clarified this with an article in *Japanese Americans: From Relocation to Redress* (Seattle: University of Washington Press, 1993).

"What she didn't tell . . ." When I started my search, I discovered that Ellen's best friend in Monticello did know that Ellen had been in Arizona. That was a helpful clue; it meant the Yukawas had either been in Gila or Poston. Her friend also recalled with chagrin that her own grandmother came out and screamed when Ellen came down to wait for the school bus one morning. "No Japs on my porch!" she hollered. "Go away!"

CHAPTER ONE

PG. 21 "They were marked . . ." ER, "To Undo a Mistake Is Always Harder Than Not to Create One Originally," *Collier's*, Oct. 10, 1943, Eleanor Roosevelt Papers (hereafter ERP), Franklin Delano Roosevelt Library (hereafter FDRL). Early in my research, I kept

running into ER! I was happy, but not surprised, to discover that she spoke out on behalf of the Nikkei. The idea of having her "speak" throughout the book gave me another powerful voice in a time when few people were willing to defend the rights of the Nikkei community.

"a date that . . ." Most people think FDR called December 7 a *day* that will live in infamy. I always thought that was what he said, but in fact he called it "a *date* that will live in infamy." Useful information if you hope to be a *Jeopardy!* contestant.

PG. 22 "December 7, 1941 . . ." *Mother & Daughter: The Letters of Eleanor and Anna Roosevelt*, ed. Bernard Asbell (New York: Fromm Int. Pub., 1988): 139–140. After finding articles by ER, I started looking for more. Just by chance, I discovered in this collection of letters that on December 7, ER was also worried that bombs might fall and she wanted her grandchildren sent East!

PG. 23 "We were filled with . . ." Commission of Wartime Relocation and Internment of Civilians (hereafter CWRIC) Testimony of Sally Kirita Tsuneishi, Los Angeles, Aug. 4, 1981, U.S. National Archives, Washington, D.C. All subsequent CWRIC Testimonies are also from the U.S. National Archives, Washington, D.C. As I mentioned on pg. 19, you will find quotes throughout the book labeled as "testimony." These statements are just a sampling of the moving accounts by 750 witnesses who testified during the CWRIC, whose mandate from Congress and the president was to investigate the policies of the government directed at Japanese Americans during World War II. All quotations marked "testimony" came from those who bore witness at the CWRIC hearings. Their words are eloquent and instrumental in leading to an apology and a payment of $20,000 to redress survivors' losses. Of course, no financial reparations could replace the years of freedom lost. Whether they favored monetary redress or not, the one message delivered consistently was that such injustice should never happen again.

"Miss Breed introduced me . . ." Tetsuzo Hirasaki, "In Memory of Clara Breed," *Footprints* (newsletter of the Japanese American Historical Society of San Diego [hereafter JAHSSD]) 3:4 (Winter 1994).

PG. 24 "December 7 was a blow . . ." Zada Taylor, "War Children on the Pacific, A Symposium Article, " *Library Journal* 67:12 (June 15, 1942): 558. American Library Association (ALA) Archives. Clara and other librarians contributed to this article just months after the war began. This article led to her first solo writing assignment. Anti-Japanese sentiments were not new to California. Clara recalled in her later ALA article "All But Blind" that ten years before the war, she had decorated the Children's Room of the San Diego Public Library with cherry blossoms, her Japanese dolls for Girls Day, and books and posters about life in China and Japan.

While the children gathered for storytime, a man came into the room and his scornful voice "boomed across the room as if from the quarterdeck of a ship. 'If I had my way, every man, woman, and child of Japanese ancestry in this country would be killed at sunup.' It was as if an electric shock passed over the room. Sparkling little faces froze into masks, remote and impenetrable." I wondered if Tets, Fusa, Louise, Hisako, or Margaret had been there that day.

PP. 24–25 "My grandfather . . ." E-mail to author from Patty Higashioka, April 22, 2003. Every family needs a family historian like Fusa's daughter Patty. She knew many stories about her family that enlarged Fusa's story. After all the help she gave me, I was surprised when Patty thanked me! In digging into the past, she had reconnected with relatives whom she had not spoken with in years, gathering some stories she never knew. In time, Patty feels this story will mean a lot to her son Ryan, who hardly got to know his grandma Fusa.

PG. 25 "My father was not . . ." Author's telephone interview with Chiyo Kusumoto Nakagawa, May 28, 2003. Fusa's daughter Patty put me in touch with Chiyo, who had many childhood stories about Fusa and Miss Breed. I later found a story in the San Diego newspaper about Chiyo and her brother running the family flower business in their father's absence.

PG. 26 "Leaving a city . . ." Poem by Kyuji Aizumi in "Further and Further Away: The Relocation of San Diego's Nikkei Community—1942," by Donald H. Estes and Matthew T. Estes, *The Journal of San Diego History* 39:1–2 (Winter–Spring 1993).

"Day after day . . ." Clara E. Breed, "Americans with the Wrong Ancestors," *Horn Book Magazine* (July 1943): 253–261.

PG. 27 "When the FBI came . . ." Author's personal interview with Margaret Ishino, Japanese American National Museum (hereafter JANM), Feb. 27, 2003.

PG. 29 "first thing before class . . ." Author's personal interview with Richard "Babe" Karasawa, Los Angeles, Feb. 26, 2003.

"on Monday, December 8 . . ." CWRIC Testimony of Sumie Barta, Seattle, Sept. 11, 1981.

PG. 30 "There were two . . ." Author's personal interview with Ellen Yukawa Spink, Raymond, CA, March 11, 2003.

"The news was . . ." "Americans with the Wrong Ancestors": 256.

"I'm not saying . . ." "Coast Given Raid Advice," quote by Mayor Fiorello La Guardia, *Los Angeles Times*, Dec. 10, 1941, 1.

PP. 30–31 "Defense on U.S. Soil Seen by Mrs. Roosevelt," *San Diego Union*, Dec. 11, 1941, 1–2. I had always heard that ER was the eyes and ears for the president, but I was surprised to discover that so soon after Pearl Harbor, she was in California, giving advice about how to prepare for attacks. She also spoke about treating the Nikkei with fairness. Her remarks were not appreciated on the West Coast. In fact, soon after this trip, she was forced to resign as Assistant Director of the Office of Civil Defense. ER was often attacked for being an activist, but that never stopped her!

PG. 31 "The Japanese mothers . . ." "War Children on the Pacific, A Symposium Article."

PG. 32 "Japanese Planes, How to Identify Enemy Craft That Might Attack the U.S.," *Life*, Dec. 22, 1941: 36–38. I had déjà vu when I found this! My brother posted this article (or one like it) on the wall of his room along with a giant world map, where he posted little flags showing major battles. Boys spent a lot of time learning to identify planes and building airplane models of balsa wood covered with tissue paper. Of course, the probability of enemy planes flying over our little town in the Catskills was zilch! Nonetheless, we had a tower behind the courthouse where volunteers watched the skies for enemy planes.

PG. 33 "Such a policy . . ." *The New York Times*, Jan. 3, 1942, 32.

PP. 33–34 "My Day," syndicated column by ER, Dec. 16, 1941, ERP, FDRL.

PG. 34 "Under the door . . ." CWRIC Testimony of Minoru Tamaki, San Francisco, Aug. 13, 1981.

PG. 35 "The day after . . ." *ALA Newsletter*, Section for Library Work with Children II: 10 (April 1942): 5. ALA Archives.

"The children came . . ." "Americans with the Wrong Ancestors": 256–257.

PG. 36 "I need your help . . ." *Rafu Shimpo*, Dec. 18, 1941.

PP. 36–37 "At approximately . . ." CWRIC Testimony of Dr. Yoshihiko Fred Fujikawa, Los Angeles, Aug. 5, 1981.

PG. 37 "With legitimate . . ." CWRIC Testimony of J. Fred MacDonald, Chicago, Sept. 22, 1981.

Hate mail, Japanese Evacuation and Relocation Study Papers (hereafter JERS), Reel 7, Bancroft Library, University of California, Berkeley (hereafter BANC).

PG. 38 "A popular journalist . . ." "The Question of Japanese-Americans," W. H. Anderson, *Los Angeles Times*, Feb. 2, 1942, A4.

PG. 40 Dr. Seuss 5th Column cartoon: Ted Geisel, aka Dr. Seuss, was generally quite liberal. But on the subject of Japanese Americans he seemed to have had a blind spot! Years later, he settled in La Jolla, California, and was a visitor to the Children's Room of the San Diego Public Library. Miss Breed's successor, Marco Thorne, told me that Dr. Seuss drew a cartoon of Clara, but I was unable to find it.

CHAPTER TWO

PG. 42 "The Japanese race . . ." Memorandum from General DeWitt to the Secretary of War, U.S. War Department, Office of the Chief of Staff, Final Report: "Japanese Evacuation from the West Coast 1942" (Washington, D.C.: Government Printing Office, 1943).

PG. 43 "We are Americans . . ." CWRIC Testimony of Kay Yamashita, Chicago, Sept. 22, 1981.

"My history teacher . . ." CWRIC Testimony of Yoshio Nakamura, Los Angeles, Aug. 6, 1981.

"As an impressionable . . ." CWRIC Testimony of Allan Hida, Chicago, Sept. 22, 1981.

PG. 44 "My Day," March 21, 1942. The Roosevelts did not always see eye to eye. On the subject of the incarceration of the Nikkei, ER opposed it and did what she could to help their cause and get them out of the camps. FDR had done many good things, but he signed Executive Order 9066, which opened the door to incarceration of the Nikkei. Finding out that FDR was not quite the hero of my childhood was disappointing.

PP. 44–45 Clara E. Breed, "All But Blind," *Library Journal* (Feb. 1, 1943): 120. ALA Archives.

PG. 45 "Japs Register for Evacuation," *San Diego Union*, April 2, 1942, A1–2.

PG. 47 "I was just 10 . . ." CWRIC Testimony of Robert Moteki, New York, Nov. 23, 1981.

"I witnessed . . ." CWRIC Testimony of Dr. Yoshihiko Fred Fujikawa.

PG. 48 "One strong rumor . . ." CWRIC Testimony of Bebe Reschke, Los Angeles, Aug. 6, 1981.

PG. 49 "I could not . . ." Tetsuzo Hirasaki, "In Memory of Clara Breed."

"Although it was risky . . ." Many of Clara's "children" brought me newspaper clippings about her. In an interview, Clara mentioned her uncle Noel. That was a great lead. I contacted the current pastor of his church and discovered that Clara's cousin Allen F. Breed was still a member there! Until that time I had been told that Clara had no living relatives. My interviews with Allen and his sister Margaret Williams revealed things I could never have known about either of the sisters.

"A Methodist minister . . ." Eleanor Breed Papers, First Congregational Church (hereafter FCC), Box 83/Carton 36, BANC. I didn't really notice the name "Eleanor Breed" on the excerpt of a diary about the FCC in Berkeley. When I did finally see it, I figured it was just a coincidence. I soon discovered that both sisters had a well-developed social conscience and were willing to do what they could to help the Nikkei families they knew.

PG. 50 "On the day before . . ." CWRIC Testimony of Hiroshi Kamei, Los Angeles, Aug. 6, 1981.

"When we got on the bus . . ." Yoshi Watanabe, "Evacuation," *Jr. Red Cross Poston High School 9th Grade Core Class Essays: History of Poston* (hereafter *Jr. Red Cross*), Vol. II, Colorado River Relocation Center Records, Box 3(7), The Huntington Library, San Marino, CA. I was searching for student voices from Poston without luck. Then Snowden Becker at JANM struck gold! When I opened the boxes at the Huntington Library, I couldn't type fast enough, so I read the essays into my tape recorder and often wept doing so. These books were meant to go to the class in Tipton, Indiana. It is not clear if they were ever sent. The students' penmanship is exquisite, and they chronicle dust storms, cotton picking, Christmas, and other events. Weeks later I found more Red Cross essays on microfilm at Bancroft Library. They had no formal name. Later I found a book called *Through Innocent Eyes* with some of these essays and more. We only had room for a small sampling.

PG. 51 "One thing that was . . ." Interview, Margaret Ishino.

"I woke up . . ." Author's personal interview with Itsuo Endo, JANM, Feb. 26, 2003.

"I used to type . . ." Author's telephone interview with Chiyo Kusumoto Nakagawa, June 2003.

PG. 52 "My dad . . ." Interview, Ellen Yukawa Spink.

"was just eleven . . ." Author's personal interview with Elizabeth Kikuchi Yamada and Joe Yamada, La Jolla, CA, March 3, 2003.

"Mrs. Ellis . . ." CWRIC Testimony of Charles Kubokawa, San Francisco, Aug. 12, 1981.

"As I passed . . ." CWRIC Testimony of Sally Kirita Tsuneishi.

PG. 54 "I wasn't very . . ." Letter to Eleanor Breed from Clara Breed, Clara E. Breed Papers, Dec. 3, 1952, San Diego Public Library (hereafter SDPL). After waiting a year to get to California, I felt so moved to be in Clara's library and holding her personal letters in my hands. The adult letters between Clara and her sister are touching and funny. In a prewar letter to Eleanor, Clara tells of visiting her uncle Noel, who was "chiefly interested in matrimony and inquires solicitously about your prospects and mine . . . says he, 'When are you going to get married?' And when I said I thought I'd wait until you had married, he said something about hell freezing over first. A minister's way of swearing. . . ." Although Clara had several serious romances and proposals that are mentioned in the letters, she never married. Her romance with a librarian from South America would have meant leaving not just her job as City Librarian, but leaving her mother, whom she supported.

PG. 55 "Thousands crowd . . ." "Cheers Mingled With Tears," *San Diego Union*, April 8, 1942, 1, SDPL.

PP. 55–56 "The scene was . . ." "Americans with the Wrong Ancestors": 257.

PG. 57 (photos) Fusa Tsumagari and her brother, Yuki; Katherine Tasaki and Tetsuzo Hirasaki, by Clara E. Breed, April 7, 1942, JAHSSD. There is something so special about the fact that Clara took pictures of her "children" that day! It is almost as if she knew these would be part of the history she would keep along with their letters.

PG. 58 "It was a real . . ." Author's telephone interview with Louise Ogawa Watanabe, May 2003.

"Taking Move in Stride," *San Diego Union*, April 8, 1942, A1.

PG. 59 "As the train . . ." Ben Segawa, "ReGenerations Project," oral history typescript, Sept. 1990, San Diego Historical Society (hereafter SDHS).

CHAPTER THREE

PG. 61 "All I remember . . ." Author's personal interview with Ben Segawa, Bonita, CA, March 5, 2003.

PG. 62 "Every one of us . . ." Interview, Margaret Ishino.

PG. 63 "Did I tell . . ." Interview, Richard "Babe" Karasawa. As a novice interviewer, I worried about my ability to get people to tell their stories. I read a few books on doing oral histories and prepared questions for each of the people I was to meet. But when Babe and others spoke, their stories took on a moving new reality.

PP. 63–64 "the horse urine . . ." Interview, Ben Segawa.

PG. 66 "I do remember . . ." Interview, Richard "Babe" Karasawa.

PP. 67–68 "Before my very eyes . . ." Kaizo Kubo, "Education Address," WRA Records, Reel 18, BANC. When I found this essay on microfilm I called Aiko Ellen Kubo to ask if she was related to anyone named Kaizo. He was indeed her brother who had died years ago. She had forgotten this beautiful piece of writing that I was able to send to her.

PG. 68 "I never dreamed . . ." CWRIC Testimony of Emi K. Fujii for her father Toshio Kimura, Chicago, Sept. 23, 1981.

PG. 69 "A long shed . . ." CWRIC Testimony, Dr. Yoshihiko Fred Fujikawa.

PG. 71 "Santa Anita Gates Open to 1000 Japs," *Los Angeles Times*, April 4, 1942, L5.

"A Chance to Prove It," editorial, *San Diego Union*, April 4, 1942.

PG. 72 "I remember . . ." CWRIC Testimony of Amy Iwasaki Mass, Los Angeles, Aug. 6, 1981.

PP. 72–73 "My Day," July 6, 1942.

PG. 73 "The them is me." Eleanor letter to Clara, Clara E. Breed Papers, July 1942, JANM. I had already seen the "My Day" column when I read the letter from Eleanor telling her mother and Clara about her part in sending the story to ER. It was complete serendipity.

"650 Japs Depart; S.F. Exodus Starts Like Giant Picnic," *San Francisco Examiner*, April 7, 1942, 1.

PP. 73–74 "My twin brother . . ." CWRIC Testimony of Thomas Minoru Tajiri, Chicago, Sept. 22, 1981.

PG. 74 "Little children . . ." "All But Blind."

CHAPTER FOUR

PG. 82 "Although the army . . . " Many people have told me that there were no schools at Santa Anita. Yet others remember classes. One can only assume that going to school was voluntary, and after the shock of being uprooted, formal school took a backseat—but there was a waiting list for piano lessons!

"We would sit . . ." Author's telephone interview with Aiko Ellen Kubo, June 17, 2003.

"At the first . . ." CWRIC Testimony of Toyo Kawakami, Chicago, Sept. 22, 1981.

PG. 85 "We were pretty sheltered . . ." Interview, Chiyo Kusumoto Nakagawa, May 28, 2003.

PG. 87 "As the elder . . ." Interview, Margaret Ishino. My interviewees were often surprised by how much I knew about them from their letters. That helped me make a personal connection quickly. They were able to expound upon details from the letters that gave me a fuller picture. For example, when I asked Margaret about all her responsibilities, she told me the stories of the lost number tag and the feeding trough she turned into a crib—stories that were not in her letters to Miss Breed.

CHAPTER FIVE

PG. 92 "Just days after . . ." "Harriet Dickson Resigns," *ALA Newsletter* 2, no. 10 (April 1942): 1, 5. ALA Archives. Taking over the chairmanship for the Newbery-Caldecott Awards, as they were known back then, was no small task, since the library was understaffed and busier than ever. In May, Clara wrote an article about the awards, urging more librarians to participate in the nominating process rather than complain about the choices made by others.

"Dear Mrs. Miller . . ." Clara E. Breed letter to Bertha E. Miller, *Horn Book Magazine*, Bertha E. Miller Papers, MS 78.B.3, F.20, April 22, 1942, The College Archives, Simmons College, Boston, MA. In their correspondence over the years, Clara and Bertha shared their enthusiasm and concerns about the world of books as well as great hopes for the postwar world.

PG. 93 "In it she wrote . . ." "War Children on the Pacific, A Symposium Article."

PG. 95 "She has given me two books." What a coincidence! *Timmy*, the book that Clara sent, was very special to me. It was the story of a floppy-eared cocker spaniel, the dog of my dreams! Every night I went to sleep with the book opened to a beautiful picture of Timmy on my pillow. It worked! My puppy, the spitting image of Timmy, arrived for the holidays that year!

PG. 96 "We American writers . . ." "Newbery-Caldecott Awards" *ALA Newsletter* 2, no. 11 (July 1942): 2. ALA Archives. I was unable to find Clara's photograph or her speech from this event. Maybe because of the war, there were fewer photos taken; maybe one day they'll turn up. The complete speeches were published in *Horn Book Magazine* (July 1942).

PG. 97 "Richard Haliburton, who crossed the Alps . . . " Another coincidence! Richard Haliburton's *Book of Marvels* was a gift my husband received as a boy, and his dream, like Eleanor's, is still to get to all the places Haliburton wrote about. All of our grandchildren are given a gift of this book for their eleventh birthdays with good wishes for a life of adventure.

"*Queen Mary*, the Cunard liner painted battleship gray now . . ." It was in the July 1942 *ALA Newsletter* that the librarian from the Berkeley

Public Library Children's Room wrote about seeing the *Queen Mary*. It was probably a one-time sighting. The *Queen Mary* usually sailed the Atlantic, but she made a trip to Australia where she was fitted out and painted as a warship. It was likely on her return with troops from the Pacific that she sailed into the San Francisco Bay.

"Eleanor told Clara about . . . the Gordons . . ." In a letter, I discovered that Clara had sent books to the Gordon children in Hawaii for Christmas. That was days before Pearl Harbor. Eleanor sent a clipping of the family and told Clara about Millie's memories of the voyage home on a ship that traveled through the night in darkness, so as not to be attacked. Years later, when Millie died, Robert Gordon married Eleanor. She was seventy-six years old and her cousin Allen was the best man. Hell had not quite frozen over!

PG. 98 "Barbed wire surrounded . . ." "All But Blind": 121–122.

PP. 98–99 "bitter feelings . . ." *Ibid.* This excerpt is from a letter in the "All But Blind" article, but it is not signed, nor does it appear in the JANM collection.

PG. 104 "Today the spark . . ." Yuki Tsumagari letter to Eleanor Breed, Eleanor Breed Papers, FCC.

"I had been . . ." Interview, Elizabeth Kikuchi Yamada. Among the treasures in Liz's home are several books that Miss Breed sent to her. Other correspondents also still have one or more of the books that she sent during the incarceration. Although most of the "children" have moved many times, these gifts from Miss Breed have been treasured for more than six decades.

PG. 105 Clara Breed letter to William F. Palmer 93.75.31 FF, Clara E. Breed Papers, Aug. 7, 1942, JANM.

PG. 107 "We departed from Santa Anita . . ." Quote from *Poston III Reunion Catalog* (1991). Collection of Elizabeth Yamada.

CHAPTER SIX

PG. 109 "Upon my arrival . . ." Chiyoko Morita, "My First Few Days in Poston," *Jr. Red Cross*, Vols. I & II. This item is reproduced by permission of The Huntington Library, San Marino, California. Chiyoko's words reminded me of my friend Ellen's description of the camps: "They sent us to places where no one would ever choose to live . . . land that no one lived on before or since!"

PG. 112 "It was brutal . . ." Marnie Mueller, "A Daughter's Need to Know" in *Last Witnesses*, ed. Erica Harth (New York: St. Martin's Press, 2001), 103.

"We opened the doors . . ." Interview, Richard "Babe" Karasawa.

PG. 115 "My oldest brother . . ." Margaret Ishino, "Executive Order 9066," unpublished memoir, author's collection. Margaret brought me a collection she had written about her experiences plus clippings she had saved about Miss Breed. In these old newspaper stories, Clara spoke of her feelings about the incarceration and about her uncle who tried to help the Nikkei in his community of Stockton.

PG. 116 "The latrine was . . ." Interview, Ellen Yukawa Spink.

"Tets was . . ." Interview, Joe Yamada.

PP. 118–119 "September 7, 1942 . . ." Tets's letter and drawing courtesy of Elizabeth Yamada.

PG. 120 "On May 1st, 1942 . . ." Miné Okubo letter to Eleanor Breed, Eleanor Breed Papers, FCC, BANC. Both Eleanor and Clara became active as members of the Fair Play Committee, an organization that worked to help the Nikkei. Among Eleanor's papers are letters from those who had strong and often angry words about their incarceration. The contrast between these letters and those sent to Clara reflect the dramatic difference between the attitudes of teenagers and young adults whose lives were put on hold.

CHAPTER SEVEN

PP. 121–122 "I have just learned . . ." Fred Bruner letter to Sen. Champ Clark, NARA RG 210, Box 277, WRA 64.200. U.S. National Archives, Washington, D.C. At the National Archives in Washington, I looked at the original letters that people addressed to their senators, the president, and the first lady. The expressions of hate became even more dreadful as I read those handwritten letters one page at a time.

PG. 125 "Katherine, like students . . ." As a former teacher, I was eager to interview some of the teachers and was curious about why they signed on. Although many have passed away, I was able to get their stories from interviews and papers that were collected by the WRA. Poston sociologists kept elaborate records, so we have first-person accounts written during the war. I also had the good fortune to talk with Barbara Washler Curry, one of the teens' favorites. Her genuine fondness for her students still rings true.

PG. 128 "As we talked about . . ." Interview, Elizabeth Kikuchi Yamada and Joe Yamada.

PP. 128–129 "A Medal for Cheesy," WRA press release, WRA Records, Reel 22, BANC.

PP. 130–131 "We heard that . . ." CWRIC Testimony of George Taketa, Chicago, Sept. 22, 1981.

PG. 133 "It was fun . . ." Interview, Aiko Ellen Kubo.

PG. 138 "About two nights ago . . ." One of the things that struck me was how well the young people of Poston wrote. Whether they were writing letters, essays, or speeches, they were gifted. I wondered if that had anything to do with the instruction they received or if it was from being avid readers. Perhaps it was both.

CHAPTER EIGHT

PG. 139 "Cold aching wind . . ." Ayoko Shintaku, "Life in Poston in Winter," *Jr. Red Cross*, Vols. I & II. This item is reproduced by permission of The Huntington Library, San Marino, California.

PP. 143–144 Dorothy Obata, "Winter Morning," *Jr. Red Cross*, BANC.

PG. 144 "Christmas won't be . . ." *Friends Intelligencer* (American Friends Service Committee's newsletter), Winter 1942. Clara E. Breed Papers, JANM.

PG. 147 Hate letters from unidentified newspapers. Clara E. Breed Papers, 93.75.26, JANM.

PG. 148 "Clara and her family . . ." I learned about the Breed's Hill connection from Marco Thorne, Clara's successor. He told me her family tree went back to the *Mayflower*. She was qualified to belong to the Daughters of the American Revolution (DAR). Long before I knew I would ever find Breed cousins, I wrote to DAR to see if Clara had ever belonged or, like ER, resigned. They had no record of Clara. Months later, when I spoke to her cousin Margaret Williams, she laughed and told me firmly that it was not an organization Clara or any of the family would have ever considered joining.

CHAPTER NINE

PG. 153 "Yes, we had . . ." Interview, Margaret Ishino.

PG. 155 "Some of my . . ." CWRIC Testimony of Yasuko Morimoto, San Francisco, Aug. 13, 1981.

PG. 156 "Loyal American citizens . . ." Elmer Davis memo to FDR, Office of War Information, *Personal Justice Denied*: 189, CWRIC.

"It is the inherent right . . ." Secretary of War Henry Stimson press release, *Personal Justice Denied*: 191, CWRIC.

"No loyal citizen . . ." *Ibid.*

PG. 158 Questions 27 and 28, *Personal Justice Denied*: 191, 192, CWRIC.

"I overheard . . ." Interview, Richard "Babe" Karasawa.

PG. 159 ". . . here I was . . ." CWRIC Testimony of Harry Taketa, Chicago, Sept. 22, 1981.

PG. 160 "My brother-in-law . . ." Interview, Elizabeth Kikuchi Yamada. It is interesting that none of the correspondents wrote to Miss Breed about these unsettling events. Younger writers may not have been aware of the strife the questionnaire created for adults. But older writers may have felt that Clara would not understand how anyone would refuse to sign yes to both questions. No one mentioned that far fewer Nisei volunteered than the government expected, and that by the following year the draft would be reinstituted. Many were offended by the idea of being segregated in an all-Nisei combat team. Others wanted the freedom to join the navy, the air force, or the marines.

PG. 161 "I have to admit . . ." Clara E. Breed, Bertha Miller letters, Bertha E. Miller Papers, MS 78.B.3, F.20, Feb. 1943, The College Archives, Simmons College, Boston, MA.

PP. 163–164 More hate mail, NARA RG 210, Box 381, WRA Records 64.502-64.503. U.S. National Archives, Washington, D.C. These letters were a chilling reminder of the racism that continued even after the Nikkei were removed. For the racists, the great hope was to send all the Nikkei back to Japan. Holding envelopes addressed to ER was special, but I also thought of how these letters must have

troubled her. She fervently believed that "we have no common race in this country . . . we cannot progress if we look down upon any group of people amongst us because of race or religion. Every citizen in this country has a right to our basic freedoms, to justice and to equality of opportunity. We retain the right to lead our individual lives as we please, but we can only do so if we grant to others the freedoms that we wish for ourselves." ER, "To Undo a Mistake."

PG. 166 "I wish you could . . ." Clara E. Breed letter to Bertha Miller, Bertha E. Miller Papers, MS 78.B.3, F.20, Aug. 6, 1943, The College Archives, Simmons College, Boston, MA.

PP. 166–167 "My grandparents . . ." E-mail, Patty Higashioka.

PG. 167 "In April 1943 . . ."CWRIC Testimony of Monica Sone, Chicago, Sept. 22, 1981.

PP. 168–170 "We were in there . . ." Interview, Ellen Yukawa Spink.

PG. 169 "I always thought . . ." (photo caption) JuJu's diary, Reel 230, Frame 94, 67/14c, BANC.

PG. 170 "There are those . . ." "Americans with the Wrong Ancestors": 261.

PG. 172 "We shared a meal . . ." "My Day," April 26, 27, 1943 and "To Undo a Mistake."

PG. 173 "The sooner we . . ." (photo caption) Japanese American Evacuation & Relocation Study Papers (hereafter JAERS), BANC MSS 67/14C, Reel 325, Pt. II, Sec. 5, Minidoka Idaho Folder P.3.00, Frame 165. After her visit, ER held a press conference in Los Angeles. It was summarized in the *Minidoka Irrigator* (May 8, 1943).

PG. 174 "Dear Mrs. Miller . . ." Clara E. Breed letter to Bertha Miller, Bertha E. Miller Papers, MS 78.B.3, F.20, May 1943, The College Archives, Simmons College, Boston, MA.

PG. 176 "Dear Miss Breed . . ." Bertha Miller letter to Clara E. Breed, Bertha E. Miller Papers, MS 78.B.3, F.20, June 1, 1943, The College Archives, Simmons College, Boston, MA.

PG. 178 "150,000 Japanese . . ." Census report. Roger Daniels, *Prisoners without Trial: Japanese Americans in World War II*, 2nd ed. (New York: Hill and Wang, 2004), 16.

PG. 179 "settle for thirty-nine . . ." Myer's remarks about thirty-nine items, *Personal Justice Denied*: 226, CWRIC.

"The outright deprivation . . ." Editorial, *Washington Post*, June 25, 1943, 8.

CHAPTER TEN

PG. 181 "I ordered material . . ." Louise Ogawa Watanabe written interview with author, May 2003. Author's collection.

PG. 183 "We gathered . . ." Margaret Ishino, "Executive Order 9066."

Maxine Davis, "The Truth About Jap Camps," *Liberty Magazine*, Aug. 7, 1943, 53.

PG. 184 "We were the children . . ." Interview, Elizabeth Kikuchi Yamada.

PG. 185 "I must have . . ." Interview, Louise Ogawa Watanabe.

PG. 186 "The summer . . ." Interview, Itsuo Endo.

PP. 186–187 "He went around . . ." and "Five to six . . ." Interview, Ben Segawa.

PG. 187 "Morale in the camps . . ." "Americans with the Wrong Ancestors": 260.

PP. 189–190 "Tomorrow more of my friends . . ." From the letters of this time period it seems clear that Miss Breed is encouraging her older correspondents to get on with their lives and leave the camps. But going out was not so simple. Fusa was the only one living with her mother; Louise couldn't convince her parents; Margaret had to care for the little ones; and Tets still hoped for his father's release.

PG. 190 "Our children are learning . . ." Naomi Wood, "Education," WRA Reel 20, BANC.

PG. 192 "To Undo a Mistake."

PG. 193 "Outside Employment Offers," JAER Records, BANC MSS 67/14C, Reel 325, Pt. II, Sec. 5, Minidoka Idaho Folder P.3.00, Frame 187, BANC.

PG. 201 John Embree, *Ibid.*

PP. 202–204 Author's telephone interview with Barbara Washler Curry, May 2003.

PP. 204–205 Democracy essays, WRA Records, Reel 18, BANC.

PG. 205 "American-Born Jap Troops," *Los Angeles Times*, Oct. 2, 1943, 1.

"I wonder . . ." "My Day," Oct. 9, 1943.

CHAPTER ELEVEN
PG. 210 "I've decided to write a book!" As a writer who has faced all these hurdles, I have to admit that this is one of my favorite letters! Katherine was wise beyond her years!

PG. 212 "To lose our . . ." CWRIC Testimony of Sasha Hohri, New York, July 16, 1981.

"All four of . . ." Ben Segawa, "ReGenerations Project."

PP. 213, 214 "We, citizens . . ." Letter to FDR from Poston Committee for Restoration of Civil Rights of U.S. Citizens of Japanese Ancestry, MSS 67/14C, Reel 234, Frame 33, BANC.

PG. 214 "For the boys, I know, it is a very delicate problem but I would much rather see them go into the army instead of to jail . . ." Louise's view of the resisters is more moderate than most. She seems to see and understand both points of view. The greater majority of Postonians considered the resisters an embarrassment. At that time more people than not believed that serving and even dying was the best way to prove their courage and loyalty. Only in recent years has the courage of those who resisted been recognized.

PG. 220 "Our family . . ." Kaizo Kubo, WRA Records, Reel 18, BANC.

CHAPTER TWELVE
PG. 221 "I remember quite vividly . . ." CWRIC Testimony of Thomas Kinago, Los Angeles, Aug. 5, 1981.

PP. 221–222 "Before the . . ." Interview, Itsuo Endo.

PG. 222 "I remember . . ." Interview, Itsuo Endo.

PG. 223 Gene Casey, "GI JAPYANK," *Collier's*, Aug. 5, 1944, 41–43.

PG. 224 "For me . . ." CWRIC Testimony of Donna Kotake, San Francisco, Aug. 11, 1981.

"I remember feeling . . ." CWRIC Testimony, Amy Iwasaki Mass.

PG. 225 "Many people . . ." "My Day," May 19, 1943.

PP. 226–227 "Remembrance," Kenny Murase, *Seasons Greetings*, Film 1932, Reel 30, 9102, WRA Records, pp. 20–21, BANC. Young adults were eager to leave camp and get on with their lives, but more than one told me that going out was also painful. This essay captures the pride, pain, and loneliness they had to deal with as they started over.

PG. 228 "I was the first . . ." Marian Muto, "ReGenerations Project."

PP. 228–229 "I left Poston . . ." Interview, Richard "Babe" Karasawa.

PP. 229–230 "Dear Friends . . ." Letter from Babe Karasawa for the Relocation Issue of Parker Valley High newspaper, *Hi Times*, Oct. 13, 1944. Looking for stories about students who had left, I found this in the Poston *Hi Times*. Babe was shocked to find it in his e-mail. Sixty years had passed since he wrote this letter. Babe loved his new school, but he still remembers that he would have been student body president if he had stayed at Parker Valley High.

PG. 230 "I remember . . ." CWRIC Testimony, Bebe Reschke.

PG. 231 "We were in Poston . . ." Interview, Ellen Yukawa Spink.

PP. 231–232 Anti-California statements, M 1342, Reel 9, Sept. 1942–Aug. 1945, Colorado River Community Analysis Reports 1-00. U.S. National Archives, Washington, D.C.

PG. 233 "Cut the throat . . ." Michi N. Weglyn, *Years of Infamy* (Seattle: University of Washington Press, 1976), 223.

PG. 237 "Should we go . . ." Poem by Yoshiko Kikuchi, in "Hot Enough to Melt Iron: The San Diego Nikkei Experience 1942–1946," by Donald H. Estes and Matthew T. Estes, *The Journal of San Diego History* 42:3 (Summer 1996). SDHS.

CHAPTER THIRTEEN
PG. 239 "Here is what . . ." Kaizo Kubo, Parker Valley High School senior essay, WRA Records, Reel 18, BANC.

PG. 241 "We did not . . ." Interview, Margaret Ishino.

"When I was honorably . . ." CWRIC Testimony of Ben Hara, Los Angeles, Aug. 5, 1981.

PG. 242 "Soon after the war . . ." In the midst of the building campaign, Clara hired the person who was to become her successor, Marco Thorne. When he was hired, Clara held up two fingers to say there were two things she wanted him to understand: "No racial discrimination on staff . . . no racial preference, either . . . and don't stand between me and my staff."

"My family . . ." CWRIC Testimony of Tadashi Tsufura, New York, Nov. 23, 1981.

PG. 243 "Life was really tough . . ." Interview, Ben Segawa.

PP. 243–244 "Miss Breed had . . ." Katherine Tasaki Segawa, "ReGenerations Project." Footnotes are sometimes one of the best parts of a book because they lead you to great finds. While reading the fine print in "ReGenerations," a collection of oral histories, I spotted the name Katherine Segawa. By then I knew Katherine Tasaki had married Ben Segawa. Now I had the adult voice of Katherine and, not surprisingly, Miss Breed was part of her story!

PP. 244–245 "After they said . . ." Interview, Ben Segawa.

PG. 245 "At that time . . ." Interview, Aiko Ellen Kubo.

PG. 246 "We wrote . . ." Interview, Louise Ogawa Watanabe.

PP. 247–248 "When we got . . ." Interview, Ellen Yukawa Spink.

CHAPTER FOURTEEN
PG. 249 "My students ask . . ." CWRIC Testimony of Grace Nakamura, Los Angeles, Aug. 6, 1981.

PP. 249–250 "I could never . . ." CWRIC Testimony of Akiyo De Loyd, Los Angeles, Aug. 4, 1981.

PG. 250 "We know now . . ." Pres. Gerald Ford's Proclamation 4417, Federal Register, Vol. 41, No. 35 (Feb. 20, 1976).

PG. 251 ". . . good words . . ." CWRIC Testimony of Sen. Daniel Inouye, Washington, D.C., Jan. 14, 1981. When I started reading the testimony from the CWRIC hearings, I looked for the names of Miss Breed's "children." I did not find them, but I knew these adult voices offered a fuller picture than the letters alone. They had the advantage of being told by those who lived it and had time to reflect on what had happened. They are among the most memorable records of the incarceration.

PG. 252 "What I wish . . ." CWRIC Testimony of Arthur Wang, Rep. Washington State Legislature, Seattle, 1981.

"Hearings set . . ." "Letter to the Editor," *San Pedro News Pilot*, July 8, 1981.

PG. 253 "How can we help . . ." CWRIC Testimony of Shirley Nakao, San Francisco, Aug. 12, 1981.

"Not surprisingly, among Clara Breed's papers . . ." Although the letter from the White House was pretty much a form letter and opened with a typo—"Dear Miss Beard:"—Clara saved it as yet another piece of her long-term involvement with the Nikkei community.

PG. 254 ". . . never talked . . ." and "Twenty thousand . . ." Interview, Ben Segawa.

CHAPTER FIFTEEN
PG. 256 "I can't find . . ." Interview, Elizabeth Kikuchi Yamada.

"The letters . . ." Tetsuzo Hirasaki, "In Memory of Clara Breed."

PG. 257 "I don't think . . ."Clara Breed interview in "Librarian Gave Hope to Nikkei Internees," by Jana Monji, *Rafu Shimpo*, May 1991. Margaret brought me this article, and in it I discovered that Clara had an uncle in California.

PG. 258 "Knowing someone . . ." Interview, Louise Ogawa Watanabe.

PG. 259 "Clara Breed not only . . ." Interview, Barbara Washler Curry.

"Whatever knowledge . . ." Interview, Ben Segawa.

"It is upon . . ." Clara Breed Papers, California Room, SDPL.

PG. 260 "How lucky I was . . ." Tets Hirasaki letter to Elizabeth Yamada, March 1989, courtesy of Elizabeth Kikuchi Yamada.

PP. 260–261 "I'm hoping . . ." Interview, Elizabeth Kikuchi Yamada and Joe Yamada.

PG. 261 "Reading is food . . ." Clara E. Breed letter to Bertha E. Miller, Bertha E. Miller Papers, MS 78.B.3, F.20, July 13, 1942, The College Archives, Simmons College, Boston, MA.

"Reading is something . . ." and "When we wrote . . ." Interview, Margaret Ishino.

PP. 262–263 "I would say . . ." Interview, Margaret Ishino.

PG. 263 "We need more . . ." Interview, Margaret Ishino.

PG. 265 Elizabeth Kikuchi Yamada, "Poston Revisited: The Colorado River," courtesy of Elizabeth Yamada.

PG. 288 Clara's letter to Tets was in an unaddressed envelope, so my guess is that she gave this to Tets directly—probably at the train station that sad day when he left. It's likely that the handwritten part refers to a gift of money that would be easy to carry.

Though we have just this one letter from Miss Breed, who knows if others will one day turn up in a trunk or scrapbook that is yet to be discovered. One can hope. But how lucky we are to have this letter that tells us so much about her. Thank you, Miss Breed!

BIBLIOGRAPHY

ALA Newsletter 2, no. 10 (April 1942): 1, 5.

ALA Newsletter 2, no. 11 (July 1942): 2, 11.

Asbell, Bernard, ed. *Mother and Daughter: The Letters of Eleanor and Anna Roosevelt.* New York: Fromm International, 1988.

Bailey, Paul Dayton. *City in the Sun: The Japanese Concentration Camp of Poston, Arizona.* Los Angeles: Westernlore Press, 1971.

Breed, Clara. "All But Blind." *ALA Journal* (February 1, 1943): 119–121.

———. "Americans with the Wrong Ancestors." *Horn Book Magazine* (July 1943): 253–261.

———. *Turning the Pages.* Kingsport, TN: Kingsport Press, 1983.

Daniels, Roger. *Prisoners without Trial: Japanese Americans in World War II, 2nd ed.* New York: Hill and Wang, 2004.

Daniels, Roger. "*Words Do Matter: A Note on Inappropriate Terminology and the Incarceration of the Japanese Americans.*" In *Nikkei in the Pacific Northwest*, edited by Louis Fiset and Gail Nomura. Seattle: University of Washington Press, 2005.

Daniels, Roger, Sandra C. Taylor, and Harry H. L. Kitano, eds. *Japanese Americans: From Relocation to Redress.* Seattle: University of Washington Press, 1993.

Egami, Hatsuye. *The Evacuation Diary of Hatsuye Egami.* Pasadena, CA: Intentional Productions, 1995.

Girdner, Audie, and Anne Loftis. *Great Betrayal.* New York: Macmillan, 1969.

Grodzins, Morton. *Americans Betrayed: Politics and the Japanese Evacuation.* Chicago: University of Chicago Press, 1949.

Harris, Catherine Embree. *Dusty Exile: Looking Back at Japanese Relocation during World War II.* Honolulu: Mutual Pub. Co., 1999.

Harth, Erica, ed. *Last Witnesses: Reflections on the Wartime Internment of Japanese Americans.* New York: St. Martin's Press, 2001.

Houston, Jeanne Wakatsuki, and James D. Houston. *Farewell to Manzanar: A True Story of Japanese American Experience during and after the World War II Internment.* New York: Bantam, 1973.

Inada, Lawson Fusao, ed. *Only What We Could Carry: The Japanese American Internment Experience.* Berkeley, CA: Heyday Books, 2000.

James, Thomas. *Exile Within: The Schooling of Japanese Americans, 1942–1945.* Cambridge, MA: Harvard University Press, 1987.

Matsuoka, Jack. *Camp II, Block 211: Daily Life in an Internment Camp.* San Francisco: Japan Publications, 1974.

Okubo, Miné. *Citizen 13660.* Seattle: University of Washington Press, 1996.

Robinson, Greg. *By Order of the President: FDR and the Internment of Japanese Americans.* Cambridge, MA: Harvard University Press, 2001.

Sone, Monica. *Nisei Daughter.* Seattle: University of Washington Press, 1979.

Tateishi, John, ed. *And Justice for All: An Oral History of the Japanese American Detention Camps.* Seattle: University of Washington Press, 1984.

Taylor, Zada. "War Children on the Pacific." *ALA Journal* (June 15, 1942): 558–562.

Uchida, Yoshiko. *Desert Exile: The Uprooting of a Japanese-American Family.* Seattle: University of Washington Press, 1982.

———. *The Invisible Thread: An Autobiography.* New York: Beech Tree/Simon and Schuster, 1995.

U.S. Commission on Wartime Relocation and Internment of Civilians. *Personal Justice Denied: Report of the Commission on Wartime Relocation and Internment of Civilians,* 2 vols. Seattle: University of Washington Press, 1997.

Weglyn, Michi Nishiura. *Years of Infamy: The Untold Story of America's Concentration Camps.* Seattle: University of Washington Press, 1976.

INDEX

PHOTO CREDITS

Great effort has been made to trace and acknowledge owners of copyrighted materials; however, the publisher would be pleased to add, correct, or revise any such acknowledgment in future printings.

COVER: Photograph courtesy of the Bancroft Library, University of California, Berkeley; drawing by Chiura Obata, Courtesy of the Obata Family

P.6: TOP TO BOTTOM, LEFT: Courtesy of Ellen Yukawa Spink; Japanese American Historical Society of San Diego; Japanese American Historical Society of San Diego; Courtesy of Elizabeth Kikuchi Yamada

RIGHT: Courtesy of Itsuo Endo; Courtesy of Florence Ishino Enomoto; Courtesy of Elizabeth Kikuchi Yamada; Courtesy of Elizabeth Kikuchi Yamada

P.7: TOP TO BOTTOM, LEFT: Courtesy of Elizabeth Kikuchi Yamada; Courtesy of Ben Segawa; Japanese American Historical Society of San Diego; Courtesy of Elizabeth Kikuchi Yamada MIDDLE: Courtesy of Patty Higashioka; Japanese American Historical Society of San Diego; Courtesy of Louise Ogawa Watanabe; Courtesy of Ellen Yukawa Spink RIGHT: Japanese American Historical Society of San Diego; Japanese American Historical Society of San Diego; Japanese American Historical Society of San Diego

P.8: Courtesy of Special Collections, San Diego Public Library

P.19: Map by Jim McMahon

P.23: © San Diego Historical Society

P.25: Courtesy of Patty Higashioka

P.28: Tribune Media Services Reprints

P.31: © Seattle Post-Intelligencer Collection, Museum of History and Industry/Corbis

P.39: Courtesy of the Bancroft Library, University of California, Berkeley

P.40: Mandeville Library, University of California, San Diego

P.42: Ham Fisher

P.43: Division of Military History, Smithsonian Institution

P.46: Japanese American Historical Society of San Diego

P.48: Library of Congress/neg.#LC-USF34-072258-D

P.49: Drawing by Chiura Obata, Courtesy of the Obata Family

P.53: Courtesy of Special Collections, San Diego Public Library

P.56: Courtesy of the Bancroft Library, University of California, Berkeley

P.57: Japanese American Historical Society of San Diego

P.58: Courtesy of Special Collections, San Diego Public Library

P.60: Courtesy of the Bancroft Library, University of California, Berkeley

P.62: National Archives/neg.#NWDNS-210-G-B389

P.64: Gift of Elizabeth Y. Yamada, Japanese American National Museum (93.75.31 HR)

P.65: Gift of Elizabeth Y. Yamada, Japanese American National Museum (93.75.31 HG)

P.66: Miné Okubo Collection

P.69: National Archives/neg.#NWDNS-210-G-B398

P.70: National Archives

P.76: Gift of Elizabeth Y. Yamada, Japanese American National Museum (93.75.HU)

P.78: Courtesy of the Bancroft Library, University of California, Berkeley

P.79: Courtesy of University of Southern California, specialized libraries and archival collections

P.83: Courtesy of University of Southern California, specialized libraries and archival collections

P.86: National Archives, El Chaparrel 1944, Poston 2 Yearbook

P.89: Courtesy of University of Southern California, specialized libraries and archival collections

P.101: Japanese American Historical Society of San Diego

P.103: Gift of Elizabeth Y. Yamada, Japanese American National Museum (93.75.31M)

P.107: Japanese American Historical Society of San Diego

P.110: Courtesy of the Bancroft Library, University of California, Berkeley

P.113: National Archives/neg.#NWDNS-210-G-A389

P.114: Courtesy of the Bancroft Library, University of California, Berkeley

P.117: Courtesy of the Bancroft Library, University of California, Berkeley

P.118: Japanese American Historical Society of San Diego

P.123: Japanese American Historical Society of San Diego

P.131: Courtesy of the Bancroft Library, University of California, Berkeley

P.132: Gift of Elizabeth Y. Yamada, Japanese American National Museum (93.75.31 ES)

P.137: Gift of Elizabeth Y. Yamada, Japanese American National Museum (93.75.31 FC)

P. 141: Courtesy of Tetsuzo Hirasaki

P.142: Japanese American Historical Society of San Diego

P.145: Courtesy of Norman Sugimato

P.148: Miné Okubo collection, print Courtesy of *The Pacific Citizen*

P.160: *Los Angeles Times*/TMS Reprints

P.169: National Archives/neg.#NWDNS-210-G-A821

P.170: Courtesy of Ellen Yukawa Spink

P.173: Courtesy of the Bancroft Library, University of California, Berkeley

P.175: Courtesy of the Bancroft Library, University of California, Berkeley

P.182: Courtesy of Margaret Ishino

P.188: Japanese American Historical Society of San Diego

P.195: Courtesy of the Bancroft Library, University of California, Berkeley

P.198-199: Courtesy of Elizabeth Kikuchi Yamada

P.203: Courtesy of Elizabeth Kikuchi Yamada

P.207: Courtesy of Miwako Yanamoto

P.217: National Archives/neg.#NWDNS-210-G-K355

P.218: Courtesy of Patty Higashioka

P.227: Courtesy of the Bancroft Library, University of California, Berkeley

P.237: Courtesy of Special Collections, San Diego Public Library

P.238: Friends of the San Diego Public Library, book Courtesy of Rhoda Cruse

P.243: Harry S. Truman Library

P.247: Courtesy of Ellen Aiko Kubo

P.248: Courtesy of Louise Ogawa Watanabe

P.251: Courtesy of Patty Higashioka

P.254: Courtesy of author; photograph by Stephen L. Oppenheim

P.257: Courtesy of Elizabeth Kikuchi Yamada

P.258: Japanese American Historical Society of San Diego

P.260: Courtesy of author; photograph by Stephen L. Oppenheim

P.261: Courtesy of author; photograph by Stephen L. Oppenheim

P.262: Courtesy of Florence Ishino Enomoto

P.263: Courtesy of Elizabeth Kikuchi Yamada

P.264: Courtesy of author; photograph by Stephen L. Oppenheim

P.267: Courtesy of Allen F. Breed

P.271: Courtesy of Louise Ogawa Watanabe

P.273: Gift of Elizabeth Y. Yamada, Japanese American National Museum (93.75.31T)

P.287: Courtesy of Lynn Eller

P.288: Courtesy of Lynn Eller

BACK COVER: Photograph courtesy of Japanese American Historical Society of San Diego; Photograph of Louise Ogawa Watanabe

Tetsuzo Hirasaki at the 1991 Poston Reunion that honored Miss Breed. Tets is holding the nameplate that he carved for her Christmas gift in 1942.

As we were finishing the final details of this book I wrote and called Tets Hirasaki again, hoping he had found a recent photo of himself. Tets never answered, but his niece, Lynn Eller, did. Just days before *Dear Miss Breed* was to go to press, she called with the sad news, her uncle Tets had died. Lynn also told me that she had a photo of Tets from the 1991 reunion and promised to send it.

Moments later I realized I had forgotten one question I had asked of everyone else. So I called back and asked if she happened to find any letters from Miss Breed among Tets's papers. Hours later, an e-mail arrived saying yes, she had a letter and she was mailing it to me. After years of hoping, it seemed I had found the only surviving letter by Clara to one of her children. It had been tucked away for more than sixty years. The letter has no date and the envelope no address because it was surely brought to the train station on that sad day in April when Clara's children left San Diego. It appears in its entirety on the next page and is a fitting end to the story of the remarkable Miss Breed.

—Joanne Oppenheim

Dear Tetsuzo,

     I am going to miss you a great deal, as you must know. You have been one of my restorers-of-faith in the human spirit. I know that you will keep your courage and humor in the weeks and days that lie ahead, no matter what they may bring.

     You said once that you were "afraid" of dissension among the Japanese. I have moments of being "afraid" of America. I want so much to have her live up to your unshaken belief in her, I want her to be just and democratic in her treatment not only of the Japanese Americans who are of course citizens, but of your father's generation.

     You people who are going to Manzanar and the other camps can help - as you have already - by proving your cooperation and loyalty, so thoroughly that even those who do not believe in your loyalty will <u>have</u> to believe in it. And do not forget for a single moment that you have real friends who trust you to meet any situation that life may bring. You have stamina and strength.

Clara E. Breed

I cannot give you a going-away present because it would be a burden to carry. Please accept this instead and perform a kindness — because I want you to have it.